JOE  T

CRUEL
WORLD

Text copyright © 2014 by Joe Hart
All rights reserved.

No part of this publication may be reproduced, stored in a retrieval system, or transmitted, in any form or by any means, electronic, mechanical, photocopying, recording, or otherwise, without the prior written permission from the author.

This is a work of fiction. The names, characters, places, and incidents are the products of the author's imagination or are used fictitiously. Any resemblance to actual events or persons, living or dead, is purely coincidental.

To all of the less fortunate and those who care for them. You are the shining examples of hope and beauty that we all can learn from and should strive for.

Special Thanks

I would like to thank Christine Clouser for her immense help with the technical side of the book. I did take some fictional liberties with the information, but Christine provided excellent insight and facts concerning viruses and their genetic structure. I can't thank you enough, Christine. And as always, thanks to my family who is in constant support of my writing as well as the readers who make my job worth doing. I love you all.

Contents

Chapter 1
Chapter 2
Chapter 3
Chapter 4
Chapter 5
Chapter 6
Chapter 7
Chapter 8
Chapter 9
Chapter 10
Chapter 11
Chapter 12
Chapter 13
Chapter 14
Chapter 15
Chapter 16
Chapter 17
Chapter 18
Chapter 19
Chapter 20
Chapter 21
Chapter 22
Chapter 23
Chapter 24
Chapter 25
Chapter 26
Chapter 27
Chapter 28
Chapter 29
Chapter 30
Chapter 31
Epilogue
Author's Note
Other Works by Joe Hart

Chapter 1

Across the Ocean

Before the plague took him, Quinn's father would say, *the world is a cruel place. Beautiful, but cruel.*

He always looked directly at Quinn when he said this, his clear gaze unwavering. Diamond blue eyes unblinking, making sure he understood.

It's like the sea, he would say, and gesture in the direction of the Atlantic that beat against the coastline, close enough to hear most days if the weather was good. *Its movement is graceful and timeless, gorgeous and hypnotizing to watch, but if you're not careful, if you don't respect it enough, it will end you like that.* And James Kelly would snap his fingers to punctuate his point each time. That brief sound would resonate within Quinn and bring pictures to mind of tomb doors being closed with a finite bang that echoed of forever.

Quinn would watch him, watch his father's lips move like they did in each movie he'd starred in, the same way he would deliver his lines with perfect timing, sometimes with a roguish smile, or deadpan and a coldness in his eyes that was never there off-set. He watched how his long-fingered hands would move, gesturing at the air or steepled together if he were lost in thought. Sometimes Quinn would catch him this way and observe him for stretches of time. James would stare out his office window at the long yard, its manicured grass and the rough walls of pine that grew rampant on the property, to where the sea met the cliffs. His fingertips would touch and rest just beneath his chin, his eyes never leaving the window, and Quinn never leaving the door while he observed him. His father's profile was perfection against the glare of daylight outside. Quinn would lock them away, these moments of silence, into boxes of memory saved for later when he would cross the path of a mirror. He would gather the courage to look at his own reflection, eventually comparing it to his father's features. But there was no comparison. There could never be.

Invariably Teresa would find him standing there, tears clouding his vision, and guide him away with soft, papery hands that always smelled of rose petals. She would kneel before him, her curled white hair feathery and so light he always imagined it floating away like smoke on wind.

I always find you crying, Quinn Michael, and there is never a reason.

I'm not like daddy, he would reply, the conversation the same since he could remember, Teresa's lined face before him, her words like balm.

You are more like your father than you know, and your tears should be reserved for true mourning, not because you want something to change. Beauty is here, she would say, and run her rose-scented fingers over his misshapen brow, down to the twisted bones beneath his cheeks. *But that is fleeting and age steals it from us all. Do you know what true beauty is?* She would ask. He would simply watch her, waiting for the words. *True beauty is doing the right thing when you know no one is looking, and that comes from here.* Her fingers would tap his chest, twice, softly. *And you, Quinn Michael, have beauty in both places.*

Then she would lead him to the kitchen, shooing the cook out so that they could have privacy while she made him cocoa or hot tea. They would sit there for an hour or more, sipping drinks while Teresa gradually drew him out of the cocoon of despair he'd spun for himself until he was ready to go outside.

The outdoors welcomed him in a way that the inside of the house never did. The large rooms, even with their vaulted ceilings, sprawling layouts, and sweeping views through massive windows couldn't compare to the air and the trees and the architecture of the Earth.

Nature drew him. It called whenever he ran outside, flying from the wide steps into the breezy Maine mornings, the pines shushing and whispering to themselves. He would stand under them some days and listen to their language, trying to discern a pattern, some telltale sign that there was more than the wind at work in their branches. Sometimes needles would drop from far above and land in his hair and on his shoulders, resting there until he plucked them away, always smelling their fresh scent before letting them fall to the ground.

But the sea was where he would always end up. The cliffs that bordered their hundred acres was highland, surrounded by a wrought iron fence that stretched in a half circle beginning at the south cliff edge and ending at the north. The property ran out into a jutting peninsula like a tongue tasting the ocean and dropped away sixty feet or more in places before leveling to a coastal shore of great, flat boulders. Quinn learned to climb down the precarious cliffs when he was only seven, his father coaching him from below, placing his feet into holds that he couldn't see until he knew the crevices by touch, finding them without effort and knowing in his heart that he could descend the bluffs in the darkness of midnight with ease.

The flat stones worn smooth by the constant embrace of the tides were his thrones. He sat upon them, governing an army of sea creatures who had hideous countenances and who worshipped him because he was the most handsome of them all. Sometimes the fantasies would fade and he would gaze out across the rolling waves, far into the horizon that hurt his eyes if he looked too long. Such amazing distance the world contained, the immensity of it all, like looking at a grain of sand upon the beach among all the others and seeing that the single grain was him in the world, nameless and adrift in the mercy of life.

Most days he spent in the solarium on the north side of the house. When the structure had been built, two years after his birth and a year and a half after his mother had left forever, his father had planned on it being a greenhouse full of foliage that he could keep blooming throughout the harsh northeastern winters. But the plants had withered despite the insulation and good sunlight, and his father had removed all but a select few of his favorites, leaving the space to become what it was now, Quinn's classroom.

Teresa had been a teacher. She normally said she'd been a teacher in her former life. When Quinn asked her what she meant, a sad smile would crease her face, touching her kind eyes, and she'd say she would tell him someday. She'd also let slip a mention of her own son, and when Quinn asked further about him, she firmly guided him on to his next chapter.

  Their lessons encompassed all subjects without definition or true structure. Some days they would spend pouring over a world map, Teresa pointing out great cities and capitals, their history unfolding from her stories in a way that always seemed like an adventure. On others they would read snippets from Shakespeare, and she would ask him what the great writer had meant after each section. Quinn would attempt an answer, and Teresa would tilt her head on her slender neck, her smoky hair tipping also, saying yes, he was right. It was only when he was twelve that he finally answered that he had probably meant several things all at once. Teresa's face had lit in a smile that followed him throughout the rest of the day, and the squeeze of her hand told him that he'd finally understood.

  At night his father would read to him after dinner, sometimes for hours in the library containing high mahogany shelves filled with books. They would rest on the leather couch before a fire crackling in the immense hearth if it was winter and holding cool glasses of iced tea if it was mid-summer. James would read, his voice sonorous and strong from years of projecting lines before a camera, the subtleties of his speech changing with each character until the story filled the room. The library would disappear around them and they would be on Mars, the red dirt glistening beneath a baking sun at their feet, or the walls would become massive trees, towering beyond sight so that their branches and leaves were lost in the blinding white of a forever sky.

  Quinn would sit beside his father, sinking toward him as the night spooled out, his shoulder gradually resting against the older man's arm until James would cuddle him in closer, stroking his hair and running his fingers over Quinn's eyes until sleep carried him away.

  These were the days of before, his life as the months became years and the world turned without him witnessing it for himself. And no matter how hard he stared across the ocean, he could never see the other side.

Chapter 2

Jackals and Buzzards

The day after his sixteenth birthday, he heard his father and Teresa argue about him for the first time.

He'd drifted off on a settee in the solarium, a book of Robert Frost poems open on his chest. Soft rain drummed against the half-domed ceiling of glass, the drops exploding as they hit only to reform into stitching rivers that flowed down the slanting wall and out of sight.

Quinn sat up and closed the book, marking his place before setting it aside. It was early evening, the sun lost somewhere behind the storm clouds and dense pines to the west. Lightning walked in a twisted stream across the sky and he listened, counting off the seconds until the thunder replied.

He made his way down the hall toward the stairs that led to the second floor and his waiting room. His muscles ached from a long run and climbing the cliffs all morning. It had been a glorious spring day, one of the first, the smell of melting ice and the air strangely warm, like an unexpected blanket placed over you during a nap.

Quinn paused, his foot on the first tread, as a voice filtered down the hall from the furthest room, his father's study. The tones of conversation were off, unsteady and varied, sounding like the cook's voice did when arguing over a recipe with the housekeeper or telling a joke. When heard from a distance, humor and anger sounded almost the same.

He walked down the hall, his sock-feet silent on the oak floorboards, ignoring the long mirror on the wall when he came even with it. He was good at not seeing mirrors now. He'd had them all removed from his room when he was fourteen and barely noticed his gliding reflection when he passed them in other areas of the house.

When he came to the T branching off to the rest of the home, it was empty. Mallory, the housekeeper, had left for the day, as well as Graham, the cook, and Foster the groundskeeper, each retiring to their respective guesthouses a short distance down the lane. The house was devoid of life save his father, Teresa, and himself, the way it was every evening. A word echoed to him that sounded like *can't,* and it was Teresa speaking. Her voice would've been recognizable to him in the middle of a tempest. Quinn edged closer to the door and saw it was open a fraction of an inch. He stopped, waiting and listening, holding his breath.

"Do you think I haven't gone over it and over it, Teresa?" His father's voice, strong but without force, tired sounding, like he hadn't slept for years and only wanted to lie down. "I've lain awake nights weighing it out, turning it over, worrying it like a stone."

"It's his life, not a stone," Teresa said from somewhere to the left of the door.

Quinn leaned forward to see if he could get a glimpse of them through the crack but saw only the darkening window looking out toward the sea cliffs.

His father sighed. "I know that. I feel like I came to a branch in the road of our lives years ago and chose one, and after walking for all this time, it may have been the wrong choice, but now I don't think I can find my way back."

"I'm not faulting you for what you did, any parent might have been tempted. The difference being you had the power to make it happen, to hide him away here, to remove yourself from the public eye, where other people wouldn't have been able to do that. But that isn't the issue; the issue is he's sixteen now."

"I know how old he is," James snapped.

Quinn blinked. He'd never heard his father truly irritated before. Upset, yes, but bark at someone like that? Never.

There was a clinking of glass, and Quinn imagined his father pouring several fingers of whisky into a tumbler he kept on his desk. He'd seen him drinking more in the last year than he ever had in his life.

"I'm sorry," James said, his tone level again. "It's hearing the number that sinks it home, how long he's been inside the walls I've built around him."

"I know, and I know how you must be feeling-"

"You don't, you can't, but that's okay. You've been like a mother to him after the pathetic excuse for one ran away to 'live her own life' as she called it. He loves you with all his heart."

"And he loves you more, Jim. Talk to him. See what he wants. There's no way you can keep him here forever."

There was a rustling sound and then a quiet clap, a ream of papers dropping onto a desk.

"The test results came back. He's not eligible for the surgery."

Quinn closed his eyes and slumped against the wall. The team of doctors had come to the house the week before, bringing cases of equipment with them. They'd drained massive amounts of blood from his arm while taking digital readouts of his facial structure. They'd even set up a portable X-Ray in the solarium, taking shot after shot of his skull, all the while his father hovering in the background, watching him. But there would be no surgery that they'd spoken tentatively of over the past six days, treading around it as if it were something priceless and breakable. There would be no hope.

"Are they sure?"

"Yes. The Fibrous Dysplasia goes deeper than they thought, deeper than two years ago when he had his last checkup. The bones aren't brittle anymore after the supplements and medication, but the deformity has grown inward."

"Inward?"

His father's sigh again, long and deflating. "Yes."

"Well, is there any danger-"

"No, they said the bones won't continue past a certain point, but the reconstruction they were promising won't be possible." James paused, the silence drawing out like a tightening wire. "I should have known. I should have guessed." Emotion clogged his voice, and there was another pause as he drank and set down the tumbler with a short bang on the desk.

5

"They'll find something. They're making new discoveries every day. We have to have faith."

"I'm running low," James said. There was the clinking of the bottle again. "I haven't had much cause to keep it in stock lately."

"You know life isn't assurances, it's chances and choices. We can choose to go on with our heads up or we can bury them in the sand, but life continues no matter what."

"Well, I'm tired of it, tired of the bullshit promises the doctors peddle, tired of waiting for the next idea to hope on. I'm tired of seeing my son, my beautiful boy, and knowing he'll never have a chance in the world. He'll never know kindness outside of these walls and fences because the truth is the world is full of jackals that call themselves people. I've seen the worst in humanity, witnessed it and might've even been a part of it at one time in my life, and there is no way I'm going to let him willingly walk out and be consumed by that."

Quinn pushed the door open and stepped into the room.

His father was where he'd pictured him, standing behind his desk, crystal glass in hand, his dark hair mussed, and a dress shirt open at the throat. Teresa was to the left, clutching her elbows with her hands, arms folded over her chest. When he entered, their eyes widened and his father set the glass down, his face falling as if receiving more bad news.

"I'm not afraid," Quinn said, locking his gaze with his father's before shifting it to Teresa whose lips pressed together into a paper-thin line.

"I'll be in the kitchen," Teresa said, moving toward the door.

"You can stay," Quinn said.

"Actually, I'd like to speak to you alone," James said, nodding once to Teresa who gave Quinn a tight smile and a squeeze on the arm before letting herself out of the room. When the door clicked shut, James made his way to the window and stared out at the storm. His hands played across the polished sill as more lightning stabbed the clouds.

"How long were you listening?"

"Long enough. The surgery's not an option?"

"No, I guess not."

"I didn't think it would be."

"I had hope."

He studied his father for a while. "I'm not afraid," he repeated.

"I know you're not, but I am. I know what's out there. The world is-"

"A cruel place," Quinn finished, moving closer to the desk. "You always tell me that. But it's also beautiful; you say that too."

James was quiet for a long time and then turned to face him. He looked older, or maybe it was simply the grayish tinge set to his features by the storm.

"Three years before you were born I was in Mali filming Standoff. It was hotter than hell while we were there and dry, so dry. The wind would blow across the plains where we were shooting and it would literally leech the moisture from you, pull it right from your skin. We would film during the daylight hours and then head back to our hotel in the evening, which was over an hour away. There were several local warlords battling in the area, over what I don't know: food, gold, drugs, everything, I suppose. Skirmishes were common, and once we even heard gunfire at night not far from our hotel. Needless to say, our security was heavy.

"One afternoon a storm rolled in, kind of uncommon for that time of year but not unheard of. If you remember the movie, everything was filmed in the desert specifically to capture the arid setting, so a rainstorm wasn't extremely useful for us. Trent, the director, called off shooting for the rest of the day, so we all packed up and started back to the hotel. I was riding in the first truck when we saw them."

James's eyelids fluttered and he looked at the floor. There was a swallow of whisky left in his glass, and he picked it up, bringing it halfway to his mouth before stopping.

"It was a little girl and a man. They were on the side of the road. He'd been shot. There was blood on his white shirt that had gone a rust color. You could see it drying in the heat and sticking to him. The girl couldn't have been more than seven, and she was starving. Her skin was plastered to her bones like shrink-wrap, and her hair was falling out. She had these huge, dark eyes that watched us as we got closer, but she never moved. She was sitting behind him, kind of holding his head up, and he wasn't conscious. His mouth was open, and for all I know he might've been dead, but I don't think he was. My driver started to slow down, and I watched her look at us. I know she couldn't see us since our windows were tinted, but she stared right at me as we came even with her. Those eyes boring into mine through the glass."

James blinked and brought the drink to his lips, pouring the whisky down his throat with a toss of his head. Quinn sat in the chair on the opposite side of the desk and perched there, watching his father.

"I told the driver to just keep going. We had a huge cooler full of ice and bottled water in the back of the truck and there was probably enough money in my wallet to feed her and her village for a week, but I told him to drive."

Thunder rumbled over the house and heavier rain pattered against the office window.

"Why?" Quinn asked. His father was a different man in the low light, not a dashing movie star but a haggard, weary soldier with dead eyes.

"Because of who I was then. That girl and the man on the side of the road might as well have been in another universe, that's how distant I felt from them. They were dirty and starving and wounded, and I was none of those. I was riding in an air-conditioned truck with personal security and a soft bed to sleep in that night. I was rich and unconcerned with the world outside of my own. Those two people were part of that outside world that was so different I couldn't relate to them. I got a sick feeling seeing them there, but it was the wrong kind of sick feeling. I felt sick at the thought of getting involved, of helping them, or leaving my comfortable world that I lived in. Being indifferent was easier. Forgetting was easier." James set the empty glass down on the desk and reached for the whisky decanter. His hand rested on the crystal stopper, but he didn't pour himself another drink. "At least I thought it was."

He glanced up and watched Quinn for a long second before looking away.

"That is the world that's waiting outside of these walls, son. That's what it has to offer. There's millions of people out there that are just like the person I used to be, who don't think past their first impressions and don't have the empathy to see who you really are. You'll be shunned based on how you look by people that can't relate, that don't know how or care."

"You can't say that. Not everyone is like that; they can't be," Quinn said. His mouth was parched, and his heart knocked against his breastbone.

"I saw it, Quinn. I was one of them. They're the people that do what I did every day. They're the ones that appear normal but hide hate and resentment below the surface. They're the ones that produce and read things like this."

James opened a drawer in the desk and scooped out several magazines. They were outdated but in good shape as if they'd been laid in the drawer years ago, untouched until that moment. He tossed them onto the desk and they spread out, fanning away from one another so that Quinn could see the covers.

They were entertainment magazines, the kind he'd seen on television over the years. They chronicled the lives of celebrities: their work, their children, even their clothing choices in such detail that it was as if they were reporting on rare, endangered species of a rainforest rather than actors and actresses living on a California coast. The magazines were all similar in the fact that their central pictures, sandwiched between miracle weight loss diet claims and the latest fashion faux pas, were of his father and himself as a young child. His father was carrying him in a bundle, hugging him close to his chest. James was youthful and even more handsome than he was now. The distinguished gray at his temples was a lush black, and even with the harried look in his eyes, they still shone with confidence and purpose on the glossy cover. Quinn could see only a portion of his own face in the picture, but it was a miniature version of how he appeared now. The child's features in the photo were uneven and slanted to one side, the bones already growing askew of proper balance. His brow was enlarged and one eye was shut, caught in mid-blink.

The headline over the picture read, *World's sexiest man has ugliest child.*

Quinn studied them each for a moment, letting his eyes run over the words, the various photos. He reached out to touch one of them and let his hand hover before drawing it back.

"It's just words," he said.

"It's not. It's opinions, people's thoughts, true feelings. These reporters loved taking pictures of me, telling the public what I was doing, who I was dating, what I was wearing. But the moment they saw you, they moved in like buzzards. I tried to continue normally, determined not to let what they were saying about you bother me. But it did. I loved you so much that when they began to close in on you with cameras and horrible words and disgust in their eyes, I couldn't take it. I brought you here and hid you away and swore never to return or let them say another unkind thing about you."

"That was your choice, not mine."

"Damn it, Quinn!" James slapped the desk with his hand and a porcelain paperweight in the shape of a dragon jumped and toppled over. "You don't understand. You haven't been out there. What if they ostracize you, laugh at you, hurt you?"

"What if they don't?"

James's brow crinkled, and he leaned away from the desk, rubbing at his mouth with one hand. The rain tapped against the window as the day fell closer to night.

"I won't take that risk."

Quinn stood and righted the porcelain dragon. Its mouth snarled at him in a permanent roar, white teeth painted red at their tips.

"I love you, dad, but someday it won't be your choice."

Quinn turned away and let himself out of the office and only allowed the tears to cloud his vision when he was halfway to his room.

Chapter 3

Four Years Past

"I'm leaving tomorrow."

The words were almost carried away by the wind and the sound of the pounding surf sixty feet below them. Quinn waited for Teresa to turn to him, but she kept her eyes focused on the shining sea. They sat with their legs dangling over the cliff's edge, his feet extending almost a full twelve inches past his teacher's.

"I know."

"How?"

"You've been quiet the last two weeks, and I could hear it in your voice yesterday when you said goodbye to your dad."

Quinn turned to the old woman, and she was old, there was no denying the fact anymore. Her hair had lost its life, and instead of wearing it in curls, she pinned it back with two tin combs etched with swirling, concentric designs in the metal. The lines in her face, merely suggestions of increasing age before, were fully embedded now, folded dark and heavy near the borders of her eyes and mouth.

"Do you think he knows?" Quinn asked.

"No, but he's your father. No matter what he says, he's known somewhere inside that you'd leave one day. Parents always know."

He turned his focus back to the ocean. A fishing trawler bobbed among the waves over a mile offshore, a dark speck that glinted, catching the sun as it rose and fell heading out to deeper water.

"Did your son leave?"

Teresa leaned forward, letting her gaze fall to the breaking waves far below them.

"You'll need to tell him when he gets home tonight; he'll want to start setting something up for you," she said, as if not hearing his question.

"Like what?"

"Like a house and a car, money, college if you want."

"I've already completed a college education, you told me yourself last month."

"There's always more to learn, Quinn Michael."

He kicked his feet and looked down at the big rocks, unchanged since he could remember. They were lucky, steadfast in their place, not unsure of anything. Not even the sea could move them if they became set somewhere.

"I wanted to leave when I turned eighteen, but there was always a reason not to. Now it's two years later and I can feel myself wavering. One minute I'll be so excited to walk through those gates, my stomach will flip on itself, and the next it'll be a stone thinking about leaving dad and you. I know why I've stayed as long as I have, and it's not because dad forbade it. I could've climbed the cliffs around the fences a long time ago.

It's fear. Fear of the unknown. And compared with how safe I am here, fear's always won out and kept me from leaving."

Quinn pointed out to where the trawler was barely visible.

"My future is like that ship. It's dwindling with each minute I stay here, and soon it will be out of sight."

Teresa smiled and patted his thigh once.

"Your future isn't that ship. It's the ocean." She put one frail arm across his shoulders. "Come on, traveler, let's get back to the house and get you packed."

When they stepped inside, his father's voice carried to them out of the living room where he sang in perfect harmony with Frank Sinatra, belting out *I've got you under my skin*. They came even with the doorway and Quinn stopped, glancing at Teresa who's mouth turned up in a grin that mirrored his own.

His father had a can of beer in one hand and was doing a graceful, sliding dance across the hardwood floor in time to the beat. His eyes shut as he hit a high note, his voice not carrying the velvety timber of Sinatra's but hanging alongside it in rough accompaniment. The song ended and on cue, Quinn and Teresa began to clap.

James spun around, his eyes lighting up before taking a bow.

"Thanks, I'll be here all week!" he yelled, hurrying across the room to them. He set his beer down and swept Quinn into a strong hug, picking him off his feet before setting him down again.

"Jeez dad, are you drunk?"

"Not in the least, my boy. Come here, Teresa."

The older woman swatted at him, the shining smile still on her face as James pulled her into the room and began to spin her while another big-band tune began to play. Teresa let out a short shriek that became laughter as they glided around the room. Quinn shook his head, watching them, his father catching his eye and winking before he dipped Teresa who responded by slapping his shoulder and laughing again.

"I thought you weren't coming home until late tonight?" Quinn said as James stood Teresa upright.

"We got done early," James said, taking a swig from his beer.

"I'm assuming the meetings went well?" Teresa said, fixing a length of hair that had come loose from one of her combs.

James grinned again, happiness ingrained into every inch of his face.

"Better than I ever dreamed."

Mallory stepped into view from the hall, a bemused expression gracing her Hispanic features.

"What is this, a fiesta?" she asked, looking around the group.

"Yes," James said. "In fact, tell Graham to cook lobster tonight and that creamy crab dip he does at Christmas. We're celebrating. Oh, and open some smoked herring too."

"All right," Mallory said, giving the three of them a puzzled smile before heading in the direction of the kitchen.

"Ish, dad, I don't know how you can eat that stuff."

"Herring's the perfect food, tons of protein and delicious besides." James gave him a playful swipe on the shoulder with his fist.

"Yeah, well, I'll stick to the lobster and crab dip."

"Me too," Teresa said.

"You two don't know what you're missing."

"We do; that's why we're not missing it," Quinn said, grinning.

James shook his head. "How about you and I take the skiff out for a run before dinner?" he asked. "She hasn't hit the water in a while."

"The skiff? Okay…" Quinn flitted his eyes to Teresa who gave a slight shrug as she finished smoothing her hair.

"Great, I'll go change if you want to grab the lifejackets from the boathouse."

"Sure."

"Meet you down there."

His father disappeared through the hall, another snippet of song floating back to them and fading as James made his way upstairs. Quinn closed his eyes and then looked down at his hands, rubbing them together as if he were cold.

"I'll see you at supper," he said, moving toward the entry. Her voice stopped him before the door.

"Don't put your plans on hold because he's happy, Quinn. He'll understand."

He nodded, not looking back and left the house.

They sailed for an hour along the shore, the canvas snapping over the sound of the wind that gusted and shoved the small boat across the waves. The spring air carried more warmth than chill in the afternoon sunshine though the salty brine that sprayed them from time to time still spoke of winter.

They didn't talk much, both of them focused on their required jobs: his father steering the skiff while Quinn ran the sail and helped turn them through the surf. *I'm leaving.* The words were in his mouth, choking him. *I'm leaving.* He'd said them so easily to Teresa, knowing that she would understand. But his father.

Quinn glanced at the older man for the thousandth time. The wind swept James's hair away from his unlined brow and his clear eyes sparkled, reflecting the sea. He could say it. He would tell him. Tomorrow he was leaving.

"Let's head in, I'm starving," James said, breaking him from his trance.

Quinn nodded, letting the words fade away with the wind as they guided the little boat toward shore.

The house smelled of boiling seafood when they returned, and Quinn's stomach growled. The soupy nausea that had accompanied him throughout their sailing, intensifying to the point of being unbearable when he started to say the words, relinquished its hold and gave way to hunger.

"Smells good, doesn't it?" James said, stifling a cough as he slung an arm around his shoulders.

"Yeah, sure does." A bout of vertigo overcame him, the same as when he glanced down sometimes while climbing. He was at the edge. "Dad, I've got to talk to you."

James stopped in the dining room entry to look at him.

"Go ahead."

"I…I'm…" His voice shook and he cleared his throat.

"It's ready you two," Mallory said from across the room. Teresa came down the hall toward them, pausing when she saw how they were standing, the expectant look on James's face.

"I'll tell you after dinner," Quinn finished.

His father studied him for a moment and then nodded.

"Okay."

Everyone dined together. Normally Mallory, Graham, and Foster, all took their dinners at their respective guesthouses, but James had insisted that they all stay. He opened two bottles of wine and poured everyone a glass, even Quinn, shushing Teresa as she objected.

"He'll be twenty-one in less than a year, plus we're celebrating," James said, pouring Quinn's glass full.

Quinn avoided Teresa's gaze as he sipped the drink, letting the alcohol drown out some of the anxiety that churned within him.

"To the future, may it bring good things to us all," James said, raising his glass. They all followed suit, and Quinn swallowed the sharp barb in his throat as his father's kind eyes locked onto his own. The older man's gaze swam with a sheen of tears before he blinked them away and drank several swallows of wine.

Midway through dinner the telephone rang and Mallory swept out of the room to answer it. She came back holding the cordless in one hand.

"It's an Alex Gregory for you, sir."

James frowned and hesitated before rising from his seat. He coughed again into the back of his hand and motioned toward the hallway.

"I'll take it in my office," he said, and left the room. Mallory set the phone down on the counter before returning to her chair.

"May be about the meeting today," Graham said, smoothing back his blond curls. "If it went as well as he let on, perhaps we'll all get raises." His Nordic face lit up in a smile and he winked at Quinn, the little golden earing he wore in his left lobe glinting in the light.

"You get paid plenty, Graham," Mallory chided. "We all know since you're always spouting numbers off."

"Yeah, try cutting grass and working in the garden sometime," Foster growled from the end of the table. "Then you'll appreciate your cool and clean little kitchen." His old, grizzled face resembled a badly assembled saddlebag. He wore a permanent scowl that Quinn had only seen fully lift once when the groundskeeper had drank too much whisky last New Year's Eve.

"Oh stop it, both of you," Teresa said. "James has always been generous and you know it."

"I was only having some fun," Graham said. Then turning to Foster he smiled. "You should try it sometime, old man. It would be such a change from your constant miserable state."

Mallory hid a laugh behind her hand, and Teresa's lips curled as she tried to fight them straight. Graham grinned into the groundskeeper's face until the older man finally let out a chuckle and tossed a bright-red lobster claw at the cook.

Quinn took a snapshot of this moment, around the table with the only family he'd ever known. Tomorrow it would be gone, only a memory, and he would be alone. Quinn smiled as Graham jeered with Foster again, but he was elsewhere, lost in what would be, already departed.

"Do you want any more?"

Quinn looked up at Mallory's plump face. She held out the platter of lobster in his direction. Foster and Graham were already leaving the table, taking their wineglasses with them into the kitchen. Quinn glanced at his plate, which still held the partially eaten food.

"No, thanks Mallory."

"Sure, let me get that for you," she said, clearing his plate.

The housekeeper left the room and then it was only he and Teresa.

"You didn't tell him." It was a statement.

"No. I couldn't, he was too..."

"Quinn, what do you want?"

"Want?"

"Yes, what do you really want, above all else?"

He was silent for a long time.

"To be happy."

"And do you think leaving this place will make you happy?"

"I don't know."

"And what's the only way you'll find out?"

"By doing it."

Teresa nodded and gave him the smile she reserved for his moments of understanding in the classroom.

"Happiness is hidden behind the fear."

Without another word, she stood and took her plate into the kitchen, leaving him alone at the table. He looked down the hallway, waiting for his father to reappear, readying the words, but he didn't emerge from his office. Quinn stood, took a deep breath and left the dining room.

The office door was shut and a fan of light spread out from beneath it like spilled gold. He knocked once and listened.

"Come in," James's voice was barely audible.

Quinn opened the door and stepped into the room. His father sat behind the desk, elbows resting on its top, hands clasped before his mouth. James looked at him and then away, his gaze finding the window and lingering there.

"You didn't finish supper," Quinn said, stopping behind the chair in front of the desk.

"Not hungry anymore." James coughed again and cleared his throat. "Is everyone done?"

"Yeah. You want me to bring in your wine?"

"No, no that's okay."

The silence stretched out between them, Quinn studying the floor and letting what he needed to say build until it boiled within him. He would just say it, get it out into the open and then it would be done, like lancing an infected wound.

"I'm sorry for keeping you here, son. For holding you back."

Quinn's jaw worked for a second without saying anything.

"It's okay. I understand why you did it."

"I don't think you do, but maybe someday you will. When you have a son or daughter of your own, then you'll know and maybe you'll be able to forgive me."

"Forgive you? You've taken care of me. You've given me everything I need."

"No, not everything. I've failed miserably there. I always thought that if I could fix the burden you were born with, change the hand you were dealt, then I could justify it, but I can't. The last years have taught me that."

Say it, tell him now.

"Dad, you don't have to-"

"I do. I need to. Everything is..." James shook his head and looked out the window again. His face was glazed in sweat and there were dark circles beneath his eyes that Quinn hadn't noticed before dinner. "...everything is wrong," he finished in a whisper.

Quinn fidgeted with the loose stitching on the chair's back, tugging it one way and then another as if it were the seam holding back the words.

"I'm sorry, you wanted to tell me something," James said, turning back to him. "You mentioned it before dinner."

Quinn bit the inside of his cheek and closed his eyes before shaking his head.

"It's nothing. We can talk about it tomorrow."

"Are you sure?"

"Yes, I'm tired and I'm sure you are too."

"Yeah, I am."

"I'm heading to bed. I'll see you in the morning."

"Sounds good. Don't forget what you wanted to talk about."

"I won't."

As Quinn neared the door, James coughed, harder this time, a short wheeze accompanying the sound like there was something caught deep in his lungs parting the air.

"Are you okay, dad?"

"Never better. Just need some sleep, I'll be fine in the morning." He smiled tightly, and Quinn nodded once before closing the door.

But in the morning he was worse.

Chapter 4

The Beginning

"He's got a fever."

Teresa stood outside his father's door, one hand on the knob as if keeping him from going inside.

"Is he okay?" Quinn asked, shifting his gaze from her to the door and back.

"He's going to be fine. His temp is only at a hundred. He must've picked a bug up while he was traveling. He had to take a public flight instead of the jet since it was being maintenanced. Those airports are cesspools of germs if you ask me."

A rasping cough came from behind the door that trailed off into a wheeze.

"Should we have Graham or Foster take him in to the hospital?"

"I already asked him and he says he won't go. Stubborn as ever."

"How about having a doctor come here?"

Teresa lowered her voice. "I was thinking the same thing. If the fever hasn't broken or is worse by this afternoon, we'll call the clinic and either have an ambulance come get him or we'll call his old physician in Portland."

Quinn had to smile. "Doctor Kain? Dad hates him."

"I know, but he's the only physician I know of that makes house calls."

Several bangs came from the kitchen below followed by a curse in Norwegian from Graham that never failed to make him smile.

"Graham's making pancakes. Go get something to eat, and I'll check on him before I come down."

"Okay." Quinn turned to move down the stairs and stopped. "I'm not leaving today."

Teresa nodded, placing a hand on his cheek. The thought of anyone else touching his face nearly made him flinch, but Teresa's fingers were soft reminders of the days when she used to pull him back from the brink of depression after seeing his reflection too often.

"Go eat and make sure you save some for me; you know how much Foster can put away."

The smell of frying batter and fresh blueberries wafted from the kitchen and his stomach murmured, but he stopped short of the dining room, pausing in the entry to the living room.

Mallory stood with a pink and blue feather duster in one hand and the remote to the muted plasma TV in the other. Her back was to him, and she didn't seem to notice when he approached and stopped beside her.

The television was tuned to CNN, a petite, blond reporter spoke into a microphone. Behind her a busy hospital bustled with activity. Nurses and patients roamed across the screen, which abruptly changed to a middle-aged man's worried face who spoke with exaggerated head movements, jerking with each word as if speaking was a titanic effort. Across the bottom of the screen a banner with red letters announced *Outbreak of flu strain reported in four states.*

"Can you turn that up?" Quinn asked. Mallory looked at him, her eyes glassy from staring at the screen. She hit a button on the remote and the room became flooded with the reporter's voice.

Doctor Douglas White, the head of staff here at Northern Madison Clinic, said as of yet the strain hasn't been identified. H1N1 has been ruled out as the virus responsible, but he stated that so far a new strain of flu is likely the cause. Over forty people have been admitted here in the last twenty-four hours, and sources report that more than a hundred are being treated throughout Minneapolis and Saint Paul. So far the symptoms include headache, nausea, vomiting, high fever, and upper respiratory congestion. The CDC has stated that so far this is not a pandemic by any means but urged the public to be as cautious as possible when in contact with someone who exhibits symptoms. In any case, we will continue to provide updates as they become available. Angela Singer reporting for CNN.

Mallory clicked the power button and the screen went dark, giving way to a shadowed reflection of the room and the two of them standing side by side. Quinn dropped his eyes to the floor.

"Do you think that is what Mr. Kelly has?" Mallory asked.

"Maybe. It sounds like the same symptoms, but I guess we won't know for a while. Teresa said if he got worse, Graham or Foster would bring him to the hospital."

Mallory twirled the feather duster around in little circles, spinning it until it was a blur of pink and blue.

"I mean, it's not the bad one. H1N1 is the worst as far as I know, right?" Quinn continued.

The housekeeper blinked and seemed to return from wherever she'd gone. She regarded him and then gave him a small smile.

"I'm sure he'll be fine, cariño. Don't worry; we'll take good care of him. I'll have Graham make his turkey soup for lunch. That should knock the sickness right out of him."

Mallory patted his arm once and then went in the direction of the kitchen where Graham cursed again, quieter this time. Quinn stood by himself in the living room for a moment, his eyes coming to rest on his distorted reflection before going to find the food he was no longer hungry for.

~

The remainder of the day slipped from the clock like water from a punctured bottle. Each time Quinn looked at it, another hour had passed. He'd gone for a run after breakfast, unable to stomach the sweet perfume of pancakes that the others huddled around in the dining room, the spring air whisking away a layer of dread as he jogged into it.

He'd run down the long winding drive, its blacktop clear of snow and ice now, the vestiges of winter melting in shaded alcoves beneath heavy pines. He passed Graham's,

Mallory's, and Foster's modest homes, each cut into a private yard that branched from the main drive. Their lawns weren't yet green, but soon Foster's plow truck would be stored away for the summer in exchange for the zero-turn lawnmower that never seemed to stop running in the warm season.

After a mile twisting through the dense forest of the property, the wrought-iron gate came into view, its top spiked with wicked points, a warning to anyone who contemplated climbing over to see what was on the other side. Quinn had slowed and stopped before the twelve-foot-high spokes, gazing up at them. He moved closer and placed his chilled hands on their bases, the steel so cold he pulled his palms away, watching to see if they would stick. The paved county road lay beyond the gate. It curved into sight to the north and then continued straight south, its centerline worn to a faded suggestion. No cars passed while he stood there, gazing at the road away from the place he'd always known. On other days when vehicles had come by, he'd always turned his face away even though at the speed they traveled, no one would have been able to see his features.

When he'd returned to the house, the main level was quiet except for soft music playing in the kitchen from Graham's iPod. He showered and dressed in clean clothes before going to his father's bedroom. Teresa was there beside the bed, a washcloth in one hand that she passed over James's face, wiping away the sweat that sprung up almost as soon as the cool moisture dried.

"How is he?" Quinn asked, coming closer.

"The fever's still there, but he's resting now. He didn't want any food but drank some ice-water."

"Good. You can take a break. I'll sit with him," Quinn said, motioning to the copy of *Watership Down* he held in one hand.

Teresa nodded. "Thanks, I think I'll lie down. I didn't sleep well last night."

Quinn sat in the chair pulled close to the side of the bed and studied his father's face. Sweat beaded and ran down from his temples, collecting in the towel Teresa had placed over his pillow. His arms lay motionless on the light blanket draped over him, and his breath came in slow, grating wheezes. Quinn reached out and took one of his hands, starting at the temperature of his skin.

It was freezing.

James moaned in his sleep, only his eyes moving beneath his closed lids. Quinn sat back, staring across the dim space of the room to where the curtains blocked out the bright day, before opening the book and beginning to read.

~

He woke with a start as the book slid from his grasp and fell to the floor. The room was darker, the slim shaft of sunlight that cut in between the drapes from before was gone, replaced by a sullen glow that barely defined the large windows behind them.

Quinn stood and retrieved the book, marking his place before setting it on the bedside table. James hadn't moved, his slumber punctuated by the boiler-whistle in his chest. All the ice had melted in the pitcher. He poured a glass anyway, fitting the bent straw between his father's lips. After a moment, the older man began to drink, his Adam's apple bobbing, the water clicking in his throat as it went down. When he was done, Quinn set the glass aside and ran a washcloth over his forehead. The skin was cool there, frigid to the touch, but sweat still rose continually. James coughed once, a drawn out sound that set Quinn's skin into prickling points. It was as if there were shards of broken pottery within his father's chest, grinding together, rearranging themselves as he slept.

When James quieted, Quinn moved across the room to the door, noting the time was after six in the evening. Teresa had appeared near four, placing a warm turkey sandwich on the table that he'd reluctantly eaten, Graham's expertise the only thing coercing the food to his sour stomach.

He left the room, closing the door to a crack before moving down the stairs. The sound of the television drew him to the living room where he found Mallory sitting on the couch with Graham and Foster flanking her.

"We need to bring him in or call an ambulance; he isn't any better," Quinn said, looking at them each in turn. None of them broke eye contact with the TV, and when he glanced in its direction, he saw why.

A map of the United States dominated the screen. At least thirty states were shaded in an emergency-red. Several were gray and only a few were white. Minnesota and Wisconsin were a solid black. The reporter's words finally broke through to him, and he braced his hand on the back of the couch.

The CDC's label of pandemic came early this afternoon when the slow stream of patients being admitted to hospitals across the country became a flood. Thirty-five states have reported over twenty thousand cases and five of them, including California and Florida, have tallied more than a hundred thousand. The outbreak appears to have begun somewhere in the mid-west, possibly Minnesota or Wisconsin. Those two states have had over a million reported cases of H4N9, as the scientists are calling it. The Mayo Clinic in Rochester, Minnesota, has been inundated with patients and has currently closed the doors for lack of room. Tents are being erected outside major hospitals in an attempt to accommodate the anticipated arrivals of the sick.

"My God," Mallory whispered. Her hand crept to her throat, and she squeezed the skin there over and over.

The screen changed from the map to the same woman who had reported the first cases earlier that day. Her hair was no longer styled and hung unkempt behind her ears. Her eyes were bloodshot, and her face held a tinge of red that her makeup couldn't obscure. Behind her the sides of an enormous hospital building shot up into the night, its walls illuminated by lights like the opening of a feature film. She cleared her throat once, listening intently to a device in her right ear before focusing again on the camera.

We have just received word that the President has ordered a nationwide lockdown of travel, including all international flights into and out of the country, and has instituted Martial Law in all fifty states.

"Holy shit," Foster said. He looked down at his hands and slowly pushed them into his pants pockets.

The CDC says it hasn't determined communicable pathways for H4N9 but says precautions must be taken in accordance with more typical strains of the flu virus such as physical contact and fluid exchange. The disease is highly contagious, and based on the information we are receiving, it is the fastest spreading flu in recorded history. As of now, medical officials are recommending all persons suffering from the symptoms of H4N9 be quarantined and kept hydrated-

Her words were cut off as a man in a leather coat and a dark stocking cap exploded into view. He shoved the reporter hard on the shoulder as he snatched the microphone from her grip. There was an instant of complete silence and then the man's voice invaded the living room, ragged and hysterical.

It's in the air, in the fucking air, man!

The camera's view dropped to the ground and only feet and knees were visible in the shot.

My kids got it and my wife and I had it within twelve hours. They're dead. They're all dead! It's in the air!

More feet invaded the scene and a rumbling sound like thunder came from the speakers, drowning out the man's cries. The screen went blank, and the noise stopped only seconds before an anchor desk appeared, manned by a wide-eyed woman in a blue dress and an elderly, regal man in a gray suit whose mouth hung open several inches. The man sputtered for a moment before nodding to someone outside of the view pane.

We're...we're going to take a short commercial break and be back with you- His speech cut off as the camera went dark and then broke into a vibrant jingle while a smiling man climbed behind the wheel of a brand new car.

Mallory fumbled with the remote and turned the TV off, leaving only the sound of their breathing in the room.

"We have to bring him in," Quinn said again, reaching toward Foster.

The older man stepped away from him before he could touch his arm, his eyes watery and strange as he looked at him and then away. Quinn blinked and then turned to Graham and Mallory who hadn't retreated but stared at him as if they were seeing him for the first time.

"Did you wash your hands?" Graham asked. His accent was more pronounced, the words rounding off at their ends.

"What?"

"After you left his room, did you wash your hands?"

Quinn shifted his gaze from the chef to Mallory who still clutched at the skin of her throat, pinching, pulling, kneading it like dough.

"No."

"Is he any better?" Foster asked. The groundskeeper had taken another step backward and stood near the doorway, one foot actually in the hall.

"Not that I can see. Look, we need to get him to a hospital now. If this flu is as serious as they're saying, he needs a doctor."

He panned their faces, the only ones he'd ever known. They were stoic and unfamiliar to him now, changed in some elemental way as if *their* bones had shifted beneath their skin, only enough for him to notice.

"What are you doing?" He asked, and his voice sounded far away. A hazy mist was gathering in the corners of the room, creeping into his vision and he shook his head.

"We need to take precautions, cariño," Mallory said, standing up from the couch.

"Like what? Isolate dad? Not get him help? We need to bring him in, now. No one's died yet. They didn't say anything about people dying from this."

"The guy that grabbed the microphone said his family died," Foster said. He didn't look at Quinn but past him at a point on the wall.

"He was out of his mind, and obviously not everyone is dying from this otherwise they'd be reporting it. Right?"

They stood around him, a circle made of strangers who said nothing.

"If you won't help me, I'll take him myself," he said finally, spinning toward the doorway.

Teresa stood there, blocking his way.

Her face glowed in the dim light thrown by the single lamp in the corner, drops of perspiration like dew on her forehead.

"I called Portland General. There was no answer," she said, and tipped forward.

Quinn barely caught her before she hit the floor.

Chapter 5

There and Gone

He carried her to her room by himself.

Graham made a move to help him, almost an automatic motion, but Quinn threw him a look and picked the old woman up without effort, cradling her like a child. She weighed no more than a bundle of blankets.

He laid her in her bed upstairs and covered her with a thick comforter. Her teeth clacked together, the sound grating against his nerves like sandpaper.

"You're okay. You're going to be okay now," he said, his voice barely carrying past his lips. Teresa made no sign that she heard him. Her teeth continued to chatter for long minutes, and Quinn checked her mouth to make sure she wasn't biting her tongue or cheeks. After a time her shivering subsided, her jaw slowing and then stopping like some component of a greater machine that was winding down. If this was his window to the world, Teresa and his father and even the others (their reactions), the engine that was the world was grinding to a halt. *Pandemic.* That word sounded too much like panic. They could find a cure, *would* find a cure, but how long would it take for everything to become normal again? Months, maybe years, he answered himself.

He left Teresa's room and walked the short distance down the hall to his father's door. The bedroom smelled of urine, and when he checked the sheets, he found his father had released his bladder without waking. It took him a half hour to change the beddings, all the while James slept on, oblivious to his surroundings. When he offered the straw to his lips, the older man wouldn't accept it. His teeth were ivory jail bars guarding his throat and Quinn was only able to dribble a bit of moisture into the side of his cheek. He went down to the kitchen and fetched another pitcher of ice water, making a quick trip around the ground floor to confirm Mallory, Graham, and Foster had all left. When he peered out of the kitchen window, there was a flit of light between the shifting trees that was Mallory's home, there and gone like a firefly winking out. The house was so quiet without the bustle of the others, the silence nearly deafened him, and he had to resist the urge to turn on Graham's iPod to break it.

In Teresa's room he fed her water that she drank, sputtering at first and coughing, the same grinding noise coming from her lungs as his father's. When she was resting again, Quinn found the cordless phone in his father's office downstairs and dialed Portland General, the nearest hospital. He waited, the line taking an extremely long time to connect, and when it did, an automatic message came on telling him that all scheduling personnel were assisting other patients and to call again later, or if it was an emergency to dial nine-one-one.

He hung up, staring at the phone's earpiece, listening to the quiet of the house. His fingers hovered over the buttons and then punched them, bringing the phone back to his ear. It rang once and then again, his stomach tightening with anticipation. Someone would answer, they had to, it was nine-one-one. He counted thirty-seven rings before hanging up only to call again with the same result.

The echo of the tolling line hung in his ear as he climbed the stairs again, his feet heavier than before. Fatigue swept over him, and he sunk into the chair beside his father's bed, running his fingers over his face. He found the one smooth place on the right side of his brow that was free of imperfections. He rubbed the spot, glancing at his father's sleeping form before staring at the floor.

"Nope, we're going," he said finally, and stood. Without hesitating, he pushed his hands beneath James's body, the frigid touch of his skin seeping through his clothes. It was like cradling a bag of softening ice. Quinn began to heave him up and off the bed, already calculating how he would get him to the garage and in the back of the SUV without stopping, when James cried out.

It was a gasping gurgle filled to the brim with pain. The pottery shards were back, but this time they were in his voice, giving way to a scraping wail that reminded Quinn of a small animal dying in the jaws of a predator. He immediately settled him on the bed again, wincing as James moaned once more before quieting into a stilted panting. The older man's jaw muscles flexed, and a new wave of sweat broke out on his forehead. Quinn wiped it away with a towel and watched his father, antagonizing minutes dropping away as James's breathing slowly returned to normal, the creases in his brow smoothing like waves returning to the sea.

He sat back, taut muscles going languid, the stress of the moment crashing down on him and then peeling away. He couldn't move him, there was no way to do it without killing him. The way his father's body felt in his hands, like a sack of rags wrapped around sharp rocks, he would puncture something internally simply carrying him to the door.

Quinn moved to Teresa's room and checked on her. She hadn't so much as turned in her sleep, and he propped her door open to the hallway when he left. The TV called to him, the promise of more terrible knowledge almost unbearable to resist, but instead he went to James's side and opened his book and began to read out loud again so that his voice filled the empty space in the air.

~

The morning dawned bright and clear, another admission of spring in earnest. The sun rose from the eastern horizon, climbing up from the depths of the ocean until it broke free, burning away a mist of fog that had settled overnight.

Quinn had slept fitfully. The chair was comfortable at first, but by the first light of day, it was an instrument of torture, its edges and cushions biting into him as if it were made of hungry mouths. He'd checked on his father and Teresa whenever he'd woken, dabbing their brows with washcloths and offering water, which neither of them drank.

When he stepped from his father's room in the early light, there was no familiar sound of breakfast being made downstairs. That was over. He would have to cook something for himself. He tried the numbers for the hospital as well as the emergency line again. Nine-one-one had the same result as the day before, innumerable tolls and still no answer, but Portland General didn't even transfer him to a recorded message; he simply received a busy signal over and over.

He ate a cold breakfast of cereal and milk while a pot of chicken broth heated on the stove. Balancing two bowls on a tray, he made his way upstairs when he finished eating and first spoon-fed some to his father and then to Teresa. Their jaws were locked tight in similar fashion, and he used the trick of dribbling some in the pocket of their cheeks and teeth to get a small portion of the broth down. He took their temperatures a short time later, first his father's, then Teresa's. After reading his teacher's he paused, staring at the numbers blinking on the display. Walking like someone in a dream, he returned to his father's room and retook his temp, waiting until the little unit beeped before reading it again.

104.5 degrees Fahrenheit.

Their temperatures were identical.

Quinn lowered his shaking hand and placed it on James's forehead. The skin was cool and moist, condensation on a thawing piece of meat. He let his hand rest there another moment and yanked it away when his fingers began to sink into his father's skull.

The cry that leapt to the back of his throat came out in a breathy moan. He hadn't felt that. It had been a hallucination. Something brought on by lack of sleep and stress. Stepping forward, he leaned in and studied the area where his palm had rested.

The outlines of his fingers were there in the skin, faint and fading but there.

He backpedaled, nearly tripping over his own feet as he fled to the upstairs bathroom, barely making it before vomiting into the toilet. His heart banged in his ears like an angered child slamming a door continuously.

"What the hell's happening?" he said, before his stomach heaved again.

When the nausea subsided enough for him to sink away from the toilet, he sat with his back against the claw-footed tub, his head resting on its curved lip. He remained there until he knew he could stand and washed his mouth out with water before moving down to the living room.

The television screen bloomed into life, the same news channel from the day before coming into focus. A man wearing a suit that looked as if he'd slept in it stood before the camera. His dark hair stuck up on one side of his head, and he kept attempting to smooth it down as he spoke.

-tion-wide panic has erupted overnight. The streets of Washington are full of protesters, many of them carrying weapons, firing guns, and clubbing those who try to subdue them. The death toll this morning is unknown since many of the major treatment centers have been unreachable, but we do know that those afflicted with H4N9 began dying late last night. The CDC hasn't released a report on their efforts to create a vaccine or what the conversion of infection to death rate is at this time, but we expect them to within the hour. Early analytical reports have stated that the mortality rate could be as high as seventy-five percent.

Quinn tried to catch the remote, but it slipped from his hand. And when he knelt to retrieve it, the strength fled from his legs and he crumpled to the couch behind him. He stared at the screen as the reporter listed off emergency centers that were still accepting the ill.

There were none in the state of Maine.

He thumbed the power button and let the room fall into silence. A gentle breeze nudged the windows and he looked outside at the cerulean sky, unblemished, the pine trees swaying gently. How would the sea look today? Aquamarine or cobalt or maybe gunmetal gray. The Atlantic never seemed to be in concurrence with the weather. It was its own dominion, independent of the sky and breeze. How would it be to get in the skiff and sail away across it? Let the waves and wind take him where they wished. Forget the broken sounds from his father and Teresa's lungs; forget the freezing, damp of their skin beneath his fingers; forget the quiet air of the house with no one speaking.

A sick, ratcheting cough came from above and he turned toward the stairs, listening to the brittle grinding sound that shouldn't have been coming from a person. Teresa, it was Teresa.

Quinn ran up the stairway taking the treads two at a time and rushed into her room. The old woman was on her side, shaking and shivering with each cough, curling in on herself like a dead leaf in a fire. He knelt at her side, throwing an arm over her thin shoulders, trying to brace her without really knowing what else to do. She hacked long and painful, her breath sounding like it was full of sand and gravel. Eventually she had nothing left, and she sagged, rolling slowly onto her back again. He gently sat her up enough to prop two pillows behind her sweating back, and when he eased her against them, her eyes were open. They were bloodshot and pain-ridden, but clearly seeing him.

"Are you okay?" she wheezed.

Quinn deflated, his air coming out in one long breath.

"You're asking if I'm okay? Yes, I'm fine."

"You don't feel it?"

"Feel what?"

"The cold?"

"No, I'm okay."

"Good." Teresa closed her eyes and was able to breathe deep without succumbing to another coughing spell. He brought the glass close to her face, offering the straw to her. She shook her head.

"Not thirsty."

"You have to drink; you're sweating buckets."

"How's your father?"

"The same, still sleeping."

"The others?"

He hesitated. "They're fine."

She nodded, her hand sliding toward his over the blankets. He took it.

"I left him," she said after a time.

"Who?"

"My son. You asked me the other day if he left me. He didn't; I left him."

Quinn frowned and waited. Teresa's chest was rising slower than before, but her fingers were strong in his own. When she spoke again, her voice was lower than a whisper, the sound of the wind in the pines.

"His name is Jeffrey. I was twenty when I got pregnant. Second year of college and his father was a married man, though I didn't know it at the time. When he found out, he threatened me. Said that if I told anyone who the father was, he'd find a way to remove me from school. Said he'd keep me from getting in anywhere else that I applied.

He was a man of power and was kind up until that point." She turned her head to the side, toward the window. The shades were open and the sky was still the seamless blue, unstitched by any clouds.

"I wanted to teach so badly, you see. It had been my dream since I was a little girl. My first teacher's name was Mrs. Felling. She was beautiful and kind and had such a way with us kids. She could get us to do anything, learn anything, and that's a real gift. Many teach but few are teachers. I was so young and stupid and scared. I knew I couldn't raise a baby on my own. So when he told me that he'd keep me from becoming what I'd always wanted, I made a decision."

Her grip on his hand tightened and she shifted her gaze back to him, her eyes clouded with memory and something else, grief.

"The couple that adopted him were from Boston. He was a truck driver and she worked in a bank. They couldn't have children of their own but wanted them desperately. We agreed on a name for him the day he was born and three days later I said goodbye to him forever."

Despite the sheen of sweat that coated her face, he could spot the tracks of her tears easily. They ran down the grooves that time had worn in her cheeks and disappeared below her chin.

"It was the biggest mistake of my life, one I never got over. He's out there somewhere and I hope he's safe. The last I heard he was a father himself with two children of his own, grandchildren that I'll never meet. And I don't deserve to meet them."

"You can't say that," Quinn said, his voice thick. "That's not true."

She coughed again, but it was feeble and the fit lasted only seconds. She appeared further away somehow, more distant than she had been moments ago even though neither of them had moved.

"Then I came here and you were my light all these years. You were such a good student, so smart. You're the son I got to raise as a second chance. You're ready for the world now. Don't be afraid. The fear…" she wheezed again, not a spasm at all but a constriction within her that didn't allow her to speak. "…it's a thief. It steals from us if we let it."

"You need to rest. Here, have some water." He tried to retrieve the glass from the table but she held his hand fast.

"Don't let it steal from you. Don't be afraid…" Her voice drifted and he saw the ocean in her eyes, a wave receding from the beach that didn't return. "…my son."

The fingers within his hand were brittle and very dry. The shine of perspiration was gone and her mouth hung open a little, her last breath escaping without any effort to draw another.

"Teresa," he said, already knowing somewhere inside where all truths are told that there would be no answer.

He rose and placed a hand against her lined cheek. Her skin was warm again, like that of floorboards resting in a setting sun, the heat draining along with the light. Words came from his mouth but he didn't know what they meant. They sounded alien to him, a language he'd never spoken before made of broken syllables amid sobs that twisted his insides into a plucked guitar string.

He sunk into the chair again and sat forward, his face resting against her hand, the scent of rose petals everywhere, the smell of his childhood long since passed.

It was forever before he sat up, his own tears drying. A dream had surrounded him, so he must have slept leaning against her bed with her palm pressed to his face. In it he had walked to the edge of the cliff overlooking the ocean. The sea had undulated in a strange way, not moving as water should, and it took him several moments to realize that there was no ocean below but only bodies floating together, dead flesh interlaced as waves of blood brought them onto the shore and drew them away.

He stood and looked at the woman in the bed, the only mother he'd ever known. She was shrunken and small, flattened in a way that made her appear like one of the blankets. When he stepped closer, he saw that it wasn't an illusion.

Teresa was sinking in on herself.

Her body was slumping inward, her features smoothing so that her face was nearly level, a two-dimensional drawing of how she looked in life. A foul odor met him and he brought his hand up to cover his mouth and nose. A scream wanted to tear from his lungs. It would rip through his chest if he didn't let it out. He struggled with himself as the room canted at his feet, threatening to slide him into a corner where he could sit and fall in upon himself just like Teresa. Collapse into nothing and be done with the nightmare.

Quinn bit down hard on the inside of his mouth, clenching his jaws until he tasted blood. The room righted itself and he breathed in the stink that filled it. Unwilling to look at what she had become, he drew the blankets the rest of the way over her form, turning the ever-present scream into a moan as he heard and felt her body implode more with the movement. The odor increased and he gagged, turning away from the bed and its shrinking occupant.

The hallway held blessedly clean air that he drank in with long breaths, filling himself over and over. As he made his way to his father's room, he slowed, pausing with his hand on the doorknob. What would he find inside? The same as what he'd just left? Worse? His stomach roiled and the urge to simply sit down nearly overcame him, but instead he turned the handle and stepped inside.

The room was dark but enough light shone in from behind him to see the rise and fall of his father's chest.

He went in and sat beside him, fumbling for a second in the dark looking for the other man's hand. And when he found it, it was warm.

Quinn swallowed, looking at his father. "Dad?"

There was a pause and quiet, longer and more silent than any he'd ever known, then James opened his eyes. He looked around the room as if studying it for the first time before his gaze slid onto Quinn. Nothing there for a long moment, no recognition, no softness or love, just a dull comprehension that he saw him.

"Can you hear me, dad?"

James licked his lips and his tongue made a scratching sound.

"Quinn."

"I'm here, dad, I'm right here."

"Run away."

"I'm not leaving you."

"You run. If there's something wrong, you run and don't look back. Run and hide."

Quinn searched his father's face for some other meaning. The man that lay before him didn't look like someone barely past fifty years old but instead closer to eighty. His hair, so lush before, receded from his forehead, creeping away to expose the withering effects of the disease on his features. Did he know where he was now? Did he know what was happening? The sickness had taken Teresa so quickly, but his father was still here, still surviving. He reached out to place a hand on his forehead but stopped and dropped it back into his lap.

"I'm going to get you help, okay? You just need to stay with me and rest."

Barely a nod, then more words that he couldn't make out echoing up from the husk his father had become.

"I couldn't hear you, dad."

James licked his lips again, the same rasping sound, a shoe being drug on concrete.

"Sorry, I'm so sorry. My fault."

"You don't have to be sorry. It's not your fault. Everything's okay. Everything's taken care of."

Quinn reached for the water and held the straw to his father's lips, but the older man coughed, liquid rumbling deep in his chest now.

"Think I'd like..." James paused, his jaw working as he searched for the strength to continue. "...a beer."

Quinn couldn't help the laugh that came out. "Okay, I'll get you one."

He started to rise but his father's hand gripped his harder, pulling him down. He then let go and reached, reached up, his arm trembling as he struggled against gravity. Quinn leaned in, noticing with alarm that the muscle in James's arm sagged like taffy inside the skin, the bones pulling taut on the opposite side. The older man's hand found his face, the fingers dry against his cheek. They flitted there, rubbing the malformations beneath his own skin, the touch beyond gentle.

"Beautiful boy," James whispered and lowered his arm to the bed. A small smile creased his cracked lips. Quinn swiped at his blurred vision, standing again.

"I'll be right back, dad."

James nodded and blinked several times at the ceiling.

Quinn hurried from the room, jogging down the stairs to the kitchen and froze in the doorway.

Mallory and Foster stood at the opposite end of the room, both wearing masks that he'd seen the groundskeeper use when painting one of the houses. Their eyes were wide above the masks and they paused when he entered the room, the heavy canvas bag between them bulging with something.

"What are you doing?" Quinn said.

Foster glanced at Mallory and then cinched the bag shut before throwing it over one shoulder. The housekeeper sidled toward the door, knocking over the pot Quinn had warmed the chicken broth in. It clanged and both Mallory and Foster jerked at the sound. He took a step closer and Foster held up a hand, his forehead pinched into horizontal lines.

"Stay back." His voice was muffled but the words were clear enough.

"What are you doing?" Quinn repeated. There was something in Foster's eyes, a fluttering that became decision as he blinked and turned toward the door leading to the front yard.

"I'll be in the truck," Foster said to Mallory.

As he left, Quinn caught sight of several water bottle caps protruding from the end of the bag that wasn't zipped shut. Mallory reached beneath the mask and began to pull at her throat.

"You're leaving?" Quinn asked. He took another step forward without meaning to, unable to help it. Mallory retreated.

"I'm sorry, cariño. Graham is sick now too and-"

"But where are you going? There's nowhere to go."

"Foster's cabin in Pennsylvania is on a mountain. It's secluded and safe."

"Nowhere is safe," Quinn said, the anger in his voice cutting through the air. "You're leaving us but there's nowhere safe out there past those gates."

"We can't stay; the sickness is here. We have to leave before it's too late." Mallory said, edging backwards and now tears ran from her brown eyes onto the lip of the mask. "I'm sorry, so sorry. We left food and water. We only took what we'll need to get there."

"Teresa's dead."

She paused for an instant and then backed the rest of the way out of the house.

"I'm sorry," she whispered, and hurried to where Foster's extended-cab Ford waited, the darker shadow of Foster himself in the driver's seat. Quinn moved to the doorway and watched them reverse until the groundskeeper could turn the vehicle around. Mallory removed her mask and stared out at him, her face streaked with fresh tears. She didn't wave as they accelerated away, their taillights flashing once before the truck rounded the first curve and disappeared.

He stood there for a long time, his hand resting on the doorjamb, eyes focused on the spot where the truck had vanished. The wind pushed its way through the trees and found his face, cool and still holding the last bite of winter. Silence, pure and unbroken.

After a while, he shut the door and stared at the kitchen counter, the partially open pantry, a muddy print from Foster's shoe. He made his way to the fridge and took out a cold can of beer from the top shelf, gripping it tight. He wound his arm back to hurl it through one of the kitchen windows but stopped, breathing hard as he forced himself to swallow the jagged lump in his throat. He leaned against the nearby countertop and squeezed the can again, waiting for it to explode in a flurry of foam. His fingers ached and a pain began to pulse behind his eyes. Maybe this was how it started.

He trudged up the stairs, opening the beer as he went. The smell from Teresa's room had crept into the hall and invaded his nostrils. Quinn closed his eyes and entered his father's room.

James lay on his side facing the window, his legs drawn up beneath him. Quinn circled the bed, pausing to grab the straw from the water glass and stopped short.

The drawn guitar string inside him tightened and then snapped.

His father's face was pale and slack, a melting wax likeness of who he had been. One arm hugged a pillow close to his still chest and his eyes were half lidded as if he were only drowsing.

A pressing hand Quinn couldn't see forced him down, his legs folding beneath him until he sat. The beer fell from his grasp and spilled on the floor, a faint chugging coming from its mouth until it was gone and all was quiet in the house except for the sound of his weeping.

Chapter 6

Three Graves

He buried them side by side beneath the biggest pine on the north lawn.
    Despite the shade the reaching branches provided, the ground was soft from the melting snow and came away in chunks with the shovel. He'd wrapped his father and Teresa in the bed sheets and carried them down once the graves were dug. As he placed them in the holes, he ignored the way the bodies felt beneath the wrappings, insubstantial and watery, as if they would pool out onto the ground at any moment and soak into the soil the way the snow had done.
    He stood on the side of the holes looking down at their shapes, letting the time slip away and the breeze chill the sweat he'd worked up digging. His mouth tried to form words, something of meaning, but every time he began to speak his throat closed, cinching off any speech. When he started to shiver, he picked up the shovel again and filled in the graves, humming a song beneath his breath to drown out the sound the dirt made when it fell. It wasn't until he finished that he realized it was the Sinatra tune his father had been singing the night he came home from his trip.
    Quinn left the shovel beneath the tree, stuck in the ground at the head of what could be a third grave. The flickering pain behind his eyes was still there but dimmer than before and his skin was warm, not cold. He didn't know if he was relieved or disappointed. At the door to the house, he stopped and looked down the driveway, dead leaves skipping across its divide. Inside he poured the last of the broth into a Tupperware bowl and covered it before walking down the silent drive.
    Graham's house was the first on the left, tucked into the thick forest behind a short turn in the narrow road. His father had spared no expense on the employee homes, building each with its own character and style. Graham's was a brick, cape cod style with two dormers and gray shutters. The chef had said his Nordic blood demanded a sauna, and James had complied upon hiring him, building a small addition onto the already completed house.
    The smoke that almost always curled from the little chimney atop the sauna was absent as he approached and Quinn sighed, mounting the steps to the front porch. He knocked hard on the front door and waited only seconds before trying the knob. It turned and he stepped inside.
    The house smelled much like the kitchen he'd just left. Garlic, cilantro, and the scent of homemade dinner rolls permeated the air, but beneath it there was something else. Quinn paused after closing the door and set the chicken broth down on the counter.
    "Graham?" Silence chased his voice from the house, and he listened for the rustle of sheets, a squeaking floorboard, something, but there was nothing, only the same quiet that filled his own home.

He moved across the wide living room and into a hallway. The smell was stronger here, choking out the aromas of food with its stench. It hung in the hall like something alive, festooning the air with a message that couldn't be denied. *Only death lives here now.*

Quinn shivered and stopped before Graham's bedroom door. It stood partially open, a slash of afternoon sunshine beating through the window and ending near his feet.

"Graham?"

He braced himself and pushed the door all the way open.

The room was in shambles.

A heavy oak dresser lay on its side, the mirror at its top shattered and reflecting the ceiling in its shards. Sets of clothes were piled and scattered everywhere as if Graham had been trying them on and discarding them in haste. Blankets and pillows were strewn across floor and beneath the bed. The bed itself was stripped bare and there were several puffs of fabric pulled up at its center.

Quinn moved into the room, stepping around the broken mirror until he stood beside the bed. The smell of putrescent fish was so thick here he could barely breathe. He placed a hand to his nose, but it did no good so he dropped it away. The mattress was partly discolored; its deep red fabric stained a darker brown in some places. When he reached out to touch it, he found that it was wet, soaking almost. A clear fluid dripped from the bedframe and added to a puddle on the floor he hadn't noticed at first. The tufts of material near the center of the bed had long scratches at their edges along with trails of red that could only be blood.

He swallowed the gorge rising up from his stomach and stepped back, stumbling over on overturned chair. The puddle on the floor, it was Graham, it had to be. He had succumbed faster to the sickness and completely disintegrated into the foul-smelling fluid. This was what was happening to his father and Teresa right now, down in the damp ground where he'd buried them.

Quinn turned and half walked, half ran from the room, sucking in great lungfuls of stinking air that only choked him. He stopped in the living room, knowing he would be sick but trying to hold it at bay. The back of the sofa was under his hand and he swayed there, drunk with the knowledge that he was now truly alone. A sound along with movement came from the rear of the house, startling him. He swung his head to the left, a cold hand clamping down in the center of his chest.

The back door eased open and then closed, banging against the frame beneath the wind's insistence.

Quinn watched it for a moment and then moved to the front door, leaving the broth on the counter.

~

He cleaned for the remainder of the afternoon, scrubbing the carpets upstairs in both his father's and Teresa's rooms, but nothing would take the smell away. Eventually he resorted to hauling the mattresses out to the backyard, stacking them near the tree line to burn in the morning. When dusk came, he showered, standing under the hot spray until it scalded his skin, his fingers rubbed raw from the brush and soap he used to clean his hands and nails.

The fridge held nothing that interested him, so he settled for a cup of tea, stirring in sugar as the last holdings of light faded from the sky. When he finally turned the TV on, the news stations were down, their logos filling up the screen. He flipped through the rest of the channels finding only re-runs of sitcoms and reality TV. He went through all of them again just to be sure and then turned the set off. The stillness of the house settled around him, and he went to the kitchen window to look out at the giant pine and the two mounds of dirt beneath it. They were only blurs of shadow now, simply another part of the landscape that would grow grass and become indistinguishable in the years ahead.

Quinn poured his tea down the drain and looked in the direction of his father's office. The internet might still be a resource, perhaps it would give him a better idea if there was anything left of the world outside the gates.

As he moved toward the hall, a humming began to fill the air and he paused, listening to the growing buzz that became a static hiss. The last nor'easter that had howled down upon them in February had sounded something like this with its relentless wind and rushing snow. The sound grew and grew until he began to crouch out of reflex, his hands coming to the sides of his head. A glass sitting on the edge of the counter pitched to the floor, exploding into a thousand pieces. The roar built, vibrating his teeth in their sockets as he realized what it was. He hurried to the front door, throwing it open to the night as the commercial airliner cruised past, its running lights blinking barely a hundred feet over the trees. It was like being underwater and seeing a giant predatory fish swim by, gliding past in search of food. The massive plane disappeared into the night, engines whining against gravity and he waited, staring after it until the concussion boomed in the distance and a glow lit the horizon in a sickly, licking orange.

The flames climbed for a long time, burning high into the dark heavens before relenting and falling into a somber radiance that would've seemed peaceful had he not known its source.

Quinn shut the door and paused at the juncture in the hallway, staring down its darkened length to the office before continuing on into the conservatory. He laid on the daybed, tucking one arm beneath his head and knew that sleep would not come, there would be no way it could. Not after today.

But after he gave the brightening stars a last look through the room's curved glass, he closed his eyes and drifted off within seconds.

~

A keening scream woke him hours later in the dead of night. He bolted upward at the sound, almost sprawling to the floor as vertigo swept over him, the embrace of sleep still strong in his limbs. The cries were high and short, screeching across the grounds in blasts that curled his guts in on themselves like coiling snakes. It was a rabbit in distress, there was no mistaking it. He'd heard it once before when a female had given birth to a litter beneath Mallory's back porch. Foster had live trapped them but one of the young had gotten pinned beneath the trap's spring-loaded door. Its cries had echoed all the way to the main house. Foster had tried to save it but it had died a day later, its spine crushed, its hind legs limp and useless.

The screams cut off as abruptly as they began and Quinn moved to the west end of the conservatory in the general direction the sounds had come from. He leaned into the glass, its surface cold beneath his palms.

The grass shone silver outside beneath the light of a half-moon. The woods were drapes of solid shadow. He watched the tree line for movement but none came. He stood there for a while, hands pressed to the glass like a patient observer at the zoo. His breath began to fog a section below his face and he reached to wipe it away as a strange sensation sprouted like a seed within him. It made gooseflesh erupt across the nape of his neck and down the backs of his arms in sickening waves. He stepped away from the glass quickly, retreating until he stood at the entrance to the conservatory. The urge to flee expanded until it was all he could feel, the same instincts that he was sure the now silent rabbit possessed in life, calling out to run, run, run.

Quinn swallowed and made his way through the dark house until he was in the living room. He wrapped himself in a thick quilt hanging over a chair and laid down on the large sofa, his eyes glancing around the room. The house ticked as it settled on its foundations. The small sounds that he knew so well were alien to him now. Each creak was a footstep, each click a doorknob turning.

He fell asleep without knowing it, sliding seamlessly into a dream of running through an endless forest, dark and twisted branches tugging at his clothes like beggars seeking change. There was something behind him but he couldn't gather the courage to look back. In the late morning, he woke covered in sweat and breathing hard, as if he had actually been sprinting only moments before. He rose and refolded the blanket before making his way to the kitchen.

When he looked out the window, he saw that the graves had been dug up during the night.

Chapter 7

Visitors

He stood beside the disturbed earth, looking down.

Both sheets he'd wrapped the bodies in were visible, the shrouds torn and tugged upward revealing a jelly-like substance caked with dirt. The soil itself had been turned and scattered into the surrounding grass, some sticking to the trunk of the towering pine. Quinn moved around the holes, trying to ignore the stench that rose from them. The smell was overlaid with an oily odor that came and went with the wind. He looked to the west to where the jet crashed the night before. A slice of gray smoke rose, cutting the blue sky into halves.

He knelt and touched the dirt. There were marks from the animal that had done this in the overturned earth. It had dug down and pulled the sheets up and after finding nothing to eat, moved on. Quinn stood and picked up the shovel that had fallen over in the night, recovering the sheets as best he could. When he was finished, he looked into the woods, his eyes growing unfocused. A bear—it had to be—or maybe a coyote. There was nothing else large enough in the state of Maine to exhume the graves overnight. The problem with the theory was the fence surrounding the property. Smaller animals could move freely between its bars but anything larger would be unable to gain access, unless it had been inside the hundred acres when the fence had been erected eighteen years ago.

"We would've seen it," Quinn said to the woods. But maybe not. Animals were reclusive, especially bears. There were deer on the property; he'd seen them many times over the years, but never anything else besides squirrels and rabbits, along with the occasional porcupine.

He turned from the woods, and just as he was about to walk toward the house, his eyes snagged on the lawn's border further down.

The mattresses were gone.

His breath hooked in his lungs and hung there for a long moment before coming out again. He walked slowly until he came even with the spot where he'd left the soiled mattresses. There were shreds of fabric strewn in the dead leaves and some tatters caught on tree trunks. A dozen yards back in the woods the sun glinted off of the twisted steel springs exposed within the remains of the mattresses. They looked like broken bodies after some horrific accident.

A worm of fear glided through his stomach. The fence had broken somewhere, fallen down over time or perhaps beneath a large bear's insistence. Quinn nodded, trying to swallow the dryness in his throat. He backed away from the woods, awaiting movement and the flash of dark fur somewhere in its depths. The rear deck bumped into the back of his legs and a groan escaped him as he fell onto his ass, the fall jarring his vision. He almost let out a laugh but cut it off, knowing how crazy it would sound.

He stood and went around to the front door as sunlight peered over the tops of the trees lining the drive. He ate a cereal bar standing by the kitchen counter, washing it down with the last of the milk. How long before he would have to go out looking for food? When he inspected the pantry, he saw that Mallory had told the truth. She and Foster had barely touched the stores within. There were two unopened cases of bottled water, multiple shelves full of canned food, and an entire corner holding Graham's baking necessities. One shelf was solely dedicated to his father's favorite Herring. He reached out to touch one of the slim containers and then turned away.

The freezer was well stocked with frozen chicken, turkey, ham, seafood, and ten pounds of ground beef. The fridge looked surprisingly empty and the reason why came to him as he shut the door. Today was Sunday. Mallory always went grocery shopping on Sunday.

He checked the TV and found the same result as the day before except now several stations were simply blank screens of darkness. Quinn flicked the power button and left the living room.

His father's office was warm and filled with light, the mahogany surfaces like dark honey, the crystal glasses glowing. He sat behind the massive desk and powered up his father's sleek desktop computer. The WIFI signal was strong in the upper right-hand corner and he clicked the Internet symbol. His father had chosen Yahoo as his homepage, and when it loaded, Quinn sat back from the screen, his fingers hanging over the keyboard and then falling to his lap.

The page was generally the same with its sidebars of ads and electronically shouted proclamations, but now at its center, instead of a rotating list of current news and photos, was a single video box, dark except for a red play triangle in its middle. There was no headline and below the box was an uneven mixture of letters and numbers running on in an unending paragraph that continued down and down as he scrolled. At the top of the page, his fingers brought the arrow over the play button on the video and hovered there before tapping it.

The video started, the camera showing a shaky frame of a pair of feet beneath a vehicle's steering wheel. It swung up and focused out of the driver's side window. The car was parked on an interstate somewhere that looked like Midwest farm country. Barren fields not yet greened by summer rolled into the distance and a string of power lines stood like sentries, their cables drooping between them. It was evening and the sun had fallen behind the horizon, its last glow seeping into the darkening sky. There was a rushing sound of static as the camera holder adjusted the zoom and then a man's muffled voice.

Do you see it? Right there on the second hill.

The camera joggled some more and then focused on a distant rise that held a tangle of brush and the outline of a lonely tree with pointed branches drooping toward the ground.

Quinn leaned closer to the computer screen. There was something strange and familiar about the tree. Its top had a bulbous look, incongruent with the rest of its thin stature. It had the appearance of being broken halfway up and its base was so spindly it didn't look strong enough to hold up the rest of its bulk. The camera dipped and came up again, a woman's voice this time saying something that he couldn't make out. The zoom engaged and the tree blurred before clearing once more, its features defining so that something within his mind forced his eyes to widen, his jaw falling open.

The tree moved.

It stepped to the side, its narrow trunk splitting in two as the camera tipped skyward. The woman squealed a warning. A thin, pale flash swung past the camera only feet outside the car's window. The video blurred and filmed a split second of the car's roof and the lower half of a man's bearded face before ending and resetting to its beginning.

Quinn sat back from the computer. His finger hovered over the play button before punching it again. He watched in silence trying to make out the words that the couple said, but they were too indistinct, too garbled. But he could hear something else clearly enough in their voices, running like a frigid river below a layer of ice. Fear. They were both terrified. The tree enlarged on the screen, impossibly taking a step to the side as the shot turned up and caught the pale thing passing the car again. Quinn paused the video, staring at the image. The thin strip outside the vehicle was bent, its middle bulging slightly with a few small dents at its joint. The entire shape looked rounded, like a white stilt bending at its center.

Quinn examined the screen for several long minutes, something stirring in the back of his mind. His lips began to tingle and he blinked, his hand reaching for the computer to start the video again.

The screeching of brakes came from the direction of the highway followed by a bang that he felt reverberate through the desk. A clicking issued from somewhere in the house and the lights went out. The computer's screen flipped to darkness, reflecting his face only inches from it along with the room behind him.

Quinn jerked, sitting back in the chair, his eyes flitting around the office. The power had gone out. The sound of the refrigerator motor winding down was the last noise and then supreme quiet invaded the house.

He stood, his legs wobbling and his stomach slewing as if it were overly full of a noxious soup. He moved down the hallway, pausing in the kitchen before continuing out the back door. The air was lighter outside, the smell of burning jet fuel no longer as pungent. Quinn breathed it in, trying to calm the nausea that rose and fell within him, a sickening tide. He looked toward the highway, listening for any further sounds but heard nothing. Only the wind spoke in the branches.

Fresh sea breeze coasted past him as he moved around to the rear of the house. He found the squat generator box and opened its access door. The generator was a large unit, capable of powering the entire house and attached garage. It was set up to turn on immediately following an outage, and it was only then he realized that it hadn't kicked on when it should have.

He examined the controls and bundles of wires running into and out of the unit. One of the buttons in the center of the side panel was labeled 'Auto Start'. He pressed it and pulled his hand away quickly. There was a sound from inside its steel shroud like dominoes snapping together. He waited for a moment and when nothing else happened, he pressed the button again. There was the same loud clicking and then silence.

Quinn stepped out of the enclosure and stared at the machine. Maybe it was out of gas? Foster had been meticulous about his work, always going the extra step to ensure that each job was done fully and correctly. But how long had it been since they'd had a power failure? A year? Two? The groundskeeper could've forgotten about the generator's maintenance, or maybe he'd been in the midst of exchanging the fuel and gotten sidetracked on another project.

Quinn stepped back inside the enclosure and found the gas spout jutting from the side of the machine. Above it was a gauge, its level reading full. He frowned and dropped his hand away from the spout's cap. For some reason, the video began to replay in his mind and he shivered before climbing back into the sunlit yard. There must be a manual for the generator somewhere, most likely in Foster's house. Maybe there was a reset that he could engage to get the machine running.

As he walked around the side of the house and started down the drive, a metallic clanging erupted from the highway. Steel on steel rang through the forest, a hollow gonging that stopped him in his tracks. It went on for thirty seconds before there was a short bang and then nothing. Quinn swallowed, waiting, waiting. His muscles were solid beneath his skin, beginning to ache from being continuously taut. There was the low hum of an engine and then the crackling of tires coming closer down the driveway.

He turned and ran.

Hurdling across the lawn he raced up the stairs and flew to the kitchen door, slamming against it and bouncing back when the knob refused to turn in his hand.

Locked.

He'd locked it on the way in earlier. He cursed and ran around the side of the building, the sound of the engine getting louder behind him. At the back door, he swung inside, shutting and locking it before hurrying to the kitchen. Standing to one side of the large windows, he waited, eyes welded to the closest bend in the drive, blood surging in his ears.

The shining chrome of a truck's grille appeared.

Quinn ducked away from the window and bent low as he hurried out of the room and down the hall to the office. Without a glance outside, he knelt by his father's desk and pulled the lowest drawer open. The gray lockbox was covered by three file folders, which he pulled out and set on the floor. *The code, the code, the code.* He'd forgotten the code. His fingers hovered over the numbers, the sound of the truck's engine getting louder before shutting off. The numbers sprang into his head as if flung there from outside. *942304.* The lid of the box popped upward and only as he reached inside did he realize that the code was his birth date backwards.

The Springfield XDM was heavy as he drew it into the light. Its black polymer grip and forty-five-caliber bore gave it an intimidating look that had impressed him years before when targeting with his father. Now the handgun shook as he pulled back the slide, barely remembering how the weapon functioned. There was a round in the chamber and the safeties were on the trigger and grip. The small flashlight attached below the barrel came on, shining against the wall, and he flinched. He'd triggered it by toggling a small pad beneath his thumb. Hitting the little switch again, he turned the light off.

Quinn snapped the lock box shut, storing it away in the drawer and moved to the office window. The entire room vibrated around him with each heartbeat. The truck was parked directly before the front door. It was a vibrant red with mud flung up its fenders in brown arcs. Its doors were open but there was no one in sight.

"Oh God," Quinn breathed, and walked into the hallway. At the doorway to the kitchen, he stopped and peered around the corner.

There were two men holding shotguns moving up the walk to the kitchen door. They were both tall and broad-shouldered, wearing stained jeans and camouflage hunting jackets. One of them wore a black bandanna over his mouth and nose, his eyes flitting to the right and left above it.

Quinn backed away from the corner and reached blindly behind him for the bannister leading upstairs. The first man came up the steps and stopped before the door. He looked over his shoulder and cocked his head to one side as if he were listening to something. Quinn's hand found the railing and he began to sidle up the stairs as his eyes landed on the drinking glass he'd used that morning. It sat in the middle of the counter, the leftover milk still wet at its bottom.

The man at the door reared back and threw a kick at the lock. The door shuddered in its frame.

Quinn ran.

He flew up the steps as the second kick hit the door and the sound of cracking wood filled the lower level. He turned in a stupid circle on the landing before opening his bedroom door. There was nowhere to hide. They would be sure to find him beneath the bed or in the closet. Another kick from the kitchen and then the sound of the door banging open against the wall.

They were inside.

Shaking, he shut his bedroom door and started for his father's room, then turned to Teresa's. Both of them were laid out the same as his own. Whispers came from the kitchen, floating up to him as if he were in a dream. The XDM almost slipped from his sweaty hand and his vision wavered. Footsteps came quietly into the hall and headed toward the office. Quinn retreated to the end of the landing and crouched, bringing up the handgun. The sights wobbled as he aimed at the head of the stairs. *Squeeze the trigger, never jerk it, otherwise you'll miss every time.* His father's voice spoke within his mind, calm, assuring. His finger tightened on the trigger as he heard one of the men speak.

"Check upstairs; I'll look around the garage."

Quinn's vision teared up, and he blinked as his eyes landed on the linen closet door beside him. Without a sound, he stood and turned the knob, slipping inside and closing the door as he heard the man climb onto the landing and move into his father's bedroom.

In the utter darkness of the linen closet, he ran his hands over the wide shelving. Rags and cleaning supplies on the lowest shelf, sheets and bedding next, extra towels and pillows near the ceiling. Quinn tucked the handgun into his pocket and found the rear of the closet and began to climb. In the hallway, the man cursed the smell and moved closer, blasting Teresa's door open with a kick. Quinn gripped the topmost shelf and blindly began to shove stacks of towels to either side. With a heave, he flattened himself onto the shelf, pulling his legs up and over a column of pillows. The gun scraped against the board beneath him and he winced, listening. Footsteps crossed the hallway outside the door and entered his room. His breathing the loudest sound in the world, he rearranged the pillows and towels before him, trying to straighten them the best he could in the dark. He laid with his back against the wall, his legs straight out, stiffening as his bed was overturned in the next room. With a final movement, he picked up a towel and flung it toward his feet, feeling it cover part of his legs, but stopping short of his toes.

The closet door opened, flooding light inside as he drew the gun out of his pocket. Between two stacks of towels, he saw the man with the bandanna step inside and flip the switch on. The light bulb directly in front of where Quinn lay remained dark, and the intruder laughed quietly behind the handkerchief before stepping inside. The man's head and shoulders were all he could see from the angle of the top shelf. Bandanna moved closer, and Quinn lost him from view completely. The man rummaged the shelves below, knocking cleaning supplies to the floor as he turned in a half-circle.

Quinn pushed the handgun through the small gap in the towels, steadying it so the grip wouldn't rattle against the shelf as his hand shook. Bandanna moved back into view holding a large comforter under one arm. He paused and turned his head to the side, his profile dark against the light streaming in from the hallway. He stood there, a statue in the doorway, listening. Quinn opened his mouth, trying to breathe as quietly as he could. His arm was beginning to ache from holding it at the odd angle before him. The sights of the gun jounced across Bandanna's skull. His finger tightened on the trigger.

"Hey Rick."

The voice came from the base of the stairs. The man turned and stepped into the hallway.

"Yeah?"

"There's a nice Tahoe in the garage. Wanna take it?"

"No, the truck'll do better on the back roads. You find anything else?"

"Nope. Didn't see any sign of anyone either. You sure someone was here?"

"The milk in that glass is still wet down there. Someone was here this morning."

"Well, they're not here now."

Rick shot a glance into the closet once more, his eyes running over Quinn's hiding place before he began to swing the door shut.

Quinn's thumb touched the flashlight switch and a blade of light sprung between the towels and hit the closing door. He jerked his thumb away from the grip and the light disappeared.

The door stopped closing and then slowly re-opened.

Rick stepped back inside the closet, examining the place on the door where the flashlight beam had landed. He scanned the space once more, searching the darkness where Quinn lay.

"Rick?" The other man's voice was closer now.

Rick cradled his shotgun, the blanket he was carrying now at his feet in a pile.

"What're you doing?"

"Thought I saw something."

"What?"

"A light or something on the door as I was closing it."

"Probably a reflection."

The silence became pregnant. Unbearable. Quinn shuddered, not believing they couldn't hear his heart thundering. He held the sight as steady as he could on Rick's forehead.

"Yeah, probably."

"The pantry's pretty full. You were right about this place."

The two men turned away from the linen closet, Rick gathering the comforter once again. They moved down the stairs and out of sight, their voices funneling up from the lower floor.

Quinn drew his arm back and rested the gun on his chest. His entire body ran with sweat, and strange colors danced on the darkened ceiling above him.

"I can't believe how that transformer went up when the car hit it. Fourth of July, man."

"Dumbfucks shouldn't have run. I wasn't going to kill them." Rick's voice was lower but still discernable.

"I bet it knocked out power to half the county."

"Probably."

"See, I wasn't kidding about the pantry. Fully stocked."

"Get the cooler and we'll take some meat from the freezer."

The sounds of the men taking his food floated up to Quinn and he closed his eyes. A heavy weariness draped over him and unbelievably he realized he could probably fall asleep right there. He could drift away and maybe roll off the shelf. Maybe Rick would come back with his shotgun and end him. Maybe that was best.

"You know, you can probably take that handkerchief off. I'm pretty sure we're immune. You look fuckin' silly anyway."

"Shut it, Dan. You have no idea if we're immune or not."

"I'm just saying, being brothers our genes are the same."

"You don't know the first thing about genes or immunity. We're lucky, that's it."

"Well, whoever lived here sure as hell wasn't. Saw a couple mattresses all tore up out in the woods. Person who was here earlier must've done that, huh?"

There was a long pause before Rick answered.

"Tore up?"

"Yeah."

"Let's get these last few bags packed up and get out of here."

"Why? You think maybe—"

"Quit talking and grab that pack of water. Let's go."

There were several more bumps and a bang followed by a loud curse. Then booted footsteps trailing away. Then silence. The truck's engine came to life and its low growl surged and then receded, its tires crunching on the drive.

Quinn lay still for a long time, and after what could've been a half hour or a day, he rolled over and pushed the towels and pillows off the shelf. He climbed down as quietly as he could and waited in the doorway, the XDM in front of him. When no sounds came from below, he made his way down to the kitchen.

It was a disaster.

Bags of sugar and salt were broken upon the floor with boot-prints tracked in them. A shattered bowl was scattered beneath the dining room table, its jagged points like curved teeth. All the cupboards and drawers had been pulled open, their contents rifled but not removed. The pantry door stood ajar, and when he pulled it the rest of the way open, the strength in his neck faded and his head sunk.

The pantry was picked clean except for his father's smoked herring. A few cans were missing and some had toppled to the floor, but they sat mostly undisturbed. He picked up the fallen tins and straightened them as he swallowed against the dryness in his throat. The rest of the stores were gone. All the bottled water, all of the fruit and the canned goods. A single can of soda lay on its side at the very back of the pantry.

When he checked the fridge, he found that the brothers had taken everything from its shelves along with most of the frozen meats. There were two boxes of frozen peaches and four bags of green beans beside a half-empty container of chocolate ice cream.

Shutting the freezer, he moved like a ghost from the kitchen to the hallway and into his father's office. The drawers to the desk were open and he shut them one at a time, carefully tucking papers and notes back inside that had been strewn on the floor. When he was done, he sat in the chair, placing the gun beside the dark computer. His blackened reflection gazed at him and he stared back. In one motion he shoved the screen violently off the desk. It flew halfway across the room and bounced once before coming to rest, unbroken on the thick carpet. Quinn stood and began to move around the desk, the smug glass of the monitor mocking him, but he stopped and sunk back into the chair.

With his face in his hands, he sobbed, the feeling of the twisted bones beneath his skin like a failed artist's sculpture. The afternoon was so bright, the sun melting the very last of the snow. A blue jay called somewhere outside, its insistent cry so mournful, echoing inside him.

When he regained his composure, he gazed out the window and watched the trees sway in the wind while one of his hands found the pistol and began to caress its grip.

Chapter 8

The Cliff

He drank the afternoon away.

 He took the crystal decanter in his father's office that was a third full of whisky to the solarium and sat back on one of the reclining chairs, resting the XDM on the table beside him. The whisky burned his throat and bloomed like a hot explosion in his stomach. He'd drank only a handful of times in his life, all of them under the supervision of his father, most of them on holidays and then only a glass or two of beer.

 The whisky was something else. It had a life of its own, plowing into his veins like hot oil. His skin tingled and the objects around him softened, their edges rounding more with each sip. A heavy weight was in the middle of his skull, pulling his head downward, but he fought against it, tipping it back to pour more of the amber liquid into his mouth.

 When there was only a thin layer of whisky on the bottom of the decanter, he threw it aside. It didn't shatter as he'd expected it to but cracked neatly in half. The booze leaked onto the tile looking like a watery bloodstain. Quinn watched it creep across the floor and slide into the channels between the tiles. His eyelids were dipped in lead, and the solarium rotated in a slow circle around him, stopping whenever he focused hard on one point. His eyes found the door leading to the backyard and the openness of the sea beyond. A lone gull cut the air and dove out of sight toward the ocean. He sat waiting for it to return, but it never did.

 The air was cooler on his skin than earlier in the day, the wind more brisk as he stumbled across the yard. He didn't spare a glance at the place where the mattresses lay in the woods, keeping his rocking vision locked on the approaching cliff. When he reached it, he slowed then stopped, his toes inches from the edge. He searched the sky and the sea but the gull was nowhere to be seen. Maybe it had plunged too far into the water and drowned or struck an unseen rock below the surface. Maybe some creature had eaten it whole without it ever knowing it was dying, gone from a world that no longer cared, had never cared.

 Quinn wavered on the edge, his gaze traveling to the foot of the cliff some sixty feet below. The slabs of rock there were angled, not sharp exactly, but peaked, easy for a smart bird like the gull to drop a shell on them and expose the meat inside.

 He tipped forward, the empty house behind him, all the ocean before him, and the waiting rocks below.

 You're ready for the world now, don't be afraid.

 Teresa's words slid through his mind and then out again. I am ready, he thought. The wind came off the ocean, nudging him backward even though he leaned into it. The rocks below spun clockwise, the whole world on a dial.

The fear, it's a thief. It steals from us if we let it.
He blinked, his vision hazing as he forced himself forward into the wind. He brought his eyes up. The last thing he'd see would be the ocean. The feeling of the breeze on his face became the same as when he and his father had taken the skiff out the last time. His father's smile in the sun. Teresa laughing as they danced in the living room. Their graves beneath the tree. Quinn stepped forward and froze.
A gull coasted a hundred feet above the water, its wings unmoving as it glided. It turned its head, two black, beaded eyes finding him for a moment before swooping lower through a draft.
Quinn fell backward onto the sprouting grass, his legs not there anymore. They were numb and useless beneath him. A great wave of dizziness washed over him and he turned, vomiting on the ground. He heaved and heaved until he was sure he would suffocate, strangled by the compressions within him. When he finally was able to draw a breath, he fell to his back, the sky so blue and vast there was no telling if it was spinning or not. The ground beneath him fell away and he was there in the azure, floating upward, a freedom coursing within him beyond anything he had ever known.

~

He awoke before dusk, the sky above taking on the purple bruise of evening. Dead grass poked through his t-shirt and a leaf crackled beneath his shoulder as he shifted. Someone had taken a hammer to the back of his skull, and when he felt it with gentle fingers, he was surprised to feel it in one piece. Sitting up, he glanced at the pile of sick beside him and his gorge rose again. His arms shook as if he'd been climbing cliffs all afternoon.
He made it to his feet and moved to the house, entering through the solarium door. Without stopping he went to the bathroom, finding the small bottle of Tylenol in the medicine cabinet. He downed three of the caplets with a cold glass of water and waited over the sink to see if the pills would make a reappearance. They stayed down and he shuffled to the living room, slumping into the couch with a sigh.
He sat there with his eyes closed, fighting the twisting snake of nausea until it finally quieted. When he glanced around the living room again, the day had darkened further. Heavy heads of thunderclouds loomed over the trees in the west, and as he stood, a low grumble issued from their direction. He moved to the kitchen, flipping the light switch on and paused for a moment before huffing a laugh exactly like Rick had done when trying the linen closet's light upstairs. Quinn went to the faucet and tried to draw another glass of water but the flow quit partway through and he groaned. The water pump wasn't working either. Only the residual pressure had allowed him a drink in the bathroom. He leaned against the sink and looked out the window into the deepening evening. The clouds were closer and very dark.
He found a flashlight in the hall closet. The intruders had rifled through the space, so he had to pick up fallen coats and an ironing board that had tipped over before grasping the thin-barreled halogen off the top shelf. As he was leaving the closet, he saw his father's favorite pair of hiking boots were gone. He slammed the door shut so hard it didn't lock and rebounded open behind him as he stalked down the hallway and outside.

It wasn't dark enough to use the flashlight yet, so he slipped it in his pocket as he walked down the drive. Cool wind slid through the trees, caressing their naked branches and sending dead leaves cartwheeling toward the sea. Quinn shivered and hunched his shoulders against the chill that ran through him.

He passed Graham's empty house, catching sight of only the top-right dormer window, its black eye finding him before sliding out of sight behind the trees. The wind gusted and died as he walked, the sky muttering again, promising rain. Something moved through the woods to his right and he stopped, his hand finding the flashlight in his pocket as he pictured the XDM resting on the table in the solarium. There was another rustle in the underbrush and then quiet. Quinn flicked the powerful light on, passing it over the place where the noises had come from. It hadn't sounded big, but maybe it was and simply light on its feet.

A rabbit exploded out of the trees and streaked across the drive.

Quinn lurched backward, his stomach already behind him, headed in the direction of the house. The brownish-gray form leapt from the left shoulder of the road and was gone among the trees on the opposite side. Its passage rattled for several seconds and then the wind rose once more, covering the sound of its flight.

He started walking again, his hand shaking as he shut the light off and returned it to his pocket. The drive bent, and on the corner, Mallory's house came into view on the right. It was a narrow two-story painted a deep shade of red. There were no trees blocking it from the drive. The lawn, always lush and well maintained in the summer, was a mess of dead grass and fallen branches. Mallory said she'd picked that particular house because she was a snoop and always had to see who was coming and going.

He didn't pause, the forlorn look of the housekeeper's home driving him onward. The first arc of lightning lit the sky and he counted the seconds until he heard thunder. Seven. The storm was getting closer. Quinn picked up his pace and in another minute turned off the main drive onto the narrow trail that led to Foster's house. The trees were very close on either side, their bases nestled in brambles of dead blackberry and wild raspberry vines. The path turned hard to the left and opened into a wide clearing.

Foster's house was log construction, chalet-style, its interlocking corners sticking out past the rest of the structure. Beneath its highest peak, a large picture window looked out onto the cleared grounds. Foster had sat with him many times over the years in the loft behind the window, gazing out at the snow-covered ground or the burning beauty of fall leaves ready to drop. He'd told stories of his younger days in the Navy, tales of huge ships and massive guns that could lob shells at targets a mile away. Quinn had listened in rapt silence, sipping at the bitter cocoa the older man always made him, too polite to ever say he couldn't stand the taste.

Quinn realized he'd stopped at the edge of the yard, his eyes locked on the house. He moved quickly across the clearing and mounted the steps, a sudden panic overtaking him as he reached for the doorknob. The door would be locked, and he would have to go back to the main house to look for a spare set of keys before returning here…in the dark. But when he grasped the knob, the door swung inward, the smell of stained logs and old food meeting him as he stepped inside. As he closed the door, he turned on the flashlight causing the darkness and shadows to break apart and flee the halogen beam.

Foster wasn't as neat a bachelor as Graham. Blankets were flung over the back of the leather couch, untidy stacks of magazines covered the coffee table, and clothes hung from the bannister running up to the second floor. Quinn shone the light into the kitchen, illuminating a pile of dishes in the sink, food dried on each one. He moved to the stairway and climbed the steps, shining the light ahead of him.

    The second floor of the house opened into the loft, its picture window looking out onto the yard and trees beyond. Wind whistled in the eaves and found cracks to hiss through. The storm was here, fat underbellies of clouds almost skimming the tallest trees in the forest. Quinn crossed the loft and entered Foster's office through an open archway. The room wasn't large and contained a small desk and rolling chair. A computer sat on the desk's top and a file system was fastened to the wall holding various bills and receipts.

    He sat at the desk, standing the light on end before opening the first drawer. Inside were rubber-banded stacks of photographs, curled and faded with time. Quinn shuffled through them, spotting Foster as a much younger man in several of them. In one particular picture, Foster held a smiling little boy in one arm, his other around a plump woman with a kind face. They were all squinting as if the sun were behind the photographer. On the picture's back *Robert, Myra, and Fred* was written in looping script. Quinn placed the picture back amongst the others. He'd never known Foster had had a family. They'd never been in any of the stories the older man had told while sitting in the loft.

    The next drawer held rows of hanging file folders, their sides bulging with paperwork. Lightning raced through the sky again outside the office window, igniting everything inside the house in a fluorescent white. He counted to five before the thunder crashed this time, the sound like massive waves hammering the coast below the cliffs.

    In the second-to-last folder, he found the generator's manual. He paged through it, the word 'troubleshooting' standing out in bold print. Maybe he could even get the generator fired up tonight if he hurried. Quinn closed the manual and grabbed the flashlight from the desktop. Outside, the first lashings of rain fell, streaking the glass in silver rivers that shone in the halogen's glow. Stepping into the loft he paused, shining the light over the places that he and Foster had sat. Ghosts of memories trailing to him through the years were replaced with the image of the man sitting behind the wheel of his truck, waiting for Mallory to leave the house for the last time. Leave *him* for the last time. And there had been no goodbye.

    A harsh scraping came from the far side of the room.

    Quinn's chest tightened and he shone the light to the furthest corner. Nothing moved but the sound continued. It was as if a tree branch were sliding along the outside of the house. *Shhhhhhhhhhhhik.*

    The sound cut off and he waited, breath suspended in his lungs, eyes wide-staring across the room. The seconds ticked by and the light's beam shook.

    Something moved past the picture window.

    He spun, only catching the faintest hint of movement out of the corner of his eye, every hair on his arms and neck standing upright. Darkness had crept from the forest and surrounded the house, the yard barely visible through the hesitant rain. What had it been? A bird zipping past? Quinn swallowed and lowered the light before flicking it off. The window became more transparent without the halogen's glow and he walked toward it, the floor creaking with each step. Lightning lit the yard, the flash far off and only providing a moment of ambient luminance. Something must have blown by the window, a piece of debris carried by the wind. Maybe it was the same thing that had slid along the wall. But it hadn't looked like something untethered floating on the air. In the brief glimpse he'd gotten, it had looked steady and lithe.

Like something walking.

A thump came from downstairs in the direction of the kitchen. The direction *it* had gone.

Quinn hurried to the stairs and clambered down them, holding the unlit flashlight like a knife. He stopped at the base of the stairway and peered around the entry to the kitchen with one eye. The window over the sink was dark, nothing moving outside its glass. He took two steps to the middle of the living room and the same sound as before came from the rear of the house. *Shhhhhhhhhhhhik.*

The image of the pistol came to him again and he turned, following the sound. It stopped as lightning flashed, immediately overlaid with a concussive blast of thunder so close it vibrated against his skin. In the brief flare, he spotted the heavy gun safe in the corner of the living room and crept toward it. Foster hunted deer every year, always taking a full two weeks off to stay at his cabin in Pennsylvania. But his guns he kept close to home.

Quinn found the safe's handle in the dark and turned it, letting out a sigh as the door clunked open. He triggered the light and swept it around the inside of the steel box.

It was empty.

Of course Foster would have taken all his weapons with him. Why had he thought otherwise? Quinn moved back to the front door and looked out into the storm. Rain fell in sheets across the yard, obscuring the road that led to the main drive. The trees swayed and sawed at the sky, their branches bony, reaching hands. A thump came from the rear of the house and he grasped the knob, his muscles trembling like those of a racehorse moments before the horn. With a lunge, he heaved the door open and sped into the rain, its touch cold and instantly soaking through his t-shirt.

He left the door standing open and tore across the yard, not looking back, only running. The rain was a solid curtain that draped the driveway from view, but he ran in its general direction, his hand gripping the flashlight that he left off. The wind sang in his ears, his breath a jagged rhythm. The driveway materialized and his feet splashed through a puddle, the water icy through his pants leg.

A tree snapped behind him.

It wasn't the creaking break of the storm doing its work on a branch. Something was following him.

He ran harder, pushing himself down the lane, rain filtering into his mouth. Quinn swiped at his eyes, trying to clear them. He gasped, sucking down more rainwater as he pelted on. He was drowning on land.

The lane widened and he almost launched himself across the main drive but managed to make the corner and keep going without breaking his stride. There was another crack somewhere behind him, but it was lost in a rattle of thunder as more lightning flared above the trees, giving him a brief view of the open drive ahead. The gun, he had to get the gun. Get in the house and get the gun. The words became a mantra in time with his steps. The air whistled past him and his feet splashed as he ran, arms pumping at his sides. The road curved, and he leaned into it, running faster than he ever had before.

Lightning flickered, illuminating the massive face of his home through the veils of falling water and a bright burst of warmth surged within him. He was almost there, another hundred yards and he would be inside. The wind shoved the trees into a fury, their tops bowing and snapping back as if trying to uproot themselves and chase after him. His feet hit the soft grass as he sped around the end of the house, and as he tried to make the last turn, his sodden shoes slipped and the world tipped to the side. Quinn fell hard on his shoulder, sliding on the soaking lawn. The air flew from his chest, pumped from his lungs by the impact. He rolled to his stomach and began to push himself up as he looked back the way he'd come.

Something tall and thin was striding down the driveway toward him.

Quinn felt his jaw unhinge as his heart stuttered. With arms he couldn't feel, he pushed himself to his feet and ran up the back steps to the door. He'd lost the flashlight and generator manual when he'd fallen, but that wasn't important. He needed the gun because what was that thing coming toward the house? It hadn't been a bear. It had been tall. Much too tall.

His hand slipped on the doorknob and he let out a hoarse moan. It was right behind him, it had to be. Its hands, its hands were huge.

The door opened and he swung inside, slamming it so hard he expected the glass to shatter in its frame. His numb fingers fumbled with the lock and finally snapped it home. Lightning erupted above the house and flared the yard into a blizzard of light.

There was nothing there.

Quinn stumbled down the hall, afterimages dancing in the darkness. His feet tried to slip again on the wood floor as he went by the stairway and he latched onto the bannister to steady himself. Wind buffeted the house, its frame protesting in groans and pops that sent shocks through his nerves with each new sound. His hands shook as he opened the door to the solarium and stepped inside.

Rain pelted the half-dome of glass in a cacophony, splattering and running rivers down its side. Familiar shapes of furniture were oblong and strange in the darkness as he navigated around them, trying to hurry without falling. The table near the reclining chair was ahead, the XDM lying on its surface. Thunder rumbled again, very close, and Quinn groped in the dark for the table's edge. He found it and ran his hands across its surface, searching for the hard polymer grip of the handgun. There was a horrifying second where his fingers met nothing, but then they closed over the heavy shape and he pulled it toward him as thunder became a war drum in his ears. His finger found the trigger and he stepped around the chair into the center of the solarium, freezing as the panes shuddered again. His skin prickled.

It wasn't thunder vibrating the glass.

His thumb found the switch on the gun's grip and pressed it. A lance of light shot from beneath the barrel and illuminated an enormous face staring down at him from the solarium's roof.

Quinn squeezed the trigger and the gun bucked. The glass pane beside the face shattered and fell in shining pieces with the rain. There was a screeching hiss that fluttered his ringing eardrums and a hand the size of a hubcap shot through the hole on the end of a skinny arm that kept coming like a snake leaving its den. Its fingers were long and pale, their tips dark and scraped raw.

Quinn tripped over a chair and fell backward, his tailbone exploding with pain as his ass met the hard flooring. The XDM flew from his grip and clattered into the dark, its light winking out. A deep reverberation, like a bullfrog croaking, filled the room. It shook the center of his chest as if massive speakers were inches away with the bass on full volume. Cold, wet flesh brushed his face and something snagged his t-shirt, yanking him to the side. Quinn cried out, his voice high and airy. He was the rabbit now, its terror his own. Long fingers curled in the fabric around his neckline and pulled, drawing him onto his feet. Lightning cut the night, and in the brief flash, Quinn's bladder released.

The thing's huge head was human, but elongated and stretched as if made of taffy. Its mouth hung open revealing spaced teeth and a lolling tongue. It was naked, its torso skeletal and distorted by its towering height. It *leaned over* the solarium, the top of its skull patched with discolored hair at least ten feet above the ground.

It adjusted its grip, releasing the hold it had on his shirt so that its thumb pressed against his breastbone and the rest of its fingers dug into his back. It squeezed.

All the air rushed from him, the vice on his chest unrelenting. The thing croaked again, an eager sound, one of anticipation and barely restrained excitement. It drew him upward toward the hole it reached through, its skinny arm hoisting him easily. Flickers of light gathered at the corners of Quinn's vision and he thrashed in its grip, the last of his air leaking out of him in a squeal. The world was losing focus, like a film heating up before a projector bulb. His arms flailed and he struck the thing's wrist, but it continued to pull him up, its mouth open and waiting. Something scraped his shoulder, and as it passed, he latched onto it, trying to stop his progress, but it came free in his hand. It was sharp and heavy and the pain that it brought as it sliced through his palm delivered a single frame of clarity that honed every detail to an edge.

Quinn raised the shard of glass and brought it down as hard as he could on the thing's arm.

The glass cut through the pale flesh, unzipping it as if there had been a hidden seam there all along. The tip glanced off hard bone and ripped free, spewing dark blood onto the rain-soaked glass. A foul blast of air swept over him, reeking of old meat, and the baritone cry exploded inches from his face, sending an icepick into each eardrum.

Then the hand around his chest was gone and he was falling back to the solarium's floor. He hit hard, the entire world jarring in his vision and there was a sharp pain in his ankle that eclipsed the burning cut on his hand. He gasped and drank the air in as rain and blood pattered around him. The thing roared again, its cry rising from the croak to a keening as it reached for him with its good arm.

Quinn scrambled back, sliding out of its reach as he searched the dark for the XDM. The sky fluttered with light, and he glimpsed the huge hand outstretched toward him, fingertips stabbing the floor as he pulled his feet away. Quinn spun and crawled to the far corner, his fingers knocking something away before latching onto it again. Glass shattered behind him and the thing bellowed, its sound filling the room, the world. Quinn turned and fired into the darkness.

It was there in the muzzle flash, hunched and striding toward him, reaching. The bullet took its index finger off its left hand above the first knuckle. The digit dropped free and fell to the floor like a worm hacked in two. Its massive face constricted in a rictus of pain and clutched its wounded hand, blood jetting free in thin spurts. Its eyes found him in another flicker of lightning, and there was something there in them, something familiar.

It leapt forward, long legs uncoiling, gapped teeth bared. Quinn fired again, the shot tearing out a chunk of flesh from its shoulder, but it kept coming. It hit him with the force of a car, sending the ceiling and floor into a spin as he flew across a table and slammed through a glass panel.

He somersaulted on the wet ground before sliding to a stop. His spine was crushed, he was sure of it. The storm bared down on him, forcing an icy whip of wind across his skin, bitter rain into his mouth and eyes. The gun, where was the gun? He raised his right hand and found that he still gripped the weapon, though he couldn't feel it. The thing in the solarium punched out two panes of glass and climbed through, its snarling face there and gone in the storm. Quinn sat up and fired a shot that went wide, blasting the window above the monster. A large piece of glass slid free from the broken frame, as it tried to struggle into the open, and sliced into the thing's back behind its jutting shoulder blades. Its cry cut the night and overrode the thunder that cracked in the sky. It flailed first one way and then the other, the heavy chunk of glass in its back snapping off as it hauled itself free of the building. Quinn steadied the gun with both hands, flipping the light on as he squeezed the trigger.

The pistol kicked, and the bridge of the thing's nose collapsed inward. Matter flew free of the back of its head, spattering the remaining glass with bits of bone and flesh. It wavered there, wobbling on its stringy arms, nearly free of the solarium for a long heartbeat, and then tipped forward onto its side. Quinn kept the gun trained on its still form as he counted. When he reached a hundred he managed to stand, his legs barely holding him. There was a hornets' nest buried in his back that sent a thousand stings up his spine as he took three shuffling steps forward then stopped. Training the light on the creature's ruined head, he stood unmoving as the rain came down around him, stinging in scrapes and cuts.

The storm faded away completely as he stared, disbelief pressing down on him until his legs finally gave out and he crumpled beside the skeletal figure, the gun's light glinting off the gold earring in the thing's left ear.

Chapter 9

Revelations

He spent the night in his own bed with the door shut and locked, a chair shoved beneath the knob.

Sleep was fleeting, coming in short spans that he woke from shaking and clutching the pistol so hard his fingers ached. The storm continued to crash around the house, howling through the destroyed solarium with a hollow voice. Near morning it moved off to the east and burnt out over the ocean, leaving the sky clear enough to see the gray edge of dawn creeping up from the water like fog.

As the room lightened by degrees, Quinn lay on his side, his back throbbing, hand pulsing in dull strobes with each heartbeat. He stared at the wall, glancing occasionally at the painting his father had given him when he was twelve. It was a vibrant watercolor of a river valley filling with the first light of day. Rolling hills speckled with trees holding the orange and reds of fall on their branches fell down to a blue river, its surface cut by the heads of rocks peeking from its depths. His father had told him it was a real place, that he'd seen it firsthand. He'd commissioned an artist to capture it on canvas, saying that a photo wouldn't have done it justice. *You have to feel it, Quinn, and the only way to feel something that you haven't seen in real life is through art.*

Quinn rose from the bed, his joints full of spiked rust. He hobbled across the room, his ankle flaring like a hot coal each time he put weight on it. He reached the painting and stood looking at it for a long time until the brushstrokes blended together into a haze.

He tore the painting from the wall and flung it across the room.

It hit the foot of his bed, the glass shattering and sprinkling the floor. The frame shifted and released its hold on the colorful canvas. The picture folded beneath itself and lay still. He breathed hard, each inhalation painful. He could still feel a giant hand squeezing his chest.

He made his way downstairs to find the sun coating the floor in the living room gold. A cool draft leaked from the direction of the solarium and he shivered, pulling on a sweatshirt hanging in the closet. He opened a can of smoked herring and sat eating it at the counter, staring into nothing. The XDM lay beside the warm can of pop, its grip in easy reach. He would never go anywhere without it again.

After choking down the last of the salty fish, he rinsed the can and threw it in the trash, which was almost full. It was starting to smell.

He stood at the kitchen window looking at the puddles shining on the drive. They were splotches of blue, reflecting the faultless sky. A chill ran through him. The puddles were the same color as the thing's eyes outside. Graham's eyes.

Dizziness swarmed him and the kitchen tilted. His briny breakfast made a leap for the back of his throat, but he gritted his teeth and breathed through his nose until it settled back in place. Fresh blood leaked from the makeshift bandage around his palm from gripping the counter so hard. He'd need to dress it properly. But first he had other things to do.

On the way out the kitchen door, he paused at the junk drawer and sifted through the contents. In the very back was a small tape measure with a maximum length of twenty feet. He held it for thirty seconds before replacing it and slamming the drawer shut and heading outside.

The day was cool despite its clarity. Quinn hugged the sweatshirt closer to him as he limped around the side of the house, waiting for the moment the solarium and the thing lying outside of it would come into view. *It won't be there. It will have regenerated somehow and dragged itself off. It's watching you right now.* The thoughts were enough to make him halt and bring the gun up from his side. He turned in a slow circle. Birds spoke somewhere in the woods, unseen in the branches. In the distance, waves crashed against rocks. When he managed to shuffle forward, the ends of pale fingers, upturned to the sky, came into view.

It lay where it had fallen; it hadn't moved overnight.

Quinn approached it, going around its side to where he'd sat the night before. He'd lost track of time after seeing the earing hanging from its distended lobe and only come to when lightning struck a tree a hundred yards from the house, showering the ground with sparks that winked out like falling stars. He knelt, steadying himself with one hand on the ground as he took in the sight.

It was even taller and skinnier than he'd thought. Its legs were long, twice the length of his own. One was drawn up as if attempting to curl into a fetal position while the other was straight, locked in a line at the bulbous knee. Its arms were equally long and would easily reach its knees while standing upright. The hands. They looked bigger in the light of day than the night before. They reminded him of enormous, pale sea-crabs. The digits were a foot in length, except for the missing left index finger that ended in a gored stump. Its torso was emaciated, that of a starving animal, ribs pronounced like xylophone bars. The bones beneath the skin resembled bamboo, its skin almost translucent and drawn tight over them like a circus tent wrapped over poles. His gaze traveled up its unreal size and stopped on its face.

The features were nearly unrecognizable. The .45 caliber bullet had destroyed an area of its upper nose and forehead the size of a silver dollar, yet even before that its countenance hadn't looked entirely human. Its head was oblong and slanted, the face stretched and uneven like a person's visage reflected in a funhouse mirror. The mouth hung open revealing tombstone teeth, chipped and sitting at varying degrees within gray gums.

But its eyes. Its eyes were Graham's.

They were half-lidded and bloodshot, but there was no mistaking them. How many times had those eyes smiled at him while slipping him a treat prior to dinner that his father had forbade? How many times had they studied a glistening sauce, seeking the exact moment to remove it from the heat? Even in death they hadn't lost their character, their Nordic blue.

Quinn sat back from the corpse, letting the unreality wash over him. The wind coasted across the grounds, picking at his clothes. After a long time, he gathered himself and stood, then walked to the big pine tree where the shovel lay in the grass.

~

He spent the rest of the morning burying the body. He dug a long trench beside Teresa's grave and pulled the thing that Graham had become into it. Dragging the corpse across the grass was like moving a pallid marionette; rigor mortis hadn't set into the muscles and joints, and its head flopped on a limp neck. It was much heavier than he'd expected. When he'd covered the last of it, he began to speak. But no words would come, so he settled for cutting three rough crosses from a stand of slender willow. When the crosses stood at the head of each grave, he waited for the tears. The crosses were so fragile and sad. But he couldn't cry. After the wind had chilled his face to the point of burning, he turned away.

~

The gate's lock at the end of the driveway was ruined. The brothers' hammer strikes had bent and twisted the box that housed the mechanism. Quinn started back for a length of rope to tie the gate shut but instead left it partially open. Maybe it was better to leave things broken now.

He found an old duffel bag in Foster's house and filled it with what food the groundskeeper had in his pantry, which wasn't much. Graham and Mallory's homes didn't yield any better since most of the food was stored in the main house. All told, he came away with a can of clam chowder, four bottles of water, two bags of salt and vinegar chips, three cans of stew, a bag of apples that hadn't turned yet, some half dried marshmallows, and a package of Norwegian chocolates hidden in the back of Graham's closet. He almost left these but at the last moment took them. Life, more so now than ever, wasn't so sure that you could leave chocolate behind.

Quinn brought the bag back to the main house and then inspected the front door. There would be no fixing it from where Rick had kicked it in. In the garage he found an ice chisel that Foster had used on the sidewalks around the house in the winter. He brought it back to the front door, measuring its length while leaning it beneath the knob. After making a mark on the wood floor, he hammered the chisel into it, breaking through the gorgeous teak until he'd created a hole to the sub-floor. He left the sharp edge jammed there and then wedged the other end beneath the kitchen doorknob. It fit tight, and after yanking on the door several times, he nodded to himself and drank down half a bottle of water.

He cleaned the solarium the best he could, sweeping glass and piling the fallen framework in one corner. The pools of blood that hadn't been touched by the rain had dried to a crusted black at the centers, fading to a deep maroon near the fringes. The rest of it had run like a monochrome painting doused with turpentine. The whole room stank of death. It smelled like a saltwater brine gone foul. He went to the bathroom to gather supplies to clean the gore but realized there was still no water. He settled for shutting the solarium door and nailing a length of two-by-four across it.

When the house was fairly secure, he gathered an armload of firewood from the garage and set it beside the hearth in the living room. In fifteen minutes hearty flames danced and sent smoke funneling up the chimney. The chill that settled over the house during the night and day without power receded from the living room, the fire's heat creeping into the kitchen and hallways.

Quinn warmed a can of chowder beside the coals, waiting until it began to bubble before eating it directly out of the container. He sat staring out the window afterward, taking a sip of water now and then. The day had grayed over as if the sky were molding. The wind continued to blow, sounding like a distant foghorn in the chimney, and it lulled him into a stupor as he gazed into the fire. He set the XDM on the couch beside him and leaned back into the couch's thick cushions. He would just close his eyes for a second. He couldn't bear their weight anymore. Every inch of his body hurt, but if he sat still, he was outside of it, outside of the pain. It was someone else's, and he was empathetic to them. But right now he was tired and needed to rest for a moment. Just a moment.

He awoke at nightfall, consciousness coming with the stiffening of his limbs and an explosion of pain in his ankle as he pushed himself upright. He blinked into the dimness of the room, the fire long since burned out.

There was something outside the kitchen door.

Awareness washed over him like a wave of ice water, his senses sharpening to needle points. The rasp of a footstep. The kitchen door shook gently and then harder before going quiet. Quinn snagged the pistol from the cushion beside him as he rose from the couch and almost sprawled in the midst of concussive pain. Every joint in his body was full of acid, but adrenaline was washing away everything but the hammering of his heart. He kept low and entered the kitchen, the XDM trained on the door. It was silent now, everything still save the wind. He moved to the window and peered out.

Evening had crept from the tree line, hemorrhaging shadows across the yard as it closed in on the house. But two darker forms moved against the wind, their shapes indistinct in the failing light. They were there, then fleetingly gone around the side of the house.

Quinn shoved away from the window and hurried down the hall to the back door. Maybe it was the brothers, back to take shelter after rethinking their situation. Or maybe it was more of the things like Graham. But they hadn't looked tall enough. As he watched through the back door's window, they appeared, merely deeper shadows against the dark. He would not let them come into the house again, no matter who they were. They wouldn't take anything from him, not now, not ever. If it was the brothers, he would get his father's boots back. With a yank, he pulled the door wide and crouched in the opening, centering the sights on the taller of the two figures.

"Stop right there."

There was the unmistakable sound of a gun being cocked and he nearly fired his own weapon, but paused as a voice, hard edged but feminine, came out of the darkness.

"I'll fucking shoot you right now. Drop the gun."

"Drop yours."

"Look, we smelled smoke and saw it above your house and came looking. That's all. We'll leave and you can go back inside, but if you come out here or make another move, I will kill you where you stand."

Quinn squinted, slowly taking in the woman's figure. She was slight and fairly tall, but that was all he could make out. The person behind her was shorter and mostly hidden, but he could see small hands clutching at the woman's waist.

"Are you alone?" he asked after a long pause.

The woman waited a long time, but the hand holding her weapon didn't waver.

"I have my son. No one else."

The little hands around her waist shifted and a small outline of a head appeared at her hip.

Quinn lowered the XDM and shoved it in the back of his jeans. He held up his hands.

"Come in. I won't hurt you."

The two shadows stayed where they were, the woman's gun still hovering on his center mass.

"There's no one else here, they all—" He let the last word fall away, and he dropped his eyes to the entryway floor. "Come in if you want," he said, and made his way back to the living room. He knelt by the hearth and stirred the ashes. Beneath the feathery soot, a single ember glowed. Quinn rolled it to the center of the fireplace and began setting kindling over it. He blew into the hearth, ashes taking flight. The ember's flare was the only light in the room, rising then falling with his insistence. After a few minutes, a flame sprang into life and began to lick at the small sticks of wood. As he was placing a larger piece of oak on the fire, the back door creaked and closed quietly. Quinn stood beside the warming fireplace and waited.

The woman appeared first in the doorway, sideling into view. A revolver, so large it was nearly comical, was in her left hand that she kept aimed at the floor. She looked close to his age and was thinner than he'd originally thought, and taller, almost as tall as he was. Her hair was very straight and very dark, hanging past her shoulders in a languid wave that nearly blended with the shadows behind her. Her face was round and ghost-white with two spots of color on her sallow cheekbones. She had a sharp nose that was incongruent with the rest of her face, though it seemed to lend an air of harsh beauty that was only more accented by her eyes that were like two sapphires reflecting the firelight. An ugly gash ran across the top of her forehead. Crusted blood dried in an uneven line from her right temple to her chin. She glanced around the large room, taking in all its corners before finding him, pinning him to the wall with her gaze. There was movement beside her in the hall at that moment and she reached for it, shielding the small shape beside her as she raised her handgun.

"You've got it!" she said, inching backward.

Quinn raised his hands, looking from one to the other, then back at her.

"Got what?"

"The disease. You're sick, aren't you?" She shot a look further into the house and then back at him as she retreated another step.

Realizing what she meant, Quinn put one palm against his face and then let his hands hang at his sides.

"No, I'm not sick. I've been this way since birth."

"Bullshit, you're just something new."

"It's called Fibrous Dysplasia. I've always looked this way." He watched her, barely visible in the darkness beyond the doorway. "My name's Quinn."

There was a long pause and then a small voice came from behind the woman.
"I'm Ty."

"Tyrus! We're leaving. Don't come any closer."

"I'm telling the truth. I'm immune, or whatever passes for immune I guess. My father had it first and then my—" he almost said *mother,* but stopped himself and continued "—teacher got it. They both died. Our cook had it too, but he…"

Quinn frowned, the images of what Graham had become playing across his mind. How the cold, pale flesh had felt beneath his fingers. "He…"

"He turned into one of them, didn't he?"

The woman was standing inside the doorway, the gun at her side again. A little outline in the hallway became a boy as he stepped forward. He was around five years old with tousled, brown hair and glazed eyes the same color of his mother's that stared past Quinn, through him.

"He turned into a stilt," the woman said.

"A stilt?"

"Because how tall they are."

"You mean you've seen one too?"

The woman huffed a derisive laugh.

"One? Try dozens."

Quinn's mouth worked but nothing came out for a moment.

"Dozens? There's more of them?"

"Are you slow too? Part of your…" she gestured at his face. "…disorder?"

"What? No, I'm just—I thought Graham was the only one."

"Sorry to disappoint you, but no. There's a lot of them. Way more than immunes."

Quinn moved to the sofa and sat, the aches in his legs and ankle muted by what the woman had told him. Ty shuffled further into the room, one hand on his mother's belt, not looking around, only staring in the general direction of the fire.

"You're really alone?" the woman asked.

"Yes. There was two others but they left."

"Were they two men?"

"No, a woman and a man. They were our housekeeper and groundskeeper. Why?"

"Because two maniacs in a truck nearly killed us yesterday. They started following us outside of Pearlton, just hovering a half-mile back, never getting closer. Then they came up fast and tailgated us for about ten miles, both of them waving for us to pull over. I would've rather chewed glass, so we kept going until they forced us off the road about a mile from here. I lost control in the ditch and hit a huge transformer. That's the last thing I remember before waking up this afternoon. When I did, all our supplies were gone. Good thing the boomer was under the seat or it would be gone too." She waved the handgun once and then slid its bulk beneath her belt.

"They were here too," Quinn said. "They came in and took all of my food and water."

"Why didn't you shoot the bastards?"

"I guess I was in shock. I didn't know what they wanted when they showed up, so I hid."

The woman's lip rose a little on one side in a sneer. "They better hope they never run into me again. Ty lost consciousness too, but he woke up before me and had to sit there wondering if I was dead until I came to."

Her jaw clenched, and the muscle in her cheek bulged as she looked away at the fire. Ty shivered once beside her.

"Come sit down by the fire," Quinn said, rising and motioning toward the couch. "I'm guessing you're both cold and tired."

"Listen, we don't need anything from you. We might stay the night just because it's not safe in the dark anymore. Looks like you've got a pretty good perimeter set up around your property, but it doesn't really matter if a stilt wants to come in." She looked out the window and then glanced at him again. Their gazes held for a moment before she looked back at the fire. "My name's Alice."

Ty inched forward, one hand still attached to his mother's waist while the other groped at the open space before him. Suddenly the glazed look in his eyes made sense.

"Here," Quinn said, stepping out of the way. "The couch is to your left."

Alice guided her son to the plush sofa and helped him onto the cushion. The little boy's face remained stoic for a beat and then broke into a shining smile.

"This is really soft," Ty said, looking about the room with his sightless eyes. He shivered again, holding his hands out in the direction of the fire. Quinn moved to get the blanket from the back of the couch, but Alice headed him off, covering her son with it before he could help.

"Are you hungry?" Quinn asked.

"Yes, really hungry," Ty said, the smile still there.

"If you have something, I can pay you for it, not that money's worth anything now." Alice said. "I'm fine, but if there's something you could spare for him."

"I'll see what I can find," Quinn said, moving into the kitchen. He picked up the flashlight on the counter and began examining his stores when he noticed Alice in the doorway, her hand on the butt of her pistol again.

"Sorry, just making sure you weren't planning anything."

"Only dinner. I'm really not dangerous."

"I kinda guessed that when you weren't able to defend your home against those jackasses."

Quinn paused in turning over a bag of chips and then shrugged. Alice shifted and fingered the pistol's grip.

"I'm sorry. I didn't mean anything. Sometimes there's no filter between here and here," she said pointing at her bloodied temple and then her lips.

"It's okay. I can assure you that I won't hurt either of you."

"Dude, you can't assure me of anything. I don't know if I'd trust God right now." She glanced around the kitchen. "In fact, I know I wouldn't."

Quinn shifted the food around in the bag on the kitchen floor and retrieved the three cans of stew and opened them. He dumped them into a large steel pan and stirred the congealed mass with a wooden spoon. Alice had moved back into the living room, and he followed her, setting the pan near the fire's edge. Ty huddled beneath the heavy blanket, only a shock of untidy hair and his face visible.

They didn't speak for a time, settling instead to simply watch the fire as the tantalizing smell of stew filled the room. Even over the popping flames, the intermittent growls of Ty's stomach could be heard. When the stew bubbled within the pan, Quinn returned to the kitchen to gather three bowls, ladling the brown and chunky mixture into each of them. He took less than half of the amount he'd dished out to Alice and Ty, eating slowly and watching them devour the meal. Ty ate with excellent dexterity, gathering a spoonful and bringing it to his mouth each time without spilling a drop. Now that the fire burned fully, Quinn could see the boy's eyes weren't exactly the same as his mother's. A thin, gray veil covered them, dimming the color that shone so sharp from Alice's. When his spoon scraped the bottom of the bowl he smacked his lips and let out a small burp.

"Ty!" Alice said.

"Excuse me. That was really good."

"Do you want more?" Quinn asked, rising from his chair across the room. Ty nodded.

"You can have the rest of mine," Alice said, beginning to empty the last of her bowl into his.

"No, there's plenty more. Here," Quinn said, picking up the pan and pouring the remainder into their bowls. Alice looked up at him for a brief second as he scraped the stew out and moved back to his chair.

"Thank you," she said.

"Thank you!" Ty trilled, his mouth full.

"You're welcome."

"Honestly, this is the first hot meal we've had in two days."

"Where did you guys come from?"

Alice hesitated, running her eyes over his face before continuing.

"Up north in Woodland Mills."

"Was it...bad up there?"

Alice shot a glance at Ty who had finished his meal and was holding the bowl politely in his lap, listening to the conversation. Alice gave a small shake of her head. Quinn rose and crossed the room.

"All done with your stew, Ty?"

"Yes, thank you. It was really good."

"You're welcome."

Quinn retrieved Alice's bowl as well and brought them to the kitchen, setting them in the sink. He flipped the water on and shook his head when nothing came out of the faucet. He made a circuit of the house in the darkness, opting not to bring the flashlight. In his father's office, he moved to the window facing the drive. The night was a blanket beyond the glass, the sky without the faintest hint of starshine. He waited, peering into the dark. There was no movement, no tall, pale shapes striding through the layers of shadow, but that didn't mean nothing looked back at him, watching and waiting for the right moment to strike.

There was a sliding rasp behind him and he spun, grabbing for the XDM.

Alice stood in the doorway, her hands raised before her.

"Sorry, didn't mean to sneak up on you."

He let the burning air escape his lungs and released the gun's grip.

"It's okay. I'm jumpy."

"I don't blame you. Must've been creepy here by yourself."

"It's my home."

"Really big place. Was your dad rich or something?"

Quinn moved to the large desk and touched the dragon paperweight, only a shape in the dark.

"You could say that."

The silence stretched between them and broke when Alice motioned toward the living room.

"He's asleep. I made him a bed on the couch. Hope you don't mind."

"Not at all. There's an inflatable mattress upstairs. I'll go get it for you."

"Actually some blankets and a pillow would work. I don't need a mattress."

"Are you sure?"

"Yeah. But I could use a drink. You wouldn't have anything, would you?"

"I think I do," Quinn said, moving behind the desk to the small liquor cabinet. Inside he located a long, slender bottle that sloshed when he shook it. After stopping in the kitchen to retrieve two glasses, they settled into the chairs across from the sofa. Ty rested beneath the comforter, his head propped on one of the pillows. The fire's glow played across his face, making his brown hair seem lighter. When Quinn glanced at Alice, the dried blood on her head looked like a black scar, marring her white skin.

"You should clean that cut on your forehead, make sure it doesn't get infected," Quinn said. "I could heat some bottled water over the fire."

"Tomorrow. It's not bleeding, so I'll deal with it in the light," Alice said, grasping the bottle he'd set on the table between them. "Belvedere, wow. Top shelf." She poured her glass half full.

"Do you want me to try and find something to mix…" His voice trailed off as she took a long drink of the clear liquid.

She shook her head and her eyes slid shut as she swallowed. "Ahh."

Quinn appraised the bottle for a moment before pouring only enough to cover the bottom of his glass. The vodka stung more than the whisky going down and brought tears to his eyes, but the warmth that bloomed in his stomach felt good.

"To answer your question, yeah, it was really bad where we came from," Alice said in a hushed voice, sitting forward to rest her elbows on her knees. "I didn't want to say anything in front of Ty." She laughed again, the same callus way she had before. It wasn't so much unkind as hollow. "When all this started happening, it was the first time I was ever thankful that he's blind. But he heard enough without actually seeing it."

"We watched some on the news when it started. It looked horrible."

"It was worse—is worse. I don't know if it's still going on or not. Everyone was dead when we left town."

Quinn paused with his drink partway to his mouth. "Everyone?"

"Everyone. Except for the stilts. There were a few of them wandering around, eating things."

Alice shivered and took another long sip of vodka.

"How did they…turn? Was there anything on TV?"

Alice shook her head. "Nothing. By the time they started showing up, almost everyone was sick. The only thing I saw was the video that someone uploaded to Yahoo."

"I saw it too," Quinn said.

"Super creepy. They're mutations of some kind. That's all I know. The disease must've affected certain people somehow and did that to them."

"Our cook, my friend, Graham, turned into one of them. I wouldn't have believed it if I hadn't seen it. He was still wearing the earring he always wore."

"Oh yeah, you can tell sometimes who they were before. Once in a while there's still a remnant of clothing on them, but most of them grew way too much to have anything on. Tattoos are still there, scars, birthmarks, some jewelry. The first one we saw was my neighbor, Mrs. Wilhelm. God, she was a pain in the ass while she was human. It was a day or so after everything went down and the media was going nuts. We live—lived—in a shitty apartment building on the north side of town and the bat was across the hall from us. She was a stinky old cat lady, but she had money. I don't know why she retired in that apartment. I know she'd always been there and her husband died a few years before we moved in. Rumor was she got paid a huge life insurance sum after her old man kicked it and she lived off of that, but she really only spent money on those cats."

Alice rolled her tongue around in her mouth as if she'd tasted something bad and then took another drink if vodka.

"She'd just gotten back from vacation, somewhere in California I think, heard her mention it to the building manager after she finished complaining about the heat not working for the hundredth time, and those cats had already started yowling again. She'd brought them somewhere while she was gone, and it was awesome not to hear them scratching and clawing on the door at all hours of the night and day. That night I'd just gotten back from The Cabinet, it's a liquor store where I work—worked—anyway, I was coming up the stairs, and there's this pale, scrawny thing crouched half in and half out of the old bat's apartment. I remember thinking that somehow one of her chairs had mildewed and she was trying to shove it out through the door. I couldn't really wrap my mind around what I was seeing. She heard me and stepped out of her apartment all hunkered down because Mrs. Wilhelm was about five foot nothing and this thing was over eight feet tall. It had a cat in its mouth, one of the tabbys. I remember the orange and white stripes on its tail and ass that hadn't been chewed up yet. Its fur was all matted down with saliva and blood. The thing just looked at me for a minute. It had pieces of gut on its chin, and it just stared at me with Mrs. Wilhelm's eyes."

Alice set her empty glass down and swallowed. She gazed into the fire not saying anything. After she'd been quiet for over a minute, Quinn cleared his throat.

"You don't have to finish; I get the picture."

"She came for me," Alice said, as if she hadn't heard him. "She spit the chewed cat out and started toward me, her long skinny legs pumping and hands touching the floor like some sort of hairless monkey. I grabbed the closest thing to me, which was one of the old fire extinguishers hanging on the wall—they were everywhere in the building—and I swung it up right as she lunged for me. It hit her in the side of the face and her head bounced off the wall as she grabbed at me. I fell on the stairs and managed to snag the bannister on the way down, but the old bat wasn't so lucky. The stairway was one of the old ones with a landing for the second floor and then for the third but it didn't turn at all. You could look down from the third floor and see the first floor landing. I was always terrified Ty would trip down them. We would've never moved into that damn place if we could've afforded somewhere else."

Alice seemed to come back to herself and looked around the room. Ty turned in his sleep and sighed. The fire cracked, and a couple of embers flew out of the hearth, fading away in midair.

"She fell and I heard her neck snap on the second landing. By the time she hit the first floor, there were bones sticking out of her skin and blood running along the treads. All I could think of was, had she gone across the hallway and visited Ty and his babysitter while I'd been gone?"

The fire eating at the dry wood became the loudest sound in the room again. Alice turned her empty glass slowly on the table.

"But they were okay."

"They were fine. His babysitter was freaked after hearing the commotion outside the door, but I was so thankful she hadn't opened it. If she had…"

"Did you leave right away?" Quinn asked, trying to keep her from focusing too much on the memory.

"Pretty much, if you don't count the time it took to put some clothes and food together. My car's a shitty Pontiac Grand Prix, but it never gave me any trouble. It would still be going if those assholes hadn't run us off the road." Her eyes swam with tears and she blinked once, long, and when she opened them again, the tears were gone. "They even took his walking cane. I don't know why or what they'd use it for, but they took it anyway. I looked in the ditches hoping they'd tossed it out after realizing they had no use for it, but it wasn't there." She sniffed once and swallowed.

"I can make him one, I'm sure. Something around here would work," Quinn offered.

"No. I'll find him one when we get going again. There'll be a medical supply store in Portland."

"That's where you're headed?"

"Yeah, well, it's a stop anyway."

"Why Portland?"

She looked at him again, tracing his face with her eyes so that it seemed like fingers were probing his features. He nearly shivered.

"My mother. She's in a home there. She's got early onset dementia."

"I'm sorry."

"Yeah, me too." Alice gripped the vodka bottle and poured one more small shot into her glass, downing it with a toss of her head. "I'm still weighing whether to go or not. I'm sure Portland will be bad, and it's the last place I want to bring Ty, but I have to know. I couldn't live without knowing."

"And if you find her, where then?"

"Iowa."

"Iowa?"

"There's a command center there. It was on the news before most of the stations went down. The government set up a huge compound inside some park or mine in Fort Dodge. They were telling everyone it was a safe haven."

"Why Iowa?"

"I'm not sure, but I think it has something to do with being centralized in the country. I'm thinking I would have set up a safe zone somewhere better than Iowa. Somewhere warmer, like Florida."

"Iowa's not nice?"

"You've never been there?"

He hesitated, almost saying, *I've never been anywhere.*

"No."

She watched him for a long moment and returned to spinning her glass again.

"I'm guessing it's the safest place in the country, if you can get there."

"If you can get there."

They both fell silent, watching the fire. Ty turned in his sleep again and murmured something. Alice rose from her chair and moved to his side, stroking his brow and smoothing his hair back. Quinn took advantage of the gap in conversation to gather the blankets and pillows from the upstairs closet. He brought them back to the living room and spread them out a makeshift bed on the floor beside the couch. Ty was quiet, and Alice had brought their glasses and the mostly empty bottle of vodka to the kitchen. When she returned and saw the blankets and pillows, she gave him half a smile as she knelt to arrange them further.

"Haven't slept in a fort bed since I was fourteen. My dad used to make them when I'd have sleepovers."

"Where's your dad now?"

Alice paused in smoothing out the comforter on the floor and then resumed.

"Thank you for everything, for taking us in. You've been great. Sorry I freaked out on you earlier. It's been one of those days."

He couldn't help but laugh. "The last week has been one of those days."

She stood and they looked at one another for a beat before he motioned to the hallway.

"There's a bathroom next to the office if you or Ty need to use it. The water's off, but we'll deal with it in the morning if need be."

"Thanks."

"I'll sleep in the office tonight if you need me."

"We'll be fine."

He stoked the fire one last time and left the room as Alice settled in beside the couch. He found a sleeping bag in the upstairs closet and unrolled it on the office floor in front of the desk. From there he could see the window and down the hallway. He set the XDM on the floor and positioned himself so that one hand rested on it and closed his eyes. The wind caressed the glass, and several times he nearly sat up to investigate a noise. But when nothing further came, he drifted off into a shallow sleep, dreaming of eyes that watched him from the darkness, unblinking and filled with hunger.

Chapter 10

Limbo

He woke to laughter.

Quinn sat up in his sleeping bag, the pistol rising with him. There was a span of seconds in which the sounds coming from the living room were completely wrong; they shouldn't be there in his house. But the prior night's events came back to him, and he relaxed, wiping away the scratching sleep in his eyes.

He climbed free of the sleeping bag, his injuries protesting, but not near as loudly as the day before. The ankle was the sorest, and he rotated it clockwise then counterclockwise, standing on the other foot. It creaked and cracked, but there was very little impingement, and the joint didn't seem to be damaged beyond a strain. After testing it with his weight once more and finding it was definitely better than yesterday, he moved down the hall.

Alice and Ty were both awake, Alice sitting at the far end of the couch from Ty, gently pinching his wriggling toes that poked from beneath the blanket as she recited a quiet rhyme. He laughed each time she gripped his feet, his face lighting with a smile that exposed his small, even teeth.

"Snapping turtle dives, under the pond, up he comes, and chomp, he's gone. Little froggy says, where did he go? Fish swims past saying look out below." Alice's voice was soft and smooth as she sang the rhyme. She recited it once more beneath Ty's giggles before she noticed Quinn standing in the doorway.

"Morning," she said, turning toward him.

"Good morning."

"Hi Quinn," Ty said, still smiling and wiggling his toes.

"Hi. Are you guys playing a game?"

"An old rhyme," Alice said, rising from the sofa.

"It's Grandpa Fischer's. He made it up," Ty said.

"Yeah. Okay, Ty, get dressed now."

Without protest, the little boy swung his legs free of the blanket and began to grope on the floor for his pair of jeans.

"They're to your left," Alice said. Ty adjusted his reach and snagged the pants and began to put them on.

"How did you sleep?" Quinn asked, moving toward the kitchen. Alice followed him, pausing in the doorway.

"Okay. I think I may've gotten a concussion yesterday. It felt like I was lying on a boat last night."

"How do you feel this morning?"

"Better. A little weak, but that might be the vodka."

Quinn poured two bottles of water into a pan and brought it to the fireplace. In a matter of minutes, he had the few leftover coals stoked into a blaze, the pan heating beside it.

"When that water's hot, you can bring it to the bathroom down the hall and clean your forehead. There's washcloths in the closet beside the door along with hydrogen peroxide in the medicine cabinet."

Alice blinked at him, her mouth opening and then shutting again. Her eyes roamed his face, and after a moment, he glanced away. No one had ever looked at him the way she did. Not unkind, but curious, probing. He was onstage and she the only audience.

"Sorry," Alice said, noticing his discomfort. "I—"

"It's okay. I know how I look."

"It's not that, I just—"

"I'll find something for us to eat," Quinn said, turning away. He rummaged in the food bag with his head down until Alice retreated from the room. After a few minutes, she passed on the way to the bathroom carrying the pan of water. Quinn cut four apples into sections and put them on plates, then opened a bag of chips, placing a handful beside the apples for each of them. He brought the food into the living room and found Ty sitting beside the glowing hearth.

"Are you hungry, Ty?"

"Yeah, really hungry."

"Okay, here you go. There's apple slices there along with some chips."

Ty took the plate from his hands and lowered it to his lap.

"What kind of chips?"

"Salt and vinegar."

"Oh, that's my favorite."

A smile tugged at Quinn's lips. "Mine too."

"Mom might be mad that I'm eating chips for breakfast," Ty whispered.

"You can blame me," Quinn whispered back. Ty grinned and began to eat.

Although he wasn't hungry, Quinn started to pick at his food also. The apples were on the verge of going bad, their flesh sandy on his tongue, but he ate them anyway. When they were almost finished with their plates, Alice returned, her hair wet and combed straight back from her forehead that now had a wide Band-Aid across it. The blood was gone, and her face was fresh and smooth. Quinn caught himself staring, and it was his turn to look away, heat rising in his cheeks.

"Chips for breakfast? I don't think so little man!" Alice play-wrestled with Ty as he tried to bring the last chip to his mouth and finally succeeded, chewing purposely with his mouth open. "You little brat," Alice teased, tickling his neck. She took up her own plate and popped an apple into her mouth. "Thank you," she said after swallowing.

"It's not much."

"It'll make a turd."

Quinn paused with his hand partway to his face and glanced at her. Ty giggled and clapped a hand to his mouth. Alice shook her head as Quinn let out a small laugh.

"I'm sorry. Old saying of my dad's. It slips out sometimes. And don't repeat that, young man," She said, nudging the still-smiling boy. He nodded once but the grin didn't fade.

When they were all finished with their makeshift breakfast, Quinn took the plates to the kitchen and Alice followed him while Ty pulled on his socks and shoes.

"I hate to ask you, but you wouldn't have a vehicle to spare, would you?" Alice said. "I noticed the other homes on the way in and didn't know if they had cars."

"You're leaving this morning?"

"We should. I spoke to my mom right after this all started. She was having a good day, knew who I was and where she was, but that might've changed by the afternoon. I would've went sooner, but it all happened so fast."

"It was like a wildfire," Quinn said, gazing at the floor. One of the brothers' boot prints was still there, faded and ghostly.

"Exactly. I have to know if she's okay or not."

Quinn glanced at her, the set to her jaw and the way her eyes lanced the room with their brightness.

"Graham has a car, but it's really small and sporty. Mallory has a minivan, since she nearly always made the runs into town for groceries." Quinn looked at his hands and then out the window. "But if you're set on leaving today, you should take the Tahoe in the garage. It's the newest and has four-wheel-drive."

"But that's your car. We can't take yours."

"I've got the other two. You guys need the Tahoe."

"Quinn, no—"

"Look, you have people to worry about and I don't."

Alice opened her mouth to say something and stopped. He turned and shuffled the dishes around on the counter into a pile, keeping his back to her.

"Why are you doing this?" she asked, her voice barely audible.

"What?"

"Helping us?"

He faced her, not able to hold her gaze for more than a second. "Because it's the right thing to do." When she merely studied him, he motioned to the rear of the house. "I'll try to get the generator running so you can take some water with you, have a shower or a bath too if you'd like." He didn't wait for a reply. Grabbing the manual from the counter and dislodging the ice chisel from beneath the kitchen doorknob, he walked outside.

The day was cool again, but the clouds were gone, and an unblemished powder-blue-sky awaited him. He stayed still for over a minute on the stoop, studying the trees and listening for any movement. When nothing but birds flitted in the very tops of the pines, he stepped down into the yard. Dew soaked his shoes within steps, but he barely noticed. There would be a lot to do to get Alice and Ty ready to leave. Then it would be just him, alone again in the big house. He and the three graves.

The wind was negligible, and the waves coasting in below the cliffs were murmurs as he rounded the house and opened the generator enclosure. After ten minutes of reading, he saw nothing that was indicative of the generator's inability to run. He tried hitting the start button again, but it merely produced the same dry click. There were four twist-locks set into a panel below the controls, and he undid them, setting the loose piece of steel to the side before crouching to look into the generator's housing. All was fuses and bundles of wires leading into darkness within the shroud. The more he studied the components, the more they blended together into one confusing mass. He sat there, staring at the alien mechanics of the machine, while all he could see was the open road beyond the gates—the breeze blowing in through the window of the Tahoe coating his skin as they drove, trees whipping past in a blur of green on either side.

He blinked, coming back to the present. His ankle throbbed from the position he sat in, and his legs were cramping. He was about to return the panel to its former position and lock it home when he spotted a wide, plastic switch set above a row of long fuses. There were no markings on or around it, and when he put pressure on it, there was resistance. He pushed harder, and the switch snapped in the direction he pressed it. There was an electrical click of contactors engaging, and the generator's engine cranked into life. The entire enclosure resounded with the machine's vibrations as the engine rose to a steady hum.

"Yes!" Quinn said, his eyes widening.

He replaced the panel cover and climbed free of the housing. With the door shut, the machine's growl became much lower, and when he rounded the side of the house, it was lost to him completely.

In the garage, he climbed into the Tahoe and keyed the ignition on. The fuel gauge sprung to a hair's width of the full mark. His father must have filled up in Portland before coming home. He found two semi-full gas cans in one corner and loaded them in the back, leaving the hatch cracked for the fumes. He was about to go into the house when he spotted a small, wooden dowel sitting on one of the shelves. It stuck out from beneath a pile of loose lumber that Foster kept for odd projects. When he pulled it free, he measured it by holding it out before him in one hand. In the drawer of the workbench, he found a roll of black electrical tape and carefully wrapped the dowel until none of the wood was visible. He tested the strength one time, bending it. It sprung back into a straight line.

When he entered the house, Alice was giving Ty a bath, the door partially open. She noticed him in the hallway and turned from where she knelt beside the tub.

"Saw the lights come on and thought I'd better get the rug rat clean before we go. No telling when he'll get another hot bath. Thank God for instant hot water heaters, huh?"

"That's for sure," Quinn said, leaning the dowel against the wall. She looked down at it then back to his face.

"I told you you didn't have to do that."

"I know. I saw it and…it only took a minute."

Alice started to say something else but stopped and turned back to Ty who was gathering bubbles before him like a sudsy blanket and running his palms over the top, popping many as he did so. Quinn hesitated for a moment and then went to the kitchen and began to clean the dirty dishes in the sink.

When the dishes were clean, he swept the floor and wiped down the counters, his hands having to do something as his thoughts wandered. Besides, Mallory and Graham would've hated seeing the kitchen this dirty.

No sounds came from down the hall. It was as if his guests had already left, the house was empty again, and he was alone. He dumped the dustpan into the garbage and stared out the window at the beautiful spring day. The trees were motionless and he could make out a few faint buds of green and red at the tips of their branches. The forest would change fast from a skeletal domain to an emerald expanse, hiding the house from the rest of the world until fall stripped the trees bare again. The snows would come along with the wind that never seemed to quit blowing during the winter. And where would he be? Here. In the house by himself, huddled around the fireplace eating whatever canned good he could find. And where would they be?

The sound of Alice entering the room brought him free of his trance and he turned to her.

"We're pretty much ready to go," she said. Her voice was even. Not unkind but not friendly either.

"I'm coming with you." The words had escaped him before he knew he'd spoken, and only the startled look on Alice's face made him realize what he'd said. "I mean, if it's okay with you, I'd like to come with. At least to Portland. There's barely any food left here, and I'm going to have to go at some point."

"No." Her reply was flat, and she crossed her arms as if barricading herself against any argument.

"You don't trust me," Quinn said, setting the broom and dustpan aside.

"I don't trust anyone except that little guy in the other room."

"If I had wanted to hurt you, I could've last night while you slept."

"You could've tried. The thing is, I don't know you or what your game is."

"I don't have a game."

"Everyone has a game."

"What's yours?"

Alice looked away at the wall and then back at him. "Keeping my son alive."

"I can help. If there's as many of those things as you say there are, then you'll need backup. Especially once you get into town."

"We don't need anyone. Do you understand?"

She spun on her heel and was about to the leave room but stopped short as Ty entered the doorway, tapping the area in front of him with the dowel.

"I found this in the hall. Did you make this for me, mom?"

Quinn held his breath, looking from Alice to Ty's small face. The boy moved the dowel around and prodded his mother's foot with it.

"Mom?"

Her shoulders dropped, and she reached out, rubbing Ty's damp hair with her fingers.

"No, Quinn made it for you."

"Oh. Thanks, Quinn! It works really good!"

"You're welcome, Ty."

The boy felt his way out of the kitchen and disappeared into the living room. Alice stood like a statue for a long minute before she faced him again.

"Just to Portland. After that we'll find another vehicle for us and we part ways. Got it?"

Quinn nodded, and Alice left him standing alone in the gentle sunshine of the kitchen.

~

He spent the rest of the morning gathering anything of use outside while Alice packed the Tahoe with blankets and towels as well as gallon jugs full of water she filled from the kitchen tap. Quinn brought the gas cans from the back of the Tahoe to Graham's garage as well as a screwdriver and hammer. He laid beneath the small sports car and pounded a hole through the bottom of the gas tank, letting it drain slowly into a large bread pan he found in the house before transferring it to a can. When the cans were full, he hauled them out to the main drive, leaving them there for when they left. The wind rose and whistled through the bare branches of the trees, its touch chilling him as he walked down the drive. He was leaving his home for the very first time. The thought brought goose bumps to his arms. He rubbed them away, but there was no way to calm the excited knot that had formed in his stomach. Even with the layer of heavy grief covering him and the insecurity the outside world offered, the sense of freedom was tangible, like something he could almost grasp and pull out of the cool air.

Inside his father's office, he found a full box of shells for the XDM and an extra magazine. He tucked them both into a small cloth bag that he slung over his shoulder and paused at the doorway before coming back to the desk. Inside the top drawer was his father's leather day planner. At the very back was a list of phone numbers. Most were marked only with a first name or initials, all of which were unfamiliar to him. At the bottom of the page were two addresses. One was a strange jumble of Spanish with a city he had never heard of while the other was in English, a town listed that Foster had told him about several times.

"Newton, Pennsylvania," he said to the empty room. With a tug, he pulled the piece of paper free and was about to stand when his gaze landed on a framed picture at the corner of the desk. It was of he and his father sitting side by side on the cliff facing the ocean. His father's arm was slung around his small shoulders. The sea was white-capped and angry looking, but their posture was relaxed, at ease with nature and each other. He couldn't have been more than ten in the picture. The memory of he and Teresa sitting in almost the exact same place only days ago washed over him, and he reached out to grasp the frame. He stopped, his fingers sliding against the smooth glass, tracing the memory for a long moment before he stood.

He rounded the desk and was about to leave the room but turned back and grasped the picture, placing it gently in the bag beside the shells. He hovered on the threshold for a long time, his eyes running over the surfaces and objects, each one spurring a memory that played out and bled into the next. When his vision began to cloud, he reached out and closed the door without a sound.

"It's hard, isn't it?"

Alice's voice startled him, and he turned to find her watching him from down the hall.

"What?"

"Leaving. I got the same way on the last trip out of our shitty, little apartment. Can you believe that?"

He nodded and looked around the house. "I'm coming back though."

"That's what I told myself too."

He made a last circuit through his home, stopping, remembering, if for only a moment. He avoided the solarium completely. The days spent with Teresa there were cherished memories, and he didn't want to taint them with how the room looked now.

At last he followed Alice and Ty out to the garage, giving the hall one last look before closing the door.

"Want me to drive?" Alice asked, leading Ty to the rear driver's side.

"Sure. I just need a minute," Quinn said, stowing his bag in the open hatch before crossing the sunlit yard.

He stopped beneath the tree at the foot of the three graves, one so much longer than the other two. He closed his eyes for a time and wavered there, an urge to return to the house and stay almost overpowering. But the invisible ties slowly broke as he knelt and put his hands in turn on the exposed dirt.

"I'll be okay," he whispered.

The sound of Alice backing the Tahoe from the garage pulled him to his feet. The three crosses stood silent in the shade of the tree. He slowly turned from his family, eyes not wanting to look away, and walked to the garage, shutting the door before rounding the house and turning off the generator. When he climbed inside the SUV, Alice gazed at him for a time before putting the vehicle into drive. Quinn watched the yard coast away and the house slide from view in his mirror.

They paused at Graham's drive and picked up the gas cans before stopping at the broken gates. Quinn climbed out and opened one side, a strange sensation running through him as he walked on ground he never had before. The road was quiet beyond in either direction, and the air was cool, full of the scent of growing things. Alice pulled through the gate and waited for him to close it behind the Tahoe. When he climbed inside, she watched him again.

"Ready?" she asked.

"Ready!" Ty called from the back seat.

Quinn let out an unsteady breath. "Ready."

Alice guided the SUV onto the open road, and he inhaled deeply as his home fell away behind them.

Chapter 11

Portland

The sun beat against the blacktop as they cruised between the blanketing forest on either side of the turnpike.

Quinn watched out the window, taking in each tree, each shadow, every animal that flitted between branches or rushed into dry grass. Ahead, the turnpike ran on in an unending line broken only by hills and the occasional curve. A few cars dotted its broad back, pulled neatly to one side or simply stalled in the center of one lane. After the first three they passed, Quinn quit trying to make out the occupants, the interiors of the cars blurred by the reflecting sun and the speed by which Alice drove. He was about to suggest stopping at the next stilled vehicle when Alice spoke.

"It's better not to look."

Ty sang to himself in the back seat, his voice a high falsetto that came out surprisingly beautiful. After a time, Quinn turned to Alice, tipping his head toward the melody that poured quietly out of the little boy.

"He's singing OneRepublic."

Alice nodded, her eyes never leaving the road. "He sings whatever I listen to or what's on the radio. He's got an unbelievable memory."

"He's got an unbelievable voice."

"I can hear you talking about me up there. I'm blind, not deaf," Ty said, as he paused between lyrics.

Quinn laughed and put a hand over his mouth while Alice's eyebrows came up and she glanced in the rearview mirror.

"You watch that sassiness, mister."

Ty giggled and began to sing again.

A stilt burst from the right-hand tree line and ran up the embankment toward the Tahoe.

"Shit!" Alice yelled, swerving hard to the left.

The stilt flew toward them. Its long, bony limbs pumping, broken teeth bared in its oblong face. Its eyes stared into Quinn's, locking there with hunger. The driver's side tires cut into the grass and gravel beside the turnpike as the stilt reached for the SUV.

They hit its outstretched arm at sixty miles per hour.

The appendage ripped off at the creature's shoulder with a wet thump, spraying Quinn's window with crimson and fleshy shrapnel. It spun once in the center of the highway and fell to its knees, a gout of arterial blood jetting out and coating the road. It stared after them, unmoving, until they crested the next hill and dropped down the opposite side.

Alice and Quinn let out a held, collected breath.

"Where the fuck did that come from?" she asked.

"From the woods. It was just there all of a sudden."

"Fuck they move fast."

"It was waiting," Quinn said, shifting so he could see through the back window. Ty had quit singing and was staring straight ahead, fingers gripping his seat belt.

"Waiting? What did it think it was going to do, rip us out of the car?"

"I don't know, but that's very aggressive."

"You can say that again."

Quinn shifted his gaze to Ty, took in the boy's stoic fear.

"It's okay, Ty. We're okay."

Ty nodded once and swallowed as he continued to twist the seatbelt. He didn't sing another note the rest of the ride to the city.

~

Portland appeared on the edge of the ocean amongst a tangle of overpasses and onramps. Quinn leaned forward as the signs announcing the city's distance counted down. The stalled cars became more prevalent here, but Alice was able to weave between them without slowing below thirty. A large cove opened up on the right and he surveyed the choppy, shining water. A half dozen boats bobbed there, tethered in place by anchors, and a long sailboat drifted past them, sails furled, its deck empty.

They took an off-ramp that pointed toward the first business district and pulled down a narrow street with dozens of cedar-shaked houses lining its sides. Ahead a small grocery store advertised lobster at eight dollars a pound. The sidewalks were deserted, the only movement a myriad of twisting pinwheels before a tourist shop. Alice took a right and drove down the street, passing dentist offices, a stone-sided restaurant, and a bakery with its front door hanging from broken hinges.

"How far to the facility where your mother lives?" Quinn asked.

"Another two miles."

Quinn's head swiveled from side to side, watching not only for the threatening movement of pale flesh but also drinking in the rich colors of the city. The houses, the storefronts, the signs of so many people and life, yet there was none. The city held a voided quality, dreamlike but so vivid he could not look away.

They came upon their first dead body while turning a corner where the street narrowed. Two cars had crashed and one had burned. The body of a partially charred man lay in the center of the street. One of his arms was charcoal-black and his scalp was blistered and purple. He faced mercifully away. Quinn was reaching toward his door handle and anticipating the cold touch of the body in his hands when Alice sped up.

"What are you—" he managed before Alice drove over the corpse.

There was a sickening double thump as the Tahoe's wheels crushed the man's skull and legs, and then they were speeding up again. Quinn's stomach rolled and his mouth opened as Alice glanced at him.

"Listen, were you present back there when that thing came out of the woods? Did you see how fast it moved? I'm sure you wanted me to stop so you could get out and pull that dead guy out of the way, but I will not endanger my child or myself because of some intangible respect for the dead. Understand? The world in which we had that luxury is gone, got me?"

Quinn turned to face the street again and nodded once.

"Mama?" Ty asked in a small voice.

"Yeah, honey."

"I gotta go potty."

"Oh for God's sake. Really?"

"Yeah."

"We'll have to wait a little bit. Can you do that?"

"I think so."

"Good."

They passed an immaculately trimmed park, tall oaks shading a playground, swings swaying without occupants. Another body was sprawled near the slides, long blonde hair ruffling in the breeze, its arms wrapped protectively around something small.

All at once Quinn could smell Graham's clam chowder, hear Mallory singing in the living room, his father talking on his phone in his office, feel Teresa's fingers brushing his face. He closed his eyes, shoving everything away, and then blinked until his vision cleared.

They rounded a curve and the road widened before encountering a bridge choked with vehicles. They stretched from one side of the small river to the other, some of them crashed into signposts while others nudged one another's bumpers. A massive eighteen-wheeler had rammed an antique shop on their side, its front end completely hidden by the building's sidewall.

"You've got to be kidding me," Alice said, slowing the Tahoe.

"Is there another way around?" Quinn asked, sitting forward.

"No. This street ends in another mile near the waterfront. Mom's home is set back on the right, two blocks in on its own street." Alice stopped the vehicle and scanned the pileup of cars. She slapped the steering wheel with her palm. "Damnit!"

Quinn waited. This wasn't his decision to make, though everything he saw said to leave this place. The rows of trees seemed to grow inward as they idled in the street, the houses with empty windows staring at them. The breeze tugged at a small flag attached to the first car's antenna blocking the bridge. It was a Boston Red Sox pennant.

"We'll have to regroup and come back," Alice said finally. She threw the Tahoe into reverse and backed into an empty drive before turning around.

"What do you mean, 'regroup'?" Quinn said as they accelerated.

"I mean, figure something else out. We need better weapons, more ammunition. If we get that, we can go on foot across the bridge and make it to the facility."

"So you won't stop to pull a body out of the way but you're going to go on foot out in the open?"

"It's my mother. What would you do for your mother?"

"I never knew her."

"Lucky you."

Quinn shot her a look, and when she didn't return his gaze, he went back to studying the various buildings scrolling by.

"We'll need better firepower anyway. Here," she said after a time, "use my phone's browser to pull up all of the gun shops in the area. Hopefully the internet's still working."

Quinn thumbed the phone on and opened the internet application, only knowing which one to touch by having played with Graham's phone over the years. After typing in 'gun stores' he hit search and touched the map option when the results appeared.

"There's one about a mile away, Thor's Outdoors."

"Are you kidding me?"

"Quite the name."

"How do we get there?"

Quinn read the directions off as Alice piloted the Tahoe through the quiet streets. Neighborhoods appeared, their lawns as well maintained as the park they'd seen. The ocean stretched away on their left, its expanse flat and calm beneath the sun. Too far out to see any details, a ship floated, only a dot amongst the blue.

After barely squeezing between another set of crashed vehicles, the green sign of Thor's Outdoors came into view, its yellow letters backed by a row of simple pine tree silhouettes. The parking lot was nearly empty save for several cars pulled tight to the front of the wide building. As they neared, the round holes in the vehicle's bodies became apparent. The glass doors of the entrance were shattered, transparent fangs hanging down in sharp points. The blaze of brass shell casings littered the ground. Alice coasted to a stop a dozen yards from the building.

"Looks like they had themselves a shootout," she said.

"I suppose this was one of the first places people came when it started to get bad," Quinn replied. "When the hospitals wouldn't take them, they decided guns were the next best thing." He studied the interior of the business. The lights were off and darkness shaded the inside after forty feet. The outlines of clothes racks and cardboard stands were the most prominent before the rest of the merchandise faded into obscurity.

"Okay, you two stay here and I'll run inside to check it out," Alice said, unbuckling her belt.

"No, mama," Ty said from the back seat.

"No. We go together or not at all," Quinn said. The finality in his voice gave him a start, and it must have surprised Alice also because she stared at him for a moment before looking past him to the waiting store.

"Okay, but the first sign of trouble, we run and get back in here, yeah?"

"Agreed."

Alice shut the Tahoe off and complete silence rolled in. They waited for nearly a minute before climbing out. Shell cases crumpled and rolled beneath his feet when he stepped to the ground. A gull sailed overhead and in a graceful turn, landed on top of Thor's sign. It leaned forward and screeched at them. Quinn drew his pistol as Alice rounded the vehicle carrying Ty on one hip while pointing the revolver with the other.

"Oh gross," she said, stopping near the front of the Tahoe. Quinn took a step forward and followed her gaze.

A bloodless, elongated arm hung down over the bumper, it's fingers snagged in the grill's holes. The opposite end was a ragged stump, worn off from being dragged.

"That's…" Quinn searched for the right word as he tried to control a bout of nausea. "…peculiar."

"Peculiar? You're an odd one, Quinn."

With the barrel of the XDM, he pried the stiff fingers free from where they'd latched on in a death grip. The appendage fell to the ground with a dry slap.

"Now that that's out of the way," Alice said, focusing on the storefront.

They moved together in a line past the bullet-riddled cars and stopped in the entryway. Glass crackled under their feet, and Alice was about to take a step inside when Quinn touched her arm.

"Wait."

"Did you hear something?"

"No, but that's the idea," he said, reaching out with the XDM toward the door's aluminum frame. He rattled the gun against it for a few seconds and then stopped, watching the gloom filling the rear of the store for movement. He did it one more time, and when nothing launched itself toward them, he glanced at Alice. Her lower lip scrunched up and she nodded once before striding into the store.

Quinn turned in a slow circle after stepping inside. The space was large, the biggest building he'd ever been in. The ceiling stretched away into steel support girders, and the walls were decorated with banners depicting smiling sportsmen casting into rivers with long poles or taking aim through scoped rifles at enormous deer. The first area was dedicated to outdoor clothing and camping gear. Next were shelves laden with fishing supplies, kayaks, trolling motors, and camouflage blinds. Most of the merchandise hadn't been touched, but there were empty hangers as well as several displays overturned, their contents splayed across the shining floor.

Alice moved without sound between the racks of clothing, her handgun sweeping back and forth while Ty held tightly around her neck. Quinn walked behind them, the utter quiet adding to the eeriness enshrouding the store.

They reached the back wall and came to the long glass cases that he assumed were supposed to display handguns like his own. Instead of shining weapons, there was only blank, red velvet. One section of glass was shattered, and there was a splash of dark blood, dripped and dried, down the front of the case. Behind the handgun displays were stands meant to hold rifles and shotguns. Most of these were empty too, but a few long-guns still leaned in their places.

"Mama's going to set you down now, honey. Stay in one place; there's broken glass." She set Ty down, and the boy didn't utter a word of protest. He waited with his hands at his sides, looking past Quinn into space.

Alice stepped between two adjacent cases and began to make her way to the rear displays when she tripped and nearly fell. Quinn moved to catch her, but she'd already righted herself and was staring down at the body she'd stumbled on. In the dim light there was no way of telling how old the man was but Quinn guessed somewhere in his thirties. Not that they could have told by his facial features even in the brightest light because everything from his mouth up was missing. The blood beneath their feet was still tacky. He hadn't been dead long.

"Damn," Alice whispered, covering her mouth and nose.

"Was he shot or...eaten?" Quinn asked, only able to take short glances at the body.

"Can't tell. Doesn't matter." Alice turned and began moving along the rifle stands. "Damn," she repeated.

"What?"

"All of these are bolt actions. There's nothing semi-auto, which is what we need."

Quinn scanned the displays, not entirely sure he would know the difference. At the end opposite the way Alice moved, a doorway opened into complete darkness. Quinn sidestepped toward it, finally flicking on the light beneath the gun barrel. The doorway opened into a small office complete with a large desk, computer, and file cabinets. Posters of different gun manufacturer's symbols lined each wall. Bloody handprints and smeared gore covered the floor. The gruesome trail led behind the desk to a narrow door made completely of steel, a heavy deadbolt positioned close to the jamb. Quinn swept the office with the light once more before stepping back into the main store.

"Think I found something," he said quietly. A moment later, Alice led Ty through the doorway and stopped on the threshold.

"What?"

"See the trail?"

"Yeah."

"I'm guessing whoever it was is still in there, but I'm betting they aren't alive anymore."

"Maybe, maybe not," Alice said, checking the seat of a leather chair near the wall before setting Ty in it. "Don't move, baby."

She crossed the office and positioned herself to one side of the door before reaching a hand out to rap twice on the steel. They waited, Quinn's light doing a shaky dance on the floor at his feet. Alice knocked again, and when there was no answer, she shrugged.

"Wait here," Quinn said, moving past Ty and back into the main store. Everything was quiet, and the parking lot remained empty save the Tahoe. He gave a brief glance around before hurrying to the aisle they'd passed on the way in. When he returned to the office, Alice gave the short, thick hammer in his hand a look.

"You think you can get through with that?"

"If I hit it right."

"You look strong, but the door looks stronger."

Quinn positioned himself beside the door after tucking the handgun into the small of his back and grasped the hammer with both hands. He gave Alice a look and she returned with a thumbs up. Aiming carefully, he wound the hammer back and swung directly for the deadbolt.

The door blasted inward, hitting the wall behind it before bouncing back.

Quinn nearly lost his balance but recovered, setting the hammer down to pull the XDM from his back. He clicked the light on again and paused.

"I think I found Thor."

The man was huge with a blood-stained belly that hung well over his beltline. He sat on the floor straight across from the door, legs splayed out in a V, head tipped back to rest against the wall. He wore black combat fatigues, his large feet hidden inside military boots. Long, blond hair hung down in two braids on either side of his head, the roots stained red from where the bullet had traveled through the roof of his mouth and out the back of his skull. A black, semi-automatic pistol, the last three inches of its barrel coated in blood, lay in his open palm.

Quinn studied the corpse for a second and then reached out, fumbling along the wall until his fingers met a switch. The room glowed beneath the light of two fluorescents set in the ceiling.

"Holy shit," Alice said, stepping into the room behind him.

It was an armory.

The walls were glazed with weapons. Handguns, rifles, shotguns, swords, knives of all lengths, and ammo. Stacks of ammo in dark, steel cases. Shelves laden with boxes all marked with the loads they carried. In the corner was a low bin containing rectangular, plastic wrapped objects the size and shape of hardcovers. Black writing graced the front of each one.

"I can't believe it," Alice said. She glanced down at Thor's corpse. "God of thunder took the easy way out, huh?"

"Appears so."

"Looks like he was wounded by someone before crawling in here."

Quinn nodded. "Must've given up and left him to take care of himself."

Alice moved to the nearest wall and brought down a wicked looking rifle with an extended magazine protruding from its bottom. She brought the weapon to her shoulder, aiming down its length before dropping it to her side. Her smile seemed to brighten the room further.

"You did good, Quinn."

~

They spent the next forty minutes making trips to the Tahoe. After walking through the entire store twice, Quinn found a small loading platform at the rear of the building and pulled the vehicle around making for a shorter route from the office. Alice picked out four AR-15s as well as three Sig Sauer handguns, explaining the benefits of each one as she handed them to Quinn to haul out. If she noticed the questioning looks he gave her, she ignored them, choosing instead to stack more ammunition in his arms.

The bin in the corner turned out to be full of MREs or, meals ready to eat, their contents displayed across the packages in small black print. They took the entire bin, and Quinn had to detach the third row seats from the rear of the Tahoe, leaving them beside a rolling dumpster. When Alice was satisfied with their haul, she picked up Ty, who had begun to squirm on his chair, and started for the door. Halfway there his small voice stopped them.

"I still need to go to the bathroom."

"Oh honey, I'm so sorry; I forgot," Alice said, turning in a circle to see where the nearest bathroom was located.

"Over there," Quinn said, motioning with his light to the far corner of the store where two alcoves were cut in the darkness. "I'll load a few more things that look useful." Alice nodded and continued through the building, pausing in the right bathroom entry to turn on the lights inside.

After they disappeared, Quinn returned to the camping area and found a black, all-purpose duffel bag. He moved along the rows, the strangeness of being where he was compounded by the fact that they seemed to be utterly alone in the city. As he took items from the shelves and stowed them away in the bag, his hands shook. Not from fear but from excitement. The bizarre exhilaration hung about him like a fog, and he chided himself, thinking of the dead they had encountered already that day, the horrifying sights he'd seen only on TV before this—though those interpretations of death were weak when compared with the thing itself: the fetid smell, the slick of blood beneath your feet, the ravaged flesh. But he couldn't deny there was something about being here, away from his home, in the company of others whom he didn't know that moved him inside. The possibility of dying was only part of what he was experiencing.

The rest was life.

He caught sight of his dark reflection in a mirror near the rear loading door and stopped. He slid a palm up his cheek and then dropped it away. For a moment he'd forgotten. Being with them had done it, the action, the danger, the sickness and fear, but mostly them—although there would always be mirrors to remind him.

He stowed the full duffel in the back of the Tahoe and glanced around the empty space behind the store. The day had warmed some, but a cool breeze coasted continually off the ocean, the air thick with salt. It could've been any day. A tractor-trailer might have rolled around the corner with a shipment. People may have jogged or walked the paved path running behind the store and around the muddy pothole a quarter mile south. But there was nothing. No movement and nobody but them.

He went back inside using his light to guide him past the office and into the main area, heading toward the dim glow coming from the bathroom. He was halfway there when a sound stopped him, his guts contracting into a painful mass.

An engine revved once, and a newer pickup coasted across the parking lot, rolling to a stop before the blockading cars. The portions of its red paint not covered by splotches of mud shone in the sunlight, and when the doors opened, the sight of Rick, still wearing his bandanna, caused a wave of déjà vu so thick that Quinn, froze in place.

Chapter 12

Run and Hide

His thumb found the flashlight switch on the gun and toggled it off.

The brothers examined the entryway, their shotguns at waist level, eyes scanning the store's depths as they waited on the far side of the line of cars. Ty's voice echoed out of the bathroom, not loud, but not quiet either. Alice answered him, just a murmur.

Quinn broke from his trance and ducked, running in a straight line toward the bathroom. As he neared the doorway, Alice emerged, leading Ty by the hand.

"Get back, kill the lights," Quinn whispered, nearly bowling them over as he forced them into the lit bathroom. His hand skittered along the wall and found a light switch, flicking it down with a snap.

"What is it?" Alice asked, instantly crouching, wrapping an arm around Ty's waist as darkness invaded the bathroom and they became only shadows.

"The brothers that ran you off the road, they're here."

"Oh shit. Those bastards," Alice whispered.

"Shh, they're inside," Quinn said.

Glass crunched beneath boots and low voices floated to them from the main area. Where would they inspect first? The bathrooms? No. The light was still on in the rear office. That's the first place they would go. Quinn inched to the doorway and peered around the corner, the pistol's grip trying to slide from his sweat-soaked palm.

The brothers were mid-way through the store, their own flashlights sweeping arcs across the shelves and walls. Quinn leaned back just as one of them turned, coating the bathroom entry with light before swinging it away. Quinn looked out again and watched the closest one, he thought it was Rick, shove a display of rain gear over.

"They're going to the back room," he breathed over his shoulder.

"They'll find the Tahoe. They'll know we're here," Alice replied. Ty whimpered once, soft and brimming with fear. Quinn watched them approach the back office and take up positions on either side of the door. His mind spun like a dervish, whirling for a way out. They were trapped. Could he sneak up behind them and kill them both before they got a shot off? He re-gripped the XDM. Could he do it? Could he take a life? Two? Alice squeezed his upper arm, trying to pull him back into the full dark of the bathroom when he saw movement out of the corner of his eye.

Four stilts were striding along the highway past the parking lot.

They were enormous. Their enlarged heads bobbed well over the seven-foot street signs that lined the road, but the one leading the pack dwarfed them all. It stood half-again as tall as the rest of them, its pale skin glowing in the sun, skeletal arms swinging in time with its stride that surpassed a car-length.

Before he had time to think, Quinn was moving. Alice gripped his arm, her nails raking furrows in his skin in an attempt to keep him where he was. His name hissed from her lips, but then he was out in the open of the store. The brothers had disappeared into the office, no doubt reveling in the armory they'd discovered. How long would it take them to wonder why the light was lit only there? How long until they saw the hammer on the desk, the broken deadbolt in the door, and do the math?

Quinn tracked the stilts as they lumbered on, coming even with the store now, the lead tilting its massive head back to sniff the air. He lowered himself closer to the floor, running bent low, stepping over fallen clothes hangers, skirting broken glass, leaping past a downed display. Then he was between the cars, sliding along their bumpers. His jeans snagged on a license plate, and he swore under his breath as the material tore along with his skin. He began to crawl, crab-walking, when he cleared the cars until he was beside the brothers' truck. His pulse jumped in his vision and his mouth gaped, breath hot and frantic blasting in and out. He stood, peeking over the truck's hood. The monsters were beyond the parking lot now, their path taking them toward the ocean. One of them made the bullfrog croak that Graham had issued the night in the solarium, and the others answered with a chuffing sound that brought the hairs to attention on the back of Quinn's neck.

With a final glance back at the storefront, he opened the passenger door of the truck and pulled himself inside. The dangling key fob in the ignition sped his heart up further. He'd been right about the brothers. They were overly confident. So much so that they didn't feel the need to lock up their unattended truck. Something in the back seat drew his attention. After he grabbed his father's hiking boots from the pile of gear that littered the space, he pressed the small panic button on the truck's keychain.

The vehicle erupted with sound.

The horn honked in short bursts, the lights flashing in strobe-like flickers. Quinn saw the group of stilts halt and spin as one, their faces turned toward the store, emaciated forms rigid. The tallest of them bellowed and began to run toward the truck.

Quinn slid out of the cab, not bothering to shut the door. He skittered between the cars and slid inside the building as the brothers burst from the back office. He had just enough time to fall flat on the floor before the lights strapped to their guns swept the space above him. He belly-crawled, knees and stomach picking up shards of glass that stung like wasps. Boots pounded the floor as he tucked himself beneath a clothing rack, sure that they'd seen him duck inside the store. But they ran past him outside, not pausing for a second.

Quinn leapt to his feet, glancing once over his shoulder to see the brothers leering, dumbstruck at the open door of the blaring truck. An instant later hungry croaking filled the air that reverberated throughout the store, and Rick screamed something to his brother as he raised his shotgun and fired.

Quinn ran on, stumbling over something in the dark, and reached the back corner of the building. Alice perched at the entry to the bathroom, Ty in her arms now, her eyes wild and looking past him. He said nothing and simply grabbed her arm, leading them across the dark store to the lit hallway. More gunfire exploded outside and there was a deep, inhuman cry of pain that mingled with one of the brothers' voices, yelling obscenities. They reached the hall and raced down it. Quinn kicked at the safety bar on the rear door and then they were outside in the sunshine, gunfire and screams following them into the open air.

They didn't speak or hesitate. Alice rushed down the concrete steps and flung the rear, passenger door open, boosting Ty inside before scrambling in herself. Quinn jumped into the driver's seat and threw his father's boots into the passenger wheel well. His thighs caught beneath the steering wheel and he realized Alice had adjusted the settings. He jammed the button on the seat down and when he could move freely, started the Tahoe. The engine roared to life and he jerked the vehicle into drive, hammering the gas as he did so. The SUV leapt forward and Quinn spun the wheel, his eyes searching frantically along the rear lot. They couldn't go around the front of the store and back to the highway. What if the stilts were still alive and decided to give chase? How far would they follow them? Or even worse, what if the brothers had survived and saw them escaping? They would know instantly who had called the stilts in with the car alarm.

A small dirt access road approached on their right, partially hidden by a sign reserving parking spaces for Thor's employees. Quinn swung onto it, and the vehicle rattled over a dozen potholes as he accelerated. The access road emptied out into an industrial park devoid of vehicles. The large buildings were dark and the streets running between them clear of obstructions. Quinn cruised a mile, doing almost sixty, and then turned up another street, bringing them into a residential development with an assortment of new homes growing out of the cleared earth. He swung into an uneven driveway and pulled past the two-stall garage and out of view of the street before stopping.

"Are you guys okay?" he asked, looking in the rearview mirror.

"We're fine," Alice said. She was still holding Ty, stroking his hair, his face buried in her shoulder. "We're fine."

Quinn let out a long breath, the humming of adrenaline in his veins quieting, but slowly so that he felt like a struck tuning fork growing still.

"That was crazy," Alice said.

"Yeah, it was."

"No, I mean what you did. You could've gotten us all killed."

"I didn't see any other choice, did you?" Quinn said, turning in his seat to face her. She held his gaze for a beat and then looked down, shaking her head.

"No, I guess not."

He watched her for a few seconds, how Ty trembled in her arms.

"I'm sorry. I didn't think; I just reacted."

Alice nodded and pried Ty away from herself enough to speak to him.

"Good thing we went potty before all that, huh, buddy?"

Ty giggled a little as Alice laughed shakily. Quinn met her eyes, and the look held for a moment that drew out, hardening into something nearly solid before she glanced away and gasped.

"You're hurt," she said, pointing to his thigh.

There was a long gouge on his right leg where the license plate had torn through his jeans and split his flesh. A little blood seeped from the bottom of the gash, and the upper half of his pants were stained red.

"I think it's okay. It doesn't hurt anyway." But as he said the words, the pain began to burn in the wound.

"Let's get inside and get it looked at. We don't want an infection now. Doctors are in short supply, I'm guessing."

They climbed from the vehicle and approached the house. It was a simple two-story with a concrete basement. It appeared newly completed. When Quinn made his way around to the front yard, there was a realtor's sign stuck in the dirt beside the curb. A sliding glass door on the back of the house gave them entry after Quinn began to pry on it with a small multipurpose bar he'd taken from the store. The inside of the house was cool and empty. No furniture adorned the living room or kitchen and the three bedrooms upstairs held no beds. When he tried the faucet in the large bathroom on the main floor, cold water poured out on his palm, turning hot when he adjusted the handle.

"We have hot water," he said, meeting Alice and Ty in the kitchen where she deposited the black duffel on the floor. "Power must still be on in most of the city."

"I guess this is as good a place as any to spend the night," she said, glancing around the room.

"I would've liked us to get somewhere a little higher and more secure."

"Me too, but I didn't see anything nearby, did you?"

"No. I don't know if it's smart to keep pressing our luck driving around town either."

Alice sighed and ruffled Ty's hair.

"No, you're probably right."

"It smells new in here," Ty said, feeling the air with his left hand.

"Here, I'll set you up in the corner, champ," Alice said, carrying him to the farthest corner of the living room. After opening a bottle of water for him, she and Quinn unloaded the necessities from the Tahoe. When they had weapons loaded and within easy reach on the marbled kitchen counter along with several MREs, Quinn moved the Tahoe tight to the rear of the house, parking it directly beneath one of the upstairs windows. From that spot, the vehicle could only be seen if someone were to round the house through the yard on either side, but from the street it was invisible. The pain in his leg intensified, and he resisted the limp that tried to implant itself in his stride. A runner of fresh blood rolled down his leg, and he felt it soak into his sock. When he stepped inside, already formulating how he would lock the broken door, Alice was at the counter, a small black case open before her.

"Come lay down, big guy," she said, patting the countertop. In the other hand she held a hooked needle that caught the early afternoon light.

"Um, you know what you're doing?"

"It's sewing; how hard can it be?"

"It's sewing a person, in this case me. Maybe it doesn't need stitches."

"Just lie down, please."

He relented and climbed up onto the wide countertop but didn't lie all the way back. There was a small scissors beside the medical kit, and he used these to clip away a large flap of jeans, exposing the wound completely.

"Shit. It's worse than I thought," Alice said, drawing a length of black thread through the needle.

"I don't suppose there's any type of pain killer in there," Quinn said.

"Nope. Not unless you count aspirin. It's pretty bare bones. There is a little numbing gel in here though."

"I'll take it."

After washing the wound off and sterilizing it with a small bottle of peroxide, Alice dabbed on the numbing gel that burned when it touched the gash but slowly leeched away some of the ache. Before she began to stitch, she looked up into his face.

"You okay?"

"I think so. Are you?"

"Yes. This is going to be painful."

"I know."

"It'll be okay, Quinn. It'll be over in a jiff. That's what mom says when I have to get shots at the doctor," Ty said from the living room.

Quinn smiled. "Thanks, Ty."

"No problem. It still really hurts though."

Alice tried to hide a grin and then raised her eyebrows in a question. Quinn nodded and she began to sew.

The pain was sharp and boiled at each point she pushed the needle through, the thread thin but severely uncomfortable as it slid through his skin. After the first two stitches he looked away, focusing on the brightness of the day in the empty field behind the development, how the brown grass nearly glowed, the twisting paths a pair of birds made through the air, the dancing flicker of a butterfly close to the trees.

"And done," Alice said, snipping off the excess thread. The stitches were surprisingly neat and there were more than he would've guessed.

"Wow, thanks," he said.

"What, you didn't think I could do it?"

"I guess I didn't know."

She gave him a small smile.

"Well, now you do."

He slid off the counter, his leg feeling somewhat like an overcooked sausage.

"Did mom fix you all up, Quinn?" Ty asked.

"She did."

"Did it hurt as much as shots at the doctors?"

"Hmmm, no, not that bad."

"Good, 'cause mom's not a doctor, you know."

"Watch that sass, boy," Alice said, cleaning up the first aid kit.

She's not, Ty mouthed, and it was Quinn's turn to hide a smile.

~

The afternoon passed into evening uneventfully. Quinn stood at the front bedroom window that faced the hidden ocean and listened for nearly an hour, one of the AR-15s leaning against the wall. No gunshots or yells or even a car engine filtered into the small development. The surrounding neighborhood was quiet as well, with only squirrels and birds moving among the branches of the trees. What had happened to the brothers? Were they dead now because of his actions? Probably. But what choice did he have? In the recesses of his heart he knew that given the chance, the two men would've gunned them all down for the contents of their vehicle.

Movement drew his attention on the next street over, and he pulled a pair of small binoculars to his eyes that he'd rested on the windowsill.

A stilt walked down the center of the neighboring street, its elongated head stuck forward, sharp shoulder blades jutting in the evening sun. It didn't look his way and continued south, stopping only to sniff the air once before disappearing through a garden in a large house's backyard.

"Anything?"

His hands lost their grip on the binoculars, and he barely caught them before they clattered to the floor. He shook his head and turned to find Alice standing in the doorway.

"Sorry I startled you."

"It's okay. One of them just went by on the next street over."

"Really?" She came into the room, stopping next to him so that her shoulder brushed his upper arm. "Let me see," she said, holding out a hand for the binoculars. He gave them to her and she scanned the houses and sidewalks methodically. Quinn looked at her, how dark her hair was compared to her skin. The delicate bones in her wrists. He'd never noticed someone's wrists before. She dropped the binoculars from her eyes and he glanced away, surveying the same area she had.

"I don't see anything now," she said.

"No, I think it kept going."

"One of them wouldn't be as much of a problem as a pack. We could handle one of them."

"Yep, they die just like we do. Where's Ty?"

"Sleeping. I made a bed in the room across the hall for him."

"Good. Did you see I parked the Tahoe below the window?"

"Yeah, why?"

"If we have to leave in the middle of the night, we can go out the window and land on the top of it. Then we don't have to go out the back door. Easy escape route."

Alice appraised him, jutting her bottom lip out like he'd seen her do when she agreed with something.

"That works. You already checked the window?"

"Yeah, it opens nice and wide, and it's already unlocked."

"Good. We'll find another vehicle we can take tomorrow before we go look for mom."

Quinn hesitated, then nodded. "Okay. When do you want to go?"

"In the morning, before noon. That'll give us enough time to get somewhere safe by sundown, and for you to get home." She looked at him, and he kept his face slack, not meeting her gaze but instead watching the quiet homes across the street.

"Perfect," he finally said.

"Perfect," she echoed and moved to the door. "I'll get some food going." He nodded once and heard her move down the hallway to the stairs. His eyes roamed the cars lining the second street over. A shadow was slumped against the steering wheel of a late model minivan. Unmoving. The entire world seemed to have stilled in the evening light.

"Perfect," he said to the empty room.

~

They ate sitting on the floor of the kitchen, Ty at Alice's side and Quinn across from them. Quinn's meal was a type of Mediterranean chicken, spicy and not at all dry like he'd thought it would be. Although they weren't able to warm the food in anything since there were no appliances in the house, everyone's food disappeared quickly, and there was little talk between bites. When they finished, Alice wrapped the disposable containers in a garbage bag she found beneath the kitchen sink and set it in a corner.

"To keep the smell down," she said when he looked at the bag.

They moved into the living room, and Quinn opened one of the windows looking out into the front yard, leaning his rifle against the wall beside it. Alice brought a blanket from the small pile of supplies in the kitchen and draped it over Ty, who smiled as she sat down beside him on the living room floor.

"It's going to get cold tonight," Alice said, hugging Ty close to her side. Quinn glanced at her and then at the gas fireplace mounted in the living room wall.

"I'll get this started," he said, moving to kneel before the glass front. "If the power's on, I'm guessing the gas will be too."

"What about the flames? You'd be able to see them from the street," Alice said.

"Not until it gets darker. Then we can pull the shades and throw blankets over the windows facing the neighborhood."

Quinn fiddled with the gas valve beneath the decorative, ceramic logs until he heard a small whoosh. He pushed the red button and listened to the distinctive click of an electric starter. Flames erupted out of the fireplace and he felt the hair on his arms shrivel beneath its touch.

"Damn," he said, sitting back. Alice made a surprised grunt and then snorted once. When he looked at her, her face was lit with the same smile he'd seen in Thor's armory. "Are my eyebrows still there?" he asked. This made Alice laugh harder, and Ty giggled. "Glad I can be of amusement," he said, moving back to his post beside the window. After a time, Alice and Ty grew quiet and only the calls of chickadees and the occasional Blue Jay filtered in from outside.

"Can we play a game?" Ty asked just when Quinn thought the boy had fallen asleep.

"What kind of game?" Alice said.

"I don't know, something fun."

"Sorry, champ. I'm fresh out of board games."

"We could play reflex," Quinn said.

"What's that?" Ty asked.

"It's word association. My dad called it reflex when I was little. Like if I say, blue, what's the first thing that comes to your mind?"

"Mom says the sky's blue, and so's the ocean sometimes."

Quinn felt his face grow hot as Alice narrowed her eyes at him. Had he just asked a blind boy what he associated with a color?

"Yeah, like that. Here, how about dog?" Quinn said, barreling on as embarrassment tried to constrict his throat.

"Friend," Ty answered almost immediately.

"There you go. Okay Alice, your turn."

"I don't want to play."

"Come on, mom!" Ty protested. Alice gave Quinn a withering look and sighed.

"Okay, hit me, Quinn."

"Blue Jay," he said, hearing the bird's shrill call again in the distance.

"Annoying," Alice said. Quinn laughed.

"Yeah, they can be that."

"Car," Ty said, sitting forward.

"Tahoe," Quinn said, glancing out of the window.

"Mom, you go. Tree."

"Grow."

"Elephant," Quinn said.

"Big!" Ty exclaimed.

"Shhh, Ty. We have to keep our voices down," Alice said.

"No fun," Ty said, half smiling.

"What? Keeping our voices down?" she asked.

"Yeah," he replied, grinning as his sightless eyes stared at the floor.

"Maine," Quinn said.

"Home," Ty answered.

"Ocean," Alice asked, looking directly at Quinn.

"Freedom," he said. "Beer."

"Good," Alice said, and Ty laughed, his head following their voices. "Steak."

"Delightful. Flowers," Quinn shot back.

"A waste. Dancing."

"Can't. Trust."

"A waste. Guns."

"Loud. Love."

"Myth. Death."

"Scary. Fire," Quinn said, glancing at the flames. Alice opened her mouth and then shut it, her eyes wide, looking past him, through him.

"I have to go to the bathroom," she said finally and stood, moving through the doorway and out of sight. A moment later there was the quiet closing of a door. Quinn watched the hallway where she'd disappeared, his brow furrowed. It was only when Ty touched his arm that he realized the boy had risen and crossed the room to him. Quinn gazed down into Ty's eyes, their focus swimming and watery. His irises were so blue and bright, even beneath the thin veil of gray film they were hard to look at.

"Bend down," Ty said, tugging his arm. Quinn obliged, tilting his head to one side to accept the secret the boy was undoubtedly about to tell him.

One of Ty's hands, small and airy, grazed his face.

Quinn jerked away, standing up so suddenly Ty nearly fell backward. The boy's eyes were as wide as his mother's had been before she left the room.

"I just wanted to know what you looked like," Ty said. His voice was small, uneven.

"Sorry. You…I'm just," Quinn said and looked up as Alice stepped into the room. She glanced from Ty to him and then back again, understanding slowly gracing her features.

"Ty, let's get you ready for bed," she said.

"But it's early, and I took a nap."

"Tyrus…"

"Okay."

Alice handed him the tape-wrapped dowel, and he shuffled out of the room, tapping with the makeshift cane. Alice hesitated for a moment and then followed him toward the bathroom. Quinn cursed under his breath and faced the window again, watching the dead neighborhood.

~

It was full dark by the time Ty fell asleep in the upstairs bedroom. Quinn had drawn all the curtains an hour before and hung an extra blanket over the window closest to the fireplace in the living room. With the flames set to low, only a slight glow rippled behind the glass, squat shadows dancing on the new carpet beyond the mantle.

Quinn sat before it, the AR-15 on the floor beside him. He'd watched the streets in front of the house until the daylight faded to nothing, like an oil lamp being turned down. The buildings blended with the trees into amorphous shapes, and the streetlamps came on near the neighboring commune of houses, scattering the shadows beneath the hedges and benches lining the sidewalks. He threw a glance at the sliding door opening to the back yard, assuring himself that the two-by-four he'd found in the garage and jammed into the frame would be sufficient as a lock.

Unless someone really wants to get in. Or some thing.

He brushed the thoughts away as Alice returned to the living room, her own weapon hanging from a sling she'd attached to it earlier in the afternoon. She sat down a step away, folding her legs beneath her like a child awaiting story time. In the flickering light, she appeared even younger. Before he could stop himself, the question fell from his mouth.

"How old are you?"

Alice turned her head toward him, coating one half of her face in light and the other in darkness.

"How old do you think I am?"

"I'm not answering that."

She smiled. "Smart guy." After a long pause, she looked back at the fire. "Twenty three. How about you?"

"Twenty."

"Not even drinking age yet."

"Nope."

"I could tell you weren't much of a drinker."

"I could tell you were."

"Touché." She fingered the stock of her rifle and turned to him again. "I'm sorry if Ty made you uncomfortable earlier. It's just how he sees people…"

Quinn shook his head. "It's fine. I didn't…"

"Didn't what?"

"Didn't want to scare him," Quinn finished, throwing Alice a look before rising to peer out of the window. When he was satisfied that the street was quiet, he sat down again.

"You wouldn't scare him. He's a whole lot more mature than I give him credit for. It's probably my fault he is that way."

"I would say that's an advantage now with how everything is. Things aren't going to get back to normal for a long time. If ever."

"Yeah," Alice said, flipping her sling back and forth with a fingertip. He watched her for a moment, gauging whether or not to ask the question that had been in the back of his mind since the night before. He glanced at her left hand, and she caught him looking. "No, I'm not married," she said, waggling her fingers. "Never was."

"I thought he might've gotten lost in all this and you didn't want to talk about it."

Alice huffed and shook her head. "I hope so, wherever the bastard is." Something told him to remain silent, so he did. After another drawn out pause, she spoke in a low monotone. "He was an exchange student from Spain, came our junior year of high school. He was going to be a pro soccer player, or 'futbol' as he always insisted. He was so cocky, so sure of himself, it was almost off-putting. But there was something else there beneath that façade. He had a love for life I'd never seen before. He wanted to see the world, try new things. The way he was so open and honest and fearless, it was disarming. Charming even," she said, stabbing a finger into the carpet.

"I got pregnant, and he left the next month. Never looked back, never answered any of my calls or emails. His parents vouched for him, always said he was 'out' or at a futbol tournament. I let them have it one day and told them that their son had gotten me pregnant and then ran away. They hung up on me and then changed their number."

"Wow," Quinn said.

"Yeah, wow's putting it fucking lightly. Not that I need a man around to run things or take care of me, actually the opposite, but I would've at least liked for him to know he had a son, that he has his hair, and that he's blind."

Alice flipped the sling hard, and it made a little snapping sound in the silent room.

"Doesn't sound like he was fearless," Quinn finally said. "Sounds like he was a coward."

Her hands quit flipping the sling and her lips opened as if she were going to make a rebuttal but a scream rang out from the street, cutting her off.

They stared at one another in the dancing light before Quinn lunged forward, scrambling with the doors and then twisting the gas valve off. The flames flickered then receded like snakes returning to their burrows. The room fell into complete darkness as another yell cut the night. Accompanying it came the deep resonance that was more of a vibration than a call.

Alice swung the sling she'd been toying with over her head and raced up the stairs, disappearing into the hall as Quinn made his way to the window. He drew the blanket aside but saw nothing moving. The scream came again. Human, definitely human.

"Quinn!" Alice hissed from the top of the stairs.

"Yeah?"

"Get up here."

He hurried across the room, tripping on the first stair before launching himself up the carpeted treads. Alice was only an outline in the dark. Her hand brushed his chest and slid down his arm to his hand. A ripple of goose bumps flowed outward from where she'd touched him, but there was barely time to register the sensation before she led him soundlessly into the front bedroom where the drapes were drawn apart revealing a swath of cold light.

"Look, across the street in the clearing," Alice said, half guiding, half shoving him to the window. Quinn stepped close to the sill and gazed out into the night. At first he saw nothing, but then movement snagged his attention, flitting in and out of the shadows in the meadow before the neighboring street.

A pair of figures ran, except ran was the wrong word—they hobbled. And after a second of scrutinizing, Quinn saw they were elderly, their hair reflecting gray as they passed through shafts of streetlight, their steps unsure and slowed by the fact that they were holding hands.

"Oh no," Quinn said, squinting, trying to see through the gloom.

The couple kept looking over their shoulders as they stumbled on, and that's when the first stilt stepped from between the trees behind them. It was hunched over, as if arthritic, but still loomed well above the two people that scurried away from it. It made the deep burping sound that now brought the image of a thick swamp filled with reptilian life to Quinn's mind. To the right, ahead of the couple, a loud bark came from the darkness and then a second stilt moved into view, this one much taller than the first, and healthy looking. It took a step toward the people, its thin arms stretching out wide as if to accept them into an embrace. It may have been a trick of the light, but Quinn could've sworn he saw a cruel smile flash across its misshapen face.

"They're trapped," Quinn said, gripping his rifle. "We have to do something."

Alice latched onto his arm as he tried to turn away from the window.

"Stop. Look," she said, pointing to the left.

Two more stilts approached from the end of the street, their long gaits pulling them toward the couple in flowing strides. Another appeared from behind the house to their right, unnervingly close and so tall it could have easily looked into the window they gazed out of.

Quinn leaned back from the glass, the sight of the stilt closest to them sending a freezing lance through his spine. They were so *quiet*. The elderly couple were in the center of the clearing now, the man's arm tight around the woman's shoulders. She was crying, long pitiful sobs of the hopeless that slid in through the windowpane. Slowly she sank to her knees, the man unable to hold her up any longer. He drew out something that glinted in the low light, bracing it with both hands at the hunched over monster closest to them.

A tongue of flame leapt from the pistol in his hands, and the stilt shaped like a question mark, straightened up and threw its head back. A deep howl of pain came from its mouth and it began clawing at its chest, but it walked on, closing the distance between it and the man. He fired again, this time at one of the stilts approaching from the left, but he must have missed since they barely broke their long strides and neither of them cried out. A warbling hiss, that sounded something like a cicada in the hottest part of summer, came from the rest of the monsters, the circle formed by their number growing closer, tighter, like a noose around the couple. The woman moaned, and Quinn could make out interspersed words of prayer between sobs. The man spun in a circle, aiming at each stilt but not pulling the trigger.

"We have to help them," Quinn said, beginning to ease the window open.

"Stop. We can't; there's too many. Besides, the shots will attract more of them." When he started to protest again, she squeezed his forearm. "We don't have scopes on these. We'll miss in the dark and they'll overwhelm us. They'll get inside. They'll get

Ty." Quinn's mouth opened to argue, but the pleading look on her face was like a shadow all its own.

Another gunshot pulled their attention back to the meadow. The injured stilt had been shot again and fallen. It crawled forward like some extended insect searching for a carcass to invade. The rest of the creatures didn't appear to be afraid of the man or his weapon in the least. They moved closer, cinching the circle smaller until they were almost in reaching distance.

The woman shook and the man stood above her, his head snapping back and forth, trying to watch all of the stilts at once. A moment before he did it, Quinn knew what he was going to do.

With a jerky motion, the man aimed the gun at the woman's head and pulled the trigger, his scream mingling with the thunder of the shot. She slumped sideways at his feet and without waiting, he tucked the barrel beneath his chin and pulled the trigger again.

The final gunshot resounded in the clearing and the man fell in a heap on top of his wife. The stilts paused before moving in closer. The tallest, that had come from behind the house next door, swiped a long arm at the next closest creature, sending it slinking back a step before dropping to its hands and knees. It brought its head down to the bodies, and even from the distance that separated them, Quinn could hear it inhale like a chef sniffing a steaming dish.

When the lead stilt lowered its head and began to feed, Quinn turned away, drawing the part in the curtains shut. His stomach roiled, and the Mediterranean chicken resurfaced in the back of his throat, tasting like an acidic semblance of its original flavor that sickened him further.

"There was nothing—" Alice began.

"We could've tried."

"They would've killed us. All of us. Who knows how many more there are out there."

"I just hope that if we're ever in a situation that bad, if someone can help, they will." In his mind's eye he saw his father watching the starving girl and the dying man on the side of the road as he drove past.

"*You* can do whatever you want after tomorrow," Alice said, walking toward the door. "I'm going to keep me and my son alive." She paused in hallway. "We should keep watch."

"I'll take the first shift," he said. Alice half nodded and vanished into the bedroom where Ty slept, undisturbed, by what had played out in the meadow.

Quinn paced downstairs and sat with his back against a kitchen cabinet, his eyes burning as he tried to block out the sounds of feeding that filled the night.

Chapter 13

Silence and Frost

The morning was overcast with interlocking clouds moving east at a steady pace.

Alice had relieved him somewhere near three in the morning, waving off his assurances that he could make the whole night.

"I'll need you alert in the morning," she'd said, and sent him to lay down in his own sleeping bag. He'd slept little and light, the first gray edges of dawn creeping beneath the curtains waking him.

They ate a simple breakfast of powdered eggs and jerky, which wasn't bad considering they had hot water to mix the eggs with. When they stepped outside, the development was quiet without so much as a single birdsong breaking the silence.

Quinn laced up his father's hiking boots and walked around the front of the house, easing up to the corner before scanning the street and meadow on its far side. There were no traces of the stilts or any sign of their late meal. The area where the couple had died was heavily trodden, the sprouting grass trampled flat. Other than a dark stain, there was nothing to show that they'd been there at all.

After loading the Tahoe, they pulled onto the street, their windows down despite the cold to hear their surroundings better. Quinn rode in the passenger seat again, his rifle between his legs and the XDM strapped in a holster on his hip he'd taken from Thor's the day before. Ty sat quietly in the backseat, his face turned toward his window, lips moving soundlessly in what Quinn could only guess was a song he sang to himself.

Quinn searched the yards and parking lots of the buildings they passed on the way back to the blocked bridge. There was no movement, human or otherwise. The emptiness filled up the city and overflowed, stretching away to the indifferent ocean that continued its forever quest of washing away the land.

When they arrived at the bridge, Alice slowed the Tahoe and swung it in a short U-turn so that it headed back the way they'd come. She motioned to Quinn to get out and then glanced in the rear view mirror.

"Honey, you wait for a second in the car, okay?"

"Okay."

Alice got out and guided Quinn a few steps away from the Tahoe before looking up into his face.

"Do you know how to get on the turnpike from here?"

"Um, no."

"Really? How many times have you been to Portland?"

Quinn licked his lips. "Not many." Alice stared at him, her blue eyes studying every inch of his face before sighing.

"Okay. You have to go back the way we came and take the first left. That'll merge into Fifth Street. Follow that for a mile and then you'll see the signs pointing to Ninety-Five. Ninety-Five goes south and then you'll see—"

"Wait, why are you telling me this?" Quinn said, cutting off her directions.

"In case something happens to me. I want you to take Ty and try to get to Iowa."

"Nothing's going to happen to you," he said, the words too fast and sounding hollow.

"In case something does, you need to be able to get out of the city. It seems like most of the stilts are still around the populated areas."

"Probably centered near military posts and hospitals. Like the one we're going to now."

She threw him a look that bordered on malicious. "This is a mental care facility, not a hospital. And it's fairly small."

Quinn nodded, seeing Ty beginning to open his door.

"Promise me," she said. "Promise you'll take care of him if something happens."

"I promise," he said, the words coming easier than he expected. Ty climbed down out of the SUV, gripping his dowel in one hand, his face trained toward their voices.

"Okay," Alice said, reaching out to grasp Ty's free hand. "We go quickly and quietly. The facility's only a few blocks on that side road. We'll go in, check the place to see if mom's there. If she's not, we leave."

"Is grandma okay?" Ty asked.

"We're not sure, honey, but we're gonna check on her." Ty's lip trembled, but he nodded and lowered his face toward the ground.

"We need anything else?" Quinn asked.

"Just these," Alice said, waving her rifle once. "Let's go."

They moved in a single line between the cars on the bridge. The air was cool and a layer of decay hung with it, thicker near the vehicles that were still occupied, their inhabitants only mushy stains on the seats inside. The river gurgled beneath the bridge.

"I'd forgotten that they did that," Alice said under her breath as they passed the last of the cars. "Turned to soup."

The feeling of his father's skull sinking beneath his fingers came and receded, and Quinn wiped his hand on his pants. "Yeah," was all he managed.

The street the facility was on branched to the right, stretching away long and narrow with old oaks growing from either side. Their branches reached high and intermingled over their heads, creating the illusion that they traveled beneath a striated tunnel. The houses were sparse here with wide lawns cut by paved drives that led to attached garages. A utility truck was stalled beside an electrical pole, its bucket half raised and empty, the driver's door cocked open. When they passed it, the same terrible odor met them like a fog and what might've been a wedding ring glinted amidst a jellied mass on the floorboard.

The street ended in a neat turnaround, its center landscaped with bushes not yet bloomed. The facility itself lay beyond, a single-story brick building with rolling lawns spanning either side dotted with birdbaths and a white fountain that still spouted water into a small pond. They stopped before the entrance, waiting for any movement from inside the structure, but the shadows remained still behind the glass lining the front doors.

Quinn glanced at Alice who gripped Ty's hand tighter.

"All right, buddy, we're going inside now. And it might smell bad for a little bit, okay?" Alice said.

"It smells bad everywhere," Ty said.

"Isn't that the truth," she said. "You ready?" she asked Quinn.

"As I'll ever be."

"Then let's go."

Alice led the way, still holding Ty's hand firmly. Quinn followed, turning back the way they'd come to inspect the empty street before moving through the door.

The smell hit him like a hammer. It was like his father's and Teresa's rooms, like the cars on the bridge, except multiplied tenfold. It was all he could do to keep from retching. The odor was in his nose, coating his throat, burning his eyes. Ty coughed once and covered his mouth. Quinn put a hand on his shoulder and squeezed. Alice moved forward, seemingly unaffected.

They were in a lobby with a square kiosk straight ahead, padded chairs lining walls hung with magazine racks. To the right side of the desk, a hallway ran away from them into darkness, a few sets of doors visible on either side. A single light burned on the desk, and when they neared it, Quinn saw a dark splash of red dried to a brown on the swivel chair before the blank computer screen. He shared a glance with Alice, and they both turned on the flashlights they'd attached to their rifles earlier that morning. Their beams cut swaths in the murk that inhabited the hallway, the sound of their footsteps much too loud. Quinn breathed through his mouth, not only to cope with the smell but also to hear any furtive movements that might've been drowned out otherwise.

The hallway spanned the entire length of the building, the right side holding rooms looking out upon the expanse of lawn that let some light into the long space. The rooms opposite them offered no views except the decorations each patient hung up on the walls. There was an abundance of these that appeared and vanished in the sweep of the flashlights: mobiles made of string and straws, finger paintings, and the occasional full-length canvas sitting on an easel. A red exit light flickered above a hallway to their right emitting a soft buzzing. Alice paused there, bringing their procession to a stop.

"My mom's room is at the very end of the hall," she whispered. "Why don't you two wait here, and I'll go check."

"No," Ty whispered back.

"I don't think we should split up," Quinn said.

A door swung open a dozen paces down the hall, its hinges emitting a brief squeak.

They froze, their lights trained on the door as it coasted to a stop. The doorway remained a frame of shadow.

Nothing moving.

No sound.

Quinn tightened his grip on the AR-15, his finger touching the trigger.

"Hello?" Alice said in a low voice.

There was a beat and then a bald head poked from the darkness followed by two dark brown eyes that flitted over them, taking them in. The man emerged from what Quinn assumed was a janitor's closet since he was inexplicably holding a mop in one hand, its head dried to a tattered pulp. He wore a dirty, blue jumpsuit, and his bare feet poked from the pant legs like two white fish. He blinked in the glare, holding up one hand to shield himself.

"Don't, don't, don't. He's not here. Doctor's not here. Not in right now. Come back later and see," the man said, looking down at the floor. He began to shift his weight from foot to foot.

"We're not going to hurt you," Quinn said, stepping past Alice and Ty. He lowered his gun toward the floor. "Are you here alone?"

The man rotated as he swayed back and forth. One hand went to his mouth and he inserted a pinkie finger between his teeth, biting down. He shook his head.

"Is there someone here with you?" Quinn asked, taking another slow step forward.

The man pulled his finger from his mouth and grinned.

"Always here, here, here, and there's room now. Any room I want. Do you know which one is yours?"

"Do you know Myra Fisher?" Alice asked. "She had a room here too."

The man's eyes traveled from Quinn to Alice.

"Marie, Marie, Marie, she lives across from me, me, me." He giggled. It was a high, splintered sound that raised the hairs on the back of Quinn's neck.

Something flashed by the window of the room to their right, there and gone in a blink.

Quinn stepped back and brought his rifle up, trying to see out the window in the room behind them. There was nothing but the long reach of dead grass, the fountain still flowing.

"Something's wrong," Quinn whispered.

"Always wrong, ping-pong, sing-song, come on," the man sang in a high voice and sprinted away from them down the hall, dropping the mop to the floor with a clatter. His blue jumpsuit flashed in and out of their lights.

"Fuck," Alice said, moving forward with Ty in tow behind her.

"Alice, let's go," Quinn said, snagging her arm.

She pulled away. "He knows my mother. Marie's her middle name." Her eyes were shining orbs in the flashlight's glow. "I need to know."

Quinn let her go, grimacing before jerking his head. They set after the man at a quick walk, his laughter bouncing off the tile floor and walls. He waited for them at the end of the hall, his back against the wall as he pushed off of it with his buttocks, letting himself slam against it before pushing off again.

"Stop that," Alice said, spearing him with her light. "You gotta be quiet."

He began to chew on his pinkie again, his upper teeth becoming red with blood.

"You said you knew where Marie was," Quinn said in as calm of voice as he could muster, the sight of the man gnawing through his own finger making his stomach flip.

"In there, in there, always in there," the man said, snapping his bald head toward the door on their right. "Go in, go see, go see, go see."

They kept Ty in between them as they moved past him. As Quinn came close to him, he realized the uniform the man wore wasn't only dirty but wet also, and the smell that came off him was palpable. He'd been soaking in what the disease had left behind.

Alice pushed the door open and stepped inside. Immediately she moved Ty to one side and stood him against the wall. When Quinn entered the room, he saw why.

A police officer lay facedown in a pool of dried blood. His face was bone white, a partial beard spattered with gore covered his cheeks. His mouth gaped open, eyes sunken and dried to crusts. His pants were pulled up above his boots and something had been *at* his legs, the teeth marks prominent in the bloodless flesh. Quinn ripped his eyes away from the body on the floor to the bed occupying the room that was stripped of everything but a thin sheet. A stained outline rested in its center, a pool of viscous jelly desiccating along its borders.

The man giggled behind them, and Quinn only had time to glance at the officer's body, the empty holster on his duty belt, before he spun and brought up his rifle.

The man had the cop's handgun trained on Ty who stood motionless against the wall, his lips moving soundlessly again, completely unaware.

"Here, we're here, come, come, come, inside, quick!" The man yelled at the top of his lungs, glee pulling his lips back from bloodied teeth.

Quinn tried to aim, but the concussion of a shot made him flinch, his sights losing the man's grinning head. There was a mist of red hanging in the air, and it coated his face like a spray of surf when he would climb the cliffs by the ocean. His right ear buzzed and his head felt lopsided, heavy with the deafness that plagued half of it. The man was gone from the doorway, and Ty still stood against the wall, covered in blood.

"Oh God," Quinn said, rushing forward. He set his gun down and gripped the boy by the shoulders, beginning to wipe the blood from his face.

"Quinn?"

"Yeah, buddy. Are you hurt?"

"I don't... don't think so. What's on me? Momma?"

Quinn glanced at the doorway and saw the man's bare feet there, splayed out, pinkie toes touching the tile. Alice stepped forward and kicked the bottom of one sole. It jumped lifelessly and laid still. She then knelt beside them both, half elbowing Quinn out of the way, and hugged Ty to her chest.

"You're okay, you're okay, you're okay," she chanted into the side of Ty's neck. Quinn rose and retrieved his rifle before shining his light on the fallen patient.

The man's head was mostly gone from the eyebrow's up. One eye had exploded and hung to the side by a strand of nerve. His mouth hung open, still grinning, a lake of blood within even with his teeth.

Quinn doubled at the waist and was quietly sick in the hall, gagging on the rotted smell of disintegrated bodies, on the blood, for what had almost happened. He wiped at his mouth and spit once before straightening. Alice moved into the hall carrying Ty. She stepped over the corpse and set her son down, rubbing his arm and hugging him to her side.

"Great shot," Quinn said.

"Thanks. Are you okay? The barrel was pretty close to your head when I fired, but I couldn't..."

"I'm fine. It's just some buzzing on that side. It's already a little better."

"Crazy fuck," Alice said, baring her teeth at the dead man. "Should've known."

"He must've killed the cop. If it were stilts, there'd be nothing left."

Alice kept running her fingers through Ty's blood-matted hair. "We can go," she said after a moment of silence. Her eyes passed over his, and Quinn glanced past the dead man to the bed. The person who had lain there and died had been small. He gave the body on the floor another look, and a chill slid from the nape of his neck to his buttocks, an icy finger tracing a path.

"Was it just me or did it sound like he was yelling to someone right before you shot him?" Quinn asked.

Alice paused in stroking Ty's hair, her eyes widening in the dim light.

The sound of the front entrance opening filled the hallway, the hinges echoing to them in a short moan.

"Turn out your light," Quinn hissed, dousing his own. The hallway fell into dappled darkness. They waited, listening, not breathing. Quinn took a step forward. The wind, it was the wind, had to have been. He motioned for them to follow, and they moved as one down the hall. The lobby was brighter than where they stood, but the sun still hid behind a blanket of clouds and didn't lighten every corner. He strained his eyes, trying to make out any movement, but there was nothing. The front doors were closed, and the steps beyond their glass were empty. They came even with the glowing exit light and stopped.

"Wind?" Alice asked, a note of hope in her voice.

A stilt stepped into the mouth of the hall, its bulbous joints bending so that it stooped down, peering in at them like a hunter cornering a warren of rabbits in a log. Its lips split revealing broken teeth.

"Go," Quinn said, pushing Ty and Alice toward the emergency exit.

The stilt rushed them, its slender body bent almost double to clear the ceiling tiles, feet hissing against the floor. The exit corridor was short, and they hit the emergency door with a bang and burst outside into daylight.

Three more stilts were moving toward them across the facility's grounds, their pale flesh the same color as the clouds. They paused as they caught sight of them then began to lope in their direction.

"Run!" Quinn yelled, swinging his rifle up. Alice scooped Ty into her arms and sprinted in the direction of the Tahoe. He fired off three quick shots, and tufts of grass whipped at the creatures' feet. He tried to find one of the monsters in the rifle's sights and was about to squeeze the trigger again when the emergency exit blasted open and the first stilt stepped out, its mouth open, teeth glinting.

Quinn put two rounds into its head.

It fell on top of him, its momentum carrying it forward. He tipped to the side, the stitches in his thigh straining, then bursting, and managed to slide away from its full weight before it pinned him to the ground. Regaining his feet, he saw the other three were closer now, lumbering toward him as fast as they could, their marionette movements clear and horrible in the light of day.

He turned and fled.

The baritone calls chased him, the air vibrating with them. *They're excited. Must not be any of the ones that got supper last night,* he thought crazily as he pelted across the lawn, trying to focus on the bottoms of Alice's feet ahead of him. She and Ty were already on the street leading from the facility toward the bridge. Movement to their right caught his attention, and he glanced that way, stumbling, as he saw two more stilts running across the grounds, their eyes locked on Alice and Ty. Quinn fired three more times, and a chunk of flesh exploded from one of the creatures' shoulders in a red haze. It spun and bellowed, putting a massive hand to the wound before finding him, its gaze boiling with pain and hatred. It redoubled its pace, blood flowing down its arm and dripping from bony fingers.

"Go! Go! Go!" Quinn yelled, glancing over his shoulder. The three behind them were closer, the distance closing with each enormous stride. He came even with Alice and Ty and his hand found Alice's arm. Blood ran down his leg, and their collective panting was a rasping soundtrack to their flight. The bridge neared, the vehicles' bright paint muted beneath the stainless steel sky. He threw another look backward and nearly cried out. The two groups had melded into one pack of skeletal limbs and flexing joints, eyes black and mouths yawning. Hungry. The Tahoe seemed to be further away with each step they took, the sound of the stilts louder, closer.

They made the bridge and sped between the cars, their footsteps slapping hard against the cement. Quinn searched the opposite side, somewhere for them to hide, but the only building was the antique shop, its front decimated by the eighteen-wheeler. For the first time, he read the script painted in bold letters on the side of the tanker: NITRO-LOCK-REFRIGERATED LIQUID. The rear of the truck was dead center of the road, blocking the middle of the bridge with its girth. A square, steel box was bolted to its end, one of two doors hanging open. As they neared it, Quinn veered off to the truck, and Alice turned sideways, still moving with Ty clutched to her chest.

"What are you doing?" she yelled.

"Just go!" he replied, swinging the second door of the truck open. The sound of the stilt's breathing filled the air, the world. He would feel their long fingers grabbing him any second just as Graham had done, their teeth biting through him. There was a number of gauges and pipes inside the truck's attachment housing, some of them covered with a thick layer of frost. A brass hammer hung from a support and he snagged this, bringing it down as hard as he could on the closest freezing pipe.

The pipe snapped off midway through and spurted a stream of liquid surrounded by white steam past his face. A portion hit his shoulder, his skin burning like nothing he'd ever felt before. He spun away from the back of the tanker, bringing his rifle up as one of the stilts lunged at him. He blew away a portion of its throat in a spray of tissue and blood that coated its brethren behind it. Its eyes flew wide, but it continued to reach for him, snagging its filthy fingernails in his shirt and tearing it partially from his chest as it tipped forward.

Quinn fell on his side, slamming to his throbbing shoulder but keeping hold of the rifle. His vision shook with the impact and his breath rushed from him. He rolled, coming up on his feet in the time it took the stilt to slide to a stop. He made it two shaking steps back before he paused, the view before him stopping him in his tracks.

The width of the bridge was covered in fog.

The liquid nitrogen spread like something alive, coating everything it touched in speckled white frost. It flowed out of the damaged pipe in an arching fountain that reminded him of the one near the facility. It ran to where the fallen monster lay, turning the already pale skin a lighter shade of gray as its warm flesh froze in a matter of seconds. The remaining stilts were backing away, the low croak running between them in a steady chorus as the nitrogen crept closer, pouring over every inch of the bridge. The tallest near the front of the pack loomed over the top of the tanker truck, its eyes finding Quinn's, locking tight. Marking him. Quinn brought up the rifle, but the creature retreated farther out of sight.

"Quinn! Come on!" Alice's cry shook him from his immobility, and he turned and sprinted the last twenty yards to the Tahoe, climbing into the passenger side as she gunned the engine and they sped away down the street.

Well-groomed yards flashed by outside his window. Houses, garages, sidewalks, pavement, more grass, trees. The trees were beginning to cause a feeling inside him, their slender trunks, long branches, reaching. He blinked, biting down hard on the inside of his mouth. His breathing slowed, his heart's pace coming down from hummingbird range closer to a human being's. Alice blew through stoplights and surged around sharp corners, the Tahoe's wheels screeching their protest. A repetitive sound came from the back seat, and he finally turned to see what was making it. Ty wiped at his nose and sniffled again, creating the scratchy sniffling, lower lip trembling. He kept running his hands over the dowel in his lap. He'd managed to hold onto it through their flight from the facility. Quinn reached back and put a hand on his small knee. The boy jumped.

"It's okay, Ty. We're going to be okay," he said. Ty rocked in his seat and nodded, biting down on his lower lip as if he knew it was betraying his courage.

Alice brought them out of the city, the last neighborhoods clinging to the sides of the streets like patches of lichen before giving way to old growths of forest that lined the turnpike. They rode in silence, slowing only to circumvent the random vehicle that blocked the highway. After a half hour, Quinn glanced at Alice and opened his mouth to speak when he saw her arms trembling, knuckles white on the steering wheel.

"Are you okay?" he asked quietly. She gave no sign she heard him, her eyes locked on the road ahead. A tollbooth approached, bordered by the first clearing they'd seen since leaving the city. The orange arm was down and blocking their lane. Quinn was about to open his door to get out and raise it when Alice put the SUV in park. She didn't look at him, instead climbing out and walking to the edge of the silent turnpike overlooking the field. She stood there, arms crossed before her, head down.

"I'll be right back, Ty," Quinn said, exiting the vehicle. He moved across the lanes, rocks snapping beneath his father's hiking boots, eyes scanning the woods surrounding the field, but there was no movement. When he neared her, he noticed her shoulders shaking and thought she was going to be sick. It was only when he stopped beside her that he saw the tears coating her cheeks. When she didn't say anything and continued to cry, staring ahead at the field, he spoke.

"I'm sorry about your mother."

She looked at him as if seeing him for the first time and lowered her face once more. Another silent sob coursed through her, and he extended his arm to put it around her shoulders before dropping it back to his side. He glanced at the idling Tahoe, Ty only a small shadow behind the tinted glass.

"I almost got him killed. The most precious thing in my life," she finally said, her voice raw. "It was stupid, so stupid to go there."

"You were only doing what anyone would," Quinn said. "I don't know what type of person wouldn't have gone looking for their own mother."

"But at the expense of what?" Alice burst out. "Ty's life? Yours? I knew she was dead already. I could feel it. But I had to check, had to satisfy that gnawing doubt. I…"

she opened her mouth to say more and just shook her head. He did reach out then, his hand finding the softness of her shoulder.

She stiffened and turned away.

Quinn lowered his hand, pressing it against his hip, unsure of what to do with it. What had he expected? For her to fall into his arms? Of course she shrank away. Who wouldn't? Maybe she feared she could catch whatever he had, like the plague was still virulent and he was a carrier.

"I'll be in the car," he said, giving her a last look. The wrapped layers of her dark hair shook once, and he left her to cry alone on the side of the road.

Chapter 14

Lonely Miles

They found an old farmhouse on the top of a hill to stay in for the night.

They'd driven for hours after Alice came back to the Tahoe, the ivory skin of her face red but clear of tears. She'd placed an unopened can of soda atop the button that raised the toll arm and they'd driven through, the lane open forever to anyone who came after them. They'd stopped only to wash off the patient's blood in a small creek beside the road, the water so cold it left them gasping as they doused their faces, hands, and hair in it.

The driveway that led to the house was overgrown, the mailbox pitted with rust and time. Quinn had spotted the 'For Sale' sign, half tipped forward to the ground like an exhausted sentry. The house itself was narrow and tall like many in New England. Faded white siding and dark blue eaves that peeled in the evening light. A field stretched out before it on the southern side, sloping down to a brambled meadow where several deer grazed, their watchful eyes finding them when they stopped near the house before going back to the ground's meager offerings.

The house was musty and empty with mouse droppings covering many of the surfaces, but the living room had a wide view of the field and drive along with a stone hearth. There were no beds in the rooms upstairs, but a dusty, pea-green sofa sat against one wall in the living room, which Ty flopped down upon and immediately fell asleep propped up against one arm, his eyes partially shut. Without speaking, Quinn and Alice unloaded what they needed for the night. As he made his way up the stairs on the last trip, he winced and stumbled, the gash in his leg brightening with pain. Alice emerged from the doorway and stopped him as he passed.

"What?"

"Why are you limping?"

"I think my stitches reopened," he said, setting down a bag full of food.

"Let's have a look."

"It's probably okay."

"Don't be dumb; that's how little problems become big ones."

She led him to a decrepit bench on the porch, grabbing the first aid kit on the way. When she stopped before him and raised her eyebrows, he glanced around the space.

"What?"

"Drop 'em, bud."

"Drop what?"

"Your pants. I'm guessing you don't have unlimited pairs from home, and you ruined the ones from yesterday."

"Uh…"

"I'm not going to take advantage of you."

"I wasn't worried about that," Quinn said quickly, unbuttoning his pants. He turned away and then sat on the bench when he'd lowered them to his knees. The top two stitches were frayed ends poking from bloodied flesh, but the rest held.

Alice didn't say anything, going about cleaning the wound with peroxide again before re-stitching the cut closed in a few deft movements. When she was finished, she gave him one of her rare smiles. It was like the sun drifting from behind a cloud the way it changed her face.

"All patched up and…what happened to your shoulder?"

Quinn glanced at the spot where the liquid nitrogen had landed. The cotton of his shirt was stiff and matted and it felt as if someone were constantly holding a flame to the skin beneath.

"Some of the liquid nitrogen got on me."

"For God's sake, why didn't you say something. Off with your shirt."

"Can I pull up my pants first?"

Alice barked her harsh laugh and nodded. He stood and after fastening his pants, drew his t-shirt off, the patch on his shoulder making him grit his teeth with the movement. There was a swollen and upraised blotch of skin the diameter of a pop can where the liquid nitrogen had hit him. It was white at the center, fading to a purple-ish brown at its edges.

"Holy shit," Alice said, stepping closer. Her breath was hot on his chest, and he raised his head, trying not to focus on the sensation. "I'm just going to clean it the best I can and wrap it. I don't think we should put any ointment on it until we see how bad it is."

"Sounds good to me," he said. Alice soaked a chunk of gauze with bottled water and began to dab at the wound, her fingers on the undamaged skin of his shoulder cool and strong. He closed his eyes and let her work, trying not to flinch or jerk when she applied pressure to the burn. He focused instead on his breathing, trying to time it with hers. In and out, calm and collected. When she finished cleaning as best she could, she taped a sterile bandage loosely over the area, allowing the burn to breathe.

"You could've been a nurse," he said, glancing at the careful work she'd done.

"And you could've been an Abercrombie model." She paused, her eyes shifting to his before packing up the first aid kit. "I mean, you're in really great shape. Do you lift weights or something?"

"I used to rock climb a lot."

"Sure. Well, hopefully that doesn't get infected. Maybe tomorrow we can find a pharmacy, upgrade our little kit here into something really useful."

"Thank you," he said.

She hesitated before zipping the pack shut. "You're welcome. Thanks for what you did on the bridge. I wouldn't have thought of that, *didn't* think of it." He pulled his shirt over his head and adjusted the fabric covering the bandage.

"I had no idea if it would work to be honest."

"But you tried anyway, so thank you."

He nodded, and they looked at one another for a long moment that broke as Alice tucked an errant strand of hair behind her ear and moved toward the doorway leading into the house.

"It's going to get chilly tonight," she said, pausing on the threshold.

"I'll find some firewood," he said. And then she was gone inside the house, and he was left only with the fresh burning in his shoulder and the twilight that crept closer over the fields.

~

He found an ancient wood box outside the back door that was partially full of decaying oak. The light was beginning to fail in the west when he got the fire going, its glow warming the open space of the room. They heated a mixture of MREs in a camp pan near the hearth after Alice tried the lights and the old electric stove in the small kitchen to no avail. Quinn woke Ty with a gentle shake to the shoulder when the food was ready, but the boy only pushed some of the meal around his plate before lying back down and falling asleep again.

"Stress," Alice said after a stint of silence broken only by the crackling fire.

"What?" Quinn asked, setting down his own half-eaten meal. The concoction of beef and beans didn't taste bad, but the texture was terrible, the mealiness catching in his throat with each bite.

Alice nodded to her son. "He's exhausted from what happened today. He didn't have to see. He knew how close..." Her voice broke on the last word, and she gazed down at her plate.

"He's safe."

"For how long? Until the next group of those things we run into?" She shook her head and glanced out the darkening window. "We have to get to Iowa. It's the only place that we have a hope."

"We'll get there, you'll see."

She looked at him, and the light played off the angles of her face, her eyes unmoving from his. His skin warmed, and he finally looked away, setting his plate on the floor.

"We didn't find another car for us," Alice said.

"No."

"And you didn't ask to be brought back to your house."

"No."

She opened her mouth to say something more but then a smile played upon her lips and she gestured to the corner of the room. "We have a visitor."

A mouse watched them from beside the couch. It balanced on its hind legs, sniffing the air, its beaded, black eyes studying them before scurrying to Ty's uneaten food. It looked at them again and then began to nibble at a piece of corn.

"I wonder if that will be us in a decade," Quinn murmured, watching the rodent's tiny paws grip the kernel and turn it.

"What do you mean?"

"If we'll be searching out scraps of what's left of the world."

"You mean if we lose."

He glanced at her and then out the window. The deer were gone and the meadow was empty with the settling night.

"You make it sound like a war."

"Isn't it?"

"The stilts are just an aftereffect of the disease. We've already lost, don't you think?"

Alice didn't reply. She moved to the fire and dumped her meal into the flames, quickly pulling her hands away before stepping back.

"They don't seem to be territorial, do they?"

"No. They almost have a pack mentality from what I've seen."

"What would you guess their numbers are? Roughly."

"There's no way of knowing really, but if I had to guess, well, let me think about it." Quinn shifted on the floor, leaning back on one hand. "If we go by how many people we saw in Portland to how many stilts we saw, we'd have a three to eleven ratio."

"But we don't know that some of the ones we saw today weren't from last night either. They're so damn alike I have trouble telling if they're male or female."

"That's true, but I don't think the ones from today were the same that..." He cleared his throat. "...that were near the development."

"Okay, so we have what type of percentage of the population dead from the plague?" Alice asked, returning to her sleeping bag that was spread open on the floor.

"They were saying seventy to seventy-five percent death rate the last time I watched TV."

"Bullshit. I didn't see anyone alive in town when we left, but there were several of those things meandering around."

Quinn shrugged. "Let's say ninety-five percent death rate then."

"Sounds closer to reality. You can't trust the news anyway. They're a bunch of lying bastards."

Quinn laughed. "That's true. So we have three hundred and seventeen million people alive after the last census and ninety-five percent of that is," he closed his eyes and rubbed the back of his neck, "approximately three-hundred million people give or take a million. That leaves seventeen million people alive. And for every three that are still human, there are eleven that aren't so..." He scrunched up his brow again, carrying numbers and shifting figures. "There's four and a half million of us and—"

"Over twelve million of them," Alice finished.

They sat in the heavy silence that pervaded the room like some oppressive fog.

"Four million of us left in the entire country. Doesn't feel like that many." She sighed and drew her legs up to her chest. "Damn it, I need a drink."

"Yeah. That would be welcome," he said, staring into the fire.

"They can't even feed on the dead since the people who got the plague turned into that stinking jelly. They'll only have live food to go after."

"I hadn't thought of that," Quinn said.

"Leave it to me to think of something gloomy." She fell silent and gazed at the fire before glancing at him again. "By the way, are you some kind of math whiz or something?"

"No. I was homeschooled and—" He almost blurted out everything to her but managed to stifle it at the last second. "We reached fairly high levels in most of the subjects."

"I guess. I'm terrible at math, always preferred art and English to algebra."

"Right brained."

"I don't know if there's anything right about it."

They sat in silence for a while, the fire crackling in the hearth, the quiet chirp of frogs somewhere off in the night. It could have been any night, any normal night. They could've been here as a family on holiday.

He shook his head, casting the thoughts away as Alice spoke again.

"There's nothing left of them, is there? The people they once were," she said.

Quinn remembered the stilts' cold stare of hatred, the hunger in their gazes as they pursued them down the street, how the thing Graham had become lifted him toward its waiting mouth.

"No, I don't think there is," he replied.

"How tall do you think they get?" Alice asked in almost a whisper. "I mean, really? The tallest one I saw was when we were leaving the apartment. It was walking along the next street, and its head was only a few feet under the stop light when it passed."

"You saw a taller one," he said, readjusting himself on the floor. "We both did."

"Where?"

"On the internet."

Her eyes widened a little and then she blinked. "How far away do you think that one was from the car?"

"Not sure, but a pretty good distance since at first I thought it was a tree standing there."

"So did I."

"I would say it was way taller than the one you saw in your town." Now they were both whispering.

A knot popped in the fire like a gunshot and they jumped.

Alice laughed under her breath. "Sitting around telling scary stories in the dark like kids."

"But now the stories are real," Quinn said, dropping his gaze to his hands.

They both fell quiet, and after a time, Alice volunteered for the first watch. Quinn curled up beside the couch on his sleeping bag, his rifle within easy reach. Ty's small snores were the only sound besides the fire chewing the oak to cinders, and the tension from the day began to uncoil inside him like a rusted length of wire. His muscles slackened, their strains relaxing to dull aches. The burn on his shoulder still flared with each heartbeat, but it was muted somewhat by the lingering touch of Alice's fingers. He imagined them there again and then pushed the thought away. There had never been room in his life for useless fantasy and there was even less in the world around him now.

Their little visitor had retreated with a small piece of bread and was gnawing on it in the corner of the room. He watched it as sleep began to draw his eyes shut, and the last thing he saw was its tail disappearing through a gap in the floor.

He awoke hours later to the feeling of fingers touching his face.

With a start, he began to sit up, his hand reaching for the AR-15, but then he made out Ty's small form kneeling beside him, only a shadow in the low light of the fire. The boy's hands traced the humped curve of his cheekbones, the incongruence of his left eye socket, the jutting point of his jaw. The urge to pull back ebbed as Ty's fingers ran down his nose and then fluttered across his forehead before falling away. Quinn lay there, frozen, waiting for Ty to begin crying or call out for his mother, but the boy simply sat beside him, looking down with eyes unseeing.

"You're different," Ty finally said. "Like me."

Quinn struggled for words, but nothing would come. Ty smiled and rose from his knees to lie back down on the couch. Within minutes his breathing was deep and rhythmic once more.

Chapter 15

Forks in the Road

"If there wasn't anything blocking the highways, we'd be there in less than a day."

Alice glanced at him from the passenger seat, the early morning sunshine settling on her hair so that it shone like oil. They were on a four-lane highway, the sides of the road still heavy with trees and brush, its stretched path through the country unblemished save for a motionless car every few miles that they pulled around without looking into. The occasional farm would appear, dormant, without movement except for a flag attached to a porch or a weathervane tattooed against the sky atop a silo. He could barely keep his eyes on the road for all there was to see beyond it. The sky, the fields, the houses. Everything so large, so open and wide. The whole world beyond the windows.

His stomach rumbled, and he placed one hand there. They'd risen early and eaten jerky since there was no hot water, and no one seemed in the mood for powdered eggs anyway. Without saying much of anything, they'd loaded the Tahoe and pulled away from the little farmhouse along with the glade it sat in. Now his appetite was returning again, the three square meals a day Graham had cooked only a memory from another life.

"Seems strange, doesn't it?" Quinn replied. "That so much could change in a few days' time?"

"Strange doesn't touch it."

"There's other people out there; we just have to find them," Ty said from the backseat. He'd awoken better rested than either of them, though Quinn knew that wasn't where the boy's unfailing optimism came from.

"You're right, baby," Alice said. "We're on our way right now to look for them."

"The army, right?" Ty asked.

"Yep."

"Like Grandpa Fisher was in?"

Alice froze and something passed across her face. The clouds that were usually there deepening into a storm before sliding away again.

"He was in the Navy," Alice corrected him, but the timbre of her voice wavered on the last word. Quinn threw her a glance before focusing on the road once again.

"And when we find them, they'll protect us, right, Momma?"

"Yes, they will."

"From the monsters."

"Yes, from the monsters."

"You're not scared of them, though, are you, Quinn?" Ty asked. He could feel the boy's small hands gripping the back of his seat to pull himself as far forward as his seatbelt would allow.

"Oh, I wouldn't say that," Quinn said. "But we can learn from the things that scare us."

"Like what?"

"We can learn how to beat them. We can learn about ourselves."

Alice shot him a look that he couldn't quite interpret.

"You mean like what makes us scared?" Ty said after a pause.

"Something like that, yes."

"Momma's scared of fire."

"Ty, that's enough," Alice said, turning in her seat. Her voice cut the air of the vehicle like a knife, and Quinn heard Ty sit back. Alice shifted again, her eyes staring out the windshield at the road that spooled away from them.

Quinn cleared his throat. "We should stop sometime soon for gas and water."

"Yeah. Next town is Belford. It's coming up in three miles," Alice said, consulting the map on her phone.

"Wonder how long the towers will hold," Quinn said, motioning to the device.

"Not sure. The power might stay on for weeks, but when that goes, I'm guessing the service will too."

"Then we'll have to consult an actual paper map." Quinn gave an exaggerated shiver.

Alice chuckled. "Where the hell are we even going to find something like that?"

Quinn reached out and tapped the glove compartment. "I put one in there before we left the house."

"You were thinking ahead. Were you doing that for us or had you already planned on coming with?"

"For you."

Alice nodded and smoothed her hair back behind her ear. "We still haven't talked about what's going to happen."

"Happen?"

"I know you're here now, and maybe you think you're some kind of knight or something…"

He glanced at her then back at the road. "What's that supposed to mean?"

"It means we were supposed to part ways in Portland."

"Not sure you noticed but Portland didn't really go as planned."

"No, it didn't, and I already thanked you for what you did but…"

"But now you want me gone."

"We don't know you, Quinn. You seem like a nice guy, but we do better alone."

Ty began singing under his breath, an airy rendition of another popular song Quinn couldn't name. His stomach roiled with hunger, and something else.

"I'm not in this for anything. I'm living in the same world you are. If you really want me gone, I'll find another car in town."

Alice wouldn't meet his gaze, and Ty continued to sing.

"In any case, it was smart thinking to bring the map," she said finally.

Quinn shrugged, begrudgingly. "My dad liked to plan; guess he passed it down to me."

"What did he do?"

His mouth began to dry and he tried to swallow what felt like grit on his tongue. *Not yet.* The sign for the Belford exit appeared beside the road and he gestured at it.

"We'll have to be careful," he said, curving the Tahoe onto the off ramp. "We can almost be sure to run into one or more of them in town."

Alice watched him for another span, but he didn't meet her gaze. Finally she focused again on the landscape and slid the AR-15 beside her into her lap.

Belford appeared with a lone gas station beside the road, a dizzying amount of plastic pinwheels made to look like flowers spinning in the grass apron before the store. A county dump truck was parked beneath the tall awning along with a red Volkswagen Rabbit. The Rabbit's door was open, and something dark lay on the ground beneath it. It was only when they pulled to a stop near one of the pumps that they saw it was a man's severed leg, still covered in dress slacks, the end that should've attached to a hip, a ragged mess of red tissue and white bone.

"Let's be quick," Alice said, her eyes locked on the bloody splashes around the leg.

"Yep," Quinn said, stopping at a pump.

When he stepped out, the air picked at his shirt, running its cool hands across his shoulders and neck. He shivered and looked up, avoiding the sight of the Rabbit and what was left of its occupant. The lights in the canopy still burned, and there were dark zeros in the digital readout of the pumps. Quinn filled the Tahoe's tank and then re-filled the half-empty gas can in the back of the vehicle, all the while watching for movement behind the plate glass of the station or in the barren field filled with the prior year's weeds.

When he finished, they left the station behind and cruised into Belford itself. The town was small with what appeared to be two main streets intersecting at its center. The outlying boundaries were filled with homes, yards beginning to green now that the snow was completely gone, dark windows gazing at them as they rolled past. A grocery store sat on the closest corner, coupons plastered against the inside of the front doors. Darkness hung inside the store, only the first rows of food visible from the street.

Quinn pulled the Tahoe to a stop at the curb, waiting for a full minute before putting the vehicle in park. They watched the street for a while, a dirty napkin and a plastic bag drifting on the sidewalk, the shine of the silver water tower looming above the buildings. Quinn leaned forward, squinting into the glare.

"What?" Alice asked.

"Thought I saw something move on the water tower."

They both scanned the scaffold surrounding the bulbous structure, its top wearing a triangular hat of steel.

"I don't see anything," Alice said, sitting back.

"No, me neither."

"Me neither," Ty said, then giggled.

Alice closed her eyes, shaking her head. "Tyrus, that's terrible." To Quinn she said, "He picked up a twisted sense of humor somewhere."

Ty continued to laugh, and Quinn glanced at her. "Yeah, wonder where?"

He scanned the street again, shooting a final look at the water tower before opening his door. Dirt crackled beneath his boots as he made his way to the Tahoe's rear and drew out his AR-15. Checking the safety, he stopped at the driver's side.

"I'll go in and have a look around, and if it's okay, we can all carry a few things out," he said. He saw Alice's eyes shift to a newer model Ford pickup a ways down the street.

"We'll load our things in that truck. You can have the Tahoe back," she said.

"No, I'll take the truck. You guys keep this. I'd feel better about you having it." Alice started to protest, but he held up a hand. "If I can't come with you, this is the only way I can help. Honk if there's trouble."

With that, he shut the door, cutting off her rebuttal, and moved to the front of the grocery store. He had to wedge his fingers between the doors and pry them apart, but once he did, they slid aside easily. He stopped in the entryway, letting his eyes adjust to the dark, his nose adjust to the stench the store held like trapped breath after the clean air outside. Quinn listened, his heartbeat the only sound in his ears. He stepped further into the store and flicked on the light mounted to his gun.

The grocery wasn't as large as some of the big chain stores they'd passed in Portland, but it still stretched further than his flashlight could reach. Many of the shelves were stripped bare, goods busted open and crushed on the floor. Three cash registers sat in designated lanes, their drawers open like surprised mouths, cash drooling over their lips. Quinn moved forward, his boots crunching chips and walnuts.

He froze as a sound came to him. Had something clicked farther in the building, or had it been an echo of his own passage? He turned and surveyed the bright street outside. The Tahoe sat where he'd left it, Alice visible in the front seat, her gun poking out the side window. Quinn waited another span before moving forward, his light swinging from side to side.

In the third aisle to his left, he found a stack of canned goods that had tipped over and rolled in every direction. Stew, soup, corn, beets, peas, chili, and more appeared in his beam. At the far end of the aisle, two cases of bottled water sat beside a cardboard box filled to the rim with food. He shined the light across its position, taking in the careful way it was packed along with the shattered jar of spaghetti sauce, two footprints leading toward the rear of the store.

Movement came from behind him and he tried to spin, bringing up the rifle, but a cold circle of steel buried itself into the soft skin behind his ear.

"Drop the gun. Do it now or I drop you." The voice was rough and deep, gravelly in a way that reminded him of people who smoked in the movies he'd watched.

"I just want to get some food," Quinn said. The gun barrel dug further into his flesh and shoved his head to the side.

"Did I stutter, boy? Put the gun down or you're dead."

Quinn lowered the AR-15 to the floor, stooping low and waiting for the moment when the man's gun would leave his head, but it didn't come. Whoever he was, he was careful. When Quinn stood again, he felt a hand fumble with the holster on his leg and then the XDM was gone too.

"You alone?" the voice said.

"Yes."

"What are you doing here?"

"Getting food, the same as you." There was more pressure from the gun barrel and then it was gone.

"Turn around." Quinn did as the voice asked, rotating in place until he faced the man.

His captor was short and stocky, the details of his face hidden in the choppy shadows thrown by the dim light. A shock of gray hair swept back from his brow in a tangled wave, and the long barrel of the shotgun he held was centered on Quinn's chest.

The man squinted and then the shotgun's barrel blocked most of his sight. Would he hear the blast that sawed most of his head away, or would it just be silent, the portions of his brain that received auditory signals already splattered down the aisle like more spilled food.

"The fuck happened to you?" the man said.

"Nothing. I was born this way. It's called Fibrous Dysplasia."

"Can you catch it?" There was a note of fear in the man's voice now, and Quinn noticed he'd taken a short step back.

"No. It's genetic."

"Don't lie to me."

"It's true."

The man backed away another two steps, the shotgun still trained on him, and a shaft of light fell on his face. He was in his late fifties or early sixties with a fresh growth of salt and pepper beard covering heavy jowls below a snub of nose. His eyes were sharpened points of green, flitting to Quinn and then to the side.

"What are you doing packing that kind of weaponry?" the man asked. His voice was still course but the edge of tension was gone.

"Haven't you seen the things roaming around out there?"

"They're people."

"They used to be."

"They're people, damn it!" The older man shuffled forward, the shotgun barrel enlarging in Quinn's line of sight. "They're working on a cure right now, right this instant. You'll see. The army'll roll in here before long and start inoculating them, change them back the way they were." His voice faded with the last sentence, barely audible in the quiet store. The muzzle of his weapon dropped also, only inches, but enough for Quinn to take a step forward.

"I really hope so. I do, because a close friend of mine became one of them, and I'd do anything to have him back the way he was." He waited, his heart kicking against his ribs hard enough to hurt. The other man lowered the weapon completely and sagged, his shoulders rounding forward.

"So many are gone, the whole damn town. You're the first person I've seen in days. They're out there, though. Maybe a dozen of them still hanging around. They run together, you know."

"I've seen them," Quinn said, his hands, palms forward, near his shoulders. The man wavered for a moment and then turned to the side, cocking his bushy head to the right.

"You ain't gonna try anything stupid, are you?"

"No sir."

"Good. You can pick up your gun."

Quinn studied him for a long moment and then bent and retrieved the AR-15 from the floor, careful to keep it pointed well away from the man.

"Can I get my handgun back too?" Quinn asked.

"Oh, sure, sure." The man said, pulling the XDM from his pocket and returning it to Quinn, grip first. "Name's Edgar, Edgar Plinton. Was the sheriff here for the past four years."

"Quinn Kelly," Quinn said, extending a hand and shaking with the other man.

"You need some food you said?" Edgar asked, gesturing toward the unlit aisles.

"Yeah, we do."

"We?" The shotgun rose several inches.

"I'm sorry, I didn't know what to tell you straight off. I'm traveling with a woman and her son. They're out in the Tahoe."

Edgar glanced over his shoulder and watched the SUV for a minute before focusing on him again. "No one else?"

"No, just us."

"I'd tend not to believe you at any other time, but finding more than a couple people these days is uncommon. You say you came from Portland?"

"I did."

"What's it like over there?"

"The same, quite a few of…" He stumbled for a second, not wanting to irritate the man. "…the people that turned, but only a few that haven't."

Edgar sucked on his lower lip. "I could've guessed. I was just hoping, that's all. The people I've seen have been less than friendly so far. That's why I welcomed you the way I did." He gazed at the floor and then brought his eyes back to meet Quinn's. "Where you going?"

Quinn hesitated. "Iowa. An army base in Fort Dodge. It's supposed to be the last stand for the military, or so we've heard."

"Iowa? I suppose it's the center of the nation, makes sense I guess. I'd ask to accompany you but my place is here. Can't leave them…" His voice trailed off, and he gazed at the darkened wall, bringing his eyes back to Quinn as if he'd forgotten he was there. "Here, let me help you load up. You can take my box; it's already full of food. I'm sure you'll want some water too?"

"That would be great, but I don't want to take your supplies from you."

Edgar nodded. "Good thing about old man Rogers who used to own this place, before he turned into a pile of goo, that is, he always kept lots of stores downstairs. There's plenty for me, don't worry about it."

They moved to the rear of the building, and Quinn carried the box of food while Edgar hauled a pack of water with one arm, the opposite hand gripping his shotgun. When he strode out of the store into the sunlight, Alice's eyes widened at the sight of the man behind him, but he gave her a reassuring nod. *It's okay, don't worry.* She adjusted herself in the seat to watch their progress as they loaded the supplies into the rear of the Tahoe.

"You're fairly well set there," Edgar said, stepping back on the curb. "Got most of the essentials anyways."

"Yeah, we got lucky, I'll say that."

"Well, I hope your luck continues," Edgar said, holding out a thick hand for him to shake again. Quinn grasped it and was about to say he needed to grab a few more things since they would be taking another vehicle, when the side of Edgar's face collapsed.

A warm spray coated Quinn's skin, and he blinked through a sudden red haze, tasting the other man's blood.

Edgar's head had fallen in, and several shards of yellow teeth hung in a congealed mass below one shredded eye. The opposite side of his face was only a gaping hole from which a torrent of blood ran. The sheriff's hand squeezed hard, crushing his fingers in a death grip. Then the man's short legs buckled, and he went down, splashing what was left of his brain matter against the sandy sidewalk.

A howling whine came from a step away, and a chunk of concrete exploded from the curb. The air beside Quinn's face was hot, and his skin vibrated with the passage of the bullet.

"Get down!" Alice screamed, and he didn't know if she was yelling at him or Ty. Probably both. Edgar twitched on the ground once and was still as all the strength went out of Quinn's legs and he slumped against the side of the Tahoe. There was another buzzing sound as a third round clipped the top of the vehicle to his left. The air was stifling, burning in his lungs as he slunk around the side of the SUV and pawed at the driver's door. The rear hatch was still open. He ran to it, whipping it down before ducking back to the open driver's door. Alice was firing from her window at the top of the water tower where the dark outline of a man rested against one of the railings.

"Gogogogo!" she yelled, and squeezed off another two shots as he slammed his door shut.

Quinn threw the Tahoe into drive and hammered the gas pedal. A hole appeared in the windshield, and the center console between them exploded in a shower of plastic. He had time to see the man on the tower waving his arm and pointing before two trucks roared onto the street behind them from an alley.

Quinn swung the SUV left in the main intersection and blazed down the street. Ahead, two cop cars were parked diagonally with sawhorses blocking the gaps between them. Quinn brought the Tahoe up over the curb and onto the sidewalk, the passenger mirror ripping away as they passed a light pole. Gunfire began to chatter behind them, and the rear window shattered, raining diamonds onto their supplies. He shifted his eyes up to see the first truck follow his lead onto the sidewalk, one figure behind the wheel while two stood in its box, both leaning over the cab with rifles pointed forward.

"Quinn," Alice said beside him. She was hunkered down, half-turned in the seat with one arm covering Ty who lay on the floorboards. "Don't let them catch us." He tried to answer but more gunfire erupted behind them and a round punched through the windshield beside the first hole.

The main street they were on exited Belford and became a county road, cracked and weathered with heavy forest to either side. Quinn accelerated off of the sidewalk and brought the Tahoe up to eighty-five. The trucks fell back but then began to close the gap, the faces of the men in the closest vehicle taking on cruel details; black sunglasses and wild hair whipping in the wind. A bald man in the rear of the first truck took aim, and Quinn slid to the side as the shot ripped the rearview mirror from its mounting. Whoops and yells came from behind them. There was an animalistic wheezing inside the SUV, and it took a moment for Quinn to realize he was making it. He swallowed, trying to calm his frantic breathing while he searched the sides of the highway. The road curved then straightened, and he pressed the pedal all the way down. The needle climbed past one hundred miles per hour. He threw a glance at the driver's side mirror and saw the trucks keeping pace behind them.

"Alice, I need you to get the map open on your phone and find a curvy road near here," he said as more shots zipped past the Tahoe like angry hornets.

"What?"

"Find a road that has curves. Do it, now!"

Alice fumbled with her phone. "There's a drive coming up on the left in half a mile, take it."

"Give us some room. Shoot back at the bastards."

Alice patted Ty once, telling him to stay down, then slowly sat up in her seat and brought the AR-15 to bear. The rifle boomed three times, filling the car with acrid smoke. Wheels screeched behind them, and the lead truck slewed across the road before coming back to center, its grille shrinking in the side mirror. A gap in the trees opened on the left side, and Quinn hammered the brakes, spinning the wheel at the same time.

The Tahoe rocked sickeningly on its springs as gravity came and went. The two wheels that had lifted from the pavement resettled, and Quinn guided them onto a small, paved drive cutting through the forest. Homes appeared and vanished behind trees as he accelerated again, glancing once into the side mirror. The mouth of the drive was empty for a beat and then filled with the bulk of the first truck, skidding sideways as they had done, before straightening out and speeding after them. Quinn focused again on the street, the adrenaline turning his nerves to livewires.

"Where's the next sharp corner?" he yelled. The air howled through the bullet holes in the windshield, coursing through the glassless back hatch. His eyes watered. Alice pulled her gaze away from the pursuing truck and punched at her phone.

"One mile, there's a sharp right-hand corner."

He nodded as another handful of bullets thunked into the rear of the Tahoe. Quinn pushed the throttle harder, the engine screaming beneath the hood.

"When I tell you, empty your magazine at them," he said, throwing a look at the side mirror.

"We won't last much longer. They're going to shoot our tires out."

"No, they're having too much fun for that. Trust me, okay?" He yanked his eyes away from the road and locked his gaze with Alice's. "Do you trust me?"

"Yes."

The bend was coming up, its sharp corner a wall of old-growth pines larger than a man could put his arms around. He pushed the gas harder.

"Quinn?" Alice said.

"It's okay."

"Quinn!"

"Shoot. Now!"

Alice spun in her seat and began blasting at the truck behind them. Quinn's damaged ear rang with each concussion, the gunshots so loud they filled up the world. The lead truck jerked to the side as Alice fired, avoiding the rounds, and revealed the second vehicle directly behind it.

The trailing truck's windshield spiderwebbed, and the left headlight burst. The front wheels jerked to the right and bit into the gravel at the edge of the ditch. The truck left the road, roared up the opposing bank, and collided with a towering oak. Quinn caught a flash of something man-shaped blasting through the broken windshield, but then the curve was there and his foot was on the brake, the steering wheel shuddering like something dying in his hands. Alice screamed, ducking low to hold onto Ty as the boy shrieked for her. The back end of the Tahoe skidded, the street like ice beneath the tires. None of them were wearing seatbelts. They would all be thrown free when the big SUV rolled and smashed into the pines. There would be pain and then nothing. This life and then the wide ocean. He could almost see his father's eyes looking at him through the cracked windshield, feel Teresa's hug.

The driveway was there on the right, his eyes finding it, latching onto it as he kept the wheel cranked. His foot left the brake and found the gas, the rear tires sliding and then catching on the shoulder of the road before peeling free. They shot off the street and onto the driveway, barely missing a conglomeration of mailboxes mounted on a steel pole. He slammed his foot down, and the brakes screeched again as they came to a stop.

"What are you doing?" Alice yelled.

Quinn threw the transmission into reverse, listening to the sound of the approaching truck over his rushing blood as he craned his neck around and stared through the empty back hatch. The remaining truck's blue paint flashed between the trees on the corner and Quinn punched the gas.

They rocketed backwards, coming even with the road as the truck passed by. The rear end of the Tahoe met the truck's passenger side in a furious impact of glass and steel. Quinn's head snapped backward, meeting the seat's headrest hard enough for flashes of light to flicker in his vision. Alice rose in her seat, and he snagged her arm, holding her tight while she tried to cover Ty with her body. There was a shriek of shredding metal and then they were still as the truck continued down the road sideways, its tires catching and turning to the sky. Sparks flew as the truck flipped over and coasted to a stop on its hood, the cab rumpled into a flattened mass.

The Tahoe's engine chugged and hissed, vibrations shaking the wheel beneath his numb fingers. He watched the truck for movement, his vision shuddering with each thunderous heartbeat. When no one climbed from the wreckage, he turned and found Alice still crouched over Ty in the rear foot space.

"Are you guys okay?"

Alice sat up, a dazed sheen covering her white face. A thin line of blood ran down from her right temple, and her eyes were clouded, blinking slow and methodical. Ty rose from beneath her, peeling himself from his mother's embrace.

"I'm okay, mom; I'm okay."

"Does anything hurt?" Quinn asked, his gaze beginning to run frantic over their forms, searching for a gaping cut or the hump of a broken bone. They were uninjured.

"I think we're okay," Alice said, swallowing. She coughed once and winced, holding her ribs. "Side hurts, though."

"Can you walk?" Quinn said.

"Yeah."

They climbed from the Tahoe, Ty from the opposite side since his door was jammed shut from the crash. The ringing hadn't left Quinn's head, and he shook it as he paced down the center of the sunlit road, cradling his rifle in both hands.

The truck ticked and pinged as the overheated metal cooled. Antifreeze and oil pooled beneath the hood, mixing into an evil, dark-orange puddle. He found the first body in the ditch. The man had struck the road and slid for a dozen yards before coming to a stop. Any features with which Quinn could've determined his age had been scraped away by the pavement. As he made to move past the corpse to the next body in the ditch, a rattling came from the cab of the pickup. Quinn moved closer and crouched beside the ruined vehicle.

Glass shards glittered everywhere on the roof of the truck. The driver's face was a mask of blood, his body hanging in a hunched lump from the seatbelt. *At least he thought to put his on,* Quinn thought absently. The noise came again, definitely not from the driver but from behind him in the less-crushed rear seat.

A woman, her eyes wide with shock lay bound and gagged on the roof of the truck. A huge, purple bruise spanned the right side of her face.

When Quinn leaned in through the broken side window, her gaze found him, and she began to moan through the simple white cloth yanking her mouth into an obscene grin.

"Nahnahnah." The woman shook her head as she tried to speak through the gag.

"It's okay; you're safe; you're safe now," Quinn said. He reached into the crushed cab, but she tried to inch away, her eyes flitting around the space searching for escape. "Here," Quinn said, kneeling further down. He held out a hand, beckoning her closer. "I won't hurt you. They were trying to kill us."

The driver unfolded from his bloody cocoon, one hand holding a pistol, blistered eye sockets two red orbs.

Quinn grabbed the man's arm and pushed it up, folding it over the rumpled door panel. The man's finger squeezed the trigger, and the gun barked once, twice. The woman screamed against the cloth. Somewhere, Quinn heard Alice yelling his name. His free hand scrabbled at the holster near his side. The XDM was there, sliding free, pushing through the open window against the man's temple.

He pulled the trigger.

He didn't hear the report, but the man went slack, his struggling arm going limp in Quinn's grasp. The pistol fell to the pavement, spinning once on its grip before falling still. He sat back and slid a few feet away from the truck, looking at the dark hole in the driver's skull, not wanting to imagine the exit wound that was surely on the opposite side, but imagining it anyway. Then Alice was there. Her lips were moving, but there was no sound, just like the gunshot. She shook him, hard, and all his senses rushed back.

"Are you okay?" she said. Her face was so close to his, her hair tickling his cheek.

"Yes."

"Can you stand?"

"I think so."

Alice got him on his feet, and he avoided looking at the driver again. Instead he focused on the woman in the backseat. There was a little blood on her white t-shirt and blue jeans, but there was no way of telling if it was hers or not. She still regarded them with frantic eyes, shifting from Alice to him and back again.

"Are you sure you're okay?" Alice asked him again.

"Yeah, pretty—"

She slapped him full across the face.

The blow caught him completely off guard, and his eyes immediately watered, the imprint of her narrow palm like a whip on his cheek.

"You almost got us killed, my son, killed!" she yelled. She was pure fury, vibrating with it, and he took a step away from her.

"I'm sorry, it was the only thing I could think of."

She opened her mouth to yell again and then closed it, her eyes running over him. The fire went out of them, and her head tilted forward. She still shook, but the anger was gone.

"I know," she finally managed. He began to move to enfold her in his arms. Something that went against every instinct but was nonetheless powerful. She allowed him to pull her close. He could smell her blood, feel her warmth against him as if he were embracing a hearth. After a moment that could've been a lifetime, she stiffened and gently pushed him away. Alice glanced around the empty road as Ty made his way past the front end of the overturned truck.

"Where's the other one?" Alice asked.

They found him farther down the street in the ditch. He'd landed in a slough of sand runoff. He lay on his back, face to the reaching branches above. In another life, he could've been called handsome with his regal nose and strong jaw, but his injuries now rendered him a sculpture of pain. His bald head was slick with blood, and the barest goatee of blond hair was stippled with gore. His ring and pinkie finger were missing from his left hand, their stumps oozing blood over ragged bone. When they approached and stopped at his side, his eyes were the only thing that moved to follow them.

"You sonofabitch," Alice said. And before Quinn could do anything, she wound back a kick and delivered it to the prone man's ribs. The solid whump of her foot connecting made Quinn flinch. The man barked a cough and clenched his jaw. As he did, his bloodied lips parted, and Quinn saw that half his upper teeth were missing.

"What the fuck, you bastard!" Alice tried to kick the man again, but Quinn pulled her back, gently, and released her when she shot him a look.

"He's dying; leave him be."

"Then we should help speed up the process," she said, bringing up her rifle.

A gurgling cough came from the bald man, and it took Quinn a second to realize he was laughing.

"Oh, it's funny? No, what's funny is you're gonna lie here and suffer, you bald fuck," Alice said, and punctuated her sentence by spitting on his face.

"Come on," Quinn said, moving back up to the road where Ty waited. "You okay, buddy?" Quinn asked him as he knelt down to the boy's level.

"I'm fine. A little scared."

"Then you're doing better than I am."

Ty held his hands in front of his pants and kept moving from side to side. "Mom," he finally said, and Alice bent beside him. He whispered something to her and she nodded, bringing him to the opposite side of the road. Quinn made his way back to the truck and crouched before the rear window opening. The woman's eyes were glazed now, and she didn't look at him when he reached in and touched her shoulder.

"We're going to get you out now, okay?" he said, but she gave no indication she'd heard him. As carefully as he could, he drew her out through the broken window until she lay on the pavement, her face slack and pale. Alice appeared beside him and glanced down at the woman.

"What's wrong with her?"

"I don't know. I think she's in shock. She doesn't seem to be hurt, other than what they did to her."

"Cut her loose and then we should go."

"I'm not sure she'll be able to walk," Quinn said, still looking down.

Alice regarded him. "She's not coming with us."

He glanced up. "What? What do you mean? We can't just leave her here. What if there's more of them back in Belford? What if they show up here and find her?"

"What if they show up and find us? We need to go. Now."

"We're not leaving her. She's innocent."

"How do you know? She could be with them and had a falling out with her beaus here and is being punished."

"If it were you, would you want me to leave you behind?" he said, moving closer to her. Alice hesitated and began to form a reply, but he cut her off. "If it were Ty?"

She closed her mouth and breathed out a long sigh through her nose before whispering to him. "My son wet his pants during this ordeal because he was so scared, and you know what he was worried about? He was worried about you seeing."

Quinn frowned. "Why?"

"Because he's a six-year-old blind boy that still thinks the world is magical and that you're our savior."

Quinn glanced over her shoulder to where Ty sat on the side of the road. His head was tilted back, and he was listening to the sound of the light breeze hushing in the branches. In his hands, he turned the wooden dowel over and over.

Quinn blinked and gazed down at his boots.

"He is my life, and I'll sacrifice anyone, including you and me, to keep him safe," Alice said. She threw another look at the woman near their feet. "We leave her as soon as she's well enough."

"Fine."

Quinn brought the woman to her feet and cut her bindings away. He untied the gag and gazed into her eyes, looking for some sign that she saw him also, but there was nothing but a profound haze on her features as thick as the fog that sometimes came in off the Atlantic.

"You're safe," Quinn said, leading her to the Tahoe. Alice was already in the backseat beside Ty, a handgun pointed near her feet.

"She can ride shotgun. And if she tries anything, she's dead. Hear me, sleeping beauty?" Alice said.

Quinn helped the woman inside the SUV and shut the door, pausing as he rounded the crushed rear hatch.

In the distance, the sound of an engine revved. Then again. Closer.

He hurried to the driver's side and climbed in. In a moment, they were barreling down the road, the wind humming through the vehicle the only sound.

Chapter 16

Respite and Rain

They drove through the rest of the morning and into the afternoon.

Quinn took random turns at first, going south, then west, then east, then west again. After they stopped near a cornfield that would never see a new crop, and heard no sound of pursuit, they continued on a turnpike, making better time than they had on the back roads. The woman stared out of the passenger window for hours and finally drifted off to sleep, her head craned back, snoring softly.

In a clearing containing a housing development like some kind of engineered mold against the land, a group of stilts milled around a small brick building. Quinn quit counting when he reached sixteen. Just before the herd was out of sight, two of them wrenched the building's steel door from its hinges and plunged inside. He thought he saw the flash of gunfire, but couldn't be sure.

In late afternoon, he pulled off on an exit and circumvented a small suburb that promised food, fuel, and hotels. On its opposite side, he followed a curving road that led past a gravel drive traveling up through a stand of trees. He waited and glanced over his shoulder at Alice who cradled Ty's head and shoulders in her lap, his eyes shut with one hand cupped to his cheek. She looked at the drive and then shrugged. *Good as any,* her look seemed to say.

The driveway wound to an opening that held a narrow, stone house. Its two stories stared down at them with dark windows but nothing moved behind them. A child's plastic pedal-bike was overturned on the greening lawn, some kind of colorful Frisbee lay beside it.

Quinn carried his rifle up the short steps and tried the knob. It held fast in his hand. As he turned, Alice bent and removed a patio block from beside the house's landscaping. Beneath it rested a rusted key, which she plucked from the rock and tossed to him.

"Pretty common hiding place," was all she said before returning to the Tahoe.

The rotting fish smell met him in the little foyer like an angry host. He pushed past it, moving carefully and without sound deeper into the house. On the left was a sitting room, ahead a spacious kitchen and dining room. A dark bathroom met him off a hallway before a compacted set of steps rose to the second floor.

There he found the previous occupants, or what was left of them.

The smell that pervaded the house came from the two bedrooms. The right one held a sleigh bed and bright red and green throw pillows that were scattered on the floor like fallen leaves. The center of the mattress was stained with the clear, jelly-like substance. It seemed to move as he watched it, and after a moment, he realized it wasn't his imagination. It was spreading out, soaking into the fabric.

They had just died. Maybe only hours ago.

The second room was undeniably a child's. A boy's by the look of it. Superhero posters papered the walls. GI-Joe's and a dozen X-Box games littered the floor. A handmade quilt, threadbare and tattered at the edges, covered the bed, its middle soaked in a short outline of a body.

Their child had died, and there hadn't been a thing they could do about it. They watched it happen, and when it was done, they went in the other room and curled up together to join him. Despite the smell, Quinn stood there, staring at the old quilt covering the boy's bed. A boy that would never grow up, never have a chance to see the world or have children of his own. He found himself wondering who had made the quilt for him, its incongruency blaring in the small room. Probably a grandparent who was gone now too.

Quinn's legs wobbled as he neared the hallway, and he had to brace himself on the bannister. After a long minute of breathing slowly, he steeled himself and returned to the parents' room, stripping the bed of its sheets and blankets. He carried the armload downstairs and hauled it outside, depositing it in a garbage can near the driveway. Alice had Ty in her arms and was gazing at the house.

"It's clear. They're gone, but only a little while ago so the smell is pretty bad." She nodded and went inside. The woman slept on in the passenger seat, her head against the window, each breath fogging a circle of glass. Quinn went inside the house, checking the lights when he stepped into the foyer. They worked. Alice had laid Ty on a loveseat in the sitting room and was covering him with a blanket when he entered.

"We have power," he said in a low voice.

"That's a plus. We all need a bath."

"Definitely." He searched the room as if the words he wanted might appear on the walls. "About back there…" His voice trailed off as Alice looked up at him. Those blue eyes, always so piercing, like being skewered no matter where he stood. "I'm sorry, but I couldn't leave her behind. I know you don't agree, but if there's not people out there willing to help one another, then what are we looking for? If that's all gone, what's the point?"

Alice gazed at him as if she were peering into the workings of some machine she'd never encountered before.

"The only thing I'm looking for is a safe place for my son. To still be here. For both of us to be immune. It's…" she shrugged. "I've never deserved him, but I'll be damned if I'm going to give him up for someone else." She glanced out the window and then back to him. "I know why you did what you did, Captain America, but that's what separates you and I."

Quinn nodded. "I'll go wake her." He moved from the sitting room to the hallway and out the door, his stomach a ball of knots. Why did he think he needed to explain himself to her? What was there to gain? Her trust? She'd already said he had that, whether he believed her or not. It was something else, some unsaid notion that rose and fell in the back of his mind, distant and then near all at once. He shook his head and jogged down the steps, stopping before the beaten Tahoe's open passenger door.

The woman was gone.

He spun, bringing up the rifle, and scanned the small yard. The trees were still and silent, nothing hid behind them and the air smelled clean, untouched by blood or decay.

118

Quinn circumvented the vehicle, checking the backseat and rear hatch. The woman was nowhere to be seen. He ran back up the steps, meeting Alice in the hallway.

"She's gone," he said, shooting a look past her deeper into the house.

"What? Where could she go?"

"I don't know. The door was open, and she was gone."

"Fuck," Alice said, drawing her handgun. "We have to find her."

They searched the first floor in a matter of minutes; there weren't many places for a grown woman to hide. Quinn glanced at the yard again before climbing the stairs.

The woman was standing in the boy's bedroom with her back to the door. In one arm she clutched a stuffed lion while in her opposite hand, the putrid jelly dripped from a closed fist.

"Ma'am?" Quinn said, as he entered the room. Alice stepped in behind him, her handgun aimed at the other woman's back. "Are you okay?" He edged forward until he could see her face. She was looking straight ahead out the window. The jelly continued to drip from between her fingers, and her mouth hung open enough for him to see her tongue moving. She was talking to herself.

"Hey, you shouldn't be up here," Alice said. She'd lowered the handgun, but still held it ready at her side.

"Come downstairs for a minute, will you?" Quinn said, putting his fingertips on the woman's arm. She jerked away and turned, really seeing him for the first time since the overturned truck. Her lips moved soundlessly, and she slowly opened her hand to let the rest of the boy's remains drool out of her palm.

"Gone," the woman finally said, her voice barely a whisper.

~

They ate in the kitchen of the strange house, their presence there somehow a violation. But, Quinn thought as he chewed the strange pasty mix that tasted of beans and celery, where would we feel welcome now in this world?

The woman had come with them after saying her one word. She'd allowed them to lead her down to the kitchen table, and Quinn had washed her hands of the foul fluid. When that was done, he heated the contents of an MRE and set it before her. She'd eaten in a trance, her motions robotic and continuous until the plate was clean. Then she'd set her fork down and picked up the stuffed lion, staring into its golden, plastic eyes.

They'd put her to bed early in the parents' room. Quinn had removed the sodden mattress and brought it to the backyard, spraying it down with a can of mineral spirits he'd found in a closet off the foyer to kill the odor. When he'd returned, Alice had made a bed for the woman out of a sleeping bag on the floor. With their urging, she lay down on it and fell asleep in a matter of minutes, the stuffed lion still tucked beneath one arm. On their way out, Alice had insisted on securing the door somehow, so Quinn reversed the knob using a screwdriver so that the locking portion faced into the hall.

Ty swallowed the last bite of his meal and belched, the sound loud and long in the hushed kitchen. A surprised look crossed his face, and he clapped his hands to his mouth.

"Excuse me."

"You're dang right, excuse you," Alice said, pinching Ty's cheek with two fingers. Quinn laughed as quietly as he could, but he thought he saw Ty shoot a furtive grin in his direction.

"Where are we at?" Ty asked, wiping his mouth with his arm.

"You mean besides in a house?"

"Yeah, mom, like what state?"

"Somewhere in New York, I think," Alice said. "Though with all the back roads we took, I'm not sure."

"How far are we from Iowa?"

"A few days, I think, unless we have anything else hold us up," Alice answered, standing to clear their plates away.

"You mean if we almost don't die again," Ty said, setting his dowel onto the table before him. Alice shot him a look and then turned her gaze to Quinn.

"We didn't almost die," Quinn said.

"They were shooting at us," Ty said, his unfocused eyes turning toward his voice.

"Yes, they were, but they didn't get us. We're safe now." Alice watched him for a moment and then turned away to the sink where she opened the tap. Ty tilted his head forward and rolled the dowel across the table. Back and forth, back and forth. Quinn opened his mouth to say something else but instead a bright collection of shapes caught his eye on the front of the refrigerator. He stood and gathered them from where they hung, suspended by the magnets in their backs, and placed them on the table before Ty. The boy heard the clatter of the plastic pieces and sat forward.

"What's that?"

"Different shapes with magnets on their backs."

"Cool." Delight filled Ty's face. "I know what a square is."

"Yeah? What is it?"

"It's got four sides like this." Ty drew a square on the tabletop with his finger.

"You got it. Can you find the square that's mixed with all the other shapes?" Quinn asked. Ty tipped his head to one side, his eyes looking off to the corner of the ceiling as his hands began to roam over the shapes. Within seconds he'd found the square magnet, tracing it with his fingers.

"Here it is."

"You got it! How about a triangle? Do you know what that one is?"

"Yep, it's a lazy square with three sides instead of four."

Quinn laughed. "That's right." Ty sorted through the shapes, producing the triangle correctly. They went through the rest of the magnets, Quinn quizzing him on the shapes he knew and explaining the ones he didn't. All the while he could feel Alice's gaze on him like heat from a fire. After Ty had memorized the shapes that he didn't know, Quinn showed him how the magnets would attract one another if slid close together. Ty giggled each time the plastic pieces snapped together, glancing in Quinn's direction, his smile as radiant as his mother's.

"Okay, buddy, that's enough for one night," Alice said after a time.

"Oh mom, we just started."

"I know, but you need a bath. You're smelly."

"Mom, I'm not smelly. I had a bath, I can't remember, but it was maybe only yesterday."

"Yeah, that's why you're not in charge of planning your baths."

"What's after bath?"

"After bath is bedtime."

"But I'm not tired."

"You always say that, and you're always asleep in under a minute," Alice said, picking Ty up from his place at the table.

"Can you tuck me in, Quinn?" Ty asked as Alice began carrying him away. Quinn blinked, shifting his eyes from the boy to Alice who stared at him and then gave a curt nod.

"Sure can, buddy."

"Yay!" Ty exclaimed, as Alice turned and brought him toward the bathroom.

Quinn sat in the kitchen, his gaze roaming around the room. Dirty dishes rested beside the sink, a magazine was folded open to an article on the counter, three marbles lay beneath a chair. He let out a sigh and stood, grabbing his AR-15 from where it leaned near the doorway before heading outside.

The yard was fading into darkness, the last light of the day cool and gray through gathering clouds on the western horizon. The wood surrounding the house was a vast trove of dead leaves and tendrils of green poking through them. Quinn moved down the driveway, pausing every dozen yards to listen. No cars, no planes, nothing. He stopped short of the road running past the driveway and waited. The sun continued its descent, and shadows began to grow like dark mildew across the ground. He returned to the house and went past the bathroom, where Ty was singing something too soft for him to hear, and climbed the stairs to the second floor. He put his ear against the master bedroom door and waited, but there was no sound from behind it. The woman was exhausted and probably still in shock. Maybe tomorrow they'd be able to coax her out of her stupor and learn more about where she was from. Alice would hate it, but if the woman could tell them where her home was, they would have to make sure she got there safely.

His thoughts were broken by the sound of Alice bringing Ty to the sitting room, and he left the woman to her slumber, descending the stairs noiselessly. When he entered the small room near the front of the house, Alice was tucking Ty in beneath a heavy blanket on the loveseat. He hovered in the doorway, setting his rifle down in the hall.

"Goodnight, sweetheart," Alice said, smoothing Ty's dark hair back from his brow. "Sleep good, okay?"

"But I'm not—" Ty paused as an enormous yawn cut his words off. "—tired," he finished.

"No, not at all. Quinn's going to say goodnight then you get some sleep. We've got a long day ahead of us tomorrow."

"Okay mom."

"I love you."

"I love you too."

Alice kissed him on the forehead before moving past Quinn out of the room. She gave him a glance he couldn't read and disappeared down the hall into the kitchen.

"Hey, buddy, you all tucked in?" Quinn asked, crouching down beside the loveseat.

"Yeah. Thanks for teaching me with the magnets. Do you think I could keep them?"

The image of the three marbles lying dormant beneath the chair in the kitchen buffeted his mind.

"I don't see why not," Quinn said. "You'll have to double check it with your mom, though."

"Okay." Ty wriggled deeper beneath the blanket, and his eyes drifted partially shut. His breathing became even, and Quinn was about to rise when the boy spoke again. "Are you going to leave us?"

"No, I'm not going to leave you. Not if I can help it."

Ty seemed to consider this. "Mom doesn't want you to leave either, not really."

"Well, we just have to take one day at a time. My dad always told me that." Tears rose to his eyes without warning.

"Where is your dad?"

"He's…he's gone."

"My dad is too. I never met him though. Mom said maybe someday. Do you miss your dad?"

Quinn swallowed the burning lump in his throat. "Every day."

"You'll see him again, right?"

"I'm sure I will."

Ty yawned again, his eyelids fluttering. "Will you stay with me until I fall asleep?"

"Of course."

"You'll watch for the monsters."

It wasn't a question. A wave of gooseflesh washed across his skin.

Quinn was going to reply, but Ty was already sleeping. He glanced at the windows, but the yard was lost to him in the darkness. He made his way to the kitchen after re-checking the front door's lock.

Alice stood at the sink cleaning dishes with a blue rag, ebony hair pulled back in a ponytail. She didn't look away from the task when he leaned his back against the cabinets beside her.

"He's sleeping."

"Good."

"Are you okay?"

"I'm fine."

"You're washing their dishes."

"I know. It felt like it was the least we could do for staying here."

He moved to the fridge, pulling it open. There were a half-dozen cold beers on its top shelf. He took two of them and popped the tops off, setting one at Alice's elbow before taking a seat at the table. She glanced at the bottle twice before drawing her hands from the sudsy water to dry them off. Quinn sipped at the beer. It was ice cold, and the carbonation burned his throat, cutting away a thirst he hadn't known was there. Alice tipped her bottle up, chugging the drink, her slender throat bobbing. She set the mostly empty beer down and stifled a long belch behind her hand.

"Now I know where Ty gets it," Quinn said. Alice wiped her lips and merely looked at him. "Sorry, that was an attempt at a joke."

"I know."

The silence spooled out between them, Alice's eyes never leaving his face, his cheeks flush and burning. He looked around the room and then met her gaze again.

"What?"

"He's getting attached to you."

"He's a great kid."

"I don't want him getting hurt."

"I understand."

"Do you?"

"Yes." She stared at him a moment longer and then came to the table, sitting down opposite him. She turned her beer bottle in circles, her delicate fingers moving gracefully. "You said you trusted me."

"What?"

"In the Tahoe before I rammed the truck, I asked you if you trusted me and you said yes," Quinn said, sitting forward.

"That was in the heat of the moment."

"So do you?"

She regarded him for a long time before spinning her bottle again.

"I guess I have to."

He settled back in his chair and finished his beer. The room continued to darken until all he could see of her was the white skin of her face and arms.

"I thought we were all dead back there," Alice said just as he was about to stand and leave the room for the first watch.

"I did too."

"You know what was overwhelming, even more than the fear?" He shook his head. "All the regrets I have came rushing back in a split second, and I thought I'd never be able to fix any of them." She laughed in her sad way. "And now I'm ashamed of it."

"Why? Because you have regrets or that they overshadowed your fear?"

She sighed. "Both."

"Everyone has regrets, and as far as I'm concerned, they're the scariest thing in the world."

"What are yours?"

He stumbled on his answer. Licking his lips, he saw her looking at him through the dim distance between them, her eyes the brightest thing in the room.

"That I didn't see more of the world before it was gone."

"It's still out there."

"But not what makes it special."

Alice huffed another laugh. "People aren't special. They never were. We're the biggest mistake in the universe. You don't think for a second this plague was natural, do you? We did this." She gestured to the quiet house. "We did all this. We're the disease, not the virus that took us out."

Quinn waited a long moment and then stood, placing his bottle in the trash near the doorway before facing her again.

"The people I knew were special, and all I can do is hope there's others like them somewhere out there. But I guess that's what separates you and I."

He turned away, snagging his rifle as he went to start the first watch.

The night passed in an onyx haze. He sat outside on the front stoop with his back against the door. The sky continued to cloud over, clamping down the darkness like a lid being put on the world. The wind picked up and tossed leaves into the air, their passage heard and felt but not seen. He retrieved a jacket from the Tahoe and shrugged himself into it, the burn on his shoulder still flaring up whenever he moved too drastically. When the time came for him to switch with Alice, he remained where he was, stolid and unmoving, senses seeking anything besides the stirring wind.

Hours later, dawn crept across the horizon like smoke from a fire that was beginning to burn there. The clouds were lower, and as the first drops of rain began to fall, he made his way inside, locking the door behind him.

Alice lay on her side next to the loveseat, one arm stretched up, her fingers holding onto Ty's small hand. He watched them sleep for a moment before continuing down the hall to the kitchen. In the pantry, he found some ground coffee and a filter for the coffeemaker on the counter. As the machine began its quiet chuckling, a thump came from overhead, and he tipped his face to the ceiling.

The woman was moving upstairs.

He waited, ready to spring to the stairs if there was further commotion, but soon her movements slowed and then ceased. A dream or nightmare. Nothing more. He refocused on the dark liquid rising in the pot and poured a steaming cup when the coffeemaker had finished its work. The smell that filled the room was so redolent of the mornings at home, his throat closed when he tried to take a sip of coffee. His father sitting at his desk going over paperwork, Graham and Foster bickering at one another in the kitchen, Mallory reading the paper before she began her cleaning for the day, and Teresa, standing at the eastern windows of the solarium watching the ocean.

"You didn't wake me."

Quinn flinched as if coming out of a dream and slopped some coffee over the rim of his cup. Alice stood in the doorway, her hair curled at the ends from sleep, face puffy but somehow alluring.

"No. I couldn't have slept." She looked down at the floor, tracing a design in the linoleum with one toe. "Do you want some coffee?" he asked.

"God yes."

She sat at the table, and he brought a cup to her, the steam rising in white tendrils. The rain abandoned its pattering and began to pound the roof. Thunder grumbled somewhere to the west. The woods around the house blurred behind silver sheets of water.

"I don't want him getting attached to you," Alice said.

"I know."

"But it's not right to deny him someone to care about."

"He's amazing. I've never met anyone like him."

"I see a lot of parallels between you two."

His eyes widened. "You do?"

"Yes. You both deal with things that you never asked for and people judge you before they know you." She fingered the handle of her cup. "Myself included."

"I understand why you'd be hesitant, I mean," he gestured at his face. "Believe me."

She shook her head. "No, that's not it, I—"

Her words were cut off by a succession of thumps and then a hard bang from overhead. They both raised their heads. A trail of dust filtered down to the floor in a thin line.

"Something's wrong," Alice said, standing up.

They hurried down the hallway, and Quinn threw a glance into the sitting room. Ty slept on beneath the blanket. They mounted the steps and were halfway up them when there was another bang and the tinkling of glass. Quinn doubled his pace and fumbled for an excruciating second with the lock before shoving the door inward.

Rain dribbled off the broken glass hanging from the window. The bedframe was flipped on its side and a full-length mirror was in pieces on the floor. The sleeping bag and blankets were a tangled mess.

The woman was gone.

"What the hell?" Alice said, coming in behind him. She crossed to the window and looked down. "She's gone."

Quinn knelt beside the bedding and inhaled. The stink was low, ventilated by the fresh air and rain, but there. The blankets were wet, the floor around them slick with fluid. His heart began to hammer. He raised his eyes to meet Alice's.

"What?" she said.

Glass broke downstairs.

Ty screamed.

Chapter 17

The Hollow Hope

Ty's scream fell and then rose again, a klaxon of terror.

Alice shouted something, but he was already moving, vaulting over the railing, air shrieking past him as he landed ten stairs down, tripping and falling the rest of the way. Quinn rolled to his feet, his ankle and shoulder burning but he barely noticed. He jerked the XDM from its holster and pelted down the hallway before bursting into the sitting room.

A stilt was leaning through the broken window that faced the front yard. A thin arm outstretched and beginning to retract, its grotesque hand gripping Ty around both legs. The boy held tight to the back of the loveseat, which was almost tipping over. The monster's eyes, so human they were startling, found him in the doorway, and a snarl split its lips revealing gray teeth.

Quinn centered the handgun on its face and pulled the trigger as it yanked hard on Ty's legs.

The shot cut the air where the thing's head had been, tearing out a chunk of window trim in a spray of splinters. The bullfrog sound gurgled from its throat but still it kept its hold on Ty's legs as it dragged him across the room toward the window. Quinn leapt forward and caught hold of the stilt's wrist, shoving the barrel against its forearm. He yanked the trigger again.

The bullet tore through the pale flesh and buried itself into the floor. An inhuman cry ripped from the stilt's throat, and it released Ty before smashing a fist the size of an ice-cream pail into Quinn's shoulder. The blow knocked him off balance and he fell, bits of glass sinking into his palm. Then Alice was there, scooping Ty up from where he lay whimpering on the floor and racing out of the room. Quinn gained his feet and peered through the open window, arms outstretched, gun shaking in bloodied hands.

The rain fell on the empty yard.

It was gone.

The air in Quinn's lungs was acid, burning with each breath. His eyes flitted between the Tahoe and the trees, then to the other side of the yard. He moved into the hallway and jerked the front door open, leading with the XDM.

Rain soaked the top of his head and then his shoulders as he stepped outside. It was cold and he shivered, turning toward the nearest corner of the house. Nothing. Sweeping back the other way, he stepped down from the stoop, blinking against the water running in his eyes. Below the shattered window was a pool of blood that led away around the far side of the house. Quinn followed it, its path beginning to run pink in the onslaught of rain. Thunder shook the air as he lunged around the corner, finger tight on the trigger, and nearly fired at a solitary birch tree, its narrow arms outstretched toward him. He swung the pistol left, then right, moving forward, his eyes darting down to the blood trail. A scratching sound came from the rear of the house and he broke into a run.

It was trying to get inside again.

Trying to get at Alice and Ty.

He rounded the corner and slid to a stop. The rain coated the yard in a wet sheen, muddying the little dirt path that led to the back door, which was shut. Quinn glanced down, finding the dollops of red, almost black in the dim light. He followed it around the next corner where it ended in a small pool. There was no blood trail continuing on. It simply ended. He turned back the way he'd come, panning the tree line. Where had it gone? It couldn't have gotten by him, not without him seeing it. He spun in a circle, glancing down at the pool near his feet, its crimson depths popping with each raindrop falling from above.

Above.

A cold, twisting fist clutched within his stomach, and the hairs on the back of his neck stiffened.

He pivoted and brought the XDM up as the stilt dropped down at him from the rooftop. The gun boomed as the creature's weight slammed into him. His shoulders connected with the earth, and it felt as if he'd fallen from a much greater height. The XDM's blood-slicked grip sprung from his hand. The stilt had fallen forward when it landed and was rolling to its feet when he lifted his head. It screamed again, its voice deep with hard edges that made his eardrums quiver.

Quinn slid backwards, hand scrabbling for the gun. The stilt rose to its full height, skeletal length unfurling. Blood dropped from its ruined arm as it lunged forward, ragged fingernails tearing through his shirt and into his skin. Quinn cried out and stretched for the gun, but the monster's long fingers closed over his throat, easily encircling his neck with one hand.

It drew him up toward its waiting mouth.

The world dimmed at the edges as his feet left the ground, his hands gripping its bony wrist. He swung a foot up, connecting with the thing's face as it pulled him closer. He kicked again, this time hitting its eye. The pressure on his throat diminished, and he fell, landing hard, knees buckling as the stilt batted him with the back of its good hand. He left the ground and crumpled into a heap when he skidded to a stop, every bone crying out inside him. The gun was somewhere to the left, but he couldn't see it. The monster loomed above, dropping toward him. He found the knife on his belt, fumbled with the strap, yanked it free as he tasted the stink of its breath.

He slashed with the blade, a last, swinging movement, his strength gone.

The stilt hovered above him, its good arm planted in the ground beside his head, eyes bulging.

Its throat was a bloody grin.

It toppled forward, more gore flowing from its neck, dropping on him like boiling rain.

He tried rolling to the side, his body full of lead, skin numb with cold. A weight fell on him, pinning him to the ground, and he gasped, heaving in a mouthful of water.

The day darkened further and then became full night as he closed his eyes.

~

Quinn came to on the loveseat in the sitting room. It was dark. A thick blanket hung over the broken window blocking out the day beyond. He sat up, wincing at the highways of pain running across his body. His head was a drum being beat from the inside with a rusty claw hammer. He put a hand to his forehead, more or less to keep it from falling apart.

"You gonna make it?"

He turned his head to where Alice sat in the corner of the room, her legs crossed, an index finger marking a page in a paperback.

"I think so."

"I'm guessing you've got a concussion. And if you tear out the stitches on your thigh again, you're just going to have to bleed. There's nothing left to stitch to."

Quinn exhaled, the teeter-totter of nausea in his stomach slowly stilling.

"How long was I out?"

"About three hours, give or take. I never wore a watch and my phone died."

"Ty?" he asked, the fog of the morning's events drawing away.

"Fine. Shook up but okay. He's eating in the kitchen."

"God." Quinn leaned back into the pillows and stared at the ceiling.

"What the hell happened, Quinn?"

"I don't know. She must've been…must've been—"

"Must've been what? That bitch turned into one of them and almost ate my son."

"She must've been sheltered. Couldn't have been exposed to the disease. She caught it here, from what was left of the bodies." His head spun, and he swallowed bile.

"Sheltered? Like hidden from the outside world." Alice stood and approached the loveseat. "Just like you, right?" Her voice was diamond-hard. Cutting. "Because of your fucking righteousness, my son almost died! We all almost died!"

He closed his eyes, letting her words lash at him. "I know."

"No, you don't. No, you don't," Alice said, coming closer. She loomed over him now just as the stilt had, hatred to match. "Your naïve view of the world is equal to poison now. Were you raised by nuns? Was that a convent we found you at?"

"No."

"Then how are you so fucking stupid?"

"I'd never left there, okay!" he burst out. His voice was too loud in his ears. "The day we drove away was the first time I'd ever been outside those grounds."

Alice stared at him, her mouth partially open, eyes prodding, probing.

"You're shitting me."

"I'm not."

"How?"

"My father was James Kelly."

She laughed. "The movie star?"

"Yes."

She laughed again and then sobered when she saw the look on his face.

"You're kidding."

"I was born like this. And instead of raising me in the limelight, he hid me away."

"Why?"

"Because he was weak!" Quinn blinked, surprised by the way his voice resounded in the small room. Blood pulsed in his ears. "He couldn't bear to see me ridiculed, so he receded from public life. He kept me shielded there, away from everyone, from everything. It was the only place I'd ever known."

Alice stepped back until her knees hit the chair she'd been sitting on and she fell into it. She looked at him for a long time and then shook her head.

"This is all unbelievable. The one fucking house I pick to overnight in."

"Well, I'm sorry you found me."

"That makes two of us."

"Momma?"

Ty stood outlined in the doorway, one hand clutching his dowel.

"Go finish eating, Ty."

"But—"

"Now."

Ty turned and retreated down the hall, the dowel tapping the floor softly.

Quinn closed his eyes and took a shuddering breath. "I'm sorry I brought her here, but I couldn't leave her like that. I had no way of knowing she was still vulnerable to the plague."

Alice stared at the wall, the muscles in her jaw clenching then relaxing beneath the smooth skin of her cheek.

"You need to get some rest," she finally said, and left him alone in the quiet room.

~

He awoke the second time to the same gray light filtering in around the makeshift curtain. Rain still fell but with much less force than before. It could've been minutes since Alice left the room, but he knew it wasn't. He'd tried to stay awake, waiting for the moment when she would return or pass by the open doorway, but the fatigue was a ten-ton anchor, pulling him deep into the trenches of sleep.

Quinn sat up, the pain in his head turned down from the blaring level of before. He stood and tested his balance, then took a step. When he didn't fall to his face, he moved into the hallway and glanced toward the kitchen. There was a light on there, and he went that way.

The kitchen was empty. A few dirty dishes soaking in dishwater. Two empty beer bottles on the table. An MRE wrapper in the garbage. He went to the sink and dipped his fingers in. The water was lukewarm.

"Alice? Ty?"

No answer.

He hurried back the way he'd come, stopping by the stairs to listen. Silence. He continued to the front door, a brick of tension expanding in his stomach. Knowing what he'd see, hating it just the same.

He opened the door.

The Tahoe was gone.

And so were they.

Chapter 18

Alone

Quinn sat on the front stoop watching the light drain from the horizon. He held a beer bottle loosely in one hand, the other on the stock of his AR-15. He'd found his duffel bag near the bathroom door. Alice had left him a dozen MREs, three hundred rounds of ammo for the rifle, fifty for the XDM, his clothing, and a case of water.

He watched the naked woods falling into darkness and almost moved to walk into it. He'd leave his weapon here, his supplies, and just walk until he found a place to rest. Or maybe something would find him first. Quinn drank the rest of his beer and tossed the bottle into the yard. The land settled into shadow around him.

When it was full dark, he went inside the house and ate one of the MREs, not bothering to read its contents. It went down without taste. When he was finished, he pulled the curtain aside from the window in the sitting room and rested on the loveseat, his rifle cradled on his lap.

The moon rose and shone behind the clouds that continued to emit rain on and off. The light was ethereal, coating the trees in silver cut with black, each new blade of grass distinguishable. He waited for headlights to slice the darkness, to shine on the house and the Tahoe to reappear. He waited for hours.

Sometime near dawn he fell asleep, dreams of demon-like figures cajoling around a fire in the center of a clearing, their voices braided into a chant that drew a cable of terror tight around his chest. Their faces were blank slates of mist, swirling as they laughed and danced around him. He was bound and couldn't move, time moving slower than it should have, succumbing to the monotone chant that was otherworldly and frightening beyond anything he'd ever known. One of the demons came closer, and he saw that it had a face. It was his father, grinning around bloodied teeth.

Quinn woke to a high-pitched chirp and swung the rifle up, centering on a robin that sat on the windowsill. It turned its head, focusing on him with one black eye as he relaxed in the cushions. It chirped again and leaped away, wings flapping madly as it soared between two trees and out of sight. It was a new day, and the sun was out, barely clearing the tops of the trees.

He ate a stick of beef jerky and drank a bottle of water for breakfast. After a quick shower, he packed a wool blanket into his bag from the master bedroom's closet, glancing around the space one last time before locking the front door and heading down the drive.

He found a log cabin-style home after traveling only a mile. Its garage was unlocked and a black Ford Raptor sat inside, as pristine as if it had come off the showroom floor days ago. Maybe it had. The thought saddened him.

He drove into the nearest town seeing nothing alive along the way save for a squirrel that darted in front of the vehicle in a near suicidal sprint. The gas station he stopped at had been looted, its glass doors and windows blown out, by gunfire or by rocks he didn't know. There were a handful of candy bars along with some potato chips left on the floor. He picked these up and returned to the Ford before filling the tank along with two gas cans he found in a storage shed beside the station.

Stopping at a blinking traffic light on the edge of the town, Quinn glanced left and right. The road was a barren stretch, punctuated by the odd vehicle every quarter mile. He gazed in each direction before punching an address into the GPS display mounted in the dash. He'd left the sheet of paper with the address on it in the ruined center console of the Tahoe, waiting for the right time to bring up his request, but that didn't matter anymore. He'd memorized the town and numbers that went with it, and now he had no one to discuss it with.

Quinn swallowed, closing his eyes for a moment before glancing at the GPS. It told him to go southwest on a road he'd never heard of. As he pulled out and accelerated, Alice and Ty flitted through his mind, and he wondered where they were on the digital map displayed within the dash, if they were safe. He supposed they were, now that they'd left him behind.

He rubbed his face, fingers finding the familiar, unnatural curves, and glanced around at the landscape flowing past. He couldn't deny the beauty of it all. The sun, the road, the trees, the fields, the towns. Each sight brand new, each place original in its own right. But everything held a tinge of disappointment. As if the colors were less today than they were the day before.

He shrugged off the thought and focused on the road. Maybe he'd drive until the drabness went away. Maybe he wouldn't stop. But there was one place he had to visit before continuing. And then again, maybe he wouldn't continue. It would all depend on what he found when he got there.

He only hoped Foster and Mallory were alive to greet him.

~

Quinn waited behind the round, sagging hay bale and watched the seven stilts examine his truck.

They were all well over eight feet, one towering above the rest that must've been upwards of twelve, their long-fingered hands poking and prodding the vehicle's paint. One sniffed at the grille, inhaling a long breath before forcing it out with a wet blast. The tallest kept turning in his direction, eyes wide and hungry, scanning the land around the road.

He'd been making good time, only having to leave the road twice to get around cars blocking the highway. But the Ford was a glutton for gas, and he'd stopped on a barren stretch where he could see a good length in almost all directions to refill the tank from one of the spare cans. When he was finished, he'd walked to the side of the highway to relieve himself, slinging his rifle around his shoulder, not bothering to close the truck's door. While he was standing there, he'd glanced back the way he'd come, the road narrowing to a dagger point in the distance before cresting a hill. At its very top, long shapes had been swaying, their movements fluid and swift. He'd cut his urination off mid-stream and began to run for the Ford when two stilts had appeared from the trees closest to the road. Without pausing they'd made a line for the truck, their deep grunts and burps becoming louder and louder.

There was no way he would have made it to the vehicle.

He'd fled in the opposite direction off the road, keeping the truck between the stilts and his flight. He'd slid behind the hay bale as they reached the truck, the first one rumbling a growl as it peered inside the cab. Within minutes the other group he'd spotted first arrived and joined them, their numbers growing from two to seven.

An hour later, they were still enamored with the vehicle. As he watched, one pulled out his bag from the backseat and tore an MRE open, its contents exploding on the pavement near its feet. Quinn re-gripped the AR-15. He raised it to his shoulder, bringing his sights to rest on the tallest stilt's head. Thirty rounds, seven of them. But only twenty yards between them and the hay bail. He placed his finger on the trigger, beginning to squeeze, but then lowered the weapon as another three pale figures emerged from the woods a quarter mile behind the truck and joined the group. Quinn's nerves frayed further as time slid by. The sun arced overhead and began its descent toward the western horizon. He watched them scatter the contents of the bag further, all the while the tallest kept pacing up and down the highway. It croaked louder than the others, and he saw that they always gave it the most space when it passed by.

All at once the leader lunged down the embankment beside the road and closed on the hay bale.

Quinn shrunk down, aiming the rifle up, a split second from pulling the trigger.

The stilt slowed and stopped on the opposite side of the bale. The wind gusted, ripping across the field. The creature reached out and nudged the bale with one hand. It rocked slightly and settled. The stilt huffed once and then turned, letting out a loud grunt. The other nine turned their heads and looked at it before lumbering away down the road. The tallest remained where it was for an agonizing second and then followed the herd.

He waited until they meandered off the highway and then counted to one hundred before sliding from behind the hay bale. The road was deserted once again. The birds chirped, and the wind slid between dead brambles in the ditch. He returned his strewn belongings to his bag and stowed it in the backseat. With a roar, the Raptor started, and he sped down the highway doing over eighty. In an hour Newton, Pennsylvania, appeared before him.

The town was tiny and built into the side of a small mountain that rose above it in a tree-studded mound. A bald swath cut down its side, the center strung with massive power lines. The highway he drove on became Newton's main street, stores numbering not more than five. A dozen houses were scattered beyond the business district, their fronts peeling paint and several open doors gaped like frozen screams. He cruised past the barren side streets and was out of the city limits in under a minute. The GPS informed him to turn right in half a mile. A dirt road appeared where the screen said it would, and he swung onto it, climbing in switchback curves through the budding trees. Every so often a driveway would branch off of the track even as it narrowed, the ditches closing in with each mile. Near the crest of the mountain, a mailbox appeared bearing a last name so familiar it took his breath away. Until then he'd been intent on the road, the destination his only focus. But now, now his hands trembled.

He turned onto the driveway, its path clear and well maintained. He searched the dirt for wheel tracks and saw nothing, but the rain could have washed those away.

One turn.

Two.

Three.

Then he saw it.

The cabin emerged in a clearing surrounded by birch trees. It was small but solid, composed of huge logs interlocked at each corner, reminding him immensely of Foster's home on his father's land. It was one level but had wide windows gracing its front, and a steep drop fell away on its opposite side that revealed the north face of the mountain. He pulled to a stop before a low lean-to that was blaringly empty, ricks of firewood stacked against its side.

The yard was silent when he stepped out, cradling the rifle in one arm. He watched the front door of the cabin, but it didn't ease open and no faces appeared in the windows. Quinn approached the house, the magnificent view of the mountainside trying to steal his attention, but he continued to the covered doorway. He knocked once, hard.

"Foster? Mallory? It's Quinn."

Nothing. No answer.

He tried the knob, but it remained solid as his hand turned around it. Quinn lifted his leg and aimed a kick at the door. Wood splintered but the lock held. One more blast from his foot and it flew inward, rebounding away from the interior wall. He moved inside to a narrow living room. The walls were adorned with pictures of mountains: McKinley, The Matterhorn, Everest. Beside each of them were smaller photos of a much younger Foster amidst groups of people, everyone adorned in climbing gear. He was smiling, his arms around others' shoulders.

Beyond the living room was a kitchen, everything in its place. In the rear of the cabin was a bedroom, bed neatly made, attached bathroom spotless, and a covered porch looking out over the vista dropping steeply away. Quinn stood beside an Adirondack chair and then sat in it, leaning his rifle against the nearby wall.

They weren't here. Had never been.

The hope that had been unconsciously building inside him crumbled, demolished by the silence and crushing knowledge that everyone he had ever known was dead.

Their faces came to him and went. They were ghosts now, nothing more. Tears clouded his eyes. Before they could fall, he rose from the chair, picking a small coffee table up as he moved, and whipped it through one of the porch windows.

The glass shattered, and the table soared out of sight, its passage echoing through the trees. He stood there, chest heaving, muscles thrumming power lines, and all the while Alice's words repeated in his mind.

That's what separates you and I.

~

He spent the night in the cabin, the air cool from the broken window. As the sun set, the valley below came alive with croaks and bellows, the cries deep and reverberating, but far away. Quinn fell asleep on the floor of Foster's bedroom with the moon gazing in through the single window.

In the morning he gathered as many supplies as he could find within the house. Foster had accrued two, five-gallon pails of rice along with twenty jugs of water. He took all of these as well as three scoped rifles and ammo to match. He considered backtracking the simplest route that Foster and Mallory may have taken, but dismissed it almost immediately. They'd left days before him, and only death would have kept Foster from reaching this place.

He drove away from the cabin at daybreak, coasting down off the mountain into a silver mist that hovered above the road. At the main highway, he paused, looking in both directions. To the left was home. He could return to it. There was some protection there, and it was familiar. To the right was complete ambiguity. The wild beyond. He gazed toward the ocean, now hours and hours out of sight, its crash upon the rocks like musical chaos. He looked ahead. A diverging road sign faced him from the opposite side of the highway. He waited only a moment longer and then turned right.

~

The day grew around him as he traveled. The Earth seemed to be coming alive with each passing hour. More green buds appeared at the ends of branches, a V of geese cruised over the highway heading north, and the temperature warmed enough for him to lower the windows and let the breeze flow across his skin.

Quinn ate as he drove, chewing every so often on a chunk of jerky and sipping on bottled water. There was no sign of life along the road other than animals, their habits uninterrupted by the catastrophe befallen to the dominant species. He tried the radio every ten miles, spinning the dial through the hissing channels. Only one station still broadcast any music, and after an hour of listening to it, it was clear that the last action the DJ had taken was to loop the same seven songs endlessly. He was about to try the AM band when the road dropped into a hollow and curved, opening to a huge expanse beyond.

A massive concrete bridge sat before him, spanning a wide river fifty feet below. The water was a murky brown, flowing fast with the winter's meltings.

Quinn brought the Raptor to a halt at its edge, gazing across the breadth of the river. The bridge itself was littered with several piles of debris. It looked as if a car crash had been cleaned up at some point. Dark stains covered the first fifty feet of the structure, and a narrow cable snaked from one side to the other at its midpoint, its ends disappearing from view over the railings. A red and brown heap lay at the far side of the bridge. When he brought up his pair of binoculars, he saw it was a deer's carcass torn asunder, its intestines draped around it in an expanded pool of dried blood.

He set the binoculars down, glancing once in the rearview mirror. The back roads had been mercifully clear, and he hadn't seen a stilt all morning.

But this bridge...

He rolled down his window and listened. Water chuckled and the wind spoke in the reaching branches of trees beside the road. Quinn swallowed, drawing out the XDM and laying it on the passenger seat before accelerating. His tires began to hum on the concrete, the sun glinting off the river below in a blazing ball of orange. As he neared the center of the bridge, he thought he heard something, a yell or a horn of some kind, and drew his foot off the gas, eyes flying to the mirrors and ahead once more.

Something was wrong with the cable lying in the middle of the bridge.

It was moving, uncoiling, straightening as he approached it. For a moment he thought it was his point of view and the movement of the vehicle playing tricks on his eyes. As he realized what was happening, he jammed on the brakes, but it was too late.

The cable snapped tight across his path, flying up and toward the truck with liquid speed.

It sunk into and through the grille, slamming him to a stop. The Raptor's tires screeched as boiling anti-freeze geysered skyward. The airbag deployed, sending a chemical dust into his eyes and mouth, choking him even as he crashed into it. He rebounded, bashing the back of his skull off the headrest.

The world fluttered, and the engine died.

He tasted blood.

His vision spun, and his ears hummed with the impact.

Quinn fumbled for the pistol even as the sounds of a motor reached him, but the gun was gone, lost somewhere in the crash. He tried to sit up, but the air bag pressed against his chest. It was full of air and his lungs had none. His leg hurt where the stitches were, the ones Alice had put in so carefully, twice. She'd be angry with him if he'd tore them again. He nearly laughed. The buzzing in his ears faded, but with it came a new sound.

Footsteps.

There was someone on the bridge. Someone outside the door, looking in through the window at him, but their features were indistinct, like the figures in his dream two nights before. The door opened.

"What in God's name are you?" a gravelly voice said.

"Please," Quinn said, trying to focus. And as his vision straightened, all he could see was the butt of a rifle. Then darkness.

Chapter 19

Sacrifice

Quinn came awake to blinding pain in his face and the douse of ice water cascading over his head and shoulders.

Reality blazed into existence as he rose from unconsciousness. His hands were bound together behind a wooden chair he sat upon. He was in a room made of cinderblocks stacked together, their borders gapped, daylight pouring between them. Crude crosses were drawn on several of the blocks in what looked like charcoal. The roof was a single chunk of ribbed steel, and there were two people standing before him. One was a middle-aged man with a gray goatee and cold eyes holding an empty ice cream pail. And the other was a woman with long, straggly, blond hair, her age somewhere near the man's but harder to determine because of the taut skin covering her face, stretched tight by high cheekbones and a broad smile.

"Can you hear me?" the man asked, and Quinn remembered his voice as the last thing he'd heard before being knocked unconscious.

"Yes."

"And it can speak, too," the blond woman said. Her voice was velvety soft, a frigid purr that sent a splinter of ice down his spine.

"You can have my supplies," Quinn said.

"Thank you, we've taken them already," the woman said.

He waited a beat, shifting his eyes between the two of them.

"Then what do you want?"

"We want our world back, demon."

"What?"

"Oh come now. We were doing so well. I'll ask the questions and you answer them. Okay?" the woman said tilting her head to one side. She came closer and Quinn could smell her, a molding flowery scent competing with rancid body odor. He looked at the man who merely glared back at him, freezing stare, eyes half-lidded.

"I was just trying to cross the bridge."

"Jimmy, can you refresh its memory on how this works?" the woman said, stepping to the side, her smile unwavering. The man lunged forward, and Quinn didn't have time to flinch.

Jimmy's fist drove into his solar plexus, and his lungs caught fire. He gasped then gagged, stomach acid racing into his mouth. He coughed and spit, the cramped muscles in his midsection slowly loosening.

"There. That's better. Now, where did you come from?" the woman asked.

"Maine," Quinn managed, though the word was more of a moan.

"Hmm, you're not fooling us, harbinger. You crawled from the cracks of the earth, divulged from the stinking bowels of the underworld."

"What?"

"Jimmy?"

Jimmy's fist connected with his shoulder this time, knuckles smacking the tender flesh where the nitrogen had scalded him. Quinn cried out as tears flooded his eyes. The pain was something alive, writhing in time with his accelerated heartbeat.

"Listen to me, beast, you have no power here in the sovereign nation of God Almighty. You will answer my questions or suffer his wrath." Spittle flew from her mouth as she spoke, some of it landing on his face as she neared him. "Do you understand?"

"Yes," Quinn breathed. Behind his back he began to feel how he was bound to the chair. The rope around his wrists wound through one wooden support. He touched the wood with his fingers. It was decoratively carved, and thin.

"Good. Again, admit that you are the cause of this plague of the body and mind that has killed so many of the unfaithful and changed the rest into creatures designed by the fallen one."

Quinn glanced past Jimmy and saw a rickety wooden door set into the building behind him. There was no handle on it. He nodded.

"I am."

Jimmy inhaled and tipped his head back, closing his eyes. He began to mumble a prayer under his breath. The woman traced the sign of the cross on her forehead, the manic smile still pulling at her mouth.

"I knew it. The moment I saw your cursed face, I knew we'd found the cause of the downfall. Jimmy, go get him. Tell him the news; tell him he was right."

Jimmy turned away and pushed at the wooden door, which swung open. No lock.

"Before you go," Quinn said, stopping the man in his tracks. "You should know you're all doomed. By bringing me here, you've killed yourselves."

The woman's smile finally faded as she looked at Jimmy. The man pulled the door shut and flexed his fingers before balling them both into fists. He stepped forward, winding back his right arm, knuckles raw and red from their prior use.

Quinn snapped both his feet up and kicked Jimmy in the chest.

The other man's eyes widened, and he made a squawking sound in his throat. Quinn felt his chair tip backward and tucked his hands beneath the seat as far as they could go as he fell. The chair hit the concrete floor, the impact jarring him. Wood cracked and he pulled hard against the ropes binding him. There was another loud snap and the bindings at his wrists loosened.

Quinn rolled to the side and felt the back of the chair come with him. Then Jimmy was above him, a short steel tube shining in one hand. Quinn drove a heel out and caught him in the crotch. Jimmy blanched, his knees unhinging. As he fell, Quinn whipped his foot around and connected with the other man's chin.

Jimmy's head rocked to the side and his eyes rolled to the whites. He crumpled backward, his skull cracking like the chair against the floor.

"Help! Demon!" the woman shrieked, and started to run across the small room toward the door. Quinn bucked his hips up and slipped his wrists past his ass, then brought his knees to his chest, threading the rope over his feet. By the time he was able to stand, the woman had escaped the room, her shrill cries like that of a wounded bird. Quinn ran to the door, banged it open and paused.

A huge, open yard spread out around him, the new grass of spring growing everywhere. Dozens of cabins lined the edges of the clearing in a circle and several massive oaks grew at its center. A long, low building to his right had a large steeple growing from its roof, a steel sculpture of Jesus hanging from its wide cross. The woman was running toward the church, glancing back every few steps, her dirty hair floating behind her. She yelped seeing him outside the structure and poured on more speed. The door of the church opened and two men stepped outside, their eyes squinting in the bright sunlight.

Quinn ran.

He pelted away, head throbbing, stomach sick with adrenaline, skin slick with sweat. A woman holding a small child opened the door to a cabin ahead of him. Her eyes bulged and she retreated, slamming the door shut. Yells grew behind him, more and more voices joining in until it sounded as if a mob were pursuing him.

He flew past the first row of cabins.

Beyond a second row was a wooden fence at least ten feet high. He would have one chance to run up it and grasp the top. He leaned forward, a high-pitched scream carrying to him from the way he'd come.

As he passed the second row of cabins and readied himself to jump, a rope snapped up from the ground, pulling tight near his ankles.

His feet hooked it and he was falling, the ground rushing up to meet him much too fast. He slammed into it, skidding forward, rocks and dirt taking bites of his skin. All the oxygen was gone from the world; there was none in his lungs. He rolled over to his side, attempting to get up.

Twin boys, no more than ten years old, watched him from a dozen yards away, their hands still gripping either end of the rope. One of them smiled at him.

A man wearing a gray, button-up shirt approached from the direction of the church followed by the woman who had been in the concrete hut. She blubbered something incoherent and sank to her knees, pulling the two twin boys to her chest as she tilted her head back.

"Praise the Lord. You boys did so good," she said, her grin stretching across her face again.

Quinn tried to get onto his hands and knees, but the man in the gray shirt kicked him back down. Soon he was surrounded by people, so many people. Men and women and children of all ages, clustering around him in a circle, their eyes flitting to him and then away. Many of their hands were clasped, their fingers intertwined in prayer. All of them were dressed the same, the woman in full-length skirts, the men in the button-up shirts and blue jeans. The circle began to move apart at the far end and a short, stocky man with silver hair strode through the gap. His eyes were shaded behind a pair of dark sunglasses, and he wore a black shirt tucked over his significant belly. He moved without hesitation, his strides purposeful and quick. He paused near Quinn's feet, the dark lenses reflecting his prone form in the dirt.

"And the great dragon was thrown down, that ancient serpent who is called the devil and Satan, the deceiver of the whole world; he was thrown down to the earth." The man spoke in a deep baritone that carried well within the circle and bounced off the fence. He squatted beside Quinn, his mouth curling up in a sneer. "Sleep now, demon, and soon we will have the truth."

Quinn tried again to roll over, but something struck him hard in the back of his head and the sun winked out into darkness.

~

"Wake up."

The words filtered down to him from a great height. A thudding ache pulsed at the base of his neck. Silence roared in his ears. Quinn blinked, a wood-paneled ceiling coming into focus. He turned his head. He was on a bed. Wide straps ran across his chest, hips, and shins. A fire burned low behind the glass doors of a stove in the corner of the room.

"Over here, handsome."

Quinn turned his head the opposite way.

The bullish man in the black shirt sat in a chair that looked like a throne beside the bed. His sunglasses were gone, and Quinn saw that his eyes were brown and deep set, piggish and watery. A peppering of whiskers covered his jowly face.

The man smiled.

"Where am I?" Quinn said. The words were too large for his mouth, his tongue thick and dry.

"My home." He sprung from his chair, moving like a much lighter man, and grasped Quinn's hand pinned beneath the strap. "Archer Tigmund, at your service. Although I should say you're at mine at the moment." He grinned again and released Quinn's fingers before re-seating himself on the velvet-covered chair. "May I have the pleasure of your name?"

"Quinn."

"Quinn, you know, I like that. Much better than Ralph. That was my given name. But I changed it. Archer is so much more distinguished and pleasant to say, don't you think?"

"What do you want with me?"

"Ah, right to the meat of it. I like you, Quinn. You're a Godsend." Archer laughed and clapped his hands, lacing his fingers together before bowing his head. "Dear Lord Almighty in the highest, we, your faithful servants of the physical world, come to you this day to offer up a tribute in representation of our loyalty to your grace. This harbinger of the apocalypse, we do now lay waste to in your name just as you cast out the most beautiful of all angels by the name of Lucifer. Lord hear our prayer."

Archer looked up from his clasped hands and smiled.

"What a load of shit; am I right?"

Quinn gazed at him and then licked his lips. "I don't understand."

Archer stood and began to pace around the bed. "Do you know where you are, Quinn?"

"Somewhere in Pennsylvania."

"Actually it's Ohio, not that it matters anymore whatsoever. Everything's gone. The government, the military, the media, everything. But not here. Here we have sanctity and preservation. It's like a damn game reserve of human beings." Archer paused and studied him. "But it's my game reserve. See, I created all this fifteen years ago. The First Church of Eternal Salvation. Has a nice ring to it, right? My father was a Lutheran minister, and he made me learn the bible front to back, cover to cover, when I was only ten. I got picked on a lot growing up, wasn't easy to be a preacher's son. That and I was a fat little fucker. But you know what I learned, Quinn?" Archer bent over him, close enough to smell the man's cologne, something sharp and tangy. "People are always looking for someone stronger than they are." He straightened and went to the stove, warming his hands above its top.

"What does this have to do with me?" Quinn asked.

"Everything, my friend, everything." Archer made his way back to the chair and dropped his girth into it. "When I started this church, I had three followers. We'd go into Cleveland, stand on the street corner, and hand out flyers. Our congregation grew over the years, but it wasn't until my good old daddy died that things really took off. See, he invested enough money to leave me a sizeable chunk with which I bought this land, built these buildings, and began to preach full-time. Now you might be thinking, where's he going with this. Well, I'll tell you, Quinn." He leaned forward, placing his elbows on his knees. "People are stupid. They're sheep. They follow anyone with a plan. But if that plan takes even the slightest detour, well, they start to look elsewhere.

"I have a sweet deal here, my friend. I'm looked to as the supreme leader in all respects. I have all the money and food that I want. And the women…" Archer shook his head and whistled between his teeth. "…there's five that share my bed right now, all of them trying to get a taste of the divine." He chuckled and his stomach jiggled.

"So you're a phony," Quinn said, slowly trying to work his hands from beneath the straps, but they were too tight.

"Hey now, that hurts. I'm an opportunist, always have been. I got pissed on when I was younger, and I vowed never to let that happen again. But lately there's been some dissent. This plague comes along and wipes out humanity, and you'd think it would be a minister's dream, right? All these people looking to me for guidance and words of wisdom. Instead they're frantic for an answer. Why did this happen? And doesn't God love us?" Archer waved his hand through the air in disgust. "Bunch of fucking whiners."

Quinn tried to slide his legs to one side beneath the strap, but there was no room to maneuver. And each time he moved, a bomb of pain would go off inside his skull. The room tilted and then leveled.

"Shit happens, that's the absolute truth, one you can live by. And I'd quit trying to get out of bed; you're going to make yourself pass out again. I'm guessing you've got a concussion, or two of them."

"So I'm your answer," Quinn said, closing his eyes as nausea surged inside him. "I'm your scapegoat."

"Damn, Quinn, you're a smart guy. I like you. I'd almost like to keep you around just to chat with. This has been really liberating for me since there's zero people that I can speak freely with." Archer rose from his seat and returned to the stove, banking it with another chunk of wood. "I know you didn't cause the plague, Quinn. I'm guessing you just have some genetic disease that made you so ugly. But my congregation's been looking for an answer, and if they don't get it soon, I'll be the one they blame. When I saw you, I planted the seed in their minds that you're responsible somehow. And Helena, the woman who was questioning you, already told everyone you confessed to being a demon and promised their demise. Your fate was sealed even before we started talking. You see, we can kill the thin bastards all day long on the bridge and it won't give the congregation what they want."

"What are you going to do with me?" Quinn asked, trying to raise his head.

Archer prodded at the fire with a steel poker, his eyes focused on the flames.

"We're going to burn you tonight, Quinn. That's the answer they're looking for."

Without another word or glance back, Archer left the room, locking the door behind him.

~

The sun crossed the window of the room in a silent arc of time. Quinn watched it glide past when he wasn't struggling against his restraints. Dizziness came and went, but the pain in his head was constant.

After hours alone, a woman entered the room carrying a glass of water. She was close to his age with dark red hair that hung down past her shoulders. As she approached the bed, her hand shook and some of the water slopped over the rim, spilling on the bed. Before he could say anything, she tipped the glass toward his mouth, pouring much too fast for him to drink. He choked and sputtered, turning his head away as the sheets beneath him became soaked. When the glass was empty, the woman hurried from the room, slamming the door behind her.

The room darkened further as the sun dropped below the horizon. Even though his nerves felt as though they were full of electricity, Quinn drifted off to sleep beneath the exhaustion of struggling to get free. When he awoke, the window next to the bed was a square of darkness, and the only light in the room came from the guttering fire. A sound rose moments later as he was trying to loosen the strap across his waist. It took him nearly a full minute to realize what it was.

People were singing outside the house.

The door to the room swung open, and Archer, along with half a dozen men, entered the room.

"We know that we are from God and the power of the whole world lies in the power of the evil one," Archer said in his booming voice. "Be not afraid, brothers; the demon cannot harm you while in my presence. He may speak in lies, so do not listen, for then you shall be at the mercy of the burning evil that we fight day in and day out."

The men surrounded the bed and unstrapped the bindings across his body. As soon as they were loose, Quinn lunged sideways, bashing his fist into the nose of a scrawny man wearing a long beard. Blood poured from the man's nose, but he merely wiped it away and helped the others grasp Quinn's arms and legs.

"Stop! I didn't do anything! I was just trying to cross the bridge," Quinn said as the men stood him on his feet and held him fast by the arms.

"You were coming to destroy the last haven of the world, demon; do not lie," Archer said, and drew the sign of the cross in the air before Quinn's face. "Come, brothers, let us proceed before it can call its brethren."

They dragged him from the room. He kicked and struggled but couldn't break free of the men's holds. Weakness pervaded his body, and each time he attempted to escape, his strength receded from him like the sun sliding behind the trees.

They hauled him out through Archer's home and into the night. Crickets chirped. Insects hummed. But above all the other evening sounds was the singing.

The entire congregation was there, all of them holding candles. Men, women, children, young, old, their faces all danced in the glow of flames held near their chests. Quinn tried counting their number but lost track as the men holding him guided him through the watching crowd. The song they sang was something he'd never heard before, all the words Latin. He'd only learned a few phrases in the ancient language from Theresa, and the congregation was singing none of them.

They pulled him past the church, the steel Jesus looking down on him from his cross. The flickering shadows thrown by the candles changed the savior's pain-stricken face into something malevolent and sneering as they passed by. Beyond the church was an open communal area ringed by tables and dozens of chairs. Several small fires burned in a broad circle, illuminating enough of the center for Quinn to see what waited there.

A post with thick rope attached through its middle sat amongst piles of dry bramble.

Quinn dug his heels into the ground, and the men forced him along. He glanced around the clearing. Beyond the sacrificial pyre was the wooden fence, a solid gate well over twelve feet high set into its length. Two guards stood watch there, rifles cradled in the crooks of their arms, their faces impassive. Several children skipped ahead of the mass, their laughter intermingling with the constant song rising from the people. Quinn threw all his weight to one side and then the other, but the men held fast, their fingers like bands of steel digging into his flesh.

They brought him to a stop before the post and its fuel beneath. He recognized one of his own gas cans beside the dry tinder.

Quinn began to shake, tremors flowing up from his feet to his shoulders and back down again. His bladder threatened to let go, but he managed to hold it as the song gradually came to an end and faded away. The gathering encircled him and stood watching as Archer stepped forward. He held a silver cup in one hand along with something that looked like a blunted spoon inside it. Liquid glinted within.

"I condemn thee, demon, of crimes against the faithful. For burdening our beautiful world with your presence and the pestilence your kind has brought upon us. With this holy water, your flesh is cleansed." Archer made a flicking movement with his wrist, and droplets of the liquid speckled Quinn's arms and face.

It burned like fire.

Quinn cried out and shook his head. The places where the water had landed were like wasp stings, burrowing beneath his skin. There was a collective gasp that ran through the crowd, and Archer turned to them, holding up the silver cup.

"You see, it cannot stand the sanctity of the church, the strength of our faith! It fears us, and in good right, for now we shall send it back to the hell whence it came!"

A roar of voices erupted from the congregation. The burns where the liquid had landed still stung, but he muscled past the pain and straightened. The people before him all had their candles raised in triumph. Some swayed in place, heads tilted back to the dark sky. Others merely stared at him, the flames they held illuminating the hatred in their eyes.

Archer motioned to the men holding Quinn, and they shoved him across the pile of brush and branches to a clear place before the vertical post. In a few quick movements, they bound him to it with the rope, wrapping his arms tight to his body and knotting it on the opposite side. When he was bound, they moved away to join their loved ones, lighting candles as they turned back to watch. Archer stepped closer, his deep-set eyes dancing, a smile pulling at the corners of his mouth.

"The acetic acid was a nice touch, don't you think?" Archer whispered, swirling the cup around in front of Quinn's face. "Pure inspiration." Quinn tried not to tremble and closed his eyes. "Thank you, Quinn, for your sacrifice. I know it doesn't mean a lot, but I really do appreciate it."

"Fuck you," Quinn said, staring into Archer's eyes. Archer shrugged and stepped back before placing the silver cup on the ground. He grasped the open gas can in one hand and began to douse the branches near Quinn's feet. With a toss, Archer sloshed some gas on the ropes binding him. The smell was overwhelming and Quinn gagged, the fumes in his nose and throat. His head floated above his body and he coughed, blinking away the tears that flooded his eyes.

It was almost here.

The pain was going to be immense. Beyond anything he'd ever felt before. How long after the flames reached him would it take to pass out? Seconds? Minutes? He shuddered and a sob escaped him. The cries of the mob rose as Archer emptied the last of the can and tossed it away. The minister accepted a long, black candle from a woman in the crowd and turned back to him.

"You came to destroy our home, our world, our faith. You have been defeated, demon, cast out by the righteous hand of God and now destroyed by his eternal servants of salvation." Archer moved forward, the candle flame licking at the air.

Quinn tipped his head back, found the stars above.

They'll be waiting when it's over. I'll be home again.

He tried to keep his focus upward and away from everything around him, but his eyes flitted down to Archer as he stopped at the edge of the pyre.

Archer winked and lowered the candle.

There was a buzzing sound and then a wet thock as Archer's throat exploded in a spray of blood and bone.

Archer's mouth dropped open, and he let the candle fall to the ground. It fluttered and went out as it hit the gravel. There was a silence, fathoms deep, and then a woman screamed.

Archer's knees gave and he fell, his head tipping back to expose the open wound at his throat. It was wide and gushing blood. He brought a hand up as if to stanch it, but let it fall away. His eyes found Quinn's, such disbelief there, and then he flopped forward onto his stomach.

Gunshots popped from the far side of the fence, and a guard near the gate fell clutching his shoulder. The congregation became a stampede of yelling people. Most ran toward the church, their cries trailing behind them as they left the circle of light. Candles fell and winked out. There was more gunfire, and Quinn squinted, trying to make out the shooter. A man with a shotgun pumped round after round into the darkness as he walked calmly toward the fence, his barrel spitting three feet of flame. He fired his last shot and waited, shoulders back, stance ready.

A muzzle flash came from twenty feet away, and his head snapped to the side, a chunk of skull spinning away like a hair-covered Frisbee. A black figure raced out of the darkness, an AR-15 swinging back and forth. There was something familiar about how the person moved.

One of the smaller fires flared, and Alice's white face turned in his direction.

"Oh my God," Quinn said as she neared. She wore black cargo pants, a black long-sleeve t-shirt, and black hiking boots. Alice swung her rifle around the yard once more and then leapt over the gas-soaked bramble.

"Hey. You look surprised to see me," she said, moving past him to the back of the post. He felt a tug on the rope binding him as she began to work at the knot.

"I…I can't…" Quinn said.

"You can't go anywhere with this fucking pole on your back; that's what you can't do," Alice replied, yanking harder. Quinn looked up, scanning the area for anyone, but it was only them and the men Alice had shot. As he watched, a bright ember floated away from the nearest fire and flew toward them. Instead of winking out, it glowed brighter and descended toward the base of the pyre.

"Shit. Alice, hurry," he said leaning forward against the rope.

"I'm trying."

The ember settled to the ground and out of sight.

He held his breath.

Nothing.

"Thank you," Quinn said, all the strength going out of his body.

Fire leapt into the darkness, flowing like it was being poured into existence. It licked up through the dry tinder, tongues of flame rising higher and higher. The pressure on the ropes stopped. Quinn jerked his head to the side.

Alice was backing away, her rifle hanging from a sling around her shoulders. Her eyes were blank, hands up in a warding off gesture.

"What are you doing? Help me!"

She glanced up at him, but the glaze upon her eyes was a mile thick. She was gone.

"Alice, get the rope off me!"

The fire rose like a wave around him, the heat growing from warm to uncomfortable to searing in less than a heartbeat.

"ALICE!"

His scream was like a physical blow. She jerked and glanced around, the fire bringing her terrified features into sharp definition. Her jaw clenched, and she rushed forward, disappearing out of his line of sight. A blade of flame lanced up from his feet, and the rope across his chest began to burn. There was the immensity of the pain, a thousand needles piercing his skin, then the rope fell away and her hand was in his.

They ran to the side and leapt over the curtain of fire. Smoke threatened to choke him, but then the air was clear and clean and he sucked it in, tasting it, drinking it. Alice stood beside him, the brightness in her eyes receding again. Her hand twitched and spasmed.

"Where? Where do we go?" Quinn said, gripping her upper arm. She looked at him, and when the fogginess of her gaze didn't clear, he slapped her hard across the face. "Where?"

"This way," Alice said, her voice thick and groggy. She jogged forward as a gunshot cracked somewhere behind them, and Alice cried out, falling to her side in a heap.

"No," Quinn said, dropping down beside her. Her right leg was tucked up close to her chest, and her hands were wrapped around her calf. Blood shone in the firelight. Another shot whistled past them, and Quinn yanked the AR-15 from around her shoulders, finding the outline of a man beyond the pyre.

Quinn emptied the magazine in his direction, and the man dove to the side, uttering a guttural cry as he landed. He didn't get up.

"Come on; we gotta go," Quinn said. He slung the rifle over his shoulder and then hauled her to her feet. She grasped his arm, and they ran across the grounds to where the fence stood.

There were two boards missing along the closest section, and they darted through the gap as more gunfire shattered the night. Rounds blasted through the boards to either side of them, splinters flying like shrapnel. Ahead, the shape of a vehicle gathered, and they raced toward it.

"Ty's inside," Alice said through a jaw locked by pain.

When they reached the car, he realized it wasn't the Tahoe. It was built lower to the ground and had narrower windows. Along the side of the fence was a dirt path that ran down a steep hill in one direction and up a substantial grade in the other. Quinn found the rear door handle, intent on simply getting Alice inside, when a round hummed through the air beside him and punctured the SUV's rear tire.

"Shit," he said, turning and pulling the trigger, but the rifle was empty. Quinn yanked the rear driver's side door open, and Ty leapt into his arms.

"Quinn?"

"Let's go," Quinn said, dragging them away from the vehicle as more shots lanced its side.

"The water, the food," Alice breathed.

"No time."

They hobbled away into the welcoming shadows. Alice's hand was an iron band around his arm, and he squeezed Ty's hand so hard he had to force himself to lessen the pressure. The trail beside the fence became rockier with savage holes and channels that tried to turn their ankles as they ran. The stars brightened as they left the glow of the fires behind, and the forest to their right thickened into something primordial.

The air beside Quinn's head heated up and then he heard the shot a moment later. Without slowing, he guided them off the trail and into the woods. A thicket of dead vine and wild raspberry cane met them, tore at their skin, as they burst through it. Ty uttered a small cry, and Quinn hoisted the boy up and over a fallen log in their way. They tore on, Alice limping beside him, Ty beginning whimper.

A hollow opened up below the side of an incline studded with mature trees. Starlight filtered through the branches, stippling the ground with dagger shadows. A darker, round shape appeared before them, and he pulled Alice and Ty behind the massive boulder, hunkering down behind its protection. He chanced a look back the way they'd come.

A dozen flashlight beams cut the darkness, their swaths ripping across trees and ground a quarter mile away.

They were coming closer.

Quinn slid down the boulder, his breath burning as he gulped it down. When he could speak he said, "We have to get up and over this hill. Can you guys do it?"

Ty nodded in the weak light, and Alice closed her eyes, her face pale as talcum. Men's voices floated to them, and when he glanced around the side of the stone, a long flashlight flickered in the place where they'd left the path.

"Okay, let's go."

He hauled them to their feet, and they set off up the hill. Twigs and leaves crackled beneath their feet, but the noise of a four-wheeler growling along the path below covered the sound. Halfway up, Alice staggered to a stop, her hand loosening on his arm. Quinn turned to her, about to ask if she needed a rest, when she tipped backward in a faint.

He managed to snag her wrist as she fell, and she crumpled at his feet instead of plummeting down the side of the hill.

"Alice," Quinn hissed in a whisper, kneeling beside her.

"Mama?"

"It's okay, buddy. She's okay."

The four-wheeler revved and crashed through a stand of brush a hundred feet below.

Quinn undid his belt and probed Alice's pant leg until he found an entry and exit hole wet with blood. He laced the belt around the wound and gently tightened it, tucking the loose end beneath itself.

A man yelled in the hollow. Something about blood.

Quinn took two deep breaths and slung Alice over his shoulders before grasping Ty's hand again.

They climbed.

Quinn's legs began to ache. Then they burned. But still they climbed. The top would never come. He kept looking at the ridge, its distance seeming to multiply with each glance. He focused on his breathing. This was nothing more than hanging a hundred feet above the black rocks of the Atlantic, waiting to find the next hand or foothold. Muscles on fire, but to quit meant death.

Ten more steps.

Five.

Three.

One.

They crested the hill, and he nearly crumbled beneath the pain and exhaustion. He allowed himself a ten count of breathing before leading Ty to the right.

The dome of the hill was covered in a layer of dry reed grass that shushed with their passing. Quinn brought them past two oak deadfalls and found a natural plain that descended the opposite side of the rise in a diagonal cut. They rushed down it and entered a sprawl of pine trees. Sounds of pursuit fell away behind them, buffeted by the evergreens. Quinn clasped Alice's legs tighter to his chest and readjusted her weight. His shoulder was numb where she rested.

"Quinn?" Ty asked.

"Shh, we have to keep going, champ. Just a little farther."

A rash of younger balsams spread out at the base of the grade, their squat forms growing so thick their branches intertwined.

"In here," Quinn gasped. The last of his energy was nearly gone. His legs were pillars of lead, lungs full of barbed wire.

They pushed through the first dozen balsams and found three larger trees surrounded by some smaller growth. Quinn wrestled them below the biggest of the three, holding up its lowest branch so Ty could sit down. He knelt and lowered Alice to the ground, letting the branches snap back into place behind and above them. He turned his head in every direction, but there was no way to see out of the hiding place, which meant there was no way to see in.

Gathering handfuls of dead needles, Quinn built a small mound beneath Alice's head and then leaned close to her, feeling her breath on his face. He checked her pulse. It was fast but steady. When he felt the wound on her leg, there was no new blood soaking her pants. He loosened his belt so that it wouldn't cut off circulation completely and waited, his fingers over the exit and entry holes.

The wound had clotted.

Quinn lay back between Alice and Ty, his breathing slowly coming back to normal. Far away, someone yelled and an engine grumbled, but it sounded as if the noises were growing fainter.

"Is my mom okay?" Ty asked when they had rested minutes that felt like hours.

"Yeah. Her leg's a little hurt, but she's fine."

"Are they going to find us?"

"No. We lost them good, buddy."

"Do you promise?"

"I promise."

"Quinn?"

"Yeah?"

"I'm really sorry."

"For what?"

"I lost my walking stick you made for me." Ty's voice constricted. "We were getting the new car and then mom said the monsters were coming, and I didn't have it with me. I left it in your car."

"Hey, hey, it's okay. I can make you a new one."

Ty sniffled, and he shifted on the ground.

"But the other one was special."

"I know. But the thing about possessions is you can replace them. Even though they're special, you can get something different and then that thing becomes special in its own way. But do you know what you can't replace?"

"What?"

"People. It's okay that you left the stick behind because you and your mom are safe, and that's the most important thing."

Ty sniffed again. "And you too," he murmured.

Quinn opened his mouth but then shut it because his own throat had closed up.

The night deepened around them, sounds of the congregation fading into silence that broke apart with frog song. There was water nearby. That was good. They might need it sooner rather than later. He hadn't had anything to drink since the woman had basically water boarded him in Archer's home. Quinn shifted on the ground and brought Alice's legs up over his own, elevating the wound. The warmth and pressure of her against him sent a shiver through is body. He swallowed and tried not to think of her face so close to him, how white her skin was, the slenderness of her wrists. But the single, overwhelming fact wouldn't leave him be. She'd come back. Somehow, despite the cutting and hardened exterior of who she was, something had gotten through.

Ty edged closer to him, and he put an arm around the boy who rested his head on his chest and drifted off within seconds. Quinn fought sleep's advances for as long as he could but succumbed sometime in the middle of the night, his rescuers breathing quietly on either side.

Chapter 20

Lost

He woke to bitter cold and the sound of wind pushing through treetops.

Quinn sat up, muscles a choir of agony. His face stung, and when he put his fingers to his cheek, the skin was crusted and drawn. Ty and Alice still slept. She had rolled over in the night and was much closer to him, one arm draped across his stomach. He ignored the rush of heat where her arm lay and moved it back to her side. When he managed to stand, he pushed through the double layer of evergreens and stepped out into the open.

Dew shone like sprinkled diamonds on every tree branch and blade of grass. The sun was barely up and his breath plumed out before him. The wind shoved rankled clouds across the sky, and on the opposite side of a narrow clearing, a doe watched him with unblinking eyes.

"Good morning," he said. The deer flicked her tail once and then was gone in two bounds, not a sound accompanying her flight.

Though his body protested, he tried to imitate her stealth as he climbed the hill they'd fled down the night before. And in the morning light, he saw how formidable it truly was. Along with the daunting height, several holes, large enough for a person to drop into, dotted its side. They could've fallen into any of them the night before, most likely breaking a bone as a consequence. He moved to the top of the rise and stopped, ready to flee at the slightest hint of danger.

The opposite side was empty. Nothing moved between the tree trunks. Off to the right, the trail lining the cult's wall ended in a tangle of brush. Four-wheeler tracks ran out from the path and came as high as where he stood but then retreated and shot off to the west.

He listened. Nothing.

When he made it back to their hiding place, Ty was awake, sitting beside his mother and holding her hand.

"Hey Ty, you okay?"

"Yeah. Mom's awake."

Quinn ducked under the branches and knelt beside Alice who looked up at him through slitted eyelids.

"No breakfast in bed?" she asked in a weak voice.

"I rang for room service but no one answered," Quinn said. She smiled.

"I knew you were more trouble than you're worth."

"Believe me, I owe you breakfast forever since I didn't burn to death last night." Alice opened her eyes a little wider and took in his appearance.

"God, your face is burned."

"It doesn't matter. Just as long as my hair looks okay."

She laughed and then winced, looking down the length of her body to her calf.

"How bad is it?"

"Not too bad. Looks like the bullet went straight through. It quit bleeding last night. Does it hurt a lot?"

"I got shot," Alice said, slowly sitting up. "Yes, it hurts a lot." She placed a hand against her temple. "Oh wow, that's not good."

"Sick to your stomach?"

"Yeah. But I'm really thirsty."

"I'll go find some water. You rest."

"Are we okay here or do we need to move?"

"We're alright for now, but we should put some distance between us and the compound before too long. Do you think you'll be able to walk?"

"As soon as my stomach calms down, I'll be good."

"Ginger ale, mom, that's what you need," Ty said.

"You're right, honey. Soon as we get to town I'm having a giant ginger ale and Jack."

"Jack?" Ty asked, tilting his head.

"Never mind," Alice said, shooting a look at Quinn.

"I'll be right back."

"Don't get lost."

"I'll try not to."

He left them beneath the cover of pines and moved in the direction he'd heard the frogs earlier. They were quiet now, but he found their shallow pond not far away concealed by a ring of budding blackberry bushes. A green scum covered the water, but he noticed some movement a dozen yards away. When he made it to the far end, he saw that a trickling stream fed the pond, dropping over polished rocks in silver drizzles. At the sight of the running water, his own thirst burned in his throat, and he laid down, pressing his face into its icy embrace. His scorched skin flared with pain and then eased, and he let out a sigh before drinking for a solid minute. He rose, searching for a suitable container to bring the water back to Alice, but there was nothing.

A gunshot rang out in the distance.

Then another. Then three more in quick succession.

Quinn ran back the way he'd come as the gunfire increased to a steady riot. He slid beneath the balsams and found Alice already gaining her feet with Ty's help.

"What the hell?" she asked, limping forward.

"Sounds like things are imploding back there."

"Let's go then," Alice said.

"My thoughts exactly."

"Here, this is the only other magazine I have," she said, pulling a thirty-round clip for the AR-15 from her pants pocket. Quinn loaded the weapon and slung it around his shoulders before helping Alice to her feet.

They made their way through the woods, Ty holding Alice's hand, Alice leaning on Quinn each time she took a step with her injured leg. They stopped at the stream and she drank, sucking the water down in long slurps while the gunfire tapered off, fading thunder in the distance. It slowed, a series of fast pops and then quiet.

One last shot echoed to them.

Alice paused from drinking and looked at Quinn before filling her mouth once more.

"This will probably make us sick, but we don't have a choice right now," she said, rising to her feet. "We don't know when we'll find water again." Quinn nodded and helped Ty cup the stream in his hands to drink.

"How far is the compound from the highway?" Quinn asked when Ty had finished.

"Far. I would say at least seven miles."

"Do you know which direction we should head to find it again?"

Alice hobbled in a circle, looking at the trees and the rise of the hill behind them.

"I think it would be that way, but I can't say for sure," she said, pointing to the south. "Since you had to drag my ass all the way up that hill last night, I'm a little disoriented believe it or not."

"He didn't drag you, mom, he carried you," Ty said.

Alice blinked and her mouth tightened into a line.

"Thank you," she said.

"It's the least I could do." She was looking at him the same way she had before, like she was taking him apart piece by piece and examining what she found. He ignored the impulse to look away and met her gaze. Held it.

"What are you guys doing?" Ty asked.

The moment broke and Alice glanced at her son.

"Figuring out where we're going."

Quinn cleared his throat. "Let's head south. I'm sure we'll run into something sooner or later."

They set off without any more discussion. The woods thickened as they traveled, the trees growing taller, their tops seeming to skim the clouds that continued to coast by. Patches of blue sky between branches, the wind in their ears, their progress slow but methodical as they leaned on one another, helped each other over obstacles. There were times when Alice would grasp his hand in her own, her fingers tightening as she hobbled beside him, and he resisted glancing at her to see if she was looking at him.

At mid-day they stopped in a glade hemmed in by towering white pine. Hunger was a hot fist in Quinn's stomach, and he surveyed the surrounding woods.

"I'm going to try to get us something to eat," he said, readjusting the rifle.

"Like what?" Ty asked.

"Probably a squirrel or something."

Ty made a disgusted face. "A squirrel? No, we can't eat a squirrel."

"Why not?"

"Because they're soft."

"They are if you cook them right," Alice said from where she sat on the ground. Ty turned his head in her direction, his mouth open. Quinn barked laughter and set off for the nearest stretch of trees.

The air was cooler beneath the wide branches of the pines, his footsteps muted on fallen needles. He watched overhead for the telltale shadow of a squirrel or chipmunk, but the limbs were devoid of any life. Even the birds were quiet here. He continued on, pushing through a stand of poplar and down a short valley that ended in a rocky stream flowing slowly, its middle only a foot deep. He was about to cross it and continue on to the other side where a promising copse of pines waited, when three long shadows floating idly in the stream caught his attention. The fish swam against the light current, their dark bodies curving lazily to keep even with its pace. Quinn edged closer to the stream, careful not to let his shadow fall upon the water. He aimed through the sights, centering on the middle and largest fish of the group, and pulled the trigger.

The rifle boomed and water flashed in the air, droplets catching the sun.

Quinn pulled the gun away from his cheek and watched as two darting shadows flew away down the stream, vanishing in an instant. Silt churned up from the bottom and clouded the water as he watched.

The white belly of a fish bobbed to the surface.

"Yes!" Quinn said, scrambling down the bank. He stepped into the water and grasped the trout, pulling it from the stream. It was over a foot long, its body a deep green, speckled with dark spots. Its gills worked feebly, opening and closing several times before stilling. When he turned its slippery length over, he could find no wound where the bullet had entered its body. The concussion of the shot had killed it. Quinn smiled, raising his eyes to the far bank.

A wolf watched him from its edge.

He froze, taking in the stark outline of its tall ears, the long snout, watchful eyes. Its coat was black with tan splotches on its chest and flanks. Its mouth opened, its tongue appearing to swipe at its chops. His fingers flexed on the rifle, and he took a step back out of the stream.

The wolf spun and bolted away, gone before he could fully register that it hadn't been a wolf at all. It had been a dog. A huge dog with a winking collar at its neck.

He jogged all the way back to the glade, a branch scratching his cheek as he went, but he didn't slow down until he was beside the small pile of branches and leaves Ty and Alice had built in preparation for a fire.

"There's gotta be a house nearby," he said, breathing hard.

"What? Where did you get a fish?" Alice said, pointing at his hand.

"Huh?" Quinn looked down at the trout, having forgotten it with the appearance of the dog. "Oh, there's a stream not too far. I shot it."

"You shot it?" Alice said, raising her eyebrows.

"Yeah. Anyways, when I looked up at the other side of the stream, there was a dog standing there with a collar on."

"A dog?" Ty asked, gaining his feet.

"Yeah, a big one. German Shepherd I think."

"Cool," Ty said.

"Where there's a dog, there's got to be a house. Can't be too far away," Quinn said.

"You're probably right," Alice said, setting the tinder aflame with her lighter. "But can we cook that fish before we leave, or are we having sushi?"

~

The trout was delicious. They cooked it on a flat rock beside the small fire, and even without any spices, the meat was rich and flavorful. When they had eaten their fill,

Alice wrapped the small remainder in a large, dry leaf and tucked it away in one of her pockets. They didn't speak, each content with having a full stomach, and Ty leaned against his mother and fell asleep in the sunshine that drenched the glade. After a time, Quinn glanced at Alice and drew a line in the dirt with one finger.

"I didn't get a chance to ask how you two found me at the compound," he said.

"It wasn't that hard."

"But I went to Foster's first and then came this way."

"I know. We went back to the house where we left you, and when you weren't there, I figured that would be the next place you'd go. The directions were in the center console. So we went there and saw you'd been there, or somebody had. I was sure it was you, so we took the most obvious route west. The bridge you crossed was the only one for twenty miles. We got there as they were hauling you and your truck away, so we went farther north and found a place to cross before coming back down to The First Church of Eternal Salvation." She said the cult's name in a sarcastic voice and made quotation marks in the air. "Bastards even had the name plastered on the side of the van they put you in. After that we waited until dark and idled along in low gear next to their stupid fence until I could see that crucifix over the top and stopped there. It wasn't long until they brought you out."

"That's amazing."

"No, what's amazing is Ty wouldn't shut up about going back to find you. Just so you know, that's the only reason I decided to come back."

"I never meant to endanger him at that house. I had no idea the woman wasn't immune."

"I know. But you trusted someone." She readjusted Ty where he leaned against her and glanced over at him. "Just don't do it ever again, okay?"

"Okay."

They woke Ty a short time later and set off again. After crossing the stream, Quinn managed to find the dog's footprints in a stretch of mud leading into denser forest. Without a machete, there was no possible way for them to move through its tangle, especially with Alice's wound that had begun to weep blood again. She waved off his offer to carry her when he mentioned it.

"I'm a little old for piggyback, and you're not carrying me like a sack of potatoes," she said, muscling past him with a limp. Instead, they circumvented the thicket, traveling east along its edge. Quinn kept shifting his gaze to the underbrush, sure that every so often he spotted a dark patch of fur or the flash of a collar out of the corner of his eye.

The day passed into afternoon and then into evening. Shadows slanted from the trees and grew long, covering twice their physical forms. The constant breeze died and with it came the renewed smells of woodland in spring: the heady scent of blooming flowers, pine sap running, the whiff of decomposing leaves.

The air grew heavy as night crept closer, and in the distance, it sounded as if a huge rockslide had given way.

"Storm's coming," Alice said. "That's gonna suck."

"I'll try to figure something out," Quinn replied.

"Yeah, if you can magic us a four-star bed and breakfast, that would be great. Oh, and a bottle of that nice vodka we had at your house."

"I'll see what I can do," Quinn said, smiling. He was about to suggest stopping beneath the bows of a tall balsam nearby when he caught the shine of something through the trees straight ahead.

"Wait here," he said, raising the AR-15 to his shoulder. He moved away, keeping low to the ground, ignoring Alice's whispered questions. He crept from tree to tree, taking cover behind each one and waiting a beat before crossing another open distance. When he had no more trees to hide behind, he eased out, bringing the rifle up at the same time.

A rusted Studebaker sat in the middle of a cleared area, the last rays of sun reflecting off a tarnished, chrome mirror. Yellowed grass reached up past its corroded fenders. Flecks of baby-blue paint shone amidst the cancerous steel. Its headlights were empty holes staring straight ahead, but when he approached its side, he saw that all of its glass was intact.

Quinn looked around the clearing, barely wide enough to house the car itself, and spotted an overgrown path stretching away into the darkening forest. A peal of thunder, this one closer, echoed in the sky. He tried the rear driver's door handle, and it opened with a shriek of protest. A musty plume of air wafted past him. The ancient upholstery cracked and split when he placed his hand on it and pressed down. Other than a gathering of dried moss on the floorboards, the interior was devoid of moisture.

When he returned to where Alice and Ty waited, the half-smile on his face silenced Alice's questions.

"I think we found our campsite," he said.

They ate the remainder of the fish inside the car as the first raindrops fell against the windshield. The woods around them settled beneath a blanket of darkness, and the sky became a mass of folded clouds.

"How far do you think we walked today?" Quinn asked, as the rain began to drum harder against the roof. Alice reclined in the passenger seat and propped her injured leg on the dash.

"My leg says three hundred miles, but I'm guessing it was closer to ten."

"That's what I was thinking."

Ty began to sing lilting tones that drifted up to them from the backseat where he'd lain down. Something folksy and sad.

"What song is that?" he asked as the storm increased and lightning splintered the darkness.

"The Biplane, Evermore."

"It sounds familiar."

"The Irish Rovers sang it. My dad loved them."

"Was he Irish?"

"Half, and half English. He said that was why he could never make a decision." The beginnings of a smile fell from her face, and she turned her head toward the window. The rain came down harder, turning the interior of the old car into a pounding cacophony.

"What happened to him?" Quinn said. He held his breath, sure that she wouldn't answer. She kept her face turned away from him, and after a long time, he knew she'd fallen asleep. He glanced into the backseat and saw Ty had laced his hands together over his chest and was breathing slow and deep. He looked like a miniature old man taking a nap. Quinn gave Alice a final look, her outline a darker shadow against the window, and readjusted the rifle beside him, settling in for the night. He was at the boundaries of sleep when Alice spoke, her voice barely carrying to him over the rain.

"He was in the Navy for fourteen years. That's why I know how to handle guns and probably why I curse so much. He had quite a few guns of his own and brought me out shooting when I was little. He was the kind of guy that never gave an inch when he thought he was right, and my mom was the same way. It made for some hard days, but they loved each other.

"One night when I was twelve, our furnace failed. Earlier that fall my dad had had it inspected, and the guy who signed off on it was a drunk. Turns out he had been drinking that morning and hadn't checked the emergency shutoff valve. A fire started in our basement, and it had eaten through the floor by the time my dad woke up."

Alice breathed deeply, steadying herself. Lightning stuttered and lit the inside of the car, turning the tears on her face into jewels.

"Part of the wall in my room collapsed when the floor started to drop into the basement. It fell on my bed and pinned me there. I remember the flames, how they moved like they were alive, like they were looking for me. Then my dad came through the smoke and shoved the wall away and I was free. I don't remember him carrying me outside. The next thing I knew my mom was holding me near the street and it was snowing and our whole house was engulfed. There were sirens and lights from the fire trucks turning the flakes red and blue. By the time they got there, all they could do was keep it contained to our yard."

She turned to him, shaking in the darkness, the rain a steady roar around them like a liquid inferno.

"He went back in. He went back in for my little sister, and neither one of them came out." She wiped at her face and sniffled, reminding him so much of Ty the night before, crying over his lost stick. "My mom didn't have early onset dementia. She had a total break with reality the night we lost them. She never recognized me again after that."

"God," Quinn whispered. "I'm so sorry."

"That's why I locked up when the fire started the other night. I can't stand it. Whenever there's one near me, I feel like I'm being watched. Like it got a taste of me that night and it won't give up until it's gotten the rest."

He searched for something to say, but there was nothing. Sometimes words were the most insubstantial things in the world. Instead, he reached out and found her arm in the dark. She jerked at his touch, but he let his fingers glide down to her wrist, over the dainty bones there, and then slide into her hand. She hesitated for a second and then gripped his palm in her own.

They sat that way for a long time. The endless rain fell around them, their breath beginning to fog the side windows. He could've remained there forever. Slowly, she released his hand and finished wiping the last of her tears away.

"I've never told anyone that," she said. "I don't know why I just told you."

"I'm glad you did."

"Why?"

"Because no one should have to carry everything alone."

Lightning flickered, and he saw the frown knitting her eyebrows together, her gaze locked on him.

"I don't get you," she said finally.

"What do you mean?"

"Nothing. Never mind." She turned in her seat, wincing as she moved her leg, and checked on Ty. "I'm so glad he can sleep. It would be so much harder if he couldn't." She settled back into her seat, trying to get comfortable.

He was about to reply when lightning blazed across the sky in a white lance, and Alice gasped, pointing out the windshield.

The dog stood watching the car from the edge of the woods.

Quinn jerked in his seat, ripping the rifle up from where it rested beside him. The last flutterings of light shone in the dog's eyes and then darkness coated the windows black.

"Holy shit," Alice said, wiping away the condensation from her window. "What the fuck is it doing?"

Quinn leaned forward, trying to see the place where the dog stood, but the night was impenetrable.

"I don't know. It looked like—"

His words slid away as lightning flared again, outlining every branch, tree, and bush.

The dog was gone.

Chapter 21

Sanctuary and Flight

In the morning they left the sunken Studebaker behind to continue rusting in its hidden place.

The overgrown trail the abandoned car sat in led them southwest, its line curving and dipping into a shallow swamp before rising again to a high stand of oaks, all green tipped and still dripping from the storm the night before. The sun rose with the same ferocity as the storm, and the day heated like an oven coming to temperature. Alice tried to walk on her own, and managed to for a while, her hand loosely holding Ty's, but near mid-day she leaned on the trunk of a tree and shook her head.

"I've gotta rest. Can't go any more right now."

"It's okay. You two take a breather, and I'll scout ahead."

"Don't get kidnapped by a cult, huh?" Alice said as he moved away. "Not sure I can come save your ass this time."

Quinn gave her a smile and walked over a slight rise that dropped into a gully. He waded through piles of fallen leaves a foot deep and climbed the other side, muscling up a short ridge before stopping. He took two steps and walked onto a hiking trail.

He stood there gazing down its length that stretched in either direction for what seemed like miles. Straight ahead the trail became a T, and across the path was a faded wooden sign, its carved letters highlighted in yellow paint.

Crowfoot County Park
Sheep's Hoof Trail Head 3.9 mi ~>
<~ Grand Falls Recreation Center 1.1 mi

Quinn stared at the sign and then closed his eyes. Only another mile and they'd be at some kind of civilization. Food, water, transportation. He turned back, marking the way with each step. As he moved, he took in the tranquility of the forest, the easy movement of the trees growing their leaves for the summer soon to come. The world had ended, humankind as a whole losing their footing on the side of the mountain of life, but here, here everything was the same as it had been for centuries. Untouched, untainted, serenity.

He was so lost in thought as he neared the place where he'd left Alice and Ty, he almost missed the sensation growing on his left side. A pressure of presence. He slowed and listened before swinging the rifle up and kneeling to steady himself for a cleaner shot.

The dog sat on its haunches fifty yards away. Its ears were erect, eyes focused on him, unmoving. It watched him for a span and then turned its head as Ty's high-pitched laughter rang out through the trees. The dog gave him another look and then rose and darted away through the underbrush and was gone.

"Wait," Quinn called out as he stood, but the Shepherd had vanished.

When he made it back to where Alice and Ty rested, Alice had her eyes closed and was seated at the base of a tree, her head tipped back. Ty turned in Quinn's direction at the sound of his footsteps.

"Quinn?"

"Yeah, buddy, just me."

"I thought I heard something else a few minutes ago."

"You probably did. Our canine friend was nearby."

"The puppy?"

"He's more of a grown-up dog, but yeah, he was here."

"What was it doing?" Alice asked, not opening her eyes.

"It looked like he was watching you guys."

She cracked an eyelid. "Cujo?"

"I don't think so. He was just sitting there, really calm."

"Did he have one of those little whisky barrels around his neck?"

Quinn laughed. "No, I didn't see one."

"Damn."

"I found a hiking trail not too far ahead, and there's a recreation area that might have a building or two we can stay in for the night and regroup."

"Wonderful. Give me two seconds."

"Mom's not feeling good," Ty said, placing a hand on his mother's shoulder.

"I'm fine, Tyrus. Give me some room to get up," Alice said, sitting forward. Quinn moved closer and knelt near her feet.

"Let me take a look at that leg."

"Kinda forward, aren't you?" Alice said, but sat back and drew up her pant leg.

The wound was puckered with blackened blood near its center, but the skin around it was a violent red and swollen. Quinn grimaced.

"I know. Let's get to the rec center," Alice said, her eyes meeting his.

She leaned on him once she was able to get to her feet, the going slow and arduous. When they made it to the trail, he glanced at her face, a mask of concentration and sweat, her pupils huge.

"I'm fine; I can make it," she breathed, and gripped his arm harder.

They set off down the hiking trail, its grade mercifully level. The sun slanted between the trees pouring golden light across the shoots of grass growing green along the sides of the path. After a half hour, the woods began to thin, and they caught glimpses of the side of a structure, its color blending with the browns and grays of the forest. The trail led to a paved turnaround and an empty parking lot, a solitary potato chip bag drifting across its expanse. The park headquarter building was two stories with bright white trim around its windows, some of which were broken. Signs directing hikers and campers alike were posted across its front and stood on posts outside the entrance. A red mountain bike leaned against the side of the building.

The whole place had a haunted look.

Quinn tried the door and it opened easily. There was a service counter straight ahead adorned with stuffed animals, t-shirts, and sweatshirts all emblazoned with the

Crowfoot County Park logo. A worn pool table rested before men's and women's bathrooms. Beside them was a set of stairs leading up to the second story. Glass littered the floor beneath two broken windows, dried blood on the edges still hanging in the frame.

He did a quick sweep of the second floor, which housed mostly boxes of dusty papers and survey maps. A sprawling desk sat before a door to the left, and when he opened it, the smell of decay hit him like a slap.

A man's body was in the middle of a small office. A shotgun lay beside him, along with most of his skull. Quinn shut the door and returned downstairs.

"It's clear," he said, coming even with an overstuffed chair that Alice sat in, Ty cuddled in her lap. Their darkened reflections looked back at them from the blank TV screen on the wall.

"Good. I'm shot," Alice said, cracking one eye open to see his reaction. He shook his head.

"Not your best work."

"Tough crowd."

"There's a..." Quinn drew his thumb across his throat and motioned to the floor over his head. "So I think we should stay down here tonight."

"Do we have power?" Alice asked.

He moved to the wall and flipped a few switches. Nothing happened.

"Back to the dark ages," he said.

"Isn't that the truth."

Quinn strode to the front desk and pulled a map from a display case, spreading it out on a nearby table. He traced a snaking line that ran from the lodge they stood in to a black dot marked 'Ferry'. He checked the drawers behind the counter, his attention on the silent vending machine in the corner of the room. After a moment, he found a stubby key in the furthest right drawer.

"There's a town only six miles from here," he said, crossing the room.

"Yeah. I don't think I could go another step there, champ," Alice said.

"Don't worry, mom; Quinn'll carry you," Ty said, patting her hair.

"Oh he will, huh?" Alice said.

"Yep. He's like superman. 'Member he carried you all the way up that hill?"

Quinn couldn't help the smile that spread across his face as he unlocked the vending machine and pulled out three bags of chips and three warm cans of soda. He brought the food to them, opening Ty's for him before settling himself on the corner of a cold fireplace.

"I'm going as soon as I'm done eating," Quinn said, chewing a handful of chips. They exploded with flavor in his mouth, and he couldn't remember something tasting so good in his life.

"What? No. You're staying here. It'll be dark in a few hours. We have to secure this place for the night," Alice said, her eyes open wide now, more alert than she'd been all day.

"I have to go. You know it," Quinn said, pointing to her injured leg while Ty munched on his chips and turned his head whenever one of them spoke.

"Quinn—"

"I'll be back before dark, no problem. And I'll leave you the rifle."

She sighed and sipped at her pop. "Never met someone so stubborn."

"Can I come with you, Quinn?" Ty asked.

"No," they both said in unison. Alice blinked and suppressed a smile. Ty frowned and continued to eat, his face toward his lap.

Quinn finished his chips and slugged the last of his soda down before setting the rifle beside Alice's chair. She unbuckled the holster holding her revolver and handed it to him.

"There's only six in that, make each one count."

"Yes, ma'am."

He was almost to the door when Ty yelled for him and came hurrying as fast as he could across the room, one hand held before him, the other out to the side. Quinn knelt and grasped his arm when he was close enough to touch.

"Don't go," Ty said, his lower lip trembling.

"I have to, buddy. It's important."

"But what if you don't come back?"

"I'll come back. You don't need to worry about that. You stay here and keep your mom safe, okay?"

The boy nodded and then leaned in closer to him, his voice dropping to a whisper.

"I wasn't asleep last night when you guys were talking."

"You weren't?" Quinn whispered back.

"No. Mom didn't tell the truth."

"About what?"

"About me talking about you after we left you. I asked why you weren't coming with us, and she told me to be quiet, so I did. I wanted to go back, but she decided to come find you." Ty turned his head toward his mother, but she seemed to be dozing again, her hand resting lightly on the rifle.

Quinn squinted at the boy and then squeezed his hand.

"I'm really glad you guys came back."

"Me too."

"Okay, go sit with your mom. If you hear anything after I leave, you wake her up, all right?"

"All right."

"See you soon, little man."

Quinn moved through the door and locked it behind him. He eyed the mountain bike leaning against the wall. It was quiet, but not fast enough to outrun anything other than a man. He walked around the side of the building, re-adjusting Alice's holster on his hip, and spotted a maintenance shed set back close to the encroaching woods. The door was unlocked, and when he stepped inside, the smell of cool concrete and gasoline assaulted him. A shape sat in the dark near the rear of the shed, and he threw the doors wider, illuminating the Honda side-by-side ATV. A key jutted from the ignition. He climbed inside the machine and turned the key, ready to return to the mountain bike, but the engine responded with an enthusiastic growl that became a hum. In a matter of minutes, he had backed out of the shed and was howling down the paved road leading away from the recreation center.

The wind coursed past him, flowing through his hair. Sunlight slipped between trees filling his sight with its honey glow. The road flew past, and he pressed the pedal down, increasing his speed. The aches and pains of the prior day's injuries retreated with the exhilaration of driving the ATV. Driveways scrolled by, mailboxes, an empty car. The road was his, and he had a clear purpose, people depending on him. The miles fled behind him, and he watched the wood lines, searching for pale skin or swaying movement.

The town of Ferry boasted a population of fifteen thousand people according to its welcome sign. To the south a great field of rotting cornstalks waved in the wind, and the north held a giant building with a sign proclaiming *Ferry Poultry Inc.* that gave off such a tremendous odor of death Quinn gagged as he passed by. The rest of Ferry, Ohio, was a conglomeration of meek, single-story businesses and homes set into the side of a sweeping hill that hadn't gained the full shade of green it would become as summer grew stronger.

Quinn slowed the ATV and stopped at the mouth of the main street running into and out of town. He waited, watching the side alleys as well as windows and roofs.

Nothing moved.

He idled forward, throwing a look back over his shoulder.

The road was empty, the sun a hand's width from the horizon.

He unfolded the map he'd brought from the lodge and studied the expanded view of Ferry. The business district consisted of four streets that intersected in a hashtag pattern. The business names weren't listed anywhere on the map. He refolded the pages and placed it in the glove compartment before urging the Honda forward.

The buildings closed in around him and seemed to grow taller, their blank windows dead eyes, the broken ones busted teeth. Water ran in a steady stream from beneath the door of a beauty parlor, flooding the sidewalk outside and a portion of the street. A woman wearing a bright yellow dress was sprawled near the front of a hardware store, her skin purplish, hair matted and tangled, obscuring her features. One of her shoes was missing.

Quinn scanned the business signs, his heart leaping when he saw the word *GUNS* in massive bold print above one storefront. He pulled the Honda to the side of the road, reluctantly shutting the engine off.

The wind was his only company on the street.

He ducked inside the store, handgun drawn.

The shelves were immaculately clean. There wasn't a single weapon left. In the rear of the store he found a solitary magazine that would fit the AR-15 along with a spilled half box of matching shells. He gathered these up, pouring them back into the container before leaving the store behind.

On the following street, two burnt husks that had once been pickups were locked together by their crushed front ends. The drivers had either escaped or been ravaged by the flames so violently that they were no longer visible. Quinn skirted the wreck and pulled to the curb beneath a flapping awning, its garish purple and orange colors bright amidst the drab surroundings. He drew the pistol again and eased inside the drug store.

An old brass bell chimed over the door as he entered, the air within the store thick with the scent of decaying food. A long, glass counter spanned the left side of the building, shining malt dispensers and candy cases lining the wall behind it. A pair of bare and graying feet protruded from an aisle on the opposite side. The rear of the store was devoted to the pharmacy, and Quinn hurried down the aisle to its white counter.

Rows and rows of shelves holding containers of pills and fluids took up the wide space. A dead computer sat atop a desk and several hundred bright green capsules were scattered on the floor. Quinn stepped on them with a popping sound and began to search the desk's drawers. He found what he was looking for, not in the desk but hanging from a thin chain attached to one of the shelf ends.

He thumbed through the pharmacy desk reference, its dog-eared pages dry and loud as he turned them. When he reached the section on antibiotics, there were dozens of choices listed. He scanned them, glancing toward the street every few minutes. The names began to blend together, their uses obscure within the subtext of medical language. He concentrated, reading each section thoroughly before moving on. When he saw the words, 'broad-spectrum', he drew a line across the page to the corresponding dosage and drug name.

"Ertapenem." He said the word, its pronunciation like chewing a bite of food too large. "Why the hell can't they name drugs something normal?" Quinn said under his breath before beginning to scan the shelves.

He found the vial of antibiotic on the bottom of the second shelf. After checking the contents, he grabbed three more bottles, tucking them into a cloth bag he spotted in the corner of the room. On the opposite side of the pharmacy, he found antiseptic, plastic-wrapped syringes, a ream of gauze, as well as a tube of burn cream. He squeezed out some of the paste onto a finger and spread it on his face, sighing with the relief it brought.

Pacing back to the desk, he spotted another row of vials secured within a glass case. When he leaned in closer, he saw they were all opiates, Morphine being the most prominent. He considered taking a few of them but decided against it. He'd been here long enough.

Grabbing a large first aid kit on the way out of the store along with two handfuls of candy bars, he paused, skirting between the aisles to an alcove holding wheelchairs, crutches, and wall full of elastic braces. There was only one of the items he sought, leaning against a row of oxygen tanks. After grabbing it, he hurried toward the door, tucking the white cane beneath his arm, and eased out into the fresh air.

A herd of stilts stood in the center of the nearest intersection.

Quinn froze, his muscles locking against joints.

There were at least thirty of them, the tallest looming above the rest so high he had trouble fathoming how tall it really was. Its head surpassed the second story of the nearest building by at least five feet, its frame so thin and rickety, it swayed with the wind.

The stilts barked and grunted at one another.

Quinn edged backward.

Three feet from the building.

His foot crunched broken glass.

The closest of them began to turn, and he bolted to the door, sliding inside and letting it close, the short jangle of the bell overhead making him wince. His heart banged in his ears covering any sounds from outside. He crouched near the door, peering through the front windows that lined the street.

A spindly leg and torso stepped into view.

Quinn slunk down, hand scrabbling for the lock on the front door, but there was none. It locked from outside. He cradled the bag and cane and crawled forward, skirting a display for shampoo as the door rattled behind him.

He didn't look back, only moved, ignoring the rustic tinkle of the bell above the door.

It was going to see him.

Quinn slid around the end of the aisle and waited, sweat trickling down his nose, down his spine. Something scraped near the front of the store. The deep croaking filled the space, then silence. He chanced a look around the shelving.

The stilt stood near the door, its long head brushing the ceiling. Its hands clenched and released over and over as it sniffed the air. Smelling. Seeking.

It moved into the aisles, feet rasping on the tile floor. Quinn lunged forward, crawling as quietly as he could to the pharmacy. Then he was through the open door, past the pick-up window, shoulder blades against the desk, breath racing in and out of his lungs. Without waiting, he sidled into the first aisle and made it to the back of the store.

There was no rear exit.

He spun in place, looking for a window, another doorway, anything.

Something tipped over in the front of the store with a crash. He used the cover of the sound to move back along the rows of drugs before setting the bag and cane down. He glanced over the top of the pick-up counter.

The stilt was closer, its long arms sweeping products from shelves as it moved toward the pharmacy. It hissed and pawed at the corpse on the floor before leaning in to feed.

Quinn ducked down, mind racing. He drew out the revolver and stared at it. There was an entire herd outside the door. They would hear a shot. He would be trapped inside as they poured in and eventually tore him apart.

Something shattered, closer this time.

His eyes roamed the space around him. Drugs, shelves, office chairs, the door (mostly glass), a rock painted a multitude of colors on the floor.

He stared at the rock.

It was a doorstop for the pharmacy entrance. It was semi-round and roughly the size of a softball. A sloppy, yellow smiley face was painted in its center.

He snaked a hand out and pulled it to him, waiting for the creature to roar. There was a tinkling of glass and then a loud sneeze. He worked himself beneath the pick-up counter and drew his feet in as footsteps came closer and stopped outside the pharmacy door.

Long seconds ticked by.

The stilt grunted and stepped inside.

He had two rapid heartbeats to decide if he would move or not.

He moved.

Quinn eased out from beneath the counter as the stilt took another step down the closest aisle. He wound back his arm and threw the rock as hard as he could at the back of its head.

The rock flew through the air and connected with the stilt's skull, the pale, hairless skin there splitting open in a spatter of blood.

It fell forward, trying to grab onto a shelf as it plummeted, but its hand met only empty air. It flattened on the pharmacy floor, arms above its head, blood dribbling down its neck.

Quinn stepped forward, putting the revolver against the slight nub of its ear, but it didn't stir. Chuffing breaths came out of its nose, and its long fingers twitched.

He turned and picked up the cloth bag along with the cane. Halfway to the front door he slowed, then stopped, staring out of the drug store's window.

Another stilt was making its way toward the store, its eyes twitching in their sockets as it left the bulk of the herd and moved with long steps in his direction.

"Fuck," he swore, his voice a hoarse whisper. He ran back the way he'd come and stepped into the pharmacy to see the prone stilt's eyes beginning to open.

The rock. Where was the rock?

There was a scratching at the front door. The bell tinkled.

The creature before him made a guttural sound in its throat.

His eyes scanned the space around him, seconds ticking down.

Quinn set the bag down and grabbed the biggest syringe he could find off of the counter. Tearing the wrapper off, he knelt before the glass case holding the opiates. His hands shook as he pulled the door open and snatched a vial of morphine from within. Quinn shoved the tip of the syringe into the rubber stopper and drew back the plunger as he crab-walked to the waking stilt's side.

He jammed the syringe into the monster's back between its shoulder blades and depressed all of the morphine in one movement.

It stiffened and issued a short grunt. Quinn peeked over the pick-up counter and saw the other stilt standing in the doorway, its head swinging from side to side. The creature before him struggled to get its wide hands beneath its shoulders, but its movements were becoming sluggish. It bared its teeth and found him with its eyes.

They were blue, like Alice's, like Ty's.

Its eyelids fluttered, and it gasped for breath, legs sliding along the floor in slow semicircles. He chanced another look over the counter and saw the stilt by the door tilt its head, but its attention was turned to the large group outside that croaked as one, their voices intermingling in a base discord.

The stilt on the floor shuddered, its muscles slackening.

The bell chimed, and the front door closed.

Quinn slumped, sliding down and lying flat. He couldn't stay here. He had to move. But at that moment, nothing was more right than the chilly tile against his back and his sweat cooling on his skin. When his breathing had returned to normal, he went to the front of the store and looked out.

The street was empty. The intersection where the herd had been was completely vacant.

The sun had dropped below the hill Ferry was built into. The afternoon shade lengthened with each minute. He gazed out at the Honda and then at the street that would take him back toward the recreation area and the lodge where Alice and Ty were waiting.

Time ticked by.

He checked the street every other minute, the bag and Ty's new cane clutched at his side. He should go now. There hadn't been any sign of them in at least twenty minutes. They'd moved on. But God, there'd been so many of them. Why were there so many? And why were they moving together?

Quinn unwrapped a candy bar and chewed.

The wind blew ribbons of sand down the open street.

He tossed the wrapper away and stood. The light had weakened. In an hour it would be full dusk.

Quinn re-gripped the bag and cane, keeping the revolver in the opposite hand as he pushed through the door slow enough not to ring the bell. The street was silent, so quiet he could hear the speckling of grit as the wind coasted across the concrete.

The Honda waited for him ten steps away.

He hesitated beneath the colorful awning. His body trembled. Fresh sweat sprung out from every pore.

Quinn launched himself forward, dropping the bag and cane into the rear hauling-bed of the ATV. He jumped into the seat and turned the key. The engine fired. He slammed the vehicle into gear and swung a U-turn in the street, sure that any second a stilt would fall upon him, reach between the protective roll-cage and rip him from the Honda. He would feel its teeth gouging into his skin, sinking through muscle and sinew before it bit through bone.

He swerved around the burnt, black pickups and hammered the gas again, glancing over his shoulder.

Nothing.

No pursuit from any direction.

The town slid past him as he gained speed.

Thirty miles per hour.

Thirty-five.

Forty.

He looked back again as he left Ferry behind, the buildings falling away as he pushed harder on the throttle. He'd made it. They'd moved on. He faced forward, a sigh of relief escaping him.

The tallest stilt stood up from the side of the road where it had been waiting and swiped a giant hand at the ATV.

Quinn cranked the wheel, the Honda listing to the right as the stilt's hand swept the roll cage, pushing the vehicle all the way over. He clung to the frame, the impact jarring his teeth in their sockets, trying to feed him to the passing pavement. Sparks flew in dazzling showers as the ATV slid off the side of the highway and spun to a stop in the gravel.

Dust was everywhere, in his eyes, his mouth, his nose. His ears rang from the screeching metal, but above it he could hear the stilt's croak, deeper and more powerful than any he'd heard before. Quinn struggled out of the capsized Honda, his vision blurred by dirt. The stilt was fifty yards away, coming fast. Its arms swung, slender legs pumping, mouth open, teeth waiting.

The gun. Where was the gun?

He scrambled around the ATV. The bag and cane were near the side of the road. The stilt stepped over them and began to run. It moved with a frightening grace, a long marionette in motion. Quinn saw the glint of steel thirty feet from the bag in the center of the highway. He waited until the stilt was upon him, its smell overwhelming.

He dove to the side, ducking beneath a reaching hand the size of a car tire. One of its ragged fingernails dug a furrow in the skin of his back, tearing his shirt partially away. He cried out and rolled to his feet, running as soon as he gained his balance. The stilt roared, and a whoosh of air passed the back of his head. His legs threatened to drop him as he pelted up the rise and tripped onto the blacktop, the revolver lying in the last rays of sun, its grip extended toward him.

He stretched, fingertips snagging the trigger guard.

Long fingers encircled his ankle and yanked him back the way he'd come. The road scratched his shoulders, and he spun the handgun around, his finger finding the trigger.

Quinn sat up and fired.

The revolver boomed, bucking like an animal in his hand. The stilt made a wheezing sound and placed a white palm over a dark hole in its chest. Its eyes bulged, too human and filled with pain. It hacked and a globule of blood spurted from its open jaws. It tried to breathe in, but a sound like a child sucking the last of a milkshake from the bottom of a glass filled the air. It released the iron grip on his ankle and took two great steps back.

It teetered on its feet for a long second and then fell like a giant tree.

The stilt crashed to the ground, landing on a jagged rock, the sound of breaking bones clear in the still evening. Its hand fell away from the hole in its chest and blood flowed from the wound, dropping to the ground like dark rain.

Quinn stared at it, watching for any movement, even a twitch of dead muscle fibers, but there was nothing. Only then did he realize he was still aiming the revolver at its flat form.

A croak came from the direction of town.

Then another.

And another.

Soon the air was alive with the other stilt's calls. Quinn pushed himself to his feet and staggered toward the overturned Honda as the first creature strode into view from behind the poultry farm.

It charged.

He sprinted toward the bag and cane, snatching them up from the highway before pelting down to the ATV. More stilts were emerging from the streets of Ferry, their height dwarfed by the distance between them. He slid to a stop beside the Honda and dropped the bag before stooping to grip the top of the roll bar. He heaved with everything he had, muscles shaking and a groan coming from his chest.

The ATV rose and then tipped to settle on its wheels.

Quinn tossed the bag and cane into the back and swung into the driver's seat. The stilt coming from the poultry farm had almost reached the edge of the property and the fence beyond. He hit the key, the engine sputtering once before grinding to life. He slammed the vehicle into drive and shot forward as the stilt leapt over the fence and climbed to the highway, its baritone cry overshadowing the howl of the motor.

He guided the Honda onto the highway and pressed the pedal to the floor. The engine whined for a moment and then hummed evenly, its speed increasing without a hitch. Quinn glanced back and saw the herd galloping behind him down the highway, all swinging, pale limbs and gnashing teeth. The Honda carried him up a short rise and then around a bend, the stilts disappearing from view.

He let himself sag in the seat, all his strength gone, washed away by the torrent of adrenaline that now receded. After another two miles, the sign for the Crowfoot County Recreation Building appeared, and he flipped on the headlights as he turned up the road and sped on.

Chapter 22

The Plague

Quinn withdrew the needle from the muscle of Alice's calf. "There. Now we'll just have to watch it to make sure it takes care of the infection," he said, rising to put the bottle of antibiotic away. Alice watched him, her face dappled by shadow and light from the fire that burned low in the hearth.

After arriving at the rec center, he'd waited in the middle of the drive, running a ball of string through pop cans he'd found in a large recycling bin behind the building. When he had enough made up to stretch across the open approach, he strung the trip wire between two trees, its center hanging six inches from the ground. All the other routes leading to the lodge were blocked by heavy brush and trees. If something came for them in the night, they'd hear it.

When he'd turned to go inside after one last walk around the building, the German Shepherd was sitting in the mouth of the hiking trail, no more than a mound of shadow amidst the growing night. He'd called to it, but the moment his voice rang out, it sprung away, vanishing in the undergrowth.

"That was really stupid of you to go," Alice said, readjusting herself in the chair as she sorted through the first aid kit he'd brought back. "You'll probably turn into one of those things now since you got scratched."

"Yeah, maybe my looks will improve," Quinn said, setting aside the cloth bag. He glanced at her until she finally dropped her gaze.

"I'm sorry. I appreciate it, but you didn't need to go."

"Really? Would you rather I chop your leg off at the knee three days from now with a hatchet we find in a barn somewhere?"

"God, you don't have to be gross. I'm trying to say thank you."

"Well, try harder," Quinn said, pulling off his shredded shirt before donning a new one with the Crowfoot County symbol emblazoned across the chest. His anger simmered, heating his face, but when he looked at Alice, she was grinning. "What?" he asked.

"You look like such a tourist."

Quinn opened his mouth and surprised himself by laughing. Alice chuckled too, and Ty raised his head from where he played in the far corner of the room, surrounded by four stuffed animals that had come from the gift shop. His new cane was by his side within reach.

"I am a tourist. Everywhere I go is the first time I've been there."

"Even with everything, it must be kind of amazing for you," Alice said. Quinn waited for a punch line. And when none came, he had a hard time answering.

"It is. As terrible as that sounds."

"It doesn't sound terrible at all. This isn't your fault. You didn't ask for this world to be waiting for you. You've got to appreciate beauty even in the worst places. I think the ones who survive will have to come to terms with that." She looked away, into the fire and stared at it like an adversary, her gaze unwavering.

"I think I can do that," he said.

"I think you've always been able to."

They were quiet for a time, Quinn watching the firelight on her face, how it clung to every angle.

"Thank you. I mean it," Alice said, finally. "You are my knight in tattered and torn armor."

"Sir Getshurtalot at your service," he said, bowing.

Alice smiled. "Come get warm by the fire."

He pulled another chair closer to the hearth and steadied the AR-15 against its arm before sitting down. The blankets he'd nailed over the windows respirated with the night air. Ty whispered to his stuffed animals.

"This is a pretty extensive first aid kit. Good pick," Alice said, placing all the contents back inside the red zippered container.

"Yeah?"

"Yep. Even has a flare gun."

"I'll remember that if we get lost at sea."

"So you didn't see anyone human," she said after a time. It wasn't a question.

"No. No one alive. Just…them."

"What were they doing?"

"Milling around. Scavenging, I think."

"But why were there so many? Why are they traveling so close together?"

Quinn sighed and rubbed his forehead. "I don't know. I was asking myself the same questions. The only answer is we were way off in our calculations about their population." He wiped at a dark stain on the thigh of his pants. "*Way* off."

"But you said they were moving in the same direction, right?"

"Yeah. They seem to be, give or take a little."

"Then what's drawing them?"

"Drawing them?"

"You know. It's almost like they're migrating. Like flocks of birds traveling south before winter or returning in the spring."

The memory of the Geese flying above the highway surfaced in his mind.

"Something like that, yeah."

"Then what is it? What's driving them?"

"I don't know," Quinn said, rising from his chair. "I can't make any sense of it. I don't even know what they are." He went to the window, pulling the heavy blanket aside enough to peer out. The dark was softened by starlight. The trees were gently swaying guards, the pop can trip line clinked quietly. He let the blanket fall into place and returned to the fire.

"They're people. Just like you and me," Alice said.

"Not anymore."

"But they were. The more I think about it the more I realize that maybe the disease that wiped most of us out wasn't the real plague. Maybe the stilts are. Maybe they're the end of everything. The very end."

"I don't think it matters anymore. Where it came from or who started it. What matters is staying alive."

"But we need to understand the why in all of this. Don't you think?"

"Yeah." Quinn's eyelids were beyond heavy, his body a thousand pounds. "I need some sleep before I try to think any more."

Alice nodded, bringing the rifle closer to her chair. "I'll take first watch."

"Are you sure you're okay?"

"I'm fine. I got a bunch of rest while you were messing around in town."

"Okay. Thanks."

He pulled a cushion off the chair he'd been sitting in and stretched out by the fire, its heat loosening the knots in his muscles, lulling him into a soundless void that he drifted through without a hint of dreams.

~

"Quinn."

He woke at once, sitting up as reality snapped into focus so hard he blinked against it. The fire had burnt down to embers, only a faint, red glow staining the room. The lodge was silent except for Ty's even breathing in a nearby chair and the gentle push of the wind in the eaves.

He turned his head toward the figure standing two strides away. Alice limped closer, her dark hair keeping her face in shadow.

"There's something at the door," she whispered, handing him her revolver. He took it from her and got to his feet, electricity running through his nerves. He made his way toward the heavy front door as a brief scratching came from its base. He shot a look at Alice, and she nodded, bringing up the rifle as he eased to the building's closest window. Clouds had moved in while he slept and smothered the stars so that a foot away from the lodge the night became a solid thing that gave nothing to his searching eyes. He sidled to the door as a board creaked on the porch. With a wave of his hand, he signaled Alice by holding up three fingers. Slowly he dropped them into a fist.

Three.

Two.

One.

He yanked the door open as Alice snapped on the light mounted to the rifle.

The dog sat before them, its ears perked, head turning from one side to the other before it licked its chops.

Quinn lowered the handgun and looked into its dark eyes.

"You want to come in?" he asked.

The Shepherd rose immediately and trotted into the room, walking a straight line to the base of Ty's chair where it sniffed once and then laid down, its head erect and watching them.

Quinn shut and bolted the door and crossed the room to the back of Ty's chair. The dog's eyes followed him.

"Well, make yourself at home," Alice said, the rifle not at her shoulder but not at her side either.

"I think he might be," Quinn said, taking in the dog's length and deep chest. It was big and powerful, plainly at ease with itself.

"You mean it lived here?"

"I'm guessing. Maybe the guy who killed himself upstairs let it out before he did it. Couldn't bear to do the same for his pet." The Shepherd shot a look up the stairs and then back at Quinn as if confirming his assumption. "And then it led us here."

"I think you're giving it too much credit. It's a dog, Quinn."

"I know, but it definitely didn't try to hide itself. If it wanted to, it could've let us pass right on by. It was like it was biding its time, seeing what kind of people we were."

They watched the dog, and it stared back at them, blinking every so often. Finally it lowered its wide head onto its paws and sighed before falling asleep.

"That's the damnedest thing," Alice said, moving to her chair. "You think it's dangerous?"

"No. Someone definitely cared for it. Look how heavy it is, how nice its coat looks."

"What a traveling fucking circus we have going here," Alice said, getting comfortable in her chair. "If we meet a juggling clown, I'm shooting his ass."

Quinn took the rifle from her to keep watch for the remainder of the night. He studied the dog sleeping soundly at the base of Ty's chair. Strange how it had gone straight to him, like it knew he was the youngest, the most vulnerable.

Where did you come from? Quinn thought.

~

The night passed without incident, and the sun rose amidst gusting wind that flapped the blankets and stirred the coals of the fire into flame again. Ty had exclaimed with fear and then delight upon waking to the giant bed of fur slumbering beside his chair. The dog had gotten up without a sound as Ty's feet grazed its back, and with Alice watching pensively, it began licking Ty's hand and then his face.

"He's nice, mom; he's nice!" Ty said, running his hands over the Shepherd's head and ears.

"Well, that remains to be seen," Alice answered, hobbling close to the fire to warm her hands.

"Can we keep him?"

"How do you know it's a he?" she asked.

"Mom," Ty said, drawing out the middle of the word as if he were talking to someone much younger. "He's too big to be a girl."

Ty's assumption proved correct when Quinn brought the dog outside. It lifted a back leg and sprayed the bottom of a highline pole beside the lodge before returning to the porch to sit and stare at him.

"So what's his name?" Ty asked, coming outside, his cane tapping before him.

"I don't know. You wanna think of one for him?"

"We can't do that. He's grown up. He's already got a name."

Quinn cocked his head. "I guess you're probably right. So what is it, big guy?" he said, addressing the dog. "Is your name Jake?" The Shepherd mirrored Quinn's head tilt and whined once in the back of his throat. "No? How about Zeke? Is it Zeke?"

"Zeke?" Ty asked.

"I don't know. I've never really been around a dog before."

"Me neither. Mom says they're dirty."

"Yeah, well Billy Bob here doesn't look dirty."

Ty giggled. "Billy Bob?"

"Sure. He could be a Billy Bob, right boy?" The dog whined and then let out a short woof.

"Just name him Flea Train and be done with it," Alice said, coming out to stand on the porch. "That's what they all are."

"Oh come on, mom. He's really nice."

"Doesn't he have a collar on?" she asked.

"He does, but there's no tag on it," Quinn said, moving down the steps. The dog came to him, panting and smiling as he petted his head. "I'm going to take a look around back."

He walked to the rear of the house, the dog remaining where he was beside the porch. Between two large propane cylinders, a makeshift lean-to sat a few feet above the ground. Beneath it were twin dog bowls. One was partially full of greenish, scummy water. The other sat beside a torn bag of dog food. Several dark pebbles rattled as he lifted it out into the light. He wiped away dust and dirt from the side exposing bright letters.

"His name's Denver," Quinn said, coming back around the front while holding up the dish. "It's right here on your bowl, isn't it, Denver?" The dog wagged his tail and came to him, nuzzling his leg before jumping to put huge paws on his chest. "Whoa! You're too big for that." He pushed the dog back down, but Denver continued to wag his tail, his entire body shivering with delight.

"Denver. Wouldn't ever have guessed that," Alice said. "Maybe it's where he's from originally."

"That could be," Quinn said, ruffling the dog's fur one more time before mounting the steps.

"We should get going," Alice said, looking at the bright cloud hiding the sun.

"I think we should wait one more day, make sure you're good to go."

"I'm good to go," Alice said.

"Alice—"

"I'm fine." There was a familiar edge to her voice that told him there would be no negotiation. "Let's leave in an hour. There's nothing to stay here for."

~

They walked to the nearest house in the mid-morning, Quinn and Alice in front with the guns, Ty behind with his cane, Denver at heal beside him. Quinn watched the dog as they moved down the declined road. Every ten steps or so, Denver would nudge Ty's hip with his shoulder, and it was only after the fourth time did he realize that the dog was keeping Ty from straying even an inch out of line. Quinn was about to say something to Alice when they came upon the driveway and turned into it.

The house at the end of the lane was massive, its top soaring almost to the tree tips. They found several cans of vegetables and fruit along with some more candy, but no weapons.

"Damn pacifists," Alice muttered before leaving the house. In the garage they found a newer GMC Sierra pickup alongside a hybrid smart-car. Alice paused before opening the door to the truck.

"Want to take the car?"

"What?"

"I'm just trying to be eco-friendly. Doing my part to save the world."

Quinn shook his head. "Get in."

They drove toward Ferry but turned south before coming within sight of the town. The day lightened but maintained its cool, gray tone throughout the afternoon. They had to stop twice to tow wrecks from the narrow country road they drove on. At the second crash, a flock of crows feasted on something in a nearby field, taking flight long enough for them to see the tattered remains of a man's jacket and pants.

It was near evening when they joined a large highway that took them northwest through a larger town. Vacant storefronts slid by, empty parking lots, the occasional dead car, or body. When they'd left the burg behind, Alice shifted in the front seat, her hands toying with the revolver.

"We should find somewhere soon."

"Definitely. I'll pull off at the next exit that looks—" But his voice faltered as they rounded a bend and the setting sun shone full force through the windshield. Quinn took his foot off the gas and coasted to a stop on the left side of the highway near a guardrail.

"What are you doing?" Alice said.

"It's," Quinn started but couldn't continue. He put the truck in park and tore his eyes away from the scene before him, checking the immediate surroundings as he opened his door and climbed out.

"Quinn, are you okay?" Alice asked.

"What's wrong?" Ty said from the backseat.

"Nothing," Quinn said, stepping away from the truck. A cool breeze trailed past him, pushing his hair back, and he swallowed, coming even with the steel rail.

A strong river flowed beneath the highway, so blue it nearly hurt his eyes to gaze into it. The water stretched between two rounded hills, their sides rich with dozens of trees that grew close to the water's edge in tiered rows, their branches beginning to green. The sun painted the dead river grass a shade of yellow as it bent beneath the wind's touch and it rippled like the water beside it. Reaching tips of rocks studded the center of the river in a zigzag like the zipper of a woman's dress.

The painting in his room at home lay before him in all its splendor.

His father's words came back to him. *The only way to feel something that you haven't seen in real life is through art.* Tears clouded his eyes, and his lower lip trembled. He sat down beside the guardrail, its cold steel beneath his palm the only sensation telling him he was here and not in his room dreaming of the day he could see the artist's rendition in person.

"Are you all right?" Alice stood beside him, and he looked up at her, blinking away the tears.

"Yeah. I'm more than all right."

"What is it, Quinn?" Ty asked, appearing at his shoulder, Denver close to his other side. "I hear water. Is it a river?" Ty gazed out over the rolling hills, not seeing the beauty that was right there before him. Quinn fought off another bout of emotion and grasped the boy's hand. *You have to feel it, Quinn.*

"You're right; it is a river. It's deep and wide with big, dark rocks in its middle. It curves between two hills that come down to meet it. The hills have trees and long grass, and the sun is shining on it all. Can you feel the sun?"

"Yes." Ty closed his eyes.

"Can you see the river?"

"Yes."

"It's all right in front of you. Everything's there."

A smile spread across Ty's small face, the sunshine lighting it like it did the grass and trees so that he looked more alive than Quinn had ever seen him.

"It's beautiful," Ty said at last.

~

They stopped for the night at a farmhouse at the end of a dirt road that cut between two fields full of greening alfalfa. At its rear, a plantation of stark trees stood in even rows, their shaded tunnels narrowing to nothing with the setting sun. There was a smell of death inside the house, but Quinn found only a dried mass in the corner of the kitchen floor. He poured a bottle of bleach on it that he found beneath the kitchen sink, and the stench subsided enough for them to breathe easier.

They brought their belongings inside and ate a meager supper of cold sweet potatoes and cranberry sauce. Denver had a bowl of dog food Quinn had packed, returning to Ty's side the moment he was finished.

"I think I'm losing weight," Alice said between bites. "If society ever rebuilds itself, I'll start my own program. 'The Apocalypse Diet: all you need is a gunshot to the leg, canned food, and overwhelming fear to lose those extra pounds'".

"You'll make a million," Quinn said.

"Yeah. At least then if we run out of toilet paper…"

Ty's face crinkled. "You mean wipe with money?"

Quinn and Alice laughed. Denver woofed once, and they all laughed harder. After he'd finished eating, Quinn took a quick tour around the farmhouse, watching the land for movement, but there was nothing, only the sharp flitting of a bat past his head and the hoot of an owl somewhere deep in the tree plantation behind the house.

He stood there as the clouds roiled amongst themselves, their bellies going from gray to black, dyed by the night. Crickets sang their endless tune, and somewhere to the east, a single coyote howled. There was no traffic trundling along the road, no planes tracing a path across the sky. He could've been the only human being alive on Earth.

He shivered and went inside.

Ty was asleep on a pile of blankets Alice had packed from the house where they acquired the truck. Denver lay next to him, one paw almost touching the boy's outstretched hands.

"Have you ever seen such a thing?" Alice said, motioning to Ty and the dog as she changed the bandage on her leg.

"No, can't say I have. They've really taken to each other."

Alice laughed without mirth.

"What's really funny is that I considered getting a service dog for him about a year ago."

"Really? I thought you didn't like them."

"I don't, but the benefit to Ty was too important. There were organizations that provided guide dogs for free, but the waiting list was over two years. There were places that trained and sold them, but the problem was the dogs were close to fifteen thousand dollars. I couldn't afford it out of pocket, so I signed up for a grant. And we were to the point for final approval when it was defunded."

"You're kidding."

"Nope. It was through the state. My income was so low we qualified. Bastards pulled the rug right out from under us. Anyone who says people applying for government assistance are lazy have never filled out any of the required paperwork; it took me almost a week to gather everything they needed. And then to have them take it away." She shook her head. "After seeing the disappointment on his face that day, I vowed never to mention a dog again until I had the flea-bitten mongrel paid for and in the house. I started saving and had about three thousand built up when everything went to shit." Alice pulled her pant leg down over the clean bandage and stared at her son. "Now he's got one, and all it took was for the world to end."

"I'd bet on Armageddon before the government any day."

She laughed and rose, carrying the rifle. "I'll take first watch."

He nodded and was about to look for a place to bed down when Alice put a hand on his shoulder. He turned to her, and she was close. So close it startled him.

"What you did today, at the river, that was…" she stared up at him. Her breath tickled against his neck. He could smell her, not a perfume of any kind, just the scent of her sweat and her hair. There was barely any light in the room, only the meager glow from the closest windows, but there was something in the way she looked at him, something in her eyes, the way her head was tilted back. It was as if—

A loud bang came from the yard. Glass tinkled.

They both flinched. She gripped his shoulder harder before releasing it. They hurried to the front door, crouching before they got to the window.

Somewhere behind them Denver growled.

Quinn brought himself up high enough to look out into the night.

"Oh my God," he said.

Chapter 23

The Cellar

A stilt loomed over the truck and shoved its hand further through the driver's window it had just smashed.

It was wreathed in shadow and only truly discernable when it moved, separating itself from the dark. Behind it, a quarter mile away, a herd milled in the field. Quinn couldn't tell how many there were, but most of the open ground was covered by slender forms, long arms swinging as they walked.

"Go get Ty and go out the back door," Quinn said. "Get into the trees and keep going. Don't stop."

"You're coming," Alice said, snagging his arm as she sidled away from the window. The stilt bumped the truck's horn, and they both jumped. The monster jerked also then slammed a fist through the rear driver's side window and continued to rummage inside.

They slipped into the living room, and Alice roused Ty, speaking so low Quinn couldn't hear what she said. Denver continued to growl, a low and menacing sound in the middle of his chest.

"Shh," Quinn said, stroking the Shepherd's ears. "Quiet now." The dog nosed Ty's shoulder as Alice helped him to his feet. Quinn grasped the first aid kit, and they started for the back door when Alice halted.

"Wait. I don't hear it anymore," she breathed. Quinn listened.

Silence.

They could be walking outside into its waiting arms and teeth.

He leaned in to Alice, putting his mouth against her ear.

"I'll check the front. Be ready to run."

He moved back through the simple house, the front entry dark and unfamiliar. He gripped the revolver.

Five shots.

Edging close to the window, he peeked outside, one eye around the window frame.

The stilt was gone, but the herd was still there, undulating like a single entity. Maybe it had gone back to rejoin them after finding nothing in the truck. What were they doing out there? So many. The group was at least twice the size of the herd in Ferry. Maybe three times, the night belied their numbers. He squinted and tried to search the areas to either side of the window.

The stilt stepped out of the darkness two paces away from the house, bowing low, its eyes finding him framed in the window.

It roared.

Quinn raised the handgun, mortaring everything inside him to keep still and aim. He couldn't miss.

He fired as it came through the glass. Its long head rocked backward, a chunk of skull vaporizing. The gunshot resounded across the field, and the surrounding area lit up in a dazzling blast of flame that shot from the barrel. Ringing filled his ears, and then something else.

Deep croaking.

They were coming.

He turned, yelling through the length of the house. "Go!" The back door opened, and they were gone before he could even make out their shapes. In the field, tall forms loped forward, long shadows beneath the starless sky. He had to buy them time somehow, give them a head start. He had four rounds left, along with his body to sacrifice if necessary. How long would his corpse slow them down? Long enough for Alice and Ty to get away? He tried to steady his hands as the stilt's footsteps and thrumming calls came closer, tried to make out his first target. It was so dark.

Dark.

Quinn tucked the revolver in its holster and ripped the first aid kit open, fingers fumbling with the orange flare pistol. He yanked it free and found one of the three tubular flares. By feel, he loaded the pistol and cocked the hammer back before standing.

Cool night air drifted in through the broken window. The herd was thirty yards away and closing. He aimed at the center of their numbers and fired.

The flare launched out of the pistol with a sizzle and seared the night in a sodium line as it sped across the distance between the farmhouse and the stilts. It blazed a path between them, their forms careening apart like water breaking on a rock. The croaks became hisses that filled the night like a kingdom of snakes.

Quinn stooped and reloaded the flare gun, shooting the second round at the greatest clot of figures.

Then he ran.

Through the house and out the rear door without looking back. The air whipped past him, his breath quickening. He sprinted into the closest row of the plantation, the sound of his passage metronomic against the many tree trunks. Sticks and grass tried to tangle his feet, but he stormed through them, twigs breaking underfoot. After what seemed like hours, he swung to a stop behind a tree, drawing the revolver.

Held his breath.

His heart wasn't where it should've been. It thudded behind his eyes, in his throat, even his arms. The farmhouse was out of the sight, only the rows and rows of trees visible in the night. A window broke. There were sounds of a door being ripped from its hinges. More croaking. Behind him he could hear soft footfalls in the distance.

He turned and ran again, plummeting through the tunnel of branches and trunks, sight jangling with each step. Ahead, a dim light swung. There and gone like the flash of the nearest lighthouse he'd watched every night at home. The light spoke a word through the blackness.

Hope. Hope. Hope.

He exploded into a clearing and nearly trampled Alice and Ty beneath him before slowing. Denver snarled and took a step toward him before he realized who Quinn was.

"Thank God," Alice said, latching onto his arm.

"They're still coming," Quinn managed between sucking breaths. Across a narrow tract of turned field, a flashlight swung.

"There's some kind of house over there," Alice said, grabbing Ty's hand. She hurried forward, and Quinn kept pace, his legs weak from the flight.

As they neared the home, which didn't seem much more than a shack of some kind, its left end much higher than the right, the person holding a flashlight shone the beam on them, and they paused with the sound of a shotgun being racked.

"Hold it right there," a cigarette soaked voice said. They stopped and stood beside one another. Alice held the AR-15 ready but pointed at the ground. "What're you doing in my field in the middle of the night?"

"We're being chased," Quinn said, throwing a look over his shoulder. The clouds had parted enough for a wedge of cold light to fall on the plantation edge. The trees stood like bristling needles in their rows.

"By what?"

"By stilts," Alice said, blinking at the glare of the flashlight.

"The hell is that?"

"The creatures. What used to be people," Alice replied, holding up a hand to block the light. "Can you get that out of our faces?"

"Why shouldn't I just drop you where you stand right now? How do I know you're tellin' the truth?"

A branch snapped in the distance, and a long hiss trailed from the trees.

"Because they're going to be here in thirty seconds," Quinn said. "Either let us inside or get out of our way." He raised the pistol from his side, aiming at the shape behind the light. The man drew the beam across them all, finally resting it on Ty who gripped Denver's collar in one white hand.

Three stilts exploded out of the plantation and paused, their heads snapping up as if catching a scent before they bellowed and ran toward them.

"Inside!" the man shouted, and fired a blast from his shotgun in the stilt's direction. They ran past him and found a weather-beaten door in the side of the house. Quinn glanced around as soon as they were all inside.

The house was a simple shed, its roof slanting dramatically to one side so that even Ty wouldn't have been able to stand up straight beneath its low end. The walls were thin, cracks as wide as his thumb open to the outside in some places. Two candles burned on the top of a great cast iron woodstove in the furthest corner beside an unmade cot. The air smelled the same as the field outside, turned soil and a hint of tobacco. Unfinished boards creaked beneath their feet.

"This won't keep them out," Alice said, spinning in the center of the room.

She was right. Quinn's eyes combed the space for somewhere to hide. He was about to lead them back outside to take their chances in the dark when the man entered and slammed the door shut behind him.

"Down here," he said, dropping to one knee. His fingers pried up a steel ring set in the floor and he pulled.

A trap door opened unto pure darkness, a single tread visible in the dim light.

Alice found his eyes, and Quinn hesitated, glancing at the man holding the door. He nodded. Alice held Ty's hand, guiding him down the steps as she disappeared into the void sideways. Denver dove after them, and Quinn heard the big dog grunt as it hit whatever floor waited. Quinn went next, hearing hurried footfalls punching the furrowed earth outside the shack.

His feet found four stairs, widely separated, then solid ground. Wooden beams ran only inches over his head, cobwebs brushing his face and shoulders. The man slipped into the cellar behind him, lowering the trap door without a sound. He shone his flashlight on a heavy, steel bolt that he threw into its housing with a clack, locking the door tight.

Wood cracked and groaned above them. The man doused his light, plunging everything into an abyss of darkness. Guttural rumbling filled the shack, vibrating the air around them. Dust rained down as heavy footsteps crossed the little house's width. Something crashed to the floor, more dust fell, and Quinn felt a sneeze beginning to build. He bit down on the inside of his cheeks and pinched the bridge of his nose. The sneeze burned in his sinuses for a harrowing moment and then receded. Someone was beside him, soft skin and hair. He ran a hand down Alice's arm, and she laced her fingers in his.

Quinn swung his free hand out, and it met rough concrete block no more than a foot away. Denver's collar jingled once and then no more. They waited, the stilts trampling the floor above them, tearing the man's home apart.

After what seemed like days, there was a loud croak from somewhere to the south, and the shambling feet receded from the planks, several more things falling in their wake.

Quiet except for their breathing.

The man flicked his flashlight on, cupping the beam in the palm of his hand. Barely any light found its way past his fingers, but it was enough to see the small room they were in.

The walls were uneven concrete block, unsealed and water-stained from many years of flooding. The floor was earth, lumped and heaved in the center of the space. There was a pile of rusted hand tools in one corner, indiscernible in their function. Other than the short angle of stairs, the room was bare.

The man went to the wall near the tools and worked on something for a moment, a soft grating coming from one of the blocks. Steel clinked. Then he returned, the shotgun cradled under one arm. He stopped at the foot of the stairs and looked up at the trap door before turning to them.

He was in his mid-to-late sixties, a curled, white beard, stained yellow around the mouth, covering his face. Wrinkles ran away from the corners of his eyes like erosion on the bank of a river, and he was mostly bald, several large age spots growing in dark patches on his naked scalp.

He illuminated each of them in turn, shuffling his boots along the dirt floor. When he came to Quinn, he froze, bringing the light closer.

"The hell happened to you?"

"I was born this way. Genetic disorder," Quinn whispered. His hand lingered on the revolver at his hip. The man grunted and stood back, lips pursing behind the dirty beard. "Thank you," Quinn said, glancing at the boards overhead. "Thanks for taking us in."

"Wouldn't have if it coulda' been helped. Wasn't much getting away from the bastards as it was." The man eyed them all again. He spit on the floor.

"We appreciate it," Quinn said. "We'll move on at first light."

There was a muted scratching sound, and the man turned his light on the corner of the cellar. Denver was pawing at a place in the corner, his nails raking the dirt up in furrows.

"Keep that dog from diggin'," the man said, taking a quick step forward. Denver looked up, glancing at all of them as Ty found his collar with one outstretched hand.

"Sorry," Ty said.

"Place is wrecked enough as it is. Don't need more damage down here." With that, he clicked the light off and moved across the room where they heard him settle to the ground. Alice squeezed Quinn's hand, bringing her mouth to his ear.

"What the hell?"

"I'm not sure. We'll just get through the night. Find another vehicle in the morning. Maybe we can make Iowa by tomorrow."

She released his hand, and they huddled together on the floor in the complete dark. Outside the stilts growled and chuffed, their bullfrog voices intermingling as they called to one another.

Alice slowly slumped closer to him and finally rested her head on his shoulder. A warmth bloomed there that spread through him, fluttering wings in his stomach.

"Are you okay to stay awake?" she asked, her voice heavy with sleep.

"Yes. I'll keep watch."

As her breathing evened and the sounds of the stilts receded further, his mind drifted, the utter blackness around him like being in the vacuum of space. He closed his eyes and opened them. No difference. The man shifted and then fell quiet. Quinn kept his hand on the revolver, finger in the trigger guard until the first light of dawn crept into the cellar through the cracks in the ceiling.

~

When it was full light, they ventured up the stairs and into the ruins of the shack above. The little house had been destroyed. Two of the four walls were gone, torn away like wreckage from a high-speed crash. Pots and pans, old newspapers, shattered wood and glass all littered the floor. Outside the sun lit the small clearing and churned earth, the greening trees in the surrounding forest tipping with the breeze. The herd of stilts was nowhere to be seen.

The man murmured that his name was Hilton when Quinn asked. He didn't say if it was his first or last. He seemed indifferent to their presence, and when Quinn suggested that they scout the immediate area, he merely fed more shells into his shotgun and headed out across the field.

Quinn followed and caught up with him after having Alice lock her, Ty, and Denver in the cellar. Hilton's eyes were bright in the light of day, their gaze roaming the earth, the trees, and Quinn's face from time to time. They moved across the field, its surface trampled by the long tracks of the stilts. When they entered the plantation, the air grew quiet around them. The birdsong that had accompanied them to that point, gone. Quinn hesitated at the border but continued after the old man when everything remained still.

When they arrived at the farmhouse where they'd left the truck the night before, Hilton stopped and slowly lowered himself to the ground. Quinn did the same, spotting movement a fraction of a second later.

Three stilts stood in the driveway, their arms at their sides, only their heads moving in a panning of the land around them.

"Damn," Quinn said under his breath.

"They're lookin' for ya," Hilton said.

Quinn glanced at him and then back at the towering creatures.

"No, they're…" He was about to say, *they're not that smart*. But were they? Were they staking out their vehicle in hopes that they would return? If they were, then was there a chance that there were more hidden and watching from other angles?

Quinn looked around, searching the plantation thoroughly. There was only the thin trees.

"We should go," Quinn said, waiting until the stilts' attention was focused on something opposite their location before standing and making his way back to the little field. Hilton followed, proceeding with a stealth that shamed even Quinn's careful treading over leaves and branches. When they were back at Hilton's home, he spoke again, producing a hand-rolled cigarette and lighter from his pocket.

"If they're waitin' there, they'll be waitin' all around. Be stupid to go traipsin' off through the woods now. Specially with a blind boy and a dog." He took a long drag on the cigarette, bright eyes squinting. "Don't like dogs."

"I'm sorry for the inconvenience, and I'm sorry for your house. If things were different, I'd help you repair it."

"Ain't a worry. Wasn't much to begin with, but it kept me dry." Hilton studied him from behind the cigarette. "What you people doin' out here anyway?"

"Trying to get to Iowa," Quinn said, looking down at the trap door.

"Yeah. What's there for ya?"

"The army, we heard."

Hilton coughed out a laugh. "Army's dead, sonny boy. Same as everything else."

"Well, that's where we're headed. We lost our map the other day and—"

"Lost your way looks like to me," Hilton said, dragging on the cigarette.

Quinn watched the other man, a tingling rising from the pit of his stomach.

"Yeah. Anyway, where are we exactly? Are we still in Ohio?"

"Nah. This be the great state of Indiana." He pronounced it, *Endiana*.

"Gotcha. You wouldn't know of any other houses nearby, any vehicles—"

"You could steal?" Hilton asked, cutting him off again.

Quinn watched the old man, shifting the AR-15 on its sling. Hilton stared at him for another beat and then broke out laughing.

"You're too tense, sonny boy. I'm just fuckin' with ya. Stealin's same as everything else in these days. Everything's forgiven." He tossed the butt of his cigarette away, not bothering to stamp it out. It smoldered on a floorboard, a razor line of smoke trailing from it.

"You're probably right," Quinn said, smiling. "We've been on the road awhile."

"Well, you're all welcome to stay as long as you need. Simply for the reason I don't want those tall bastards coming down on my head again if you try to leave too soon." Hilton barked another laugh and then motioned toward the rickety cot overturned in the corner. "Give me a hand so there's somethin' to sleep on down there, will ya?"

~

The day passed in a humid blur, the close air warming by ratcheting increments in the cellar. Hilton began to speak more and more as the hours went by, his mood improving so that he smiled most of the time when he talked. He had been a truck driver in his former life, years ago, he said. Never married, no kids. He belonged to the road until a bad back kept him from sitting for long periods of time. When he could no longer make a living driving truck, he came here to his father's land and constructed the shack that sat above them. He said it was therapeutic to get away from the trappings of society. Raise his garden in the solace of each day and read in the evenings. He had no electricity, no running water, no indoor toilet, but he made do.

"Really, things didn't change for me much when everything happened," Hilton said, smoking another cigarette. "Walked into town one day a month ago, things were fine. Went back last week, everyone's dead."

"It really happened fast," Alice said. She sat against the wall watching Ty play with an interlocking steel puzzle Hilton had given him earlier. The pieces slid together in a maze-like pattern. By turning and twisting them into the correct shape, they would come apart.

"I guess we really shoulda' seen it all comin'," Hilton said. "World was shit and just got worse as the years went by. Can't keep takin' line and not expect to get a hook in your hand eventually. Not that it was such a stretch, most people changin' into monsters." He gave Quinn a fleeting look and chewed on the cigarette that poked from his beard.

They passed around the last bottle of water from Quinn's bag and shared two melted candy bars. In the evening, they heard the passage of several stilts through the woods beside the shack. Their calls were absent, but they could hear the snapping of branches, feel the heavy footfalls through the foundation. After the sounds faded away, Quinn approached Hilton who was arranging the dirty cot in a corner.

"I think we'll have to stay another night, if it's okay with you. I don't think it would be safe enough today to travel any distance," Quinn said.

"That's more'n fine. Apologies about how I acted earlier. Wasn't myself. Not used to guests," Hilton said, straightening. "Got a feeling we should douse the lights early tonight, not make a spectacle of ourselves."

"Sounds good. Thank you again," Quinn said, putting out his hand. The older man shook it.

"No thanks needed. 'Bout time I do some good deeds." He grinned at Quinn, and there were two teeth missing from the top left side of his mouth. Quinn felt his upper lip curling. Hilton's hand was clammy and cool, like something already dead, but his smile was genuine and radiated warmth.

Quinn made his way back to the opposite side of the room and sat down beside Ty who was still working on the puzzle.

"Getting anywhere with that, champ?"

"Maybe. I thought I had it figured out a little bit ago, but now I'm not sure."

Quinn stared at Hilton who sat on the cot and flopped onto his back, closing his eyes with one last look around the room. The old man's age spots gleamed with moisture. Quinn imagined them moving like black amoebas on the petri dish of Hilton's scalp.

"Got it!" Ty exclaimed in a quiet voice. He held the two pieces of puzzle out in triumph.

"Great job, honey," Alice said, stroking his hair. "We'll have to find more of those for you. I've never seen one like that before."

"Made it myself," Hilton said, and they all glanced at him. Quinn had thought the man was sleeping. "You can have it if you want, little one." He didn't open his eyes.

"Really?" Ty asked.

"Wouldn't lie to ya."

"Cool! Thank you, sir."

Hilton smiled and then rolled toward the wall. Soon soft snores drifted from him, and he broke wind loudly. Alice put a hand over Ty's mouth before the laughter could slip out and shot a look at Quinn, a bemused smile on her face. Quinn shrugged and pulled out the revolver, rotating the cylinder around and around. Four shots left. He glanced at Hilton and then back at the brass shells before holstering the weapon and standing.

Quinn moved across the room and inspected the pile of tools. They were all rusted beyond use. Screwdriver tips blunted, saw blades clogged, chains coiled like snakes, hammers orange and pitted. Above the pile was a hole in one of the cement blocks, its edges rounded and smoothed. He ran a finger inside it. Nothing but the hollow center of the block.

"What are you doing?" Alice asked. He came back to her and sat down.

"Nothing. Looking around."

"You haven't slept yet, have you?"

"No."

"You must be exhausted. Lie down for a while, I'll keep watch."

He leaned closer to her. "Something's wrong."

"What do you mean?"

"With him," he said, nodding toward Hilton.

"He's eccentric and a hermit. Probably hasn't talked much with people in years."

"I know, but there's something wrong with him. His eyes."

"Quinn, what choice do we have? Those things are still around, it's almost dark, and we have no idea where the next safe haven could be."

Quinn grimaced and rubbed his brow. God he was tired.

"I know. Okay, let's just get through the night. We leave first thing tomorrow."

"Agreed. Now go to sleep. I can handle myself. Where are the matches? I want to light a candle before I can't see at all."

He handed her the small matchbook that he'd brought down from upstairs. She drew one of the matches across the striking strip and lit a candle. The darkness slowly lifted, light flickering on the block walls barely revealing the supports above them.

Alice handed him back the matches, and he laid down near Ty, his head resting against the floor. He didn't think he'd be able to sleep with the lump of dread that pulsed in the base of his stomach, but exhaustion gradually drew him deeper into darkness. His eyelids were immovable weights that drifted lower with each second. The candlelight wavered in his blurry vision before winking out like a firefly.

~

"Quinn."

The whisper woke him like a dousing of ice water. He opened his eyes and blinked several times because there was no change. He was blind. Somehow he'd gone blind while he slept and now the world was only darkness.

A hand touched his shoulder and he jerked.

"It's me," Ty whispered.

Quinn looked around, searching for the boy's face in the darkness. The candle had gone out. He remembered Alice lighting a candle. There was a muffled clink of steel across the cellar.

"What's wrong, buddy?"

"Denver was digging. I got him to stop, but what is this?" he asked, taking Quinn's hand in his own. Ty guided his palm to the rough floor, over a rock, and onto something half-domed and smooth. He could feel loose dirt around the object where the dog's paws had pulled the earth free.

Denver whined.

Quinn felt the object again. It was buried several inches beneath the cellar floor. It was dry, crusted with soil. His fingers met two depressions filled with dirt.

"What is it?" Ty asked again.

Quinn got on his knees and dug in his pocket, searching for the matches he knew were there. He got them out, fingertips prying one from the pack. He folded the cover over, pinning the match between it and the striking strip. He pulled.

Flame fluttered and flared, pouring light onto the hole where a human skull stared up at him, eye sockets packed with dirt.

"Shit!" Quinn said, dropping the match. His mind flooded with possibilities in the half second it took him to grab for the revolver at his hip—that wasn't there.

A flashlight clicked from across the cellar and shone on him. Denver growled once, deep and long.

"Shut it," Hilton said, pinpointing the dog with the beam he held in his left hand. In his right he gripped the revolver. Alice lay on Hilton's cot, eyes clouded with pain, her wrists bound by the rusted chain he'd spotted earlier in the pile of tools. Her mouth was gagged with a strip of dirty cloth.

"Hilton, what are you doing?" Quinn said, rising to his feet.

"What's it look like, pretty boy? Huh?" Hilton said, bringing the weapon to bear on his chest. "Shouldn't have slept so hard."

"Momma?" Ty said. Alice moaned a word through the gag.

"Damn, what a fortuitous meeting this was," Hilton said. "To think, I was under the impression that I'd never get to have any more fun, and you people waltz onto my property."

"Hilton, I don't know what's going on, but you need to give me my gun back."

The old man laughed. "Don't act fuckin' stupid. You know exactly what's going on. Your shitheel dog over there dug up my last project, just when I was figuring out a plan for all of you." He gestured in a semicircle, and Denver growled again, punctuating the rumble with a deafening bark.

"Shut up!" Hilton yelled, pointing the gun at the dog. Ty scrambled sideways and put an arm around Denver's neck, but the dog continued to growl. Quinn searched the area around him. Save for a small rock near his left foot, there was nothing in reach.

"Hilton, please, let us go. You have no reason to hurt us. Just let us up the stairs, and we'll leave you be."

"Wrong again, sonny boy. I have every reason to hurt you."

"Why?"

Hilton grinned, his missing teeth a black hole in his mouth.

"Because I can." He turned and set the flashlight down before grabbing Alice by the hair, bringing her off the cot to her feet. She let out a strangled cry, and Quinn took a step forward. Hilton pressed the barrel of the gun against her temple and cocked the hammer.

"Don't," Quinn said, taking another step. He heard the desperation in his voice and so did Hilton who raised an eyebrow.

"We got some feelings for this pretty gal, do we? Okay then, now we have some ground to stand on. I'm going to kill all of you eventually, but I'll let you decide who goes easy and who doesn't, how's that?" Hilton said.

Quinn tried to keep his hands steady as he raised them.

"You don't need to do this."

"Aww, enough of that bullshit. We're past that. This is happening. Now are you gonna choose who gets a bullet and who gets the saw blade or am I?"

Quinn looked at Alice and then glanced at Ty who crouched beside Denver, the dog's neck outstretched, muzzle full of fangs. He licked his lips, staring at the revolver, trying to remember.

Finally he let out a sob and dropped to his knees before Hilton.

"Shoot me. I don't care about them," Quinn said.

Hilton pointed the handgun at him. The barrel looked a mile long in the shadows cast from the flashlight.

"Well, I didn't figure you for a coward, but there's one inside us all. Sometimes he just needs some proddin'."

Alice choked his name past her gag, eyes huge and full of disbelief.

"Quinn, what are you doing?" Ty asked as he lost his grip on Denver. The dog took a step forward, releasing another explosive bark. Hilton aimed the gun at the Shepherd, but when Denver didn't come any nearer, he shifted his attention back to Quinn who let his face crumple with another sob.

"Please shoot me; I can't stand pain." Quinn brought his hands forward in supplication. "Please."

He said the last word as a whisper and closed his eyes.

"Well, that makes it easier for me," Hilton said, stepping closer. He placed the gun barrel against Quinn's forehead. "The bitch and the little one will be more fun anyway. Night night, handsome."

Hilton pulled the trigger.

The hammer fell. Nothing happened.

Quinn slapped the gun away from his head and jumped to his feet, slamming his fist into Hilton's gaping jaw. There was a crack loud enough to resound in the dead air of the room, and the flashlight spun away on the floor. Quinn launched himself at the older man who grunted in pain as he fell onto the stairs behind him.

Ty screamed something, and Denver barked again.

Quinn found the soft flesh of Hilton's neck and locked his hands around it, pressing his thumbs deep into the man's jugulars. Hilton swung a fist up. Quinn's ear detonated with pain and tears rushed from his eyes, blinding him. Instead of caving in to the impulse to let go, he held tighter and brought his forehead down on Hilton's nose.

Blood spurted black in the low light.

Quinn let go with one hand and hammered a fist into Hilton's shattered nose.

He hit him again.

And again.

And again.

The old man coughed out a spray of blood that speckled Quinn's face and went slack. He slid down the stairs and lay still at their base.

Quinn stood back from the crumpled form, lungs heaving, blood dripping from his knuckles, his face. He reached down and plucked the revolver from the floor and holstered it before going to Alice and Ty who stood beside Denver. Quinn untied the gag and drew the filthy cloth from her mouth.

"Are you okay?" he asked.

"Oh my God," she said, her voice raw. "Yes, I'm fine. What the hell happened?" She staggered, and he helped her ease to the floor.

"He's a psychopath."

"I can see that. I meant why didn't the gun go off?"

"There was only four live rounds in the cylinder. Before I went to sleep, I set it so the hammer was on the first empty, just for safety's sake." Quinn grabbed the flashlight and shone it on the chain that bound Alice's hands.

"But how did you know he hadn't readjusted it?" she asked.

"I didn't."

He set to work on the bolt and nut holding the chain tight around her wrists. The chain came free, and Alice rubbed the ragged skin there, slowly trying to stand. Quinn steadied her on one side with Ty on the other.

"He hit me on the side of the head," Alice said. "We were talking in low voices since you both were asleep. He was being really pleasant, even charming. I had the rifle. And then he moved so fast I couldn't react, couldn't even scream. He hit me, and I woke up on the cot a minute or so before you struck the match."

Quinn shone the light on the shallow grave, the skull a dull yellow in the beam.

"How many more do you think are down here?" Alice asked in a low voice as she hugged Ty to her side.

Quinn shook his head and was about to answer when a heavy footstep thumped on the floorboards directly above them.

There was a deep croak that shook the air around them, and the trap door began to jump on its hinges.

Chapter 24

Royal

Wood groaned and splintered as the door was wrenched upward.

Quinn flicked the light off. He grabbed Alice's hand in the dark and then managed to find Ty's shoulder. Without a word, he led them around the perimeter of the cellar, stopping in the narrow space behind the stairs as the trap door was torn completely away and the stench of rotting fish filled the air. Denver began to growl but fell silent as suddenly as he'd started.

Quinn reached to the side, finding the edge of Hilton's cot. He stretched, feeling with shaking fingers until he brushed the stock of the rifle near the wall. The base rumble came again, and a deeper shadow in the darkness glided down the stairs.

Quinn froze.

It was an arm. Thin and crooked with a long-fingered hand at its end. It slid down into the space like a snake hunting its dinner. With a jabbing motion, the hand encircled Hilton's leg and drug him up from where he lay. The old man's head bounced once on the top stair, and Quinn heard him mumble something incoherent.

They waited another moment, then Quinn grasped the rifle and pulled it close, leaning in to Ty and Alice.

"We have to move," he whispered. "We're trapped if it comes back."

Hilton moaned somewhere above them and then began to scream.

"Now," Quinn said.

He went first, climbing the stairs into the cool air of the open night. A half moon hung midway in the sky, the wink of some ancient, alien god. In the field, three stilts were tearing at something between them that writhed and rasped out words filled with agony.

Quinn helped Ty out of the cellar, holding his hand as Denver came next and Alice last. He motioned to the woods behind the shack, and Alice led the way, Ty trailing behind her with his hand locked to Denver's collar. Quinn shot a final look back in time to see Hilton separate three ways, dark, ropy things falling to the turned earth at the creatures' feet.

They ran.

They plunged as one into the woods, flying past gnarled pines, their feet cushioned by decades of fallen needles. The moon followed them, lighting their way. They traveled steadily down, the forest tumbling into a gully scarred by a silver stream. They splashed across it and paused on the other side, listening for sounds behind them.

Silence except for the chuckle of water.

Quinn took the lead, finding a side hill less steep than others that took them back up into a bramble before disgorging them onto a gigantic field. Its openness staggered him for a moment, and he stopped, each breath full of daggers.

"There," Alice said, pointing to a tall, curved shape at the field's far end. They ran toward it. As they closed in, it was revealed as a spine-broken barn, its sideboards hanging like loosened teeth.

The odor of old hay and decaying wood met them as they stepped through the open doorway on its closest end. The barn was mostly empty, an ancient tractor pinned beneath its roof near the center, leaning lumber at its sides, hay bales released of their bindings everywhere on the ground. They moved to the middle of the structure where a split door opened off to the field, its upper half swung wide. Quinn stopped and surveyed the expanse, no movement from the opposite tree line. He counted to five hundred and then turned away, sitting down on a rusted bucket near the others.

Ty curled next to Denver who sat rigid, head upright and watching. Alice rested beside her son, her hand stroking his hair.

"Everyone okay?" Quinn asked.

Alice huffed a laugh. "Peachy."

"I don't want to go back there," Ty murmured. "That man was scary even though he was pretending to be nice."

"We won't go back," Quinn said.

"I threw away his puzzle," Ty said, and nuzzled closer to Denver's dark coat. In less than a minute, he was asleep.

"It was an anchor for the chains," Quinn said after a time.

"What?" Alice said.

"The hole in the block near Hilton's cot. He unscrewed something out of it when we first got down there. It was an anchor to secure the chains to the wall."

Alice shuddered. "What a sick fuck."

"It's like the damned were spared in all this," Quinn said, gazing out through the open door to where the moon hovered. "We've only met a couple decent people, and they died almost immediately. It's almost like God left them here to suffer."

"We're suffering," Alice hissed. "My son is suffering, and he doesn't deserve it." She brushed Ty's hair back again. "There is no God," she said after a long time.

Quinn stared at the floor until Alice rolled onto her side, hugging Ty to her. He rose from the bucket and stood near the door again, watching the night rotate toward dawn.

Hours later, when the sky was beginning to lighten in the east, he noticed a quiet sound coming from inside the barn. It was a stuttering wheeze, like a light wind teasing the eaves of a house. It took him over a minute to realize Alice was crying.

He went to her and knelt down, placing a hand on her shoulder. She resisted for a moment but finally rolled toward him. Her face was streaked with tears, and she wiped her nose before shaking her head.

"I'm fine."

"You always cry when you're fine?"

She swallowed, letting out a long sigh as more tears coursed down her cheeks.

"I would've picked Ty," she said.

"For what?"

"For that bastard to shoot first. Knowing what was coming, I would've rather seen him die quickly, and I feel inhuman for even having that thought."

"You can't blame yourself for that. Anyone would've made that choice in your position."

"No. They would've found a way to get free. They would've bided time until they could escape. But my mind was blank, and my head hurt so much I couldn't think of anything. All I could see was my beautiful boy being tortured by that madman, and I couldn't stand the thought of it."

Beautiful boy. Alice saying his father's words was almost too much for him. He rubbed her shoulder as she continued, her voice uneven.

"All my life I tried to be strong, to shove everything and everyone away that got too close. I let my guard down once and got burned. But when Ty was born, that was it. The wall I'd built crumbled, and even though I patched it, it was never as strong again." She looked at the boy's sleeping form. "I can't lose him, Quinn, I can't, and I feel like he could slip away at any time."

"That's not going to happen."

"You can say that." Her tone was suddenly venomous. "There's nothing for you to lose."

Quinn's brow furrowed, and he looked down. "My father told me once that the greatest evil in the world was indifference, that until we sloughed off our apathy and replaced it with empathy, none of us were safe." He looked up at her, lowering his voice further. "We're not damned and we're not dead and I still have a lot to lose."

Alice sniffed. "You're a fool."

"Definitely. But I know one thing that's stronger than your wall."

"What's that?"

"Hope."

He stood and paced back to the door. The sun was sliding from beneath the land, its edge blood red. He watched it rise and tapped the rifle's grip with a finger. Tomorrow was here.

~

They set off an hour later with empty stomachs. Their food was gone along with their water and first aid. Alice's scalp was cut and bloody, but it had stopped bleeding and she was able to walk on her own without dizziness tossing her to the ground.

They followed an overgrown path away from the sagging barn that wound past an empty foundation that might've once supported a house. Now all that it held was an inch of black water and leaves from the prior fall. The day became humid as they walked, the air clinging to them like an extra set of clothing. The trail led through a stand of birch dressed with willow brush before emptying out on a county road. The lanes were barren in both directions, nothing but heat mirages wafting up in the distance like the land itself was boiling.

"How long until we get to Iowa?" Ty asked as they walked. His hand rested on Denver's collar, the dog leading him solely now without the help of either Quinn or Alice. The transition had been seamless. The boy and the dog were a team.

"Pretty soon," Quinn said.

"How soon?"
"Like really soon."
"Today?"
"Not today."
"That's not really soon, Quinn. That's really long."
"How about tomorrow?"
Ty seemed to consider it. "Denver wants to get there today."
Quinn and Alice laughed. "He does, does he?"
"Yep. Do you think I could ride him?"
"What? No, you can't ride Denver," Quinn said, unable to keep from laughing.
"I don't think he'd mind. He's big enough."
"He probably wouldn't mind, but I'm not sure he'd hold you," Alice said, kicking a rock off the side of the road.
"Mom, he can't hold me; he doesn't have any arms."
This made Quinn and Alice lose it again. He glanced at her, catching her eye for a split second and she smiled. It felt good to laugh after the night before. The sun warming their backs, the fresh air, the open road. It all culminated to a near giddiness inside him. They were alive, despite everything that had happened.

The road looped through a spattering of trees that grew on the edges of uncultivated fields. They came to a set of railroad tracks, and Quinn stopped, walking perpendicular to the road along the rails for fifty yards.

"What are you doing?" Alice asked, shielding her eyes from the sun. Quinn paused and bent down, picking something up from between the rocks that filled the gaps of creosoted timbers. He came back and flipped her a dull, flat object. She caught it.

"Flattened penny?"

"We haven't seen any driveways for over two hours of walking. Kids usually put pennies on tracks. If there's kids around here, there must be a house nearby."

Alice gazed at the smashed penny and tried to hand it back.

"Keep it," Quinn said, beginning to walk again. "It's your lucky penny."

"I could use some luck. And some coffee. And a steak. But mostly luck."

Ty walked ahead of them, Denver's nose dropping to the pavement every few minutes. The dog's tongue hung out, a long strip of pink.

"You've seen me cry more than anyone else has now," Alice said quietly as they followed the boy and his Shepherd.

"I should feel special."

"Or worried." She glanced sideways, studying him again, and he felt heat rise to his face that had nothing to do with the climbing temperature of the day. He fumbled for words that weren't there, but then she'd moved past him, picking up her pace until she strode beside Ty. Their voices floated back to him, and he gazed up at the unbroken blue bowl above.

~

They came to the first house before mid-day. It was barely set off the road, a ramshackle patching of tin and plywood. A dead dog lay in the yard at the end of a chain, swarms of flies lifting from its body as they mounted the porch steps. Inside was a blotchy stain three times the size of a person beside a ragged EZ chair. The house smelled of rotting food and dirty laundry. They found half a dozen boxes of Mac-N-Cheese along with two cans of baked beans. Quinn procured a can opener from a kitchen drawer, and they ate the cold meal in silence at the cluttered table covered with bills and cigarette ashes.

In the leaning garage was a car covered by a huge, white drop cloth. A stack of wide tires encircling chrome rims stood in a corner. An impressive array of mechanic tools lined the wall with some strewn about the floor. Quinn walked to the edge of the sheet covering the car and tried to tug it free, but before he could really pull, the cloth began to slide toward him, gathering speed as it went. He stepped back, drawing the revolver as it fell to the floor.

"Holy shit," Alice said from beside him.

The car sat on blocks, its empty wheel wells giving it a skeletal look. It was low and sloping in a powerful way that struck a bell inside Quinn's chest. Shiny, black paint covered its entire length, polished to a sheen that reflected everything in the room. A spoiler grew from the long hood and bright strips of chrome shone from the bottoms of the doors and bumpers.

"What is it?" Quinn asked, approaching the machine.

"It's a Dodge Challenger, either a seventy or a seventy-one," Alice said, moving forward to run her hand along a fender. "My dad was restoring one when…" Her voice trailed off, and she moved around the front of the car. She cleared her throat. "Pop the hood, will you?"

Quinn opened the heavy driver's door and found the hood release. Alice pushed the hood up and whistled.

"That's a three-eighty-three big block. This is a brand new engine. Look at the exhaust and the plug wires. This thing hasn't even been out on the road yet," she said, her words a tone of awe.

"Didn't know you were into cars," Quinn said.

"I'm into this car. Look at how sexy she is."

"Mom," Ty said from the other side of the garage.

"Sorry, honey, but this is one fine piece of craftsmanship."

"What is this kind of car doing in a place like this?" Quinn asked, moving around the vehicle.

"I'm guessing whoever lived here was a mechanic. You'd be surprised how many of them have side projects like this."

"But how could he afford it? You saw the inside of the house."

"Not all of us can live on private estates in mansions, dear."

"That's not what I meant. I—"

"Priorities, that's how he afforded it. He ate macaroni so he could buy the perfect carburetor."

"Seems strange," Quinn said, eyeing the Challenger.

"Everyone sacrifices something for what they love." She glanced at him and then leaned into the driver's seat. "Keys are here. Should we see if she runs?"

"Do it, mom," Ty said. Denver woofed.

Alice twisted the key. The starter engaged, and the engine turned over with a throaty groan before catching. It chugged to life, idling loud in erratic pulses like an irregular heartbeat. Alice stood from the seat and smiled.

"It sounds like it's running rough," Quinn said over the throbbing engine.

"It's supposed to. It's been tinkered with for racing. It barely idles because it wants to fly." She grinned. In that moment, with exhaust flowing into the close space of the garage, blood matting her hair to the side of her head, she had never looked more beautiful. That smile.

He blinked, coming back to himself. "Don't you think it's a little loud?"

"Some of the trucks we've driven have been almost as loud," she said, stooping to turn the vehicle off. "At least with this, we're riding in style." She turned to Ty. "What do you think, buddy? Should we take this car or look for another one?"

"This one," Ty said, a smile spreading across his face. "I like how it sounds."

After checking the engine to make sure it was full of coolant and oil, they put the wheels on with a socket wrench. The interior was in rough shape, the dark leather cracked with stuffing poking through in yellow clumps. The floorboards were dirty and little strippings of wire were scattered every few inches. With nothing to put in the trunk, Quinn moved to the garage door and opened it, glancing in all directions before coming back to the car. When he got there, Alice was already in the driver's seat.

"Nuh-uh, not today, bud. You're riding shotgun," she said, jerking a thumb to the seat beside her. Once he was in, she backed out and lined the car up with the open highway. The sun was apexing in the sky, the shadows nearly extinct. "I really shouldn't do this, but what the hell," she said.

Alice slid the shifter back. Her feet twitched beneath the dashboard, and Quinn was sucked back in his seat as the engine roared and the wide tires shrieked. They rocketed forward, and Ty let out a high peal of laughter as Alice accelerated through the gears. The landscape beside the car fled past, trees and brush only blurs, a wooden bridge there and gone. When Quinn glanced over at her, one end of her mouth was turned up in a grin.

Eventually the road lost its straight line and began to snake through several rough hills that spilled down to the highway. Alice slowed and eased the Challenger around the curves as if she had grown up driving the car. She rolled her window down, and her seat was far enough forward for Denver to poke his head into the open air. His tongue lolled, eyes taking in the speeding scenery.

They drove into the golden afternoon without hindrance, filling the car up with gas at a large, silent farm that appeared to the north. The hills gave way to fields again that wouldn't be planted, last year's crops withering away in stolid silos. Quinn watched the land coast past. So much to see and take in. He drank the scenery with his eyes, opened his hand to catch the passing air in his palm like a harried creature that couldn't stay, each mile the furthest he'd ever been from home.

It was closing in on dusk when they passed the sign welcoming them to Illinois. They hadn't seen a single stilt the entire day, not even a glimpse of a thin moving line on the horizon or striding across any of the miles of open fields. As they crested a rise, a shallow valley opened below them, cupping a small town in its bowl. Several buildings and houses were lit, glowing warm in the failing day. On the far side of the valley, a line of wind turbines cranked steadily, their white blades chasing one another like an endless game of tag. Above them a large house was a stark cutout against the sky, lights blazing, its bulk resting on a rise overlooking the burg below.

"Turn here," Quinn said, pointing to the right at a gated driveway. Alice idled up to the wrought iron and stopped. Quinn climbed out and walked to the gate. It swung open with a push. They trundled up the curved drive, the house staying hidden until they reached the peak. It was a sprawling single story, its roof lined by filigreed railings. Long black tire marks lay in several rows before the attached garage doors. The inside of the garage was empty save for untouched camping equipment stacked against one wall and over a dozen folding lawn chairs. Quinn searched the house and found only scattered papers in an office along with a mixture of twenty and fifty-dollar bills. Everything else was in its place.

He raised the garage door with the touch of a button, and Alice backed the car inside. Denver brought Ty into the spacious living room lined with three enormous picture windows looking down upon the town. Alice began to check for weapons while Quinn searched the kitchen. He opened a pantry door, and a smell wafted out that instantly transported him home. He closed his eyes and inhaled, smiling.

When Alice returned to the kitchen, the coffee was already brewing. It drizzled into the pot in strong, brown streams, steam rising in delicious, scented tendrils.

"Oh, my, God. You found coffee," she said, coming to his side.

"You mentioned you could use some. Sit down and I'll pour you a cup."

She sat at the breakfast bar that halved the kitchen, watching him fill a mug full of the brew. He set it down before her, and she brought her nose so close to the liquid he was sure she would scald its tip.

"That's better than cocaine," she said, bringing the cup to her lips.

"You've tried cocaine?"

She sipped and swallowed, smiling as she closed her eyes.

"No, but I'd bet anything I'm right."

Quinn found the access to the roof in a hallway off of the living room. A wide stairway led up and out a pair of storm doors to a patio and outdoor kitchen, complete with brick oven and bar. The sun was setting, and it bathed the valley in tepid red light that receded across the land like bloodletting in reverse. He gazed at the beauty of it for a time before checking for other routes onto the roof. There was an extendible access ladder attached to one sidewall. In less than a second, they could have a way off the roof and back to the garage. They would sleep on the roof tonight.

He carried up a stack of blankets from the ground floor, lining the reclining lawn chairs with them before leading Alice and Ty up. Denver patrolled the entire roof and then settled on the patio stone beside Ty's chair before drifting off to sleep. As darkness crept closer, Quinn started the gas grill in the outdoor kitchen, ignoring Alice's questioning look before going to the main floor and returning with three frozen packages.

"You're kidding," Alice said as he dropped the porterhouse steaks onto the table and began unwrapping them.

"Guess that penny really was lucky."

"You keep giving me things like coffee and steak and you're going to get lucky."

Quinn dropped the fork he was using to pry the steaks from their containers and banged his head on the grill as he bent to pick it up. Alice giggled and walked away to circle the perimeter. He couldn't help but watch her, the graceful way she moved.

They ate beneath a twilight sky filled with purple clouds. The steak was phenomenal, and Quinn even managed to find a dusty bottle of wine in the basement cupboard that tasted like smoke from a campfire mixed with cherries.

The wind spun the turbines until they could no longer make out their bright fins. There was no sound from the town below, only the lights in homes that people had left on before dying or trying to run from the wave of sickness that they had no chance of outdistancing. Frogs took up a chorus somewhere down the side of the hill, their throaty voices filling the night.

Ty sang them a quiet song while petting Denver's broad head, the dog's eyes never leaving the boy. They watched the clouds soar past while wrapped in blankets, their stomachs full for the first time in days. When Ty finished singing, they golf-clapped, and he stood taking a small bow.

"I think I'm going to lie down now," Ty said, cuddling in the blankets on his chair. "Can Denver sleep with me tonight?"

"Honey, he's too big," Alice said, tucking him in. Ty drew his legs up leaving a long space at the bottom of his chair.

"There, now there's room."

"Ty…"

"Pleeeeaase?" The boy let the word draw out as he clasped his hands before him. Alice sighed. Ty smiled and snapped his fingers. "Denver, up."

The dog rose from his place beside him and climbed onto the chair, curling into as small a shape as he could manage. His tail thumped as Alice surveyed them both.

"Unbelievable. It's like I've got two kids now."

"Thanks, mom!" Ty called before burrowing deeper in his covers. "Goodnight, Quinn."

"Goodnight, buddy. We'll get to Iowa tomorrow."

"Think so?"

"I know so."

Ty grinned and lay back on his pillow.

"Will we?" Alice said, coming back to the table. She refilled her glass of wine, taking a long drink from it.

"If tomorrow goes as good as today did."

"Ha, now you jinxed it for us."

"Hope not. You can really drive that car, by the way."

"What, you think women can't drive?"

"No, but you really seem to enjoy that one."

"I do." She paused, running a fingertip around the rim of her glass. "I thought about my dad a lot today."

"I bet."

"He would've loved cruising like that."

The frogs became sporadic and finally quieted after a time. The clouds washed away from the moon, its light draping everything in silver.

"You ever thought about ending it all?" Alice asked, not looking at him. She gazed down into her wine glass, swirling it with one hand.

"Yeah, I have. More than once," Quinn said. He'd only had one glass of wine, but his head buzzed with its presence. "But I only was serious after all this happened. I was going to jump off the cliff behind our house. I had nothing left. Everyone I'd ever really known was dead."

"What stopped you?"

"Teresa's..." he paused. "My mother's words. She was the only mother I ever knew. I remembered something she said."

"What was it?"

"To not let fear win."

Alice turned her glass again and then stood, moving to the edge of the roof. Quinn followed and leaned against the rail beside her.

"How about you?" he asked.

"Every day," she said staring straight ahead. "Ever since the night of the fire. I was basically an orphan from that day forward. I didn't think I could be more alone, even in death." She tipped her glass, slugging her wine in a few gulps. "I don't believe in God. I think that beyond this life there's just darkness." She snapped her fingers, and he was reminded of his father saying how cruel the world could be. "We wink out, and there's nothing left of us, just memories."

He waited awhile, letting the breeze slip past them. Again, he was aware of her scent and how close she was, her arm brushing his at times.

"Can't memories be enough?" he said.

"What do you mean?"

"My father and friends are all gone, but I remember them every day. They haven't faded."

She smiled sadly and tossed her wine glass into the darkness. It shattered on something hard below the house.

"Ty's the only reason I keep going. Other than that..." She started to turn away, but he put a hand on her arm. She stopped, staring up at him.

"I've lost everything too, but I didn't die along with everyone else and you didn't either and neither did your son. You're special," he said, letting her arm go. "for more reasons than you know."

He expected her to scoff or walk away, but she did neither. Her hand came up to his cheek and touched it, her fingers softer than he'd expected. He steeled himself, trying not to jerk away, as she ran her fingertips over the jutting bones and slanted chin, trailing her hand down to his neck. Goosebumps spread out from the contact, running in sheets down his back and chest. He started to lean in, closing the distance between them that was a thousand miles, and less than inches, but stopped. She was watching him again, studying him with searching eyes that cut to his center. She was seeing him, even with the low light. Seeing the imperfections, the incongruities, the ugliness.

Quinn stepped away, and only then realized he was gripping her shoulder with one hand.

"I'm sorry. I..." he shot a look at her, her face impassive, giving him nothing. He brought his gaze to the floor. "Would you mind taking first watch?"

"No, that's fine," she said.

"Thanks."

He moved to the reclined lawn chair and lay down, covering himself with blankets. His hands were shaking. Halfway through situating himself, he began to rise again, but settled back down, staring up at the clearing sky and the cold sprinklings of stars that winked at him as if they knew secrets that would never be told.

~

They woke with the first morning rays that streamed through the trees to the west. Quinn avoided Alice's gaze as much as possible as they packed every useful item in the house they could find. Quinn found a smart phone and charger, and after bringing the device back to life, saw that the satellites still worked somewhere miles above the earth. Each of them took a short but welcome shower, and Quinn shaved off the heavy growth of beard that had accumulated over the past days. He avoided his reflection, slicing away the scruff by feel alone. Afterwards they ate a mostly silent breakfast and loaded the Challenger. Soon the massive house dwindled in their rearview mirrors.

"I liked that place," Ty said as they reached highway speed and took a route that bypassed the valley town.

"Yeah, why's that?" Alice asked, glancing back at him.

"It felt safe."

"Nowhere's safe," Alice said. Quinn glanced at her, but she held her eyes steady on the road.

The Challenger growled, pulling them on through the day. They stopped once for gas and had to detour three times. Twice because there were bridges out, blown wide by what appeared to be explosives, and the third from an impassable tunnel jammed full of dead cars and darkness. The last time they backtracked for forty miles before finding another route.

When they stopped beside a lonely field of dandelions to relieve their bladders, Alice held Quinn back on the side of the road while Denver led Ty to a stand of narrow trees.

"I'm sorry about last night," she started. "I had a lot to drink, and my tolerance is way down."

"Nothing to be sorry for. I overstepped my bounds; won't happen again."

"Quinn—"

"No, it's fine. Everything's fine. We're making good time, huh?" he said, walking away. She didn't reply, and he crossed the ditch and relieved himself before coming back to the car.

They reached Fort Dodge in the late afternoon. The town grew above the treetops in a smattering of brick and brownstone squares. A clock tower gazed down upon the streets, its cyclopean form looming above the rest of the buildings.

They entered the town from the east, idling into a barren industrial park lined with chain link fencing around its border. They waited, scanning the rows of buildings.

"Where is the military installation supposed to be?" Alice asked.

"It looks like there's three mining locations according to the map. One might be a processing plant. That one's on the southwest side of town."

"Where are the other two?"

"One's southeast and the other is northeast. The last one's out in the middle of nowhere." He glanced at her. "That's where I'd put a refugee center if it were me, get out of the city and off the beaten path."

Alice nodded, still staring at the buildings.

"Strange that we didn't see any of them again today," she said. "Kinda gives me the creeps."

"It gives me the creeps seeing them," Quinn replied.

"So what's our plan? Do we try to find the army before dark, or do we overnight in one of the buildings here and go looking in the morning?"

"I'd hate to be without cover when the sun goes down," Quinn said.

"Me too," Alice said.

"Me three," Ty chimed in.

"Okay. Let's find somewhere secure and get inside. I'm starving," Alice said, pulling forward.

They glided down the aisles of buildings. Many were barricaded by the same chain link that surrounded the rest of the park. Others were wide open, overhead doors gaping, windows shattered and jagged.

"Damn, I vote for that one," Alice said, drawing even with a distributing company. The garish, electric signs advertising liquor and beer above its main entrance were dark, but the building looked solid with only a single, unbroken window in its front.

"I'll take a walk," Quinn said, opening his door. He brought the rifle with him, checking its load before crossing the business's yard. The front door was locked, and when he peered in through the window, he saw it was also barricaded. A second steel door within the entry was shut tight. Quinn moved around the side of the building, pacing along its seamless block wall. On the backside there was a single door that wouldn't budge. When he looked closer, he saw that the latch had been welded solid to the frame. The opposite side of the building was an open loading dock for trucks to back into, its long promenade of concrete empty save for a stack of pallets in one corner. Quinn took two steps onto the loading dock and stopped.

A smeared bloodstain ran in a swath to one of the overhead doors.

He knelt beside it, dipping his fingers into one of the larger blotches of gore. It was still wet.

Quinn stood and moved to the door, following the blood trail. Smeared handprints covered its bottom edge, jets of crimson spattered near its base. Quinn stood to one side of the door and pushed upward.

It slid easily.

He dropped into a crouch, flicking the rifle's light on. Cases of beer stacked on pallets glowed in the glare along with a river of blood that led away into the darkness of the warehouse.

"Shit," he said, glancing over his shoulder at the sun. It was nearly touching the horizon. With two deep breaths, he pushed the door up its track enough to crawl beneath it and went inside.

The ceilings were high and lined with rows of darkened fluorescent lights. With the stacks of spirits on every side it was like being in a cavern of some sort, their heights soaring above him like stalagmites. He swept the area, the fresh blood shining back at him from the floor. He walked beside it, glancing up and around with each step. His boots clicked on the polished floor, the loudest sound besides his heart. The trail wound through two more stacks of booze and then dribbled into a narrow stream before ending completely.

Quinn shone the light into an alcove straight ahead of where the blood trail ended. A middle-aged man with short blond hair lay in the shadows beneath a large shelf loaded with vodka, his shoulders propped up against the wall. His eyes were partially lidded, and he held a dark handgun in his dripping fingers.

"Stop," he said, his voice weak and hollow in the air of the warehouse.

"I'm not going to hurt you," Quinn said, keeping the AR-15 trained on the man's chest.

The man laughed, a quiet, wet sound. "Good; that's good."

Quinn lowered the rifle enough to illuminate the man's legs.

His left foot ended in a ragged stump that oozed blood into a broad pool. As Quinn watched, the man's arm slumped to his side, and his eyes rolled up into his head.

~

They ate a cold dinner of cheese and sliced sausages along with several cans of beer they'd taken from an open container. They sat in a semicircle on the floor, Denver lying between Ty and Alice on his side, soaking in the coolness of the concrete. Quinn kept glancing over at the man's prone form, his head resting on a rolled up blanket, leg elevated and secured on a steel chair they'd found in the front office.

After the man passed out, Quinn had seen he'd been holding a makeshift tourniquet with his free hand, and without the pressure, the stump began to bleed freely again. He'd retied the bootlace the man had used, staunching the flow to almost nothing, before running outside to direct Alice to the rear loading dock. Once they were all inside, they'd repositioned the injured man and poured a small amount of water in his mouth that he managed to swallow. After that, he'd become completely unresponsive, the rising and falling of his chest the only movement.

They'd found a stockpile of food, weapons, and ammunition in one of the offices along with a meager first aid kit that had already been pilfered of anything useful. A hiking backpack leaned against one wall near the food and weapons, its many pouches bulging with enough supplies to keep a single person going for more than two weeks.

Alice drained the last of her beer and set the can aside before motioning to the man. "What do you think happened to his foot?"

Quinn glanced at Ty and then back to her, lowering his voice. "I think it was bitten off."

"Me too."

"Yeah. Looked like teeth marks in the flesh around the wound. Not that you can really tell since infection's already setting in."

"He's not going to make it," she said.

"No, I don't think so."

They cleaned up their wrappers and cans and checked on the man again. His face was pale and dry, but when Quinn put a hand to the man's forehead, he nearly yanked it back with shock.

"He's burning up."

They tried drizzling more water in the man's mouth, but he merely coughed it back out. His breathing began to take on a liquid wheezing, so they let him be and made their own beds up for the night.

"You think one of us has to keep watch?" Alice said, tucking Ty into a sleeping bag.

"I think it's okay if we all sleep tonight. This place is locked down really well. Any problems and we can scoot right out the door and into the car."

They were quiet for a time as they lay down on their own blankets. The darkness around them was complete.

"Wonder what he was doing here," Alice said finally.

"Surviving, like the rest of us."

"Almost looks like he was planning something."

"Like what?" Quinn asked.

"Like a trip."

He listened to the man's labored breathing a dozen yards away. That could be any of them lying there, wounded, dying. How would it feel to know beyond any doubt that you were going to die? The idea was one thing, but the fear, the fear was all encompassing.

"This fort-bed thing is getting kind of old," Alice said, breaking the silence.

Quinn chuckled, and she laughed too after a moment.

"I can't believe we made it," Alice said.

"Me neither."

"Not really what you would've picked for your first road trip, huh?"

He smiled. "It's not what I had in mind, no."

She was quiet for a long time. "Thank you for everything you did to get us here."

"You're welcome. Thanks for saving my life a hundred times."

"Ditto." Her blankets rustled, and he imagined her turning toward him in the dark. "What if there's no army there tomorrow?"

The question caught him off guard. Not because he'd never thought it but because he'd been thinking it for days.

"Then we find a safe place somewhere else."

She settled again with more shushing of blankets.

"Goodnight, Quinn."

"Goodnight."

Sleep eluded him like a beggar with a stolen scrap of bread. He would begin to drift off then the steel loading doors would shift in the wind letting out unfamiliar clanks and clicks. Each time he would bring his hand to the butt of the revolver before relaxing again. Much later, when he'd finally found a position that was partially comfortable, another sound roused him. It was reedy and low, as if it were coming from the bottom of some pit. He sat up, images of a thousand stilts surrounding the building filling his head. Instead, he slowly made out words filtering through the darkness.

"I Royal."

Quinn rolled to his feet and found the rifle. He flicked the light on, and it brightened enough of the space for him to move without the fear of sprawling over a low crate. He walked to the man's side and saw that his eyes were open, the irises obscured by a thin membrane, like a fog hanging over a valley.

"Here, have some water," Quinn said, picking up the bottle sitting nearby on the concrete. He tried to bring it to the man's cracked lips, but he turned his head away, refusing.

"I Royal," he breathed again, and tried to raise one of his arms.
"Your name is Royal?" Quinn asked leaning closer.
"Royal."
The man opened his mouth wide and took in a long shuddering breath before letting it wheeze out. He spasmed several times as if trying to cure a case of hiccups, and then fell still, the last of his air leaking from between his teeth.

"Damn it," Quinn said, checking his pulse. Nothing. He put his hands on the man's chest in the CPR position but then sat back. He was resting now. How cruel would it be to bring him back?

He stood and found a dusty sheet draped over a stack of whisky cases. He shook it out and gently spread it over the man's body.

Royal.

Quinn retrieved the rifle and moved past Ty and Alice toward the front offices. Denver's dark head rose, and after a moment, the Shepherd padded silently after him.

In the office with the supplies, Quinn sat down and began to open the heavy pack leaning against the wall. There were fire-starting materials, extra clothes, emergency blankets, spare magazines for the two pistols and four rifles that sat on the floor, along with a bladder filled with water. All of the pockets contained similar survival items, except for the topmost. When he opened it, he first thought that the man had packed sheaves of paper for more fire-starting fuel, but after a moment of inspecting them, he saw he was wrong.

He studied the pages after settling to the floor, Denver dropping onto his side next to him. Absently, he scratched the dog's ears as he read, page after page of information, facts, numbers, first-hand accounts, surveys, and data. As he unfolded another page, a plastic ID card slid free and fell to the floor. He picked it up, studying the dead man's face along with the words beneath it. He frowned, flipping the card over, but there was nothing on the back except an imbedded row of numbers with a bar code below them. He set the ID aside and scanned the folded document, eyes flickering across meaningless tangles of numbers and terms. At the very bottom were two signatures. The first was strangely familiar, as if it were the name of a character from a book he'd read years ago.

The other signature stopped his heart between beats.

He stared at the name, and time seemed to slow. Denver grunted beside him, and the page began to tremble in his hand. It couldn't be. There was no possible way.

Footsteps came from the warehouse and neared the office as Alice materialized out of the darkness and stopped in the doorway, her eyes still bleary with sleep.

"What are you doing?"

Quinn folded the paper, tucking the ID card inside it once again.

"Going through his things," he said, his voice hoarse and shaky. "He's—"

"Dead. I saw."

Quinn gathered up the rest of the papers, replacing all of them in the pack, save for the one holding the ID, which he jammed in his pocket.

"Did you sleep at all?" she asked as he rose and stretched his aching spine.

"A little. Not much. Is it daylight yet?"

"Just before dawn."

"We need to go. We need to find the army, now." He grabbed the pack and the rifle, handing the latter to Alice as he moved past her into the dark of the warehouse.

"Okay. Any reason you're so raring to go?"

"We just need to get there," he said over his shoulder as he made his way through the sections of alcohol.

"Quinn, slow down. Let's take a second—"

"No, damnit! We're going now!" His voice rang throughout the open space and came back to him. Hearing the frantic sound of his words along with the stricken look on Alice's face was enough to sober the racing anxiety burning a hole in his chest.

"What's going on?" she asked. "You're starting to scare me." Ty sat up from his bed and called to Denver quietly before walking beside the dog to stand near his mother.

Quinn's legs grew weaker and weaker as he pulled the paper from his pocket and flipped it open, catching the ID as it slid out. He held it before him as if it were something foul that he couldn't stand to touch.

"We need to find the army because my father's signature is on this piece of paper the dead man was carrying."

Chapter 25

The Army

They drove through the gray dawn, its light choked with bruised clouds that hung low and heavy with rain.

They'd spent an hour packing the Challenger with supplies that the man in the warehouse had accumulated, their talk limited to the necessities since Quinn had shown Alice the signed page. There was no mistaking his father's writing, the loop of his e's and the long tail of the y were all Quinn needed to know it wasn't simply someone with the same name or an attempt at a forgery. The paragraphs above his father's hand gave them no clues as to what the document signified. The language was unmistakably medical in origin, but other than that, the page was a shard of a sculpture without any definable shape.

"Do you think he was sick before he caught the plague?" Alice asked as the last buildings of Fort Dodge passed by on their left. "You said he came home from a business trip right before everything happened, right?"

"Yeah," Quinn said, prying his vision from the road ahead.

"Maybe it wasn't a business trip at all. Maybe he was getting treatment."

"I don't think so. He never had more than a cold all my life. He wasn't sick; he would've told me."

"Parents don't tell their kids everything."

"I know, you never tell me anything," Ty muttered from the backseat.

"Oh stop it, Tyrus. You're the most informed six year old I know."

"I'm almost seven!"

"You won't be seven for another nine months."

"That's pretty close, though. Right, Denver?"

The dog woofed once.

"See?" Ty said, crossing his arms.

Alice rolled her eyes. "Now I have to argue with a dog too."

"Take this next right coming up," Quinn said, studying the smart phone's display. Alice turned the car onto a beaten county road, its surface pockmarked with attempted patches of potholes and frost heaves.

"But the guy, Harold Roman, was definitely military, right? I mean, that ID had nothing but his photo, his name, and clearance number," Alice said.

"If I had to guess, I'd say military, but who knows," Quinn said. "Turn left on the next road."

The landscape around them was featureless grasslands only beginning to green. The sky continued to descend, the clouds churning above the treetops. In the distance, the land humped into a broad hill, and dots of abandoned vehicles began to appear. They weaved in and around them, doors yawning open, windows broken, a sprawled and bloated body on a tailgate.

"What's that smell?" Ty asked, covering his nose.

The air thickened with each mile they drove, the stench of the plague's rapid decomposition like a clinging curtain hovering above the land. Ahead, the line of vehicles became a mass that choked the road as well as the dirt track snaking around the base of the broad hill. A business sign had been knocked down and a torn banner waved in its place, only a handful of words discernable on its flaccid surface.

United States Ar
Zon
Only nec belongin
Milit guiden
Stay inside your ve

Alice pulled to the side of the road, and they stared at the lane strangled with hundreds of cars and trucks all parked at different angles like a portion of rush hour traffic had detoured here and then fallen still indefinitely.

"Holy shit," Alice said. She sighed and let her face drop into one hand before rubbing her temple. "If they're—"

"Let's not get ahead of ourselves," Quinn said. "We need to check out the compound before we make any decisions."

"You ever see that movie where the family drives all the way across the country to go to an amusement park but when they get there, it's closed?"

"Yeah."

"That's not like this at all," Alice said, climbing out.

They armed themselves, and Quinn strapped Roman's pack on. They left the rest of the supplies with the car, locking it before moving along the ditch lining the dirt drive. They walked past car after car. Many were intact, their windows rolled tight as if the occupants had merely paused here to get out and sightsee. There were no bodies visible, inside or out, along the road. Only the chirp of insects and the sounds of their passage accompanied them. The stagnant line of vehicles curved, and they followed their arc, stopping as one as the scene opened before them.

"What is it?" Ty asked, gripping Denver's collar.

It was a warzone.

The vehicles past the point where they stood were torn masses of steel and shattered glass. The road became a battered field, studded with debris and cratered to a lunar quality. A chain link fence had been erected beyond the devastation, topped with spools of razor wire, but it too lay mashed to the ground in countless places, support posts leaning like weary soldiers. Past the fence was a five-foot concrete barricade made of interconnected pieces like those separating the center of a four-lane highway. It's top was painted a bronze that shone in the cool light of the day. Many of the sections were tipped over or crumbling, cracks spanning from bullet holes like eggs ready to break. Beyond the first ring of concrete, a second much higher barrier stood, interspersed by vacant, steel guard towers and scaffolding.

Everything was silent and still. Unmoving.

"Damnit," Alice swore, sweeping the entire area with her rifle. Quinn took several steps forward and cupped a hand to his mouth.

"Hello!"

His call echoed across the grassland and returned to them. A crow called from a solitary tree at the base of the hill, its voice mocking.

They waited and then picked their way forward through the divots and piles of blasted steel that they realized had been cars and pickups. Strands of clothing were buried beneath tossed sand, a child's backpack hung from a twisted fender by one frayed strap. They stopped at the first concrete barrier, and Quinn saw that the top wasn't painted bronze as he'd first thought.

It was covered in brass shell casings.

They were everywhere. They littered the ground outside the barrier, and inside, they rose like miniature sand dunes. Every ten paces there was a semi-bare spot on the ground, and he realized this was where the shooters had been standing.

"What happened here?" Quinn said, brushing the shells with his palm. They tinkled like steel rain as they dropped to the dirt.

"I don't want to know," Alice said, reaching out to grasp Ty's free hand.

"Let's go this way," Quinn said, motioning to the east side of the barriers.

They crossed over a collapsed portion of concrete and walked between the two perimeters. The ground was covered with spent ammunition. Here and there were dried mats of blood turned black with time. Similar stains splashed the higher concrete walls as well. Flies carried on a continuous humming all around them.

The barriers curved and then straightened in a corridor that stretched away and over a short rise. The piles of shells continued out of sight. They stopped near a toppled section as the first drops of rain began to fall. Quinn glanced at Alice who stared back at him, her mouth a pale gash.

"They're not here, are they?" Ty said. Denver sat on his haunches, his eyes watching the top of the nearest barricade. Alice knelt beside Ty, still holding his hand. She brushed his hair away from his brow and opened her mouth to reply when Denver began to growl.

"Put your hands in the air! Do it, now!" A deep voice yelled from somewhere nearby.

Quinn flinched and instinctually brought his rifle up as he ducked. A shot ricocheted off the pillar next to him.

"I will not ask again! Put your hands up!"

Quinn let the rifle hang from the strap draped around his shoulders and slowly brought his hands over his head. Alice and Ty did the same beside him. There was a scraping rasp and a door painted the exact same color as the concrete, opened in the barricade fifty yards away. A soldier dressed in full military fatigues and boots sidled into the channel, a short-barreled rifle centered on them. Another soldier emerged behind him, his weapon sweeping the area around the barriers and then back to their position. Quinn eased himself around and stood to his full height.

"Don't fucking move!" the closest soldier said. The man was near enough now Quinn could see hard, green eyes beneath the helmet he wore. A rash of brown stubble covered a handsome face, and when he moved, it was with practiced fluidity and confidence.

"Thomas, got anything in the area?" the nearest soldier said, never turning his head away from them. The voice from above called out a moment later.

"Negative. All clear."

"Is there anyone else with you?" the soldier asked.

"No, it's just us," Alice said.

The soldier scanned them all again, his eyes flitting to Quinn's face and holding there for a long time before looking down at Ty and Denver who's fangs were bared white beneath peeled lips.

"Put your weapons on the ground and step away from them."

Quinn glanced at Alice who looked back at him, a thousand unsaid words in a single gaze. He nodded, and they stripped their rifles free, along with the revolver and Roman's pack, laying them on the piled shells.

"I'm going to search you. If any of you move in a way that displeases the soldier above you, you will be shot. Do you understand?"

They all nodded, and Quinn heard Ty draw in a shuddering breath. The soldier moved forward and patted them down while the man behind him kept a bead on them, his gaze locked on Quinn's face.

"They're clean," the first soldier said, stepping back. He lowered his weapon but kept his finger on the trigger. "Where the hell did you folks come from?"

"Maine," Alice answered. "Can we put our fucking hands down now?"

The soldier's eyebrows rose and he nodded. "Yes, go ahead."

They lowered their hands, and Ty stroked Denver's head and back, smoothing his hackles that stood upright, until the big dog licked his chops and sat down near the boy's feet.

"Maine?" the second soldier repeated.

"Yes, Maine. We heard about the safe zone before everything went to shit and drove here," Alice said, bringing Ty close to her side. The soldier turned to his companion and shrugged.

"Unbelievable you got here unscathed," he said after a pause.

"We didn't get here unscathed," Quinn said. "There was plenty of scathing."

"I see. Well, no offense, buddy, but can I ask what's—"

"It's a genetic disorder that affected my facial bones. I've had it since I was born."

The soldier studied him for a moment and then turned to Alice. "You corroborate this, ma'am?"

Alice laughed bitterly. "Yes, I corroborate. Now, are you going to let us inside, or do we have to hoof it back to our vehicle and find the real army?"

The soldier eyed them all for another beat and then offered his hand.

"Lieutenant Garret Wexler. This is Private Weston Murray. And the man up above is Private First Class Robert Thomas. Welcome to U.S. Army Safe Haven Number 81, or as we call it, Camp Terra Verde. Murray, kindly gather the people's weapons, and I'll show them inside."

"We can't have our guns?" Alice asked.

"No, ma'am. Civilians are not allowed to carry weapons within camp," Wexler said, ushering them toward the battered steel door set into the barricade. They stepped inside, and Quinn couldn't help faltering, his eyes widening at the sight.

Innumerable rows of low, white tents were set on the crusted soil. They stretched away in unending lines, some collapsed upon themselves while others were larger and stood above their counterparts. The circumference of the barriers was immense, the walls running in a huge loop that he lost sight of as it dipped down and curved to the west. A half dozen tanks sat across the immense yard as well as four large transport trucks, their rear ends open and empty. Machinegun turrets were folded back in upright positions every twenty yards atop the walls, and a narrow band of steel scaffolding ran in a half circle along the north, west, and east of the perimeter, giving access to the turrets. The soldier Wexler had identified as Thomas stood on one edge of a platform above them, a long sniper rifle notched against a hip. He watched them as they entered and spit a string of tobacco juice to the ground fifteen feet below. The wind carried the rotting scent past them as more rain began to fall.

"You good for a bit, Thomas?" Wexler called without looking up.

"Yeah. Send me up an umbrella. Better yet, send me up Sergeant Collincz." Thomas grinned, and Murray, who had just entered the camp carrying their weapons, broke into laughter. Wexler half turned toward them and cocked his head to one side. He waited until both soldiers quieted, and Thomas faced the fields outside the walls. Wexler shifted his attention back to them and then nodded toward a long, green tent beside the transport trucks.

"Follow me, please."

Thunder rolled across the sky like an unseen avalanche as they kept pace behind the Lieutenant and ducked beneath the flaps into the tent. Inside were two plastic folding tables surrounded by chairs along with a bank of computer equipment, screens all dark. A rack of rifles hung from one wall, stacks of army-green plastic ponchos lining the ground beneath them. A half-eaten protein bar sat on the edge of the closest table, and Wexler picked it up, biting off a chunk before unsnapping his helmet.

"Apologies, but I'm going to finish my lunch if you folks don't mind," he said, lowering himself into a chair.

Quinn gazed around the mostly barren tent to the raindrops pelting the dry ground outside sending up puffs of dust. He caught Alice's eye, and she stared at him, holding her hands out, palms up. *What's going on?* He shrugged and turned to Wexler who was finishing his protein bar.

"Sir, can you tell us what's happening here?"

Wexler crushed the wrapper and flung it into a plastic bin beside the table. He looked at them all before sighing.

"Not exactly what you expected after traveling all this way, I'm sure."

"Fucking A," Alice said, placing her hands on her hips. Wexler appraised her and smiled before rubbing the close-cropped hair on his head.

"When the disease titled A4N9 became labeled as a pandemic, the United States government began setting up quarantine zones as well as safe havens across the country. This one was completed first as a centralized location." He paused and looked at them all. "It was also the *only* one completed."

"What?" Quinn said.

"The disease moved too fast for the other havens to be finished. The kill rate was unbelievable. Just when we thought the worst had passed, another wave of sickness would roll over. Millions upon millions of infected dying in their homes, the streets, their cars, everywhere. And then we began to see *them.*" Wexler scratched the stubble on his jaw and gazed down at the floor.

"You mean the stilts," Quinn said.

"Stilts? Yeah, that's a good name for them. We never really had an official title to call them, never received any protocol." He laughed, but it held no humor. "Never received a lot of things."

"That's where all the shells came from outside, isn't it?" Quinn said, ice water pooling in the pit of his stomach. "You were shooting at them, weren't you?"

Wexler nodded without looking up. "The last strings of refugees were coming in five days ago. The quarantines broke down as soon as they were established. Everyone was sick. Those who weren't were immune, simple as that. We didn't realize what was coming, we had zero intel. And then they were just there, all around us." Wexler fumbled in his pocket and drew out a crumpled pack of cigarettes and a lighter. He lit the smoke and drew hard on it, expelling a white plume into the air as the rain drummed harder on the tent. "We took hundreds of them down, but they kept coming until dark and then they just vanished, pulled away their dead. I saw a few eating their own, but the worst thing was the people coming in were caught in the crossfire. Some were dragged off, but a lot got blown to pieces during all the fighting." Wexler coughed and pinched the bridge of his nose. "That's when I had the most men under my command."

"Lieutenant, where is everyone? Where's the refugees and the rest of your troops?" Quinn asked in a low voice as lightning slit the sky's belly. Wexler took another drag on his cigarette, the smoke turning his eyes a sick, milky green as he stared through it.

"They're dead. We're all that's left."

Chapter 26

Questions and Answers

"What do you mean you're all that's left?" Alice asked, her voice rising in pitch. "You're all that's left of your company?"

"We're all that's left of the United States Army, ma'am. When this shit went down, they had cases springing up in Russia, England, Germany, Australia, and Canada. Deployments went everywhere, but we were all given comm codes to reach the other havens. That's how I know they were never finished. There were mass AWOL reports at first and then everyone was sick. The last haven I heard from was in northern Texas, and the Captain in charge there was delirious with fever. He said the things people were becoming were the future and there was no resisting them. Those that were immune were the damned and they'd be the ones to suffer the most."

Quinn crossed his arms to keep them from shaking. *I wonder if we're the damned?* "There's got to be other posts out there. Someone must've survived," he said.

"Listen bud, I manned the comms myself until most lines dropped off the grid. The last contact we had with the outside was three days ago. There's been nothing but silence ever since."

"Oh my God," Alice said, and slowly sat in a chair. She pulled Ty into her lap, and Denver slumped to the ground near her feet.

"We suspected it was bad, but…" Quinn waved his hand at the rain-pelted dirt, his throat closing up.

"It's global," Wexler said, finishing his cigarette. He crushed it beneath the sole of his boot and stood. "The scientists had just started to scrape the surface of the virus when it all collapsed." He surveyed them again. "Did you see anyone else alive out there?"

"Yes. They were mostly hostile," Alice said, not looking up. "But there were a few."

"We've had two small bands of renegades come through, both repelled easily, but then we had numbers and firepower. We burned through ammo during the fight with the tall bastards because we figured we'd have another transport come in within a day. None ever came."

"So you three are it?" Alice asked. "You're all that's left?"

"We have two more. One is Sergeant Collincz. She's over attending to Doctor Holtz in the rear of the compound."

"What about him?" Quinn asked, pulling out the ID card with Harold Roman's picture on it. "Did you know him?" Wexler took the card from him and glanced up.

"Where did you get this?"

"I found it in the pack I was wearing earlier. Roman was hiding in a distributing warehouse on the east side of Fort Dodge. He'd been injured, looked like a stilt bit him. He died in the middle of the night," Quinn said.

Wexler grimaced and turned the ID card over and over in his hands.

"He disappeared three nights ago while on watch. He was a lab technician from Minnesota, showed up right when we were first setting camp. We had to recruit him to help watch the walls after everyone died. I was sure he'd been taken."

"He was also carrying this," Quinn said, opening the paper with the medical terminology on it. Wexler read through it and after a moment, shook his head, handing it back.

"Doesn't make a lick of sense to me."

"I can't understand it either, but that's my father's signature on the very bottom."

Wexler took out the pack of cigarettes again, pulling one free before rolling it between his fingers. "You could try showing it to Holtz, but don't get your hopes up."

"Why's that?" Quinn asked.

"Because he's lost touch with reality the last few days. He's a military doctor and was working in a lab here on base when everyone started developing the fever and dropping dead. He tried everything that they sent him as far as vaccines and even made quite a few of his own, from what I understand, before his wife fell ill." Wexler tucked the cigarette away for later. "When she died, he became unstable, didn't sleep for days and started babbling nonsense to anyone that came within earshot. He's been asleep for over twenty-four hours, and we've been taking turns checking on him."

"I'd like to see him," Quinn said.

"Me too," Alice said, coming to her feet.

Wexler gazed at them and then out at the rain before standing to grab several ponchos off the floor.

"You're going to need these. It's a bit of a walk."

~

They trudged through the curtains of rain as the wind tried to tug the plastic ponchos from their bodies. Thomas gave Wexler a short signal from the wall before resuming his vigil of the surrounding land. They made their way down the first row of tents, the openings flapping in the wind like beckoning hands. Denver eyed each one warily as they passed as if he expected something to rise from inside.

Wexler lead at a brisk pace, not looking around, head down, hands gripping his weapon. The land slowly sloped away, gradually at first and then more quickly. An access road, packed solid by dozens of tires, ran parallel to the north wall, disappearing from their view as it made a sharp turn and dropped away. The rain fell harder until they could only see a dozen strides ahead, the water undulating like a living thing. Lightning flashed again, and Quinn made out a low, dark building a hundred yards away, its features hidden by the storm. Beyond that was something he couldn't quite understand, his mind fumbling with the information relayed in the brief blast of light. They hurried toward the building. It was only when they were close enough to see the plastic windows set in its sides and the light glowing within that he realized what lay beyond the building itself.

The land completely dropped away into nothing fifty paces past the shelter. He had the impression of an unfathomable hole without a bottom and then the wind shifted, obscuring everything into a rain-washed haze.

"Inside!" Wexler said, holding the door open for them. Ty and Denver went in first, Alice following. Halfway through the entry, she slipped on the slick partition, her arms flying out to steady herself. Quinn stepped forward, knowing he couldn't catch her, but then Wexler's arm was there, wrapping around her mid-back and holding her close. She glanced up at him, her eyes wide and he smiled.

"Okay?" he asked. She nodded and regained her footing before going inside. Quinn looked down at the ground as he passed the soldier. Wexler held the door for him saying, "Careful, it's slippery."

"I got it," Quinn said, stepping inside the building.

The structure was steel-framed construction with heavy poles secured in the earth, cement surrounding their bases. The shell was a tough canvas, its sides dotted with plastic widows beaded with rain. Medical equipment was everywhere. There were five cots, all missing their bedding, against one wall while the very front of the building was dedicated to computers and slim machines attached to them with snaking cables. A plastic curtain hung in the center of the space and a light shone behind it. A dark figure, only a smudged outline that moved toward them, drew a break in the curtain aside.

The soldier was a woman, mid-thirties with a round, pretty face framed by blond hair that she wore in a tight ponytail. She was shorter than Alice and heavier with a suggestion of muscularity beneath her uniform. Her eyes widened as she spotted them standing behind Wexler. Her gaze slid to each of their faces, her mouth partially open.

"They came in a little while ago," Wexler said. "From Maine."

"You're kidding," Collincz said, looking them over. "My God, that's unbelievable."

"They've come to speak with Holtz."

"About what?"

Quinn stepped forward, holding out his paper. "Harold Roman had this in his pack when we found him. He's dead," Quinn said when Collincz's eyes snapped up at the man's name. She gave a quick nod and dropped her gaze to the text on the page. "That's my father's signature on the bottom."

"Doctor Alex Gregory?"

There was something about the name that tolled a bell in his mind again, something about the way Collincz said it.

"No, James Kelly."

"*The* James Kelly?" Collincz asked.

"If you're referring to the movie star, then yes." Both soldiers ran their gazes over his face before passing a look between them.

"I don't understand any of this, but I'm guessing Holtz will," Collincz finally said. "Come with me; we'll see if he's still awake."

She led them back through the plastic sheet to the rear of the building, which had so much lab equipment they might as well have walked into a government research facility. There were glass containment vestibules with protective rubber gloves hanging from their sides, vials upon vials stacked in centrifuges, beakers, microscopes, and powerful overhead lights that were all darkened. An electric lantern on a nearby table threw bleached light against everything in the room. In the furthest corner was a simple cot covered with black woolen blankets. A tall man with a shock of white hair and a few days' growth of matching stubble on his long face lay beneath the covers. His eyes were open, and he stared at the ceiling that the rain continued to hammer against. Beside his bed was a simple steel tray holding a paper, pen, and a worn leather wallet. Collincz brought them to the man's bedside and leaned into his line of sight.

"Doctor Holtz? There's some people here to see you." Holtz's glazed stare never wavered. "Doctor? Could you maybe talk with them for a bit?" When the man didn't so much as blink, Collincz held the sheet of paper with the signatures on it before his eyes. "Does any of this make sense to you, sir?" Holtz looked through the paper, a drop of saliva gathering at the corner of his mouth. Collincz held the paper steady for another few seconds and then stood back from the prone man.

"I'm sorry," she said, handing the sheet back to Quinn. "He was completely comatose for over a day, and when he woke up, he took a few sips of water and chicken broth before becoming catatonic. I have no clue as to whether or not he'll snap out of it. He could be like this for another hour, or…" She let her sentence trail off as another bolt of lightning ripped through the sky.

"I'm hungry," Ty said in a low voice.

Collincz smiled. "I bet you are. How would you like a bowl of soup to warm you up and some dry blankets to cuddle into?"

Ty nodded, his face turned toward her voice. "That would be great!"

"Good. And what does your dog like to eat?"

"He'll have soup too."

"Ty," Alice said, frowning. The two soldiers laughed, and Ty grinned slyly.

"How about some lunchmeat?" Wexler said. "We have some that's going to go bad in a day or two."

As the soldiers busied themselves preparing a meal and places to sit, Quinn moved to Holtz's cot and looked down at the old man. His eyes were brown and bloodshot with layers of wrinkles surrounding their edges. His skin was like papyrus: jaundiced and so thin it looked as if it would tear at the slightest touch. Quinn leaned over him, feeling Holtz's gentle breaths on his face.

The doctor's eyes met his own for a split second before unfocusing again.

"Quinn?"

Alice's voice so close made him jerk.

"Yeah."

"What were you doing?"

"Seeing if there's anything worthwhile here," he said, moving past her. "C'mon, let's eat."

~

The rain continued through the afternoon, the sky hanging low and heavy, split only by the occasional streak of lightning. They ate cold sandwiches and hot tomato soup followed by a chocolate protein bar identical to the one Wexler had consumed earlier.

"Eat as many as you'd like. And don't worry," he told them as he tossed the bars across the small folding table. "We've got plenty of them."

Quinn and Alice took turns relating their journey with the intermittent comment from Ty to fill in the small things they missed. When they were finished, Wexler and Collincz cleared the table and set up three more cots in the center of the rear room.

"You can stay as long as you like," Wexler said, opening his cigarette pack again. "We've got enough rations available for over a year, and as long as it keeps raining like this, we'll have water too." He lit the smoke and took a long drag before motioning to Collincz. "Sergeant Collincz has been staying here for the last few days caring for Doctor Holtz. She'll get you anything you need. The toilet's in the front corner, shower on the opposite side, though there's no hot water."

"Where are you going?" Ty asked.

"I gotta go keep a lookout up front, bud," Wexler said, patting him gently on the back. He shot a look at Alice and smiled, his handsome features becoming more so. "But I'll be around."

Quinn watched Alice return his smile with her own, heat flaring in her alabaster skin. He pretended to see something of interest across the room and moved there, toying with the edge of a rumpled plastic tarp until Wexler said his goodbyes and vanished into the rain-soaked day. He tugged harder on the corner of the tarp, and it dropped to the floor, revealing a decaying stilt's arm lying on a dissection tray.

Quinn stepped back, covering his nose as the smell wafted from the rotting flesh. The arm was folded at the elbow and wrist, its skin flayed away in precise lines and pinned back by aluminum clamps revealing the musculature and white bone beneath.

"It always creeped me out too," Collincz said, stepping up beside him. "A week ago this whole lab and three others like it were full of techs and doctors like Holtz. He was in charge, though. He was the brains the military was counting on. When those things started showing up, he had groups go out and harvest samples from the dead ones before the others dragged them away and ate them or whatever they did after dark."

"What was he doing with the tissue samples?"

"Trying to determine how we became them," she said, pointing from her chest to the disembodied arm.

"Did he figure it out?"

"Not that I know of. He was making progress, from what I understood, in the days before his wife passed, but then he shut down. That was it for possibly finding a cure. Not that it mattered by then. Everyone was dying or dead." She looked out the window still drizzling with rain. "We didn't stand a chance, and the higher-ups seemed to know it too."

"What do you mean?" Quinn asked.

She appraised him for a moment. "You saw all those tents set up on the way down here, right?"

"Yeah, why?"

"They were for the refugees that would undoubtedly show up once the government started broadcasting this location as a central haven. But they served two purposes." Collincz ticked off her fingers. "One, obviously for shelter; and two, they doubled as body bags. Just pull the stakes and yank on the right edge and the whole thing folds over itself containing whatever's inside."

Quinn licked his lips and glanced down at the floor. "What was the reason for setting up the haven around a mine?"

"They said it was for fresh water collection. There's always groundwater forming in a mine and then there's the runoff from rainstorms like this one."

"But's that not the real reason, was it?" Quinn asked. Collincz shook her head, watching him. "It was for the disposal of bodies."

She nodded. "We were running one big burial ground. That open mine a hundred yards from here was supposed to be the biggest mass grave in the world. While all the officials ran off to their bunkers, we were supposed to deal with the mess." She looked away and began to chew on her lower lip. "We hauled thousands of bodies down there before they dissolved completely. That's what the smell is that hangs over this place."

"My God," Quinn said. He leaned against the table. "They never thought there'd be a cure, did they?"

"No. They folded their cards and left the table before we knew what had happened. I think Holtz must have known what was going on all along, but he kept at it. He was sure there was a cure."

"He's still alive. He's immune to the disease. That has to mean something."

"I thought that too," Collincz said, taking a deep breath. "I had hope, right up until my fiancée's unit was taken out by a herd of those things." She smiled sadly and cleared her throat before turning away. "Let me know if you need anything else."

~

They spent the evening playing with a set of dominoes they found in a cabinet. Alice helped Ty set up rows of them, guiding his hands through the motions of how to create corners and curves that would fall when the first was pushed over. Soon Ty was creating long, intricate lines, a look of concentration pinching his face.

"I need more of them," he said after a time.

"I'm sorry, honey," Alice said. "There's only the one box."

"I could make really good ones with a bunch of boxes."

"I know you could. You're doing amazing with them."

Quinn sat a short distance away, staring at the U shape Ty was building on the table, his eyes glazed. Alice pulled her chair closer to him, swatting him on the knee.

"You look like you're a thousand miles away," she said.

"I was."

"Good place?"

"Not really, no."

"You're thinking about your father?"

"Yes."

"I'm sure there's an explanation."

"You're right. And I need to find out what it is."

"Quinn, there could be a million reasons why your dad's signature was on that paper."

He turned to her. "Roman was a lab technician from Minnesota. Alice, Minnesota was where the plague originated."

"That doesn't prove anything."

"It proves enough for me to…" He caught himself as Ty tipped over the first domino and watched as they all fell in a liquid motion.

"For you to what?" Alice asked. He hesitated.

"For me to go there."

"What? No, that's insane. Why would you leave to go back out there? This is the safest place we've found. We have multiple layers of protection, trained soldiers with guns, food, shelter. Where else could be safer?"

The images on the documents swam behind Quinn's eyes, and he opened his mouth then closed it before sighing.

"You're right; this is the safest place for you and Ty. But I won't be able to move on until I know."

"Sometimes knowing isn't the answer," Alice said. Her voice was beginning to sharpen, her eyes taking on the hard glint he'd seen so many times over the past days, the determination he so admired. "Sometimes it's better to let things be."

"You're right. But this isn't one of those times," he said, and stood from his chair. Ty had stopped playing and was listening, his mouth downturned at the ends. Denver watched from beneath the table and even Collincz had paused from trying to feed Holtz some broth. He moved out of the back room, pushing through the plastic curtain before crossing the front space and out into the open air.

The rain had tapered off and only the lightest of mists fell giving the world a spectral quality. He walked through it, past the side of the building to where the open mine began in earnest.

It looked like an Aztec pyramid in reverse. The hole's depths were stepped in wide ledges, each signifying a level that the mine had reached and pushed past. The concrete walls erected around its perimeter were dwarfed by distance, but he could still make out their unbroken edges. As the hole deepened, its middle area lessened, but the very bottom of the pit was still immense. He thought that the entire town of Fort Dodge might fit inside the expanse.

He stood there for a long time. Now there was no sea or rocks below him, only a manmade scar in the earth. He could see across to the other side, something he'd never been able to do with the ocean. Across was another barricade he would have to pass. Beyond that was the open land he would have to traverse. And perhaps past that he would find answers.

He waited until all the light had faded from the day before returning to Holtz's building. Another storm was approaching on the heels of the last. Its angry face of clouds broadened and spit curses of lightning and thunder as it came.

The inside of the building was warmer, and he didn't realize he was wet and cold until that moment. He paused at the thin divider before turning back and setting up a wide cot in the front portion of the building. The darkness was almost complete. The electric lantern had been turned down to a dull glow, and the windows were lighter shadows in the walls.

Quinn stripped out of his clothing, and hung them to dry on the back of a chair before showering quickly beneath a stream of cool water in the small partition against the wall. After drying off, he slid into the cot, draping one of the heavy blankets over him before curling an arm beneath his head. He closed his eyes to the rippling pulse of lightning and answering thunder in the distance.

He came out of a dream where a field of white tents wrapped around humanesque shapes wriggled and squirmed like an unending plane of maggots. Moans swirled through the air, all of the voices coalescing into a hum of misery that became his name.

"Quinn."

The whisper wasn't from his dream. It came from directly beside him.

Alice sat on the edge of his cot, her shape so familiar that he knew it even before the lightning strobed through the windows illuminating her face. She wore a black tank top and matching underwear, her hair a cascade of darkness across the white skin of her back.

"What are you doing?" he asked, beginning to sit up. She placed a cool hand against his chest and stopped him from rising.

"All those times I was looking at you and you thought I was staring at this," she whispered, letting her hand trail up his neck to cup his face. "I was wondering."

"Wondering what?" he asked. Heat had blossomed where she'd touched him, spreading outward, downward. His heart was beating so hard he was sure it would rupture at any moment.

"I wondered why you were helping us. I wondered why you were so kind to me and my son. I wondered how you had come by the most beautiful eyes I had ever seen." She leaned closer to him, only a shadow against the backdrop of darkness. "And I wondered what it would be like to do this."

She kissed him.

Her lips were soft but strong, moving against his own with gentle pressure. The slick wetness of them was unlike anything he'd ever experienced. He reached out, unable to keep from doing so, and put his hand on her shoulder, pulling her closer, feeling the velvety smoothness of her skin. She responded by kissing him harder, her lips more urgent in their movements. Her tongue danced out and slid against his teeth, and he couldn't help but let out a soft moan.

Alice drew back and pulled the blanket away from him before climbing into the cot. She laid against him, her slender length almost too much to bear. He inhaled deeply, trying to keep control of the heat building in his lower belly.

"I've never…" he breathed, her hair brushing his chest and face as she kissed his neck.

"I know," she murmured. "I'll be gentle; you'll survive." Lightning washed the building again, her eyes dancing in the nimble light.

She peeled her clothing away and then removed his so that they were naked against each other, their skin pressing together as they embraced once again. Her hands moved over his body and then guided his fingers over hers. He explored her, not able to experience enough of her skin. Slowly, she eased herself up and grasped him, before lowering herself down in a settling of pleasure so deep he nearly cried out with it.

"Shhh, not yet," she said, coming close to him, her breath tickling his ear. She began to move above him, stroking his neck and chest. He clung to her, beginning to shake with a need so great and deep that it became exponential, building upon itself until it was a tower from which he dangled over an infinite drop filled with ecstasy. Alice moaned his name and arched her back before closing the gap between them, their bodies melding into one. There was a tightening inside him that ratcheted up until he thought he would burst. Alice whispered his name and said now, please, please, now, now, now and then he was shuddering with a release so profound all the sound in the world ceased. In the quivering silence, they held each other, spiraling down until he felt like he had returned to the ocean, drifting on his back in gentle waves that rose and fell beneath him.

It seemed like hours before he was able to speak.

"I—"

"Don't," she said, putting her fingers to his mouth. "Just hold me."

"Okay."

He laid there with Alice pressed against him, aware of every inch of her body, the rising and falling of her chest, the strand of her hair that rested on his temple. He drifted away, the illusion of being on a sun-warmed raft in the middle of the sea carrying him into sleep.

They woke in the early morning hours, both of them moving sinuously against one another, enjoying the heat and closeness. Pallid light streamed in through the window, the day smothered beneath a blanket of hovering clouds.

"Good morning," Alice said, nuzzling his neck. Quinn smiled, drawing a fingertip up the small of her back.

"Morning. Did that all happen?"

"Every second."

"Wow."

"Yeah."

"I'm sorry I couldn't—" Quinn waved his free hand. "—hold off more."

"God, Quinn. For your first time, you were, something else..." she trailed off.

"You're just being nice."

"Am I ever 'just being nice'"?

"No, I guess not."

"I'll take that as a compliment."

He fell silent for a while, lying still, looking up at the dingy canvas above them.

"You know, I don't expect anything for helping you and Ty. I hope—"

"That I didn't pity-fuck you?" she asked, raising herself onto an elbow." No. I didn't. And don't ever ask something like that again."

"Okay. It's just hard for me to believe because..." he gestured at his face. She leaned forward and kissed him on the lips. It was gentle and sweet.

"Believe it."

They fell silent for a long while, a few raindrops tapping against the roof.

"Alice, I know you're going to hate me for it, but—"

"You're leaving anyway, right?"

He shifted, looking her in the eyes. "How'd you know?"

"Because I knew there was no changing your mind last night when you walked out of the room. And because I know I'd do the same thing if it were my father."

"I would stay, and you don't know how much I want to, but then it would be like I'm still living behind that fence in Maine. I'd be trapped everyday knowing that he might have had something to do with all this. I'd never be free, not really."

She nodded against his shoulder. "Everyone I've ever cared about has left me," she whispered. "Everyone but Ty, and I know someday he'll leave too."

"I'm coming back," he said.

"You'll try."

216

"I will."

There was the sound of movement in the other room, someone stirring in their blankets. They rose from the cot and dressed quietly, Quinn staring at her as she donned her clothes, a sense of disbelief still clinging to the memory of their lovemaking, like some glorious fever-dream. She caught him looking at her and gave him a mock disapproving look. He smiled, and they crept to the plastic barrier and peered through.

Doctor Holtz was sitting on the edge of his cot holding his wallet. He looked up at them and blinked. The sound of his dry tongue rasping across his lips was audible.

"A chimeric virus. That's how they did it," he said, slowly nodding.

Chapter 27

The Storm

They gathered around Holtz as if they were half-frozen adventurers stumbling upon a fire. Collincz woke at the sound of the doctor's voice and leapt to her feet, straightening her uniform that she'd slept in. Holtz gazed around at them, his movements hesitant and slow.

"How long?" he asked Collincz after she'd handed him a bottle of water. His voice was still rough, but held a sonorous quality tinted with a slight British accent that Quinn was sure would resound powerfully in a lecture hall.

"About thirty-six hours or so."

The old man nodded and ran his fingers over his wallet again. He began to open it but stopped.

"How many are left?" he said.

"Thomas, Murray, Wexler, and these three that came in from outside yesterday."

Holtz looked around at them, his eyes hovering on Quinn's face the longest.

"You're the one with the paper, aren't you," Holtz said after a time. Quinn nodded, coming forward.

"Yes, but how did you know that? You were…"

"I thought it was a dream when I woke up. But now that I see you, I know that it wasn't. Someone showed me a paper, held it before me?"

"I did," Collincz said.

"Do you still have it?"

Quinn dug in his pocket and drew out the page that was beginning to roughen from being handled so much. Holtz took it from him and read, holding the paper only inches from his nose. When he was finished, he looked up at Quinn but didn't hand the page back.

"Where did you get this?"

"From a man named Harold Roman. He was from this camp. We found him right before he died in Fort Dodge. It was in his pack. My father was James Kelly," Quinn added.

"I see."

"Do you know what it means?"

"Oh yes. In fact, it's so familiar it's almost like finding something that you hadn't known you'd lost."

"What do you mean?" Quinn said, grabbing a nearby chair and pulling it closer to sit in. The others did the same, seating themselves in a semicircle around the doctor's bed.

"It means the answer I've been looking for was right before my eyes the whole time." He cleared his throat. "When this all began, and my wife and I came here, we had all the samples and test subjects we needed. There was always a sick person turning up or being quarantined in different areas of the camp. Now, from the start, I suspected we were dealing with a virus, a very special virus, but a virus just the same. The problem was when we began to study the samples, we found only a simple strain of flu."

"Flu?" Alice asked. "Like stomach flu or what?"

"No, not stomach flu but a strain of influenza. It appeared to be exactly like the type that makes its rounds every winter all over the world. But instead of only a handful of people dying, we had hundreds of millions." He paused again and turned his wallet end over end. He opened it and shut it. "It baffled us to say the least. But the most interesting aspect was hidden within the strain of flu. There were two latent protein impressions within infected humans, but only one remained within the mutated population. Now, one of the proteins in the humans we understood because of the extreme immune reaction that occurred within nearly all infected. This produced the high fever. But it also was a type of concealment for what the protein was doing."

"And what was that, doctor?" Collincz asked.

"It was creating an enzyme that dissolved healthy bone structure." Holtz shifted his eyes to each of them. Quinn rubbed his hands on his pants, recalling the softness of his father's forehead beneath his fingers. "This increased the fever beyond known medical records, which in essence liquefied the body from the inside out over a period of time. Bones, organs, musculature, everything broke down and continued to dissolve even after death. The end result, as I'm sure you're all aware, is a viscous, foul smelling liquid."

Holtz took another drink of water as the pattering of rain increased on the roof. Denver whined, and Ty, who had been listening raptly, stroked the dog's ear.

"But what does this have to do with the paper Roman was carrying?" Quinn asked.

"Everything," Holtz said. "One of the first terms you'll come upon on that page is adenovirus. Do you know what that is?" Everyone shook their heads. "An adenovirus is basically a gutted virus. Its proteins have been extracted or modified for genetic purposes. Genetic research has made huge leaps and bounds in the past decades, and many scientists are only beginning to grasp the full potential of the power gene therapy encompasses. The adenovirus in question was disguised as a flu virus carrying the two types of proteins I mentioned before as well as a heavy dose of human growth hormone. You see the genes from the flu virus were present and easily recognizable. This was why it baffled my colleagues and I so much. These other proteins were integrated among the flu's typical contents that enabled it to reproduce and metabolize within a host. Chimeric is the correct term for what we found though we didn't realize it at the time. It was basically an adenovirus shell containing the flu genes as well as the proteins I mentioned. As I said, we know that the first protein destroyed healthy bone structure, but the second was designed to rebuild it."

Silence hung in the air for a beat before Quinn rubbed the side of his face and leaned forward.

"So you're saying this virus was engineered?"

"That's exactly what I'm saying, dear boy."

"But why?" Alice asked.

Holtz's eyes darkened, and in the gray light, he seemed not just old but ancient.

"I can only tell you what I believe," he said. "From my studies, and with this new revelation, I can only conclude that the anomalies were the end result of a genetic undertaking such as the world has never seen before. It appears to me that they were designed to evolve from any healthy human being through the virus to be used for God knows what purpose by their creators."

"You mean as weapons," Collincz said.

"I would assume so, yes," Holtz said. "What those poor people have become are strong, fast, seemingly remorseless killing machines. The genes encoded by the virus produced proteins that went far beyond reforming normal bone structure, as well as affecting the subject's humanity, among other things. They would be an expendable and valuable resource in any ground conflict because of their inherent ability to instill fear among an enemy."

"Holy shit," Collincz said as she dropped her face into her palm.

"Can you create some kind of anti-virus now that you know what you're dealing with?" Alice said. "Something that could bring these people back from what they've become?"

"Actually, my dear, the term is anti-viral, and unfortunately that would take several months under a full-scale effort by many skilled scientists in a well-equipped lab. And of course we have none of those, not even the time." Holtz sighed. "In any case, an anti-viral would most likely kill the host."

"So that's it. We're totally fucked," Alice said looking around. "Because the damn government wanted a new biological weapon to play with, now we have herds of monsters roaming the country."

Quinn pulled his gaze from the filmed window and focused on the doctor again.

"They're moving in the same direction; I'm not sure if you knew that or not," he said, gauging the doctor's reaction.

Holtz frowned. "I didn't."

"Do you know why that would be?"

"No. They could be forming a new hierarchy and migration pattern to fit their needs. From my tests here, they are susceptible to climate change. They'll burn. They'll freeze. So I would guess they will move south when the weather turns cold this fall."

"Every group we've seen in the last five days has been moving northwest," Quinn said.

"That's peculiar to say the least," Holtz replied. "But I don't have the foggiest what it could mean. The only other factor that's interesting is the name opposite your father's," he said, tapping it once with a fingernail. "Doctor Alex Gregory. He's a brilliant geneticist, fairly young for his field. I've read several of his studies. He was at the forefront of the genetic community. The last I heard, Gregory was working for a private company called Genset." Holtz looked at him, eyes unwavering. "Genset's lab headquarters is located in southern Minnesota."

Quinn let his gaze slide to the floor. The name, there was something about the name. It echoed of memory that was barely out of reach. He strained for it, but it slipped away each time, sliding through the fingers of his mind like smoke. For some reason, the taste of seafood rose with the doctor's name—Graham's excellent lobster and shrimp drenched with butter and lemon. The smell of home.

All at once, the memory came rushing back.

He'd been trying to tell his father he was leaving. Teresa's encouraging looks. The phone ringing. Mallory returning to the dining room. *It's an Alex Gregory for you, sir.*

"Oh my God," Quinn whispered, looking around at all of them. "Oh my God." He began to tremble, and Alice rose from her spot to kneel beside him, her touch barely registering.

"What is it?"

"He called my dad," Quinn said, voice thin and reedy. He swallowed. "Alex Gregory called my dad the night he got sick."

Chapter 28

The Highway Calls

Quinn stared out at the dismal morning, fog rising from the earth like vengeful spirits.

A hand slid into his, and he intertwined his fingers with Alice's. She stood beside him, but he couldn't find the courage to look at her.

"You'll try, right?" She said finally.

"I will. Nothing could keep me from coming back."

"You won't run off with the next hot survivalist chick you run into?"

He smiled and turned to her. "No."

"Better not. Or I'll hunt you down."

He leaned in and kissed her, the act so foreign he half expected her to shove him away. She didn't. She kissed him back, fiercely. When they parted, she looked into his eyes and tugged once on his shirt.

"Go say goodbye to that boy in the other room. He's going to miss you."

Ty was playing with Denver on the floor near Holtz's cot. He was putting a finger on one of the big dog's front paws and holding it there until Denver playfully snapped at him. Ty laughed and then switched to the other paw. Quinn watched him for a few minutes. He could stay. He could walk back and tell Alice that he didn't have to go. The past was what it was, unchangeable and now alien. They could carve out a life here, and he could try to forget. He could try.

He knelt beside Ty and gently touched his shoulder.

"Hey, buddy."

"Hey."

"Having fun?"

"Yeah."

"Are you upset?"

"Yeah."

"Why?"

"Because you're leaving, aren't you?" Ty turned his face up, and his blue eyes were unfocused, looking past him. But there was so much in them that it overwhelmed him.

"I'm sorry, I have to."

"You don't. You could stay. Mom likes you; I know she does. She came back for you, remember?"

"Yes, she did, and so did you." Quinn put his hand on the back of Ty's neck and drew him to his chest squeezing him tight. The boy stretched an arm around his back. "Thank you for being so brave all this time." They sat that way for a long span, the wetness of Ty's tears soaking through the front of his shirt.

"Will you come back?" Ty asked, his voice muffled.

"Yes. I promise."

"Don't get lost."

"I won't."

Quinn released him and wiped the tears from his small face before ruffling Denver's ears. "Keep them safe," he said to the dog. He stood and walked out of the room.

Alice wasn't in the front area, and he hadn't expected her to be. Collincz and Holtz waited by the door.

"You're sure Wexler will give me a vehicle?" he asked as he donned a poncho.

"He'd better. We have more Humvees than people now," Collincz said. She put out a hand and he shook it, doing the same with the doctor.

"I hope you find what you're looking for," Holtz said, giving his hand a final squeeze.

"Me too," Quinn said, and stepped out the door into the gentle rain.

He walked quickly with his head down, focusing on the muddy ground and the sluicing water that ran the opposite way toward the pit. He watched the streams flow past, taking sediment away to be deposited somewhere new.

When he made it to the front of the enclosure, he saw that Thomas stood on his perch. He was looking through a set of powerful binoculars at something beyond the barriers. The soldier didn't turn toward him as he headed for the tent Wexler had brought them to initially. He glanced around for Murray, but the other man was nowhere in sight. When he ducked beneath the tent's enclosure, he saw that Wexler was sitting at the table with his head tipped to one side, his back to him, fast asleep. Quinn hesitated but continued on, he couldn't wait any longer.

"Lieutenant? Sorry to wake you. I was wondering if I could ask a favor. I need to borrow—"

Quinn's words died in his throat as he came even with the other man.

The left side of Wexler's face was missing.

Shattered bone and shredded tissue hung from a ragged exit wound beside his nose. He'd been shot point blank.

"Fuck," Quinn said, stumbling back. His hand grasping the back of a chair and sliding off. Vomit geysered to the back of his throat, but he swallowed the nausea down, the world tipping beneath his boots. It was Murray, it had to be.

Quinn ran out of the tent, head swiveling, searching for some sign of the murderer. The fog was empty save for the infinite rows of tents stretching into oblivion and the steady tap of rain.

"Hey. Hey, Thomas," Quinn hissed as he neared the narrow staircase that led to the sniper's perch. Thomas turned toward him, eyebrows drawn together in a scowl. "It's Wexler, he's dead," Quinn said as he reached the top of the stairs.

"I know. I killed him," Thomas said, and kicked Quinn in the chest.

Gravity ceased.

There was a blessed moment of weightlessness and then the savage bite of steel stairs in his back. He rolled once, feeling his scalp tear above his ear then his feet hit the ground, legs buckling as he collapsed to his side.

His vision roiled as if stirred from within his skull. A tattoo of pain throbbed in his back. When he managed to raise himself onto an elbow, the wet ground tilted beneath him.

Thomas's footsteps clanged down the stairs as another sound built in the air. It was a deep revving layered by other throaty grumbles. The noise climbed and climbed until it overshadowed Thomas's approach. The soldier stopped a foot away and looked down at him.

"Man, you are fuckin' ugly. Think I improved your looks by booting your ass down those stairs."

The sound outside the walls slowly died, one by one, and he realized it was engines, many engines all growling together. Footsteps came from behind him, and he had enough strength to turn his head and see Murray moving toward the steel door set in the concrete.

"Remember what he said. He's interested in him, so don't kill him," Murray called as he unbolted the door and swung it wide. He stepped outside and yelled something Quinn didn't understand. The fog was slowly lifting from the ground, but it was growing in his head. Hot wetness drenched the side of his face and pooled near his collar. He sat up and tried to climb to his hands and knees, but Thomas pushed him over with a boot.

"Stay the fuck down or I'll put a round through that fucked up face of yours."

Murray returned from outside the wall, and Quinn wiped at the blood that was beginning to run in his eye. There was someone with Murray, many someones. People streamed through the door, their clothing dirty and torn, faces grimy, hair greased. Most were men, but a few women mingled with them, their eyes cold and narrowed as they spotted him lying on the ground. He counted twenty of them before they split into two groups, making room for a solitary figure that strode through the doorway, stopping several paces from where Quinn lay.

The man was bald, with a healing gouge along the top of his scalp. He wore a blond goatee, and it rippled around his mouth as he smiled revealing the empty space where his upper teeth should've been. He sauntered closer and knelt beside Quinn, bringing his face close to his.

"You sure have one of those unforgettable faces," the man said. His voice was like gravel sliding on concrete. A wave of chuckling rolled through the mass of people behind him, but he didn't stop looking at Quinn. "You believe in serendipity, my friend? Because finding you here is nothing less than a miracle." The man stroked his goatee with his left hand, and Quinn saw the clotted stumps sewn shut where his ring and pinkie fingers were missing. "Left me to die in that ditch and stole my bitch." Laughter again from the group. He stood and drew out an automatic pistol, turning to where Thomas watched.

"You Thomas?" the man said. Thomas nodded, stepping forward to hold out a hand.

"And you're Bracken." They shook.

"So this is Murray?" Bracken said, pointing at the other soldier.

"That's me," Murray said.

Bracken raised the pistol and shot Murray through the forehead. Brain matter flew in streamers out the back of the man's skull, and his eyes crossed before falling to his knees then his face. Bracken turned the pistol on Thomas whose mouth hung wide, his hands open at his sides.

"Don't shoot me! Don't, please!" Thomas yelled, holding his palms out.

"Tell me why I shouldn't," Bracken said, tilting his head to one side.

"Because I got you in. I guided you here. We have a deal. Please. I can fight. I know my way around the camp better than anyone."

"We'll see about that," Bracken said after studying the soldier for a time. "Vince, relieve this jarhead of his weapons."

Quinn searched the area for a way out, but feet were filling up his vision, encircling him as he turned. He wiped at his eye again, clearing it of blood, and gazed up at Bracken who stood over him. The man looked a thousand feet tall, taller than any stilt.

"What'd you do with my property, friend? You keep her for yourself? Kill her when you were through?"

"She turned," Quinn said, spitting coppery saliva onto the ground. "She'd never been exposed to the virus."

Bracken seemed to consider this. "That makes sense. Her and her husband and boy were holed up in a cabin way off in the boondocks. It's a shame. She was sumptuous."

"What do you want?" Quinn asked, shooting a look toward the far end of the compound. The rain fell in light curtains, and the wind tugged at the tents. There was no help coming.

"To carve out a life in this new and exciting world, that's all." Bracken cocked his head. "And you, you tried to take that from me. Do you know how much pain I endured recently?"

"Not enough," Quinn said.

Bracken kicked him in the shoulder sending him back to the ground. Spangles of light spun at the edges of his vision, and he gasped with the agony that flooded the place where the man's boot had landed.

"Plenty," Bracken said. "But I'm not a cruel man. I won't leave you to die in some ditch drowning in your own blood. I'm not like that. This world needs a new God since the old one is dead." He lifted the pistol and centered it on Quinn's head. "And I plan to be merciful."

Quinn spun on the ground and threw a kick at Bracken's leg. It connected, sending the man off balance. The gun fired, mud kicking up beside Quinn's elbow. He made to launch himself to his feet when several fists pummeled his head and back. He curled in on himself as a kick caught him in the thigh dropping him to the wet ground.

"That's enough. Just hold the fucker," Bracken said. Rough hands grasped Quinn's arms and hair locking him in place. The gun barrel pressed against his forehead, and through the red-tinted glaze that covered his eyes, Bracken leaned closer. "You're a fighter; I'll give you that. But the good fight is done."

The barrel pressed harder.

Quinn closed his eyes, picturing Alice and Ty, his father, Mallory, Graham, Foster, Teresa.

A base thrumming filled the air.

The barrel's pressure diminished.

The croak came again followed by others.

Quinn opened his eyes and looked past the throng of people to where Thomas ran toward his perch. The soldier's boots clanged up the metal steps to the top of the barricade. He froze. And even across the distance through the falling rain, Thomas's words were clear.

"Oh my God." The soldier twisted toward the group. "You led them right to us!"

A giant hand snaked over the top of the concrete barrier and encircled Thomas's head. It flexed, and there was a sound like an egg cracking on a tabletop. The arm yanked the soldier's limp body up and over the wall in a flail of lifeless legs and arms.

Cries erupted from the marauders, and the hands that held Quinn released him as they grabbed for weapons. Bracken had turned partially to the side, his pistol still inches from Quinn's face.

Quinn whipped his hand up and grabbed the gun by the barrel, snapping it one way and tipping his head the other.

The gun went off. His hand jerked with the recoil, heat flaring in his palm. He tightened his grip and twisted, yanking the pistol from Bracken's fingers.

He rolled to the side as Bracken launched a kick at his chest. The gritty mud dug into his skin, but he kept moving, his momentum bringing him to his feet. Bracken had something in his hand. It flashed silver as he leapt forward, driving the long-bladed knife toward Quinn's heart. Quinn sidestepped and swung the pistol around, connecting the handle with the side of Bracken's head. The man stumbled as Quinn tossed the gun up, spinning the grip into his palm.

Bracken turned, slicing the air with his blade.

Quinn fired.

The knife blade carved a path an inch from Quinn's stomach before falling to the ground. Bracken brought both hands up to his chest where a perfectly round hole pumped dark blood onto his shirt. His eyes found Quinn's, surprise and disbelief filling them to their brims.

Bracken stumbled backwards and tipped off his feet, thudding to the ground in a splash of bloody water and moved no more.

The air was filled with shouts and gunfire, but below it all was the deep, sickening vibration coming from outside the walls. Quinn ran several yards to his left and dove behind a semi-collapsed tent before rising enough to look around.

Bracken's army was on the walls and firing through gaps in the concrete pillars. They yelled incoherently—no real orders or defined direction, only panic and disarray. Several of the men were turning in circles searching for something. And when one of them spotted Bracken's lifeless body, they ran to him, crouching by his side before standing and scanning the tents.

Quinn ducked back down. Rain dripped off his nose, and he rubbed the blood from his eyes again before chancing another look. The two men were closer, their attention torn between the tents and the battle raging behind them. One of them yelled something, and a round shredded a hole in the tent beside Quinn's head. He brought the pistol up and fired twice at both men, re-centering the sights after each recoil. There was a cry of pain as one went down clutching his stomach. The other turned and ran, firing blindly over one shoulder.

Quinn stood and was about to run toward the opposite end of the camp when one of the tall barricades began to rock. Long fingers wrapped over its top and pulled. The barrier tipped and fell outward, tearing away the weak supports that bound it to the others on either side.

Beyond the wall was a sea of pale flesh.

Thousands of stilts lurched toward the walls, their long bodies twisting and turning as they clawed their way forward.

The first stilt stepped into the compound and roared. Someone shot it through the chest. It cried out and fell to its knees, swiping a woman off the scaffolding as it dropped. The woman screamed and hit the ground hard on her side. She tried to regain her feet, but even from the distance he stood, Quinn could see her arm hanging away from her body at an odd angle. The wounded stilt reached out with the last of its strength and pulled her to its mouth, biting the top of her skull off, her scream drowning in its throat.

More of the creatures streamed through the gap in the wall. The fighters held for a beat and then scattered, running from the stilts in every direction. A twenty-foot-tall beast snatched a man from the ground and gripped him in both of its skeletal hands before wrenching him apart at the waist. A smaller stilt had cornered two men who'd run out of ammo, its arms spread apart as if herding cattle. One of the men tried to run tight to the wall and was flattened as the barricade he was passing tipped forward and hammered him to the ground.

The open space of the compound was awash with stilts feeding and people running. Pure chaos.

Quinn ducked low and ran.

He pelted down the rows of tents, breath stinging in his chest, back and head aching from where he'd hit the stairs. Screams of the dying behind him mingled with the stilt's roars, chasing him as he fled.

Collincz appeared through the rain, her rifle centered on his chest as he skidded to a stop.

"What the hell's going on up there?"

"They're inside; we have to go!" Quinn panted, taking off around her.

"Who's inside? What about the others?" she asked, running beside him while throwing looks back over her shoulder.

"They're dead; they're all dead."

A body sailed over Collincz's head and crashed through one of the last tents in a row. It ragdolled to a stop, and he barely registered that the corpse was decapitated before barreling past it. There were a few more stuttering barks of gunfire behind them and then more cries of pain echoed out of the mist.

Ahead, the doctor's building materialized, and Alice was standing in the doorway, eyes wide at the sight of them running toward her.

"Go! We have to run. Get Ty," Quinn said, sliding to a stop. Alice dashed inside as Holtz moved toward them, his face drawn tight, skull-like in the dim light.

"What is it?"

"They're inside the walls. We have to move. Now!" Quinn said, grasping the older man by the arm. He pulled the doctor into the rain as Alice appeared carrying Ty, Denver trotting behind her. Without a word, she transferred Ty to him, and he hugged the boy close as he turned to Collincz.

"Is there another way out?"

A scream cut the air followed by a rumbling croak. Collincz glanced to the front of the compound. Quinn grabbed her uniform and jerked her forward.

"Is there another way out?" he said, his face inches from hers. She blinked and then nodded.

"There's a reinforced access door at the very back behind the mine."

"Let's go," he said, beginning to skirt the tent. Alice kept pace beside him, but they halted as Collincz yelled something.

The soldier was standing between them and Holtz, who wore a sad smile. He had drawn his wallet out and pulled a picture from inside.

"Doctor, come on!" Collincz called.

"I think that I might be of more use here since I was unable to do my job properly." He glanced down at the photo before looking at them again. "Godspeed," he said, and ducked back inside the tent. Collincz made to move in his direction when a man came hurtling out of the rain, his eyes wild, mouth open. A hand reached out from the mist and plucked him off the ground like a child playing with a toy. The man didn't have time to scream before the stilt swung him up and bashed him into the ground headfirst. He remained rigid for a second, his legs and torso sticking up from the mud, then fell sideways in a pile of lifeless flesh. The stilt that killed him gazed at his body for a second and then looked up at them, its lips pulling back from yellowed teeth.

Collincz raised her rifle and shot it through the eye. It dropped where it stood.

Another tall form emerged through the rain. Then another.

"Go," Quinn whispered to Alice. They ran.

The mine opened up in a yawning of earth so deep it made him dizzy to look at it. The ground between the edge of the pit and the concrete barricade narrowed as they went, their footsteps and breathing the only sounds now. Quinn glanced over his shoulder at Collincz who jogged behind them. As he watched, she stopped and dropped to a knee before firing three controlled bursts from her rifle. Something croaked near the doctor's tent and then a concussive blast shook the air.

They stopped and spun, seeing a plume of fire rise from where the medical building used to be. It licked into the soaking air before falling away, steam rushing up in its place. They turned and continued on the path, its width dwindling the further they went. Ty's arms were locked around his neck, face buried against his shoulder, and he cradled him, muscles beginning to burn. They followed a curve in the mine's edge and slowed, climbing over a small washout that held loose sand and rock. On the other side, the land sloped, narrowing to a glorified ledge. Quinn took a tentative step onto its slim offering.

The ground slid away.

They were falling, sliding down amidst tumbling dirt and sucking mud. Alice let out a shriek, and Quinn tried to stabilize himself and Ty by falling to his back. For a horrifying second, gravity threatened to flip them forward into the abyss of open air but then they were stopping, his feet gaining purchase. Alice tumbled beside him on all fours, barely holding onto the shelf they rested on. Collincz and Denver were nearby still on their feet.

They had fallen down to the next step in the inverted pyramid, the following drop beside them almost double the first descent and twice as steep.

"Everyone okay?" Quinn asked in a low voice. They nodded their assent, except Ty who only clung tighter to him. "Let's go," he said, leading the way along the new level. The mine wall began to curve more as they hurried along its lip. Quinn peered ahead trying to make out the rear face of the pit, but the rain was falling harder, obscuring everything to a silver vapor. He kept his eyes on the ground ahead of them, looking for the signs of another weak spot that would send them all tumbling to their deaths below. After minutes that seemed like hours, Collincz called out and they stopped. She made her way to Quinn and glanced around, her blond hair plastered to her skull.

"The door's somewhere near here," she said, squinting against the rain. "Let's try climbing up at the next possible route." He nodded and was about to take a step when Alice grabbed his arm.

"Look," she said, pointing down into the depths of the mine.

Tall shapes were moving across its floor, barely discernable through the storm. There were hundreds of them.

"Oh God. They smell the bodies," Collincz said, raising her weapon. Alice grasped the soldier's arm, and they moved forward as one. After another minute, they came to a chasm of larger rock running perpendicular to the ledges. It looked like some kind of drainage channel. Quinn placed his feet on a heavy boulder and tested it. It didn't shift.

"Get on my back, buddy," he said, kneeling down. Ty swung around, re-gripping his arms around Quinn's neck and digging his knees into his sides. Quinn stepped out on the column of rock and began to climb. "Put your hands and feet where I do," he said over his shoulder to the women. He moved slow and sure, testing each hold before placing his weight on it. Luckily the section of rock wasn't completely vertical but ran upwards in a steep slant. As he climbed, he was transported back to a cliff ledge overlooking the ocean, searching for the right place to secure himself. He gave in to the vision, ignoring the ache in his muscles, the choking pressure of Ty's arms around his neck, the rain slicking the holds, the throbbing roars in the mine below.

Then he was at the top, pulling himself onto a wider expanse of dirt beside the barrier. A short distance away was a broad steel door set between two of the pillars, a heavy iron bar bolted across its middle.

Quinn gently released Ty to the ground and turned to help Alice up the last feet of the slope. Collincz came next and then Denver, who climbed up the rock in a surefooted lunge of muscle. When he turned around, Collincz was already at the door, digging for something in her uniform pocket. The rain pounded down, and he hugged Alice and Ty tight to him, relishing the feel of them safe for a moment. Below, the grunts and croaks of the stilts filtered up to them.

"Hopefully they haven't surrounded the entire compound," Collincz said, pulling out a small ring of keys. She selected one and shoved it into the lock securing the bar across the door. She turned it, and the lock popped free.

A stilt lunged out of the rain and swiped Collincz away from the door.

She flew into the open air over the mine and fell out of sight without a sound, her blond hair waving as she plummeted.

"No!" Quinn yelled, bringing up the pistol. The stilt bellowed, opening its mouth wide as it charged. He fired twice, both bullets blasting teeth apart as they ripped through the stilt's mouth and out of the back of its skull. It fell forward, bouncing off the edge of the pit before rolling down and out of sight.

There was more movement along the path ahead, long forms striding forward.

Quinn grabbed the bar on the door and yanked it up and away. He grasped the handle and pulled. The door opened into a rain-drenched field. Alice raced past him carrying Ty, and Denver followed, bounding out through the open door. Quinn aimed at the next stilt that appeared through the rain, the shot punching it in the chest as the pistol locked open and empty. He shoved the gun in the back of his pants and slammed the door shut behind them.

He ran.

In a few steps, he caught up to them, and they fled across the field. Over his shoulder, the door remained closed until the last time he looked and could no longer make out its shape through the rain.

The field sloped downward and entered a slash of poplar, their white trunks scarred with black knots. They plunged through the forest, which opened to a field already green with sprouts only inches high. Across the plain was a driveway leading to a farm, its red silo towering above the flatness of the land.

"There," Quinn gasped, relieving Alice of Ty's weight. They rested for a minute, listening for the sounds of breaking branches above the rain. When they continued, Ty shook with cold against Quinn's chest, and Alice was limping heavily.

They made it to the farmhouse, breaking a pane of glass in the front door to gain entry. It was blessedly warm and dry inside without a hint of decay in the air. Quinn set Ty down and found a blanket to cover him with while Alice searched the pantry for food.

"We need to leave as soon as possible," Quinn said on his way to the attached garage.

"I know," Alice replied, not looking up from where she gathered canned goods and boxes of crackers.

Along with a newer model Chevy pickup, there was a faint stench in the garage. In the empty space beside the truck, he saw its source. Two empty nooses hung from a rafter, their loops cinched to the size of a fist. Below them on the floor were two sets of crusted clothing and glasses in separate piles beside a pair of overturned chairs. Quinn looked at the clothing for a while and then checked the truck for keys.

The keys weren't in the ignition but hung from a peg near the entrance to the garage inside the house. By the time he returned to the kitchen, Alice had found a plastic bag and filled it with as much food as it would hold.

"There's no water here," she said, gathering a stack of blankets.

"That's okay; we'll find some on the way."

Quinn checked the sodden fields through the porch windows before they loaded the truck and popped the overhead door. He threw it up on its tracks and backed the truck out before closing the garage again. Alice had noticed the clothing on the floor and looked at him as he climbed back into the cab.

"Just felt wrong to leave the door open," he said.

They rolled down the driveway and turned onto a county road that led to a paved highway heading north, each mile leaving Fort Dodge farther behind.

Chapter 29

Ground Zero

Quinn pulled the truck to a stop in the marina parking lot and looked around the mostly empty space.

They'd driven for four hours straight, taking highways and side roads away from the interstates that had become cluttered with more and more stalled or crashed vehicles the closer they got to Minneapolis. Closer to Genset's headquarters.

"What are you doing?" Alice asked, sitting up in her seat. She'd drifted off the last twenty miles and only woken when he stopped the truck.

"This is where you guys get out," Quinn said, not looking at her.

"What?"

"I can't ask you to come with me to that building. I have no idea what I'll find there."

"You don't have to ask; we're coming with you." Alice's voice was ragged with sleep but hardening with each word.

"No. I'll get one of these boats set up for you guys, and you're going to get on it and take it out into deeper water and anchor. I'll go to Genset and come back here when I'm finished."

"Screw that noise. Look at me, Quinn," Alice said. He did. "After what just happened back there, you want us to split up again?"

"That had nothing to do with this. That was beyond anyone's control. But I'm choosing to go to that building. I need to know what my father was doing."

"I understand that, but you're going to have to get used to the idea of us coming with you." She crossed her arms and stared at him, unblinking, impassive.

"I want to come with," Ty said. "And so does Denver." The dog let out rumbly woof. "See?"

Alice tipped her head to one side and raised her eyebrows.

"See?" she echoed.

"Damn it, this is not negotiable. Of all the things that happened to us, most of them weren't avoidable, but this is. You don't need to be put in harm's way again. You need to be somewhere safe."

"Like I said before, nowhere's safe. The best thing we can do now is stick together."

Quinn glared at her, fiddling with a loose string hanging from the steering wheel cover. "I never thought I'd hear you say that," he said finally.

She shook her head and sighed, but smiled. "Me neither."

Quinn looked out over the gray water lapping at the boats. He closed his eyes.

"Okay."

They spent a half hour searching the marina for a boat that had adequate fuel and room for the three of them and the dog. They located a sleek, twenty-foot yacht at the farthest end of the marina that fit their needs. In the bottom living area below deck, he found the dried remains of a man in a bed, only his underwear and some fillings were left within the sheets. The keys to the boat were in a pair of pants lying on the floor, and he found a nine-millimeter pistol in the bedside drawer, its magazine a little over half full. After disposing of the remains, they brought their bag of food and blankets on board, and Quinn test-started the engine, its chugging rumble answering as soon as he turned the key.

"Why are we taking a boat from here?" Alice asked when they were finished and returning to the truck.

"I have a hunch that they don't care much for water. We haven't seen any swimming or crossing lakes anywhere. I think it might be safer traveling the river for a while." His voice must have betrayed something because she watched him for a long time before looking away.

Genset headquarters was located in a business complex outside the city of Hastings, only a fifteen-minute drive from the marina. They consulted the smart phone's map judging the best route to take before pulling away from the docks.

The streets they traveled on were empty. Water streamed along the gutters and dropped into grates, houses reflected their passing in dark windows, everything quiet. No one spoke and even Denver seemed to be waiting.

They turned into the business complex and spotted the Genset building at once. It was a high, two-story structure, its front plated with reflective glass that mirrored the ashen sky. They drove across the asphalt parking lot and stopped before the entrance. The genetic lab was surrounded by stretches of cleared land, several business buildings in the distance rising up from the ground like the heads of buried giants. Quinn surveyed the area and drove in a circle in the parking lot before stopping again before the door.

"Looks clear," Alice said.

"That's what worries me."

"We definitely left that large herd behind. Even going full speed, it would take them another four hours or so to get here."

"I know. But if this is ground zero, where are all the people that turned?"

"Maybe they migrated like the others we saw," Alice offered, turning in her seat.

"Maybe."

The rain had let up for a time when they were locating a boat, but now it fell again in steady layers. They waited for another five minutes without talking before Quinn opened his door.

"Maybe you guys should stay here, just in case," he tried again.

"Maybe you should give up a lost cause when you see one," Alice said, climbing out of the car.

The rain was even colder than before, and they rushed through it to the solid awning over the entrance. Several lights glowed within the building, and a card reader mounted to the side of the door blinked a red LED. Quinn dug in his pocket and brought out Harold Roman's ID and slid it through the reader slot.

The door clicked open.

They stepped inside.

Quinn drew the pistol he'd taken from the boat and glanced around. They were in a high-ceilinged lobby. A dark waiting area sat to the right, magazines spread across a low table, padded chairs against the wall. To the left was an unmarked steel door painted the same color as the wall. Ahead was a long reception desk, business card holders, pamphlets, and pens adorning its top. Before the desk was a towering glass sculpture of a DNA strand, its round base filled with water. As Quinn stepped closer, he saw that it was a fountain, the double helixes drilled with holes for water to drip through.

Their footsteps echoed on the marble flooring as they approached the desk. To either side there were double doors leading farther into the building. The rectangular windows set within the doors were dark.

"One or two?" Alice asked.

Quinn moved past the desk and peered through the left door's window. A hallway lay beyond, doors closed on both walls. But there was something on the floor and ceiling, something uneven and stretching the length of the hall where it disappeared into darkness. Quinn squinted, trying to discern what it was. He tried the door, but it was locked. When he looked for a card reader, he found none. There was only a standard lock set in the door's handle.

He moved away from the entrance, watching the small window the entire time, waiting for movement to slide past it.

They closed in on the other set of doors. Just as he was about to swipe Roman's card across the reader beside them, Ty paused, holding Denver back.

"Momma, I don't like it here," the boy whispered. Quinn and Alice turned to him. He looked so young in the dimly lit lobby, so small.

"I know you don't, honey," Alice said, shooting Quinn a look. There was something there and gone in her expression. Unease. He felt it too. The whole building gave off a chill as if the temperature had dropped below zero the moment they stepped through the doors. They shouldn't be here.

Quinn faced the doors again and swiped the card.

The locks clicked open.

They pushed through the doors into a hallway twice the width of the first he'd seen. The same strange shadow grew on the ceilings and floors as well as the walls. At first he had the wild impression that roots from some gigantic tree had invaded the building, shoving tendrils further and further inside. The shapes were humped and irregular, their ends coming to rounded points, all heading toward the doors they entered through.

"What the hell is that?" Alice said.

"I don't know."

There were offices to either side, and at the very end of the corridor another door without a window waited. Quinn leaned into the first room to the right and slid his hand along the wall until it met a switch.

He flipped it up.

Light bloomed within the office, spreading part way down the hall.

Alice sucked in a breath.

The 'roots' were gnarled tangles of white growths, their surfaces pocked with spongy holes and sharp protrusions not unlike a coral reef. Quinn moved to the center of the hall and knelt beside a patch of the material. He reached out and was about to touch it when Alice spoke.

"Quinn, don't."

He glanced at her, standing in the office doorway, light outlining her as she clasped Ty to her side. He drew his hand back but leaned closer to the floor. The growth gave off a faint odor of decay, dry but still potent in a way that a rotting vegetable smells when forgotten in the rear of a pantry. He ran his gaze across the protrusion where it met other coils that joined and became a larger mass that disappeared through broken sheetrock and disturbed ceiling tiles. Its composition nudged something in his mind, almost coming into the light before drifting away. His eyes narrowed in concentration, and all at once recognition tightened every muscle in his body.

The substance on the floors, walls, and ceilings was bone.

He rose and stepped away from it, wiping the hand he'd almost touched the osseous growth with on his pants. Alice found his eyes, questioning him as he turned and shook his head. He looked around the large office. It was made to be a comfortable space, the walls a calming beige trimmed with browns and tans. An executive leather chair sat before a sprawling desk that held a touchscreen computer console mounted within the wood at an angle comfortable to anyone sitting in the chair. There were large cardboard boxes on the floor filled with white confetti that he soon recognized as shredded papers. When he opened the desk drawers, only empty space met him, files hanging limp and thin on their rails. The same went for the file cabinet in the corner of the room. Every paper in the office had been destroyed.

"There's nothing here," he said, sliding the last drawer shut. He moved to the computer screen, bringing it to life with a fingertip. Username and password bars appeared, a curser blinking in the first box. Quinn stared at the screen, his fingers hovering over letters. Slowly he curled his hands into fists, arms shaking.

"Let's check the other office," Alice said, guiding him away from the mocking screen.

The opposite room was smaller and less elegant but yielded the same results. Shredded paper was strewn across the floor in twisted and torn strips as if the person performing the task had been in an extreme hurry, treading amongst the fallen fragments. He tried the computer console in the smaller office and attempted every combination of letters and numbers he could think of that had any significance to his father. None of them worked.

He picked up a stapler and wound his arm back, ready to throw it through the glass of a painting hanging on the wall, but Alice grasped his wrist. Gently, she brought his hand down, and he loosened his grip on the stapler.

"There's nothing here," he said, shoulders going slack, his strength seeping away with his anger. "They scrubbed everything."

"I know. I'm sorry."

"What the hell were they doing here?"

"I don't know." She ran her hand up his arm, her touch light and soothing. "Maybe it's gone like everything else."

They stepped back into the hall, and his gaze trailed along the shoots of bone that disappeared behind the door. The last unchecked door. One more barrier between him and what he wanted.

He moved toward it, Roman's card already out of his pocket, the reader beside the door glowing red. His hand was on the knob, card sliding, door unlocking.

He turned the handle and stepped inside.

The room was long, stretching away in banks of stainless steel counters and tables covered in microscopes, square canisters, centrifuges, and several unfamiliar boxy pieces of equipment, their digital gauges still lit with numbers holding no meaning. A partial bank of fluorescents glowed at the far end of the room, throwing cold light like freezing water across the floor. To the left, a wall grew to the ceiling, its lower half solid block and steel while its upper was completely glass. The bone growth spanned the entire length of the room, its twisted calcifications reaching between tables and chairs, encompassing others within its folds like magma flowing around a formidable rock it couldn't melt. Somewhere rain pattered.

Quinn moved farther into the room, taking small, careful steps over arms of bone that reached everywhere. A growl simmered within Denver's chest.

"Quinn, what are you doing?" Alice asked from close behind.

"There's something here," he whispered. "Can't you feel it?" She didn't answer, but her steps followed him as he made his way to the opposite end of the room.

The partition between the rooms held a broad set of sliding doors near the back wall. They gaped open like jaws caught in a death cry. The second room was unlit, and the meager light from the fluorescents reached only feet into its space before succumbing to its void. A cool breeze drafted from somewhere as Quinn closed in on the doorway leading to darkness. He paused as he reached the entry, the smell of rot stronger in the air. At his feet, he noticed a layer of grime trailing into the adjoining room from behind him. He bent closer and saw that the dirt was an overlayment of giant footprints leading into and out of the lab.

He stood, his hands shaking as he searched the lower part of the wall, finding a knob mounted on a steel plate.

"Quinn?" There was an edge of worry in Alice's voice, a tone of warning. But he could stop the movement of his hand no more than he could control the arc of the sun.

His fingers gripped the knob.

Spun it.

Light spread like a wave from the fixtures in the next room.

He stared at what waited in its center and tried not to scream.

Chapter 30

The Belly of the Beast

Alice stepped up beside him. As her eyes focused on what lay beyond, he clapped a hand to her mouth, stifling the cry that tried to break free.

It was clearly an operating room. There was a medical bed against the right wall, stripped and unused. A large light, hooded by reflective glass, hung from the ceiling by an articulating arm. The far end of the room held a counter and a bank of temperature controlled containers, all of them linked to one another, their doors marked with labels too small to read at a distance.

The rest of the area was occupied by mounds of bone.

It grew outward from the center of the space, great sheets of it climbing the walls and smothering anything beneath. The ceiling was completely gone, pieces of broken tile laying everywhere as if a bomb had detonated nearby. In its place the bone threaded between supports and cables, its white mass spliced with light fixtures and steel struts. But the middle of the room held their complete attention, the sight nearly beyond comprehension. Quinn stared at the spectacle, transfixed and trying to quell the mounting horror that grew like a tsunami inside him.

The bone piled to over five feet at the center of the operating space, and protruding from its top was a man's upper body.

He was slumped toward them, his neck bent forward, chin on chest, his tangled hair askew. One arm was completely encased by the bone while the other remained free. Below his chest he seemed to be fused with the mass of calcification.

"Oh my God," Alice whispered as she drew his hand away from her face.

"What is it?" Ty asked. Neither of them answered.

Quinn stepped through the open doorway, pausing for an eternity as he listened. Only the dripping of water met his ears. Slowly, he made his way across the room and approached the corpse, Alice and Ty's footsteps following his. He stopped a pace away from the man and dropped into a crouch, tipping his head to one side to get a better view of the dead man's face.

He had been in his late forties, and handsome. Even with the cold pallor of death, his features were lean and defined, his cheeks covered in sparse stubble as well as his strong jaw. He wore a blue, button-up shirt, the tie at the throat loosened and trailing down where it disappeared into the osseous fibers. Over the shirt was a white lab coat, the breast unmarked by a nametag or threaded embossing. Quinn studied the man for a time, examining how the bone melded with his clothing, and he assumed the flesh beneath.

"Who are you?" Quinn whispered.

The man's arm whipped out, and a cold hand grasped his wrist.

Quinn couldn't stifle the yell that leapt from his throat as he jerked away, breaking the icy hold. He stumbled back, bumping into Alice who grabbed his shoulders, steadying him.

The man's arm hung in the air, suspended there as if it had always been. His body convulsed, and he stiffened, his head tipping back on his neck until he looked at them with hazy eyes.

"Holy shit, he's alive," Alice said. Quinn stepped forward and cautiously approached the partially cocooned man.

"Can you hear me?" Quinn asked. The man gazed around the room, eyes half-lidded, lips blue and parted. He began to shiver. Gradually the tremors ceased, and he swallowed, looking down at his free hand before bringing his gaze up to Quinn's.

"You," he said, voice like sandpaper on glass. The way he said the word turned a spigot of cold water on in Quinn's bloodstream. "You're here."

The skin on Quinn's neck prickled, scalp cinching tight. The man licked his dead lips and took a deep breath before offering a weak smile.

"It's nice to finally meet you, Quinn."

The strength went out of Quinn's legs, and he slumped to the floor in an area where there was no bone. Then Alice and Ty were beside him, their hands on his shaking arms. Denver whined and licked his ear.

"H-how do you know my name?" Quinn said, his voice hoarse and unfamiliar.

The man blinked, swaying in his encasement of bone.

"You were the only thing your father ever talked about."

"How did you know my father?" Quinn said, raising his voice.

"Quiet," the man whispered, "You'll wake him."

"Wake who?"

"Rodney. He's sleeping, but he'll be awake soon."

Quinn glanced around the operating room looking for a figure concealed in the thin shadows or beneath a table in the adjoining lab. He flinched as the man's fingers grazed his face, and he pulled away from the frigid touch.

"I'm sorry, but after all this time, seeing you in person…" The man's voice faded, and he coughed, a low wheezing sound with almost no force to it. It was like listening to wind hiss through the leaves of a tree.

"Who are you?" Quinn repeated. He tried to compose himself, to steady his bearings, all the while seeing that the man's eyes were nearly colorless, the iris a sickly shade of gray matching the sky outside.

"My name is Alex Gregory, and I was a friend of your father's."

"What did he have to do with this?"

"We were best friends in college," Gregory said, his voice gaining some strength, but still he spoke in hushed tones. "He called me two years ago and offered to set up a lab to advance my work. The amount of money he was offering, I couldn't say no."

Quinn looked around the room, a burning lump filling his throat.

"So this was just another investment of his, another place to make a profit?"

"No, you misunderstand, Quinn."

"I think I understand very well. I'm guessing he caught wind of some government program through his connections and saw dollar signs. He commissioned you to undertake the genetics side of it, and somewhere along the line, it went horribly wrong.

Am I close?" He'd slowly gained his feet during the tirade, the anger and adrenaline cocktail pumping through his veins like a drug, heightening the indignity, the outrage. Everyone dead, only suffering for those who were left, and why?

"No, you're not," Gregory said, beginning to tremble again. "This was not a government project. Genset was privately funded solely by your father."

"Why would he try to make monsters out of people?" Quinn said. "What purpose would it serve?"

"The abominations that were created in the aftermath were not the goal; they were an outcome of a mistake." Gregory sagged, his neck slackening so that he stared at the floor, breathing hard.

"If they weren't what you were trying to create, then what were you doing here?"

Gregory managed to raise his head high enough to look him in the eye.

"Your father was trying to cure you."

Quinn felt like he'd been kicked by a horse. The air buzzed, and he lost vestibular sense. The ground was the sky and then it reversed, sending him into a dizzying tailspin.

"What?" was all he managed, all he could get himself to say.

"When all of the surgeries for you were ruled out, he came to me. He knew I was trying new gene therapy strategies, —that I was on the forefront of discovery—and asked if there was any way to help with your condition. He wanted a normal life for you so much, Quinn; it was his sole ambition. He built this place, gave us tens of millions for a budget, all for you."

Quinn lowered himself to the floor as the world continued to whirl around him.

"I don't understand…why?" he breathed.

"Because he loved you. More than anything or anyone. He was driven beyond any man I've ever met." Gregory paused, glancing around the operating theatre as if he'd heard something. They all listened too, but there was nothing but the hum of the lights and the rain. "We began work on mice, then moved on to primates, slowly verifying what route we needed to take to get to the end goal. It became clear early on that a virus would be necessary for the delivery of the genetic program."

"A chimeric virus," Quinn said, recalling the information Holtz had told him.

"Yes. An adenovirus holding a common flu virus gene. We mutated the gene responsible for transmission so it could never become communicable." Gregory swallowed and shook again as if fighting off another coughing episode. "But something went wrong with our first test in a human."

"You said you were working with primates. How did you ever get clearance to go ahead with human testing?" Alice asked.

Gregory seemed to focus on her for a moment before sliding his gaze back to Quinn.

"We didn't. Your father pushed the tests forward. I told him we needed another two years of clinical trials after gaining licenses, but he couldn't be dissuaded."

"But what did he hope to achieve with all this? You said so yourself that the surgeries were out of the question. How was this virus supposed to help me?" Quinn asked.

"The chimeric virus—" Gregory said, pointing his free arm at a coolant cell at the furthest end of the row, "—held a protein for dissolving healthy bone tissue and another, that was purely experimental, for rebuilding it, along with a dose of human growth hormone to promote the generation of cells. We were going to concentrate the virus in your facial bones and then make an organic cast replicated from your father's bone structure. The cast would have been implanted on your skull and the secondary protein would have rebuilt the bones according to the cast."

Quinn swayed before the man. The rain was calling him. He could walk into it and let it soak his clothing, wash away the swirling shock that cloaked him. He could forget.

"You could've stopped him," Quinn said, tears blurring his vision. "You could've prevented all this."

"You're right. I could have. But my own aspirations were too great. We went ahead with testing on our first human candidate. His name was Rodney Fairbanks. He was an Iraq War veteran. He'd been involved in drug trials for years, especially concerning post-traumatic stress disorder. We offered him more money than he'd ever received before.

"The initial tests were very promising. Your father was ecstatic when he left that day."

For a moment, Quinn was lost in the memory of his father dancing with Teresa in their living room, Frank Sinatra's voice surrounding him completely.

"But something went wrong," Quinn said.

"Yes," Gregory replied. "The gene that encodes the contagion protein must have reverted after interacting with Rodney's cells. It became an actively replicating virus once more. Every person that came into contact with him that day carried it from this building out into the world."

"My father flew home that day on a public flight," Quinn said. "He gave it to everyone. He helped spread it across the nation."

Gregory shuddered and nodded. "It killed nearly everyone it came in contact with. The virus caused an enormously high fever that we were able to control in this laboratory, but worldwide they had no idea what they were dealing with. The abominations were a genetic anomaly I only partially understand. A genetic factor allowed a significant portion of the population to weather the fever, but they lost their humanity in the process. The abnormal growth of the bone, skin, and musculature, was caused by the experimental protein combined with the HGH. It was something we never anticipated."

Some of his father's last words floated back to him. *Sorry, I'm so sorry. My fault.* Now he understood what he'd meant.

"Goddamn you. Goddamn you both," Quinn said.

"I'm sure that He has," Gregory said, looking up. His eyes darted around and his jaw clenched, the muscles of his face bulging beneath the pallor. "He'll be awake soon, and they'll return before long. You don't have much time."

"Who will? Who will be awake soon?" Alice asked.

"Rodney. He sleeps deeply part of the day, but he feeds the rest of it. I was trying to save him when he began to change and I...I couldn't escape." Gregory lowered his voice further. "I've tried not to eat what they bring, but he hurts me. He's tied into my nervous system, and oh God, he hurts me." Gregory gestured weakly around them, and a prickling sensation crawled up Quinn's back like a many-legged insect. He let his eyes slide over the growth of bone flowing everywhere in the building, its reaching points crawling down the hallways, seeking ever outward.

Quinn began backing away.

"Please, you have to kill me, please," Gregory begged.

"Who is he controlling?" Quinn asked.

"Them. All of the abominations that can smell the pheromones he produces. They communicate with the others through scent and tell them his wishes."

"What does he tell them?" Quinn said, fear running him through like a lance.

"Come to me, come to me, come to me," Gregory whispered. "They hunt and bring him food, and I have to eat it—you don't know what I've had to eat." The doctor began to sob and he suddenly convulsed as if hooked to ten thousand volts. His head snapped back, eyes rolling up in his skull while his mouth gaped open and a creaking moan slipped from him. It was a sound of distilled pain, the cry of the damned.

"Quinn, we have to go," Alice said, grabbing his arm. She was looking down now, down at the tracks on the floor that led to the center of the room. So many tracks.

"Kiiiilll mmmeeeeeeee," Gregory hissed, eyes jittering in their sockets, his arm outstretched and shaking.

Quinn brought up the handgun and aimed at the man's forehead. The sights wavered as the doctor's jaw clenched so tight they could hear his teeth cracking in his mouth. Quinn squeezed the trigger but then released it and moved across the operating room to the far wall.

"What are you doing?" Alice said.

"I have to be sure," he said, opening the last refrigerated cell on the counter. Inside were four vials of clear liquid. He grabbed the first and pulled it out, ripping the drawer in front of him open. Inside were all manner of sterile instruments in plastic wrappers. He rifled through them, a clock ticking down in his mind. Gregory screamed behind him. The syringes were at the very back of the drawer, and he drew one out, tearing the package with his teeth. He fumbled the plastic cap off the needle and plunged it into the rubber stopper at the end of the vial. He retracted the plunger, filling the syringe, and threw the vial across the room.

Somewhere far away, a stilt roared.

Quinn jammed the needle into Gregory's neck and depressed the liquid.

His eyes bulged, and all of his wind rushed out, sliding from between his broken teeth. A small amount of blood dribbled down his chin, and he seized again, muscles becoming bands of iron before slackening.

"Quinn!" Alice yelled as she pulled Ty out of the room and headed toward the door they'd entered through. He began to follow and looked back when he reached the divider between the operating room and the lab.

Gregory was slumping forward, further than he should've been able, and Quinn saw that the bone around him was softening where it met his clothes. The doctor raised his head, eyes clear now locking onto Quinn's, the pain in them washed away.

"Thank you," he whispered.

Quinn turned and ran.

Alice, Ty, and Denver were waiting at the locked door. He drew out Roman's card and was about to slide it through the reader when another croak echoed into the lab. Quinn turned, squinting down the passage that led out the back of the room. There was a small amount of light filtering in at the rear wall.

"Wait a second," he said and sprinted through the lab and down the hall. It turned a corner at a door marked 'roof access' before opening up to the field outside the end of the building. There had been a fire exit door there once, but it had been torn away and lay scratched and bent on the grass. The rain continued to fall in an unending drizzle.

Through the storm, he saw the first of them on the horizon.

In a span of seconds, there were dozens more. Then hundreds.

They ran toward the building with a single purpose. He could feel their calls in his bones.

Quinn bolted back the way he'd come, sliding on the slick floor as he raced toward the lab door.

"We have to go, right now," he said, slicing the card through the reader. They pushed past the door and ran down the hallway pausing again before bursting into the lobby. Quinn glanced out through the tall windows lining the front of the building and slid to a stop, grasping Alice and Ty as he did.

Two stilts were striding toward the truck. They were too close; they'd never make it.

"Damn it," Alice said, her hair whipping as she looked around the building. Ty's hand trembled in his own and Denver whined and paced before them.

"The roof. If we can get on the roof, maybe we can distract them long enough to jump onto the awning and then down to the truck," Quinn said.

"No, if we go outside they'll kill us," Alice said.

"If we stay in here, we're trapped. They won't leave until they've dug us out. Those doors aren't going to hold them. There's hundreds of them out there," Quinn said, gripping her arm hard. She searched his face and looked out at the stilts near the truck. They picked at it with long fingers, and it rocked on its springs.

"Okay," she said.

They retraced their steps, the air humming with deep vibrations. When they arrived at the lab, things were dropping from the ceiling around them, and it was a split second before Quinn realized it was Rodney collapsing from where he'd grown. They raced down the rear hall and stopped at the door leading to the roof. Quinn yanked on the door without looking outside, but Alice must have done so since her grasp on his arm tightened.

"Quinn…"

The door was locked.

"Quinn…" More urgency in her voice.

"Stand back," he said, shoving the pistol against the gap between the door and its frame near the handle.

He fired.

The gunshot was deafening, but when he tugged on the doorknob, the door swung free toward them. He shoved them into the dark stairway, a last look at the pale mass of lurching flesh, closer now, so much closer.

He lunged through the door, slamming it behind him. There was no way to re-lock it so he ran, ripping up the stairs two at a time. At the top landing, Alice had unlocked the outside door and already spilled onto the roof. As he made the landing, a fire extinguisher caught his attention on the wall. He tore it free of its mooring and sprinted onto the roof.

The roof was covered with rock and felt spongy beneath his feet. He neared the waist-high edge and looked over.

The field behind the building was filled with stilts. They poured like a tidal wave across the earth, arms swinging, heads tilted up, mouths open and belching roars.

"Is the front clear?" he yelled over his shoulder.

"There's a few around the truck!" Alice called back.

"Get down! Don't let them see you!"

He tossed the fire extinguisher over the side as the first stilts neared the building. He took aim, breathing, locking the sights on the red steel canister. The sights shook. *Don't let the fear win.*

He squeezed the trigger.

The extinguisher jumped and spewed a stream of thick, white smoke into the air. The stilts nearby staggered away from it, the rest slowing and hanging back as the cylinder arced out even more of its contents. Quinn dashed around the side of the building banging the pistol on the concrete lip as he neared its front. The stilts surrounding the truck looked up at him, glaring through the short distance that separated them.

"This way you ugly fuckers!" Quinn yelled and ran back the way he'd come. He only had to wait a moment to know that they'd taken the bait. They came into view, their eyes finding him as he pelted to the rear of the building. "Jump when it's safe!" he yelled, but didn't look back to see if Alice had heard him. The fire extinguisher was fizzling its last, and the herd approached it, coming closer like an army of thin apes. One of them reached out and batted the canister against the building. When it merely rolled a few inches into the grass and fell still, they flooded through the open doorway while others reached up, trying to grasp the edge of the roof.

He chanced a look over his shoulder just in time to see Alice lock eyes with him as she climbed onto the roof's lip. Their gaze solidified into something almost tangible and then broke as she jumped.

Two giant hands latched onto the roof and pulled, a snarling face appearing behind them. Quinn shot the stilt through the head, bringing down four more before turning and running as fast as he could toward the front of the building. He vaulted the wall, hoping that he'd estimated correctly, and fell over the side.

The awning was there, slamming beneath his feet. He nearly lost his grip on the gun but realigned himself with the truck before leaping toward it. Denver was lying on his side in the truck's bed. Quinn dropped like a stone beside him, his feet hitting the back of the truck with an impact that buckled his legs and rattled his brain. His knees impacted the steel bed and he cried out, but his voice was lost in the revving engine and the peel of rubber on the wet asphalt.

The truck rocketed forward as the first stilt rounded the building. It swiped a hand out and caught hold of the tailgate. Quinn rolled to his side, as the monster began to climb into the truck, and fired, the bullet tearing into the stilt's chest. It barked in agony, sending spittle onto Quinn's shirt before losing its grip and sliding away to the road. Quinn sat up in time to see the entire herd, their numbers past the thousands, pursuing them on spindly legs. Alice accelerated, and their forms began to shrink.

Quinn sagged against the steel and slumped lower, coming even with Denver's snout. The Shepherd snuffled wetly against his ear.

"You're a good boy, Denver, good boy." He petted the dog's thick fur and noticed the ugly angle of his left hind leg. "Shit," Quinn said, sitting up to examine the injury. He placed his hand on the leg, and Denver whined with pain, drool lining his dark lips. "It's okay, boy; it's okay. We'll get you better; we're safe now."

He scooted forward until he could peer into the cab of the truck. Alice rolled down the left rear window, and he stood up, legs throbbing, rain stinging like wasps.

"You guys okay?" he called.

"We're fine. Ty scraped up his knees and elbows."

"I'm okay!" Ty called. "Denver's hurt. I heard him yelp when he landed."

"He's going to be fine," Quinn said.

"Are you alright?" Alice asked.

"I'm okay. You remember how to get back to the marina?"

"I've heard of a backseat driver, but you're not even in the cab."

He grinned and sat down.

A sallow arm flew inches over his head and blasted through the back window.

Everything was movement and sound.

The truck swerved. Ty screamed. Alice yelled something, and Denver growled as he launched himself up onto his feet.

The tallest stilt Quinn had ever seen ran behind the truck, its height soaring over thirty feet. Its limbs were like white ropes, bending and flexing as it kept pace with the vehicle. Quinn raised the gun and fired, the shot going wide over the monster's shoulder. He pulled the trigger again.

Empty.

Denver latched onto the stilt's wrist as it withdrew its arm, its hand clutching Ty around the chest. The big dog bit down, bone cracking in its jaws. Ty screamed again, his cries brimming with pain and intermingling with the stilt's roars. The truck jerked again, and Quinn's head connected with a wheel well. His vision swung, and he put out a hand as Ty was dragged from the backseat, his legs kicking broken glass in glittering pieces. There was blood on his small face, his unseeing eyes stretched with terror.

The stilt dragged Denver along with Ty to the back of the truck.

"Quinn!" Alice screamed.

He found his feet, the world still pin-wheeling. The stilt roared and tried to bat him from the truck, but he crouched, feeling the passage of air over his head. Quinn took a step and brought his foot down as hard as he could on the slender arm holding Ty just before the point where it rested on the tailgate.

There was a loud snap of bone.

The stilt screeched, the sound making his eardrums ripple.

Denver shook his massive head.

Blood spurted across the truck bed, and the stilt tripped and toppled. It fell in a tangled heap on the highway, rolling, as skin and flesh were peeled away against the blacktop. Quinn pulled his eyes from the sight and dropped to his knees beside Ty who lay on his back, soaked in crimson. The stilt's hand still gripped him around the chest, and Denver yanked on the shredded meat where the wrist ended. Quinn pried the spasming fingers from around Ty's torso and jerked it out of Denver's clutching jaws. He tossed the splayed hand over the side of the truck like an enormous spider before pulling Ty into his lap.

"Is he okay?" Alice screamed, not watching the road at all.

"I've got him!" Quinn yelled. "Are you all right, champ?"

Ty shuddered and coughed, spitting out the stilt's blood that had found its way into his mouth. He vomited and Quinn held him, wiping at his face. There were several small lacerations on his cheeks and forehead that bled freely.

"Are you okay?" Quinn asked again when the boy had quit gagging. Ty settled into his arms and slowly nodded.

"I think so."

"Any pain inside your stomach or chest?"

"Nuh-uh, not really."

Quinn sighed and pulled him closer, kissing the top of his head. "You're okay; I gotcha now."

"I think I wet my pants," Ty said in a small voice that barely carried over the wind and rain that lashed them.

"I think I did too, buddy," Quinn said. The tiniest of laughs escaped the boy, and Quinn hugged him tighter as they flew down the highway through the storm.

Chapter 31

Up the River

They spent that night anchored in the center of the St. Croix River.

Quinn steered them to the middle of a broad expanse that could have passed for a lake, except for the constant current trying to bring them downstream. They cleaned their wounds, disinfecting the cuts on Ty's face along with setting Denver's leg as well as they could. The huge dog laid still through the whole procedure, snarling only once near the end when Quinn moved his leg slightly to wrap it tighter. Despite her assurances that she was fine, Alice had sprained her ankle in the ten-foot drop from the awning to the truck. She joked that it couldn't have happened to the leg she'd gotten shot in and how Quinn was going to have to carry her most places from that point on. He said he would gladly oblige.

The following days were easy and quiet. They cruised north up the river, passing patches of dense forest and large suburbs alike. Once a group of stilts spotted them coming around a bend near a campsite. The tallest of the herd had waded up to its thighs in the water before roaring impotently at them while they passed well out of reach. Ty had at first shrank from the creature's cries, but as they faded, he stood and stuck his tongue past his lips in the direction of the diminishing sounds.

They all shared the master bed at night with Ty curled peacefully between them and Denver lying on his own blanket near the mouth of the hold. On the third day, after they'd circumvented an impassable damn by scouting and finding a smaller boat on its other side, Alice sat next to Quinn as he guided them across a wide lake, all the while consulting the phone's mapping application that miraculously still functioned.

"Why didn't you just shoot him?" she asked after a time.

"Who?"

"Gregory. You pumped him full of the virus instead."

Quinn chewed on his bottom lip. "I wanted to be sure. If I'd just shot him, there was no guarantee it would've killed whatever Rodney had become. I took a chance thinking that re-injecting him with the virus would dissolve the bone again. I couldn't stand the thought of that thing controlling the stilts, having them do its bidding. I couldn't leave Gregory like that either. Even though he probably deserved it."

She nodded and wound a piece of stray fishing line around her finger before looking at him again.

"Where are you taking us, captain?" she asked, pinning him with one flash of sapphire eyes.

"I'm not a hundred percent sure yet."

"Bullshit. You're not fooling anyone. You know exactly where you're going. You've known since we stopped at the marina."

He hesitated but only for a moment. "When Harold Roman was dying, he said something to me."

"Okay."

"He said 'I Royal'. I thought he was trying to tell me his name was Royal. But he wasn't. He was trying to say Isle Royale."

"Isle Royale? What's that?"

"It's an island off the coast of northern Minnesota in Lake Superior. That's what most of the documents and maps were about that he had in his pack. You were right; he was planning a trip. He knew more about the stilts and their biology than most people, and he figured that that island would be one of the best places for refuge."

Alice watched him for a long time and then glanced at Ty and Denver who rode on the floor together in the bow.

"How would we survive there?" she finally asked.

"It's got a population of moose as well as an interior lake with fish, not to mention Lake Superior on all sides. There'd be plenty of food. The island itself is fifteen miles offshore, and I don't see any of those things swimming that far, especially with how cold the water temperature typically is. In the winter, we won't have to worry about them at all since they'll have to migrate south to keep from freezing to death. There's visitor lodges there that we can live in, plenty of wood to burn." He studied her face, how the sunshine lit her hair into a raven flare each time the wind caught it. "What do you think?"

She stared ahead at the water glimmering beyond the boat. He waited, content to watch her rather than the scenic landscape that slipped past them. After a time, she turned back to him.

"I think I'm in love with you," she said. His jaw slackened and he blinked. Alice laughed, tossing her head to one side and leaned in, kissing him firmly on the lips. When she drew back, she smiled and stroked the side of his face. "Let's go to your island."

Epilogue

3 Years Later

The lure splashed, hitting the water in a spray that caught the late fall sunlight.

Ty began to reel, jigging the rod with an expert hand as he felt the bump of a fish testing the bait. He froze, slowly bringing up the slack line until it tightened, the jerking tug transferring through the rod into his hands. He snapped his arms up, setting the hook and began to reel again, the tension of the fish making him whoop with delight.

"Another one?" Quinn asked, casting his own line out again into the lake.

"Of course."

"Oh listen to you, great white fisherman."

"You're just upset that a blind kid can out-catch you."

"And you're pretty cocky for someone who's only been fishing for three years."

Ty laughed and drew the whipping perch out of the water, catching it as it swung toward him on the end of the line. In a matter of seconds, he had the fish off the hook and strung on the shining stringer that trailed into the water at their feet. The other four fish swimming in place that were threaded there flipped indignantly until he released the chain holding them.

"So that's four to one," Ty said, baiting his hook before casting it out again in a graceful curve of line.

"You're gonna beat me again," Quinn said. He scratched at the thick beard covering his face, still not fully used to the feeling of it there even after growing it for over a year.

"Are you going to take me to shore when you go this time?" Ty asked.

"Absolutely not."

"But I'm almost ten," he protested, jigging his rod harder.

"You're barely nine."

"But you said yourself that you hadn't seen one of them in almost two years."

"That doesn't mean that they aren't there."

Ty fell silent for a long time. The air was already cooling, winter's breath coursing in from the west. Soon the snow would begin to fall, their journeys outside of the main lodge limited to gathering firewood from the extensive pile ricked against the back wall and to the portable fish house that they would erect once the ice was thick enough to stand on.

"Do you think we'll ever live back on the mainland again?" Ty asked, pulling Quinn away from the preparations he was going through in his head. The question caught him off guard, and he looked at the boy, growing tall now, his steps steady and sure on any of the hiking trails that snaked across the island like a child's treasure map.

"Do you want to go back?" Quinn asked.

Ty jigged the rod, tipping his head to one side, looking so much like his mother in the sun.

"Not really, I guess," he said finally. "Do you think about them a lot, your dad, Teresa, everyone you lost?" Ty asked after another pause.

"Yes, I do."

"And you miss them?"

"Very much."

"But you'd never want to go back to your home where you grew up?"

Quinn wound in his line and secured it to the pole before coming close to Ty and embracing him.

"This is my home."

They brought the fish up to the four-wheeler that waited for them on the trail beside the lake and climbed on, Ty holding onto Quinn's waist as they rode back to the lodge. When the low buildings came into view through the trees, Quinn guided the four-wheeler close to the first one, stopping beneath the heavy boughs of a pine.

"Can I clean them?" Ty asked, picking up the stringer.

"Absolutely; less work for me. Don't cut yourself."

"I won't. Here Denver!" The great German Shepherd rose from the bed on the rear deck of the lodge and trotted to the boy, the hobble in his hind leg barely noticeable. Ty grabbed the bar of the upraised collar Quinn had designed, and the dog lead him in the direction of the fish-cleaning shack farther down the shoreline. Quinn watched them go, something tightening in his chest at the sight of them walking away.

The sun was beginning to slide behind the tall trees that lined the bank, casting fire across the water in undulating waves. He moved down to the lake's edge, walking out onto the dock that jutted into the cold water. He stood there for a long time, looking across the lake, the land he knew was there unseen. He closed his eyes, and for a moment, he was back, listening to the water rush against rock, the breeze caressing his face, the ocean before him.

He heard her approach and only opened his eyes after she'd slipped an arm around his waist.

"What are you doing out here?" Alice asked.

"Dreaming dreams."

"Are they good ones?"

"Not as good as the one I'm living."

The whole world was quiet save for their breathing, the lake's eternal movement, the sun's descent. She glanced up at him.

"You're reliving it all again, aren't you." When he didn't reply she continued. "Honey, stop. You have to quit this," she said, guiding his head down to hers. She kissed him, held his face in her hands. "Your father loved you beyond anything."

"And it destroyed the world," Quinn said, swallowing. "Because of how I am."

"It's not your fault. After all the times we've discussed it, after what you've put yourself through, you know you couldn't have done anything different, you know that."

"It doesn't change anything."

"Listen to me. You brought us here. You made a life for us. We wouldn't have survived without you."

"You would have been fine. You're the toughest person I've ever met."

"No, I'm not. The boy in that little shack over there is, but he wouldn't be here today if it weren't for you." She brought her lips to his again and then gazed into his eyes, looking from one to the other. "Remember what you told me a long time ago? About hope being stronger than anything?"

He nodded.

She brought his hands down to the slight swell of her belly.

"I haven't forgotten."

Author's Note

As always, thanks so much for reading. I appreciate you coming along on yet another journey. I hope the ride was as fulfilling for you as it was for me to create.

The idea for Cruel World was born of an image that came to me out of the blue some time ago of a boy sitting with his father in a room full of books. The boy was afflicted with a deformity that kept him from doing all the typical things that someone his age would have partaken in. He did not go to school, he didn't play with other kids, he had no one besides his doting father who wanted only to protect him from the cruelty outside their walls. The original title I had for this story was The Bookseller's Son.

What evolved from there became Cruel World. Of course my singular idea transformed into something frightening and thrilling as is the nature of my contemplation. I wanted to know how someone who was cut off from the outside world, someone dubbed as a physical 'monster', would deal with being released from his sanctuary/prison into a world filled with real monsters, both human and not.

I have unending respect for the resiliency of those who suffer from some type of physical or mental disability, and hope that I conveyed my admiration throughout the book. Those of us who are blessed with healthy bodies and mental abilities should reflect more upon the notion of lacking such traits that are often taken for granted. The suffering that many endure goes unnoticed at times, and just by realizing how fortunate many of us are would go a long way in the extension of kindness and empathy.

Once again, I hope you've enjoyed the book, and if you have feedback, I would love to hear from you in the form of a review, an email, or by reaching out via social media. Thank you for your company and I hope to have a new place for us to go soon if you're up for the ride.

Joe Hart
November 2014

Other Works by Joe Hart

Novels

Lineage
Singularity
EverFall
The River Is Dark
The Waiting
Widow Town

Short story collections

Midnight Paths: A Collection of Dark Horror

Short Stories

"The Line Unseen"
"The Edge of Life"
"Outpost"